"Land presents a larger-than-life hero with a dark past, a risk taker accompanied by a sidekick so skilled in killing as to seem infallible. Their spectacular ride, global in its dimensions, will enthrall all thrill seekers. Highly recommended."

—*Library Journal*

"Rich, real, believable . . . Pulsating with rhythm . . . Propels you along page by page at an unrelenting pace. Jon Land knows exactly what he's doing."

—Steve Berry, *New York Times* bestselling author of *The Charlemagne Pursuit*

"Here, at last, is another fast-paced, conspiracy-riddled, page-turning yarn from Jon Land that you won't be able to put down until you swallow it whole. . . . *The Seven Sins* is so exquisitely constructed that you literally can't stop to catch a breath. I loved every callous, murderous, conspiracy-rich moment of it."

—*The Providence Journal*

"A sizzling summer page-turner to devour while sunning on the beach."

—*Bookreporter.com*

"The kind of high-velocity thriller that just won't let you put it down. Relentlessly inventive and delightfully complex . . . Pure fun."

—T. Jefferson Parker, *New York Times* bestselling author of *L.A. Oulaws*

"Enter a world of high stakes, high money, and high excitement with Jon Land's *The Seven Sins*. A must-read for anyone who loves mystery and adventure, and a super bonus for anyone who loves the ever-involving realm of human history and psyche as well!"

—Heather Graham, *New York Times* bestselling author of *The Dead Room*

"A 'Sin'-tillating ride."

—*Las Vegas Weekly*

THE
SEVEN SINS

The Tyrant Ascending

JON LAND

A TOM DOHERTY ASSOCIATES BOOK
NEW YORK

This is a work of fiction. All of the characters, organizations, and events portrayed in this novel are either products of the author's imagination or are used fictitiously.

THE SEVEN SINS: THE TYRANT ASCENDING

Copyright © 2007 by King Midas World Entertainment, Inc.

All rights reserved.

A Forge Book
Published by Tom Doherty Associates, LLC
175 Fifth Avenue
New York, NY 10010

www.tor-forge.com

Forge® is a registered trademark of Tom Doherty Associates, LLC.

ISBN-13: 978-0-7653-5438-9
ISBN-10: 0-7653-5438-1

First Edition: June 2008
First Mass Market Edition: June 2009

Printed in the United States of America

0 9 8 7 6 5 4 3 2 1

For my mother

Youth fades; love droops, the leaves of friendship fall;
A mother's secret hope outlives them all.

—Oliver Wendell Holmes, "A Mother's Secret"

ACKNOWLEDGMENTS

It's been too long, too long since we last met and too long since I had a story to tell you.

But first there are people to thank for helping me to tell it better and giving me the chance to tell it at all. That list starts with the Forge Books family headed by Tom Doherty and Linda Quinton, dear friends who publish books "the way they should be published," to quote my late agent, the wondrous Toni Mendez. Paul Stevens, Elena Stokes, and Jodi Rosoff were all there behind this one, and there's no better editor anywhere than Natalia Aponte. Natalia always knows what I'm trying to say and excels at helping me say it better.

An answer to any question, meanwhile, remains only a phone call away thanks to the now-retired Emery Pineo, my former junior high science teacher and still the smartest man I know. My father, Mark Land, helped with the gambling scenes, and my new agent, Henry Morrison, always provides a calm voice in the midst of whatever storm I'm facing.

Those who have been with me before will notice a much different tale this time out, which brings me to my final and most important acknowledgment. The story of Michael Tiranno is inspired by Fabrizio Boccardi, whose fascinating life and true rags-to-riches story became the inspiration for this book. Someday you will be able to visit the *real* Seven Sins Casino and Resort. Until then, this book will have to suffice. So let's turn the page and begin.

Nothing so weak and unstable as a reputation for power not based on force.

—Tacitus, *Annals*, Book XIX

CONFERENCE CENTER

POOL DECK

RETAIL VILLAGE

DESERT INN ROAD

SERVICE/MAINTENANCE

EXIT

PARKING

EVENTS ARENA

VEHICLE ENTRY/EXIT

HOTEL/CASINO PORTE COCHERE

ENTRY

N
W E
S

THE SEVEN SINS

SITE PLAN

0   100   200

SCALE IN FEET

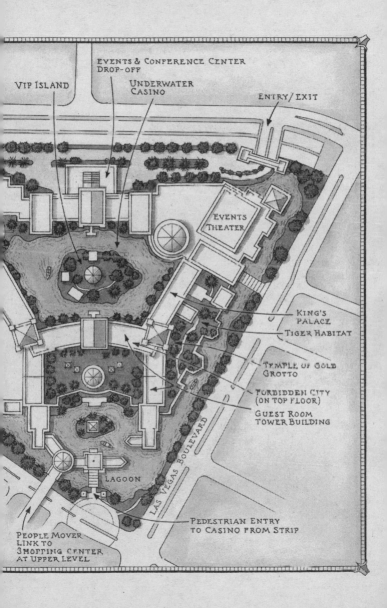

VIP ISLAND

EVENTS & CONFERENCE CENTER DROP-OFF

UNDERWATER CASINO

ENTRY / EXIT

EVENTS THEATER

KING'S PALACE

TIGER HABITAT

TEMPLE OF GOLD GROTTO

FORBIDDEN CITY (ON TOP FLOOR)

GUEST ROOM TOWER BUILDING

LAS VEGAS BOULEVARD

LAGOON

PEDESTRIAN ENTRY TO CASINO FROM STRIP

PEOPLE MOVER LINK TO SHOPPING CENTER AT UPPER LEVEL

THE SEVEN
SINS

PROLOGUE

THE BOY

THE AEGEAN SEA, 74 B.C.

"She's out there all right, Captain. Hiding from us."

Captain Ali-san Kubivaros wondered if his first mate, Simirah, was as good a prophet as he was a crewman. The fog before the *Belas* seemed like an impenetrable wall, and with visibility nonexistent even he knew it best to keep his ship's speed slow at midday. Had Kubivaros believed in omens, the suddenness by which this bank had appeared would have disturbed him greatly. As it was, he was concerned only with finding the corn ship that had strayed off course here in the Aegean Sea between Delos and Crete.

"I heard the creak of her sails off the port bow," Simirah insisted. "Must have caught wind of us and come about."

All Kubivaros's instincts told him to steer straight down the center channel for Crete, not pursue this fool's errand of additional plunder. After all, he had just off-loaded on Delos the crews of three captured ships. Nearly three hundred men in all had been held for days in the vast holds of the *Belas*. Some had died from thirst but most had survived in decent enough condition to bring a hefty price.

The stout and balding Kubivaros hardly fit the dashing figure of a legendary seaman, but in every port of call that knew his name he was considered the greatest Cilician pirate of his time, perhaps ever. Yet he nonetheless loathed trafficking in men rather than goods. The large and unwieldy corn ships were like lumbering spiral-shaped warehouses at sea. They carried hundreds of tons of Egyptian wheat to Italy, their oversized frames and slow speed making for easy and profitable targets. Selling men into the service of wealthy Romans, though, meant separating them from their families forever, even as Kubivaros longed to return to his. The irony chewed at him, but was nothing a glass of wine couldn't settle.

This feeling was something different. Ten years as a pirate, the last two as captain of the *Belas,* had honed his instincts and taught him to make greed his ally, not allow it to consume him. A corn ship this far off course more than felt wrong; it *was* wrong. It didn't take a lifetime at sea to tell Kubivaros that.

Still he stopped short of ordering the *Belas* to steer out of the fog bank that had enveloped her. In years past, in times before Kubivaros's birth, pirates would have counted their blessings, along with their gold, and sailed for home. But these were not those times. Events had conspired to turn the tables in wine dark waters like these to the point where the Cilicians practically owned the Mediterranean and Aegean seas.

The powerful Seleucid Empire, which had long controlled the seas thanks to the huge swatch of territory it ruled through Syria, Mesopotamia, and Persia, had started to disintegrate after 150 B.C., when Alexander Belas, after whom Kubivaros's ship was named, blazed a bloody trail to the throne. Added to that was the fact that Roman noblemen needed slaves to work their fiefdom-sized plantations, called *latifundia,* financial motivation for the Roman navy to give pirates free reign of the seas.

Crete, the Baleares, and Kubivaros's own homeland of western Cilicia became homes to thousands of pirates, serving as their bases of operations. The wars between the Romans and King Mithradates VI further destabilized Asia Minor and gave especially the Cilician pirates added power that men like Kubivaros seized passionately. As captain of the *Belas,* he need fear nothing, which made it all the more strange that today, mired in this fog bank, he feared *something.*

Thanks to an especially rich plunder, formed of legendary spoils now safely buried in Crete, Kubivaros need never have set foot off land again. But the life he had chosen was about what he kept in his heart as well as his ship's holds. And that more than anything prevented him from seeking safe passage out of the fog bank.

"There, sir!" Simirah beamed. "Her main sail's in view off our port bow!"

"Then bring us about," Kubivaros said without hesitation, feeling the familiar fire stoked within him. "And let's have our way with her."

Quick and agile, the *Belas* sliced across the sluggish corn ship's route, leaving the prey no choice but to heave sail and stop.

"*Aganta!*" Kubivaros roared, ordering his crew to hold fast.

With that, the *Belas*'s strongest mates slung baling hooks across the corn ship's deck rails, effectively fastening the two ships together, before the soon-to-be-imprisoned crew could react. Kuvibaros watched as his archers poised in the prow of the *Belas*, prepared to take aim at any of that crew foolish enough to fight back, but none did. It never failed to surprise him how men were so willing to submit to capture and slavery if it meant saving their lives. For Kubivaros, death would have been far more welcome.

The seized corn ship might have dwarfed the *Belas* in breadth but their heights were only slightly dissimilar, allowing the raiding party led by Kubivaros to board with only a meager climb. He stepped onto the corn ship's deck to find her crew kneeling in submission. Kubivaros walked among them, boots skirting their fingers and knees. His heart hammered in excitement, all regret and trepidation vanquished by the rush of victory surging through his veins.

"Who calls himself captain of this—"

Kubivaros heard a hiss pulse through the air an instant before arrows cut down the men on either side of him. He whipped his sword from its scabbard and swung to find Roman legion soldiers swarming onto the decks everywhere around him in full battle gear wielding shields, swords, and spears as well as bows. Overwhelmed by the onslaught, his archers on board the *Belas* fired off a wildly errant burst before being cut down en masse by a flood of arrows that sliced through the fog wafting between the two ships.

Kubivaros rushed toward the youngest crewmen he had foolishly taken on the boarding party. Merely boys, they were ill-prepared for any battle, much less against the soldiers of Rome. His dormant skills as a swordsman returned with a flourish, his blade taking down three of the enemy, but not before two of the boys fell screaming at his feet. Kubivaros dropped his blade to comfort them as they died in the moments before he was taken captive. A pair of soldiers twisted his arms harshly behind his back and jerked him to his feet. Grimacing in pain, Kubivaros watched in silence as the ranks of the Roman soldiers parted to allow a young man of almost feminine beauty to slide through, approaching the pirate captain with a narrow grin that struck a chord in his memory. His heart continued to hammer, though in fear now.

"Do you know who I am?" the young man asked.

"Caesar," Kubivaros replied, recognizing him as the rich Roman prefect he had kidnapped on two separate occasions, four years apart.

"I forgave you the first time," Julius Caesar told him when they were face-to-face. "I promised I would not forgive you the second."

The first time Kubivaros had ransomed him for twenty-five talents. The second time Caesar insisted the ransom be doubled, but warned if he wasn't released immediately he would hunt the crew of the *Belas* down and kill them all. The pirates had laughed off the threat, then rejoiced in the poems and tales Caesar had shared with them during their time together, more as mates than as captive and captors.

As if to respect that relationship, Caesar stopped short enough of Kubivaros to invite the captain to draw his sword and be slain in battle if he so chose. And the way the impish young man held his own sword at the ready, the captain had no doubt at whose hands his death would come.

Instead, though, Kubivaros did something he never deemed himself capable of doing: he sank to his knees before the man who had twice been his prisoner.

"Take my life," the captain implored him, "but spare my men."

"Your men *are* your life. And all of you will hang for not heeding my warning."

Kubivaros looked into Caesar's eyes and saw nothing but black, bottomless holes. "And if there was a way to beseech you to be merciful—"

"Then I would listen to it."

"A treasure, a treasure more vast than anything you can imagine." Kubivaros saw something in those black eyes before him change. He sensed hope. "The spoils of a great plunder that will assure any man who holds them a power fit for the gods."

Caesar loomed a bit closer. "You believe I need such spoils?"

"I believe they could only make you stronger."

The black eyes flashed. "Go on."

"I will make you a map. To the spot in Crete where the treasure is buried."

"And in return . . . ?"

"I ask only that you be merciful."

"You'd take me at my word?"

Kubivaros nodded subserviently.

"Then, Captain, you have it."

Standing before Kubivaros, Caesar studied the hastily scrawled map, matching up the scale and landmarks to his knowledge of Crete. He nodded in satisfaction as he tucked it inside his robes.

"Very good, Captain Kubivaros," he said, cocking his gaze to the head of the Roman legion who had accompanied him. "Prepare the gallows for them."

Kubivaros's eyes bulged in shock. "You . . . you gave your *word*!"

"That I would be merciful." Caesar nodded. "And I will honor it. By cutting your throats before I hang all of you, so you won't suffer."

When it was over, and the last of the slain crew of the *Belas* had been tossed overboard, the head of Caesar's Roman legion bowed reverently to him.

"Should we plot a course back to Rome?"

"No," Caesar told him, again regarding Kubivaros's map. "Crete."

CENTRAL TURKEY, HIGH SUMMER, 1957

"One of the greatest treasures ever known to man," Professor Rodney Young said simply.

"That is what you expect to find, Professor?"

Young turned away from the open shaft dug out of the excavated burial mound to face the official from Turkey's Bureau of Antiquities. "That's what brought me here, Mr. Saltuk."

Young adjusted the sweat-soaked bandanna tied round his long, thin neck. Standing alongside the thirty-foot mound left him no protection from the midday sun, now at its peak, baking the air and scorching the ground along with Young's pale skin. Occasionally the wind would whip huge plumes of dust into the air that pasted Young's face and hair with grit no amount of washing seemed able to remove. Sometimes he could feel it down his throat and on the inside of his mouth, to be ground between his teeth.

"If my suspicions that the king known as Mita," Young continued, "gave birth to the legend of King Midas, I expect we are about to uncover one of the richest finds in history."

Karem Saltuk, dwarfed by Young's lanky, six-foot frame, looked neither impressed nor convinced. "People have been searching for the lost treasure of King Midas, the man who could turn anything he touched into gold, for centuries, only to find it to be a myth, just like him."

"Perhaps because they didn't know where to look," Young said, a strange sense of assurance creeping into his voice.

For relief from the dust as much as anything, Young poked his head back into the shaft toward the work crew that were nearly finished excavating the opening of the tomb. A tenured professor at the University of Pennsylvania, he was here on behalf of the school's Museum of Archaeology and Anthropology and couldn't help but imagine the wing that would be created to display this find if his suspicions were right.

"Midas created gold," he told Saltuk. "Mita, according to my research, acquired it."

"A rather important distinction, Professor."

Young's crew had used a drilling rig to bore deeply into the excavated mound uncovered above the modern village of Yassihöyük. What Young suspected to be the burial chamber had been found fifty yards below the upper surface. To access it, his team had first dug a horizontal trench into the side of the mound, then tunneled through a double wall of tree logs and timbers, the last of which were about to be breached.

Young had never learned to embrace the difficult work forged in hot, stale air within cramped confines under the sparse light spilled by battery-operated lanterns hung from tunnel walls. The task was further complicated by the need to be painstakingly deliberate through every step of the excavation process. Patience was paramount, efficiency sacrificed in favor of caution lest the secrets of the find be damaged or compromised.

"Your *myth* places Midas a ruler around 700 B.C. Archaeologists and historians have confirmed that King Mita was a powerful leader at the same time in Phrygia, a region in what is now central Turkey and includes its capital of Gordion." Young paused dramatically. "Here."

"So if you're right . . ."

"If I'm right, the vast riches of the man who was the *real* King Midas are about to be unearthed."

As if on cue, Young's two most trusted excavators clamored toward him down the shaft. They gestured backward, their excited mutterings through dirt-choked mouths indicating they had at last broken through to the tomb. Young took their place in the cool shaft, enjoying his rightful stature as the first to actually enter the tomb.

"Well, Mr. Saltuk," he said to the man from the Bureau of Antiquities. "Myth or legend. Shall we find out?"

Saltuk followed Young along the shaft's slight downward slope. They reached a ladder and Young took the rungs quickly, switching on his flashlight, as they approached the opening.

Crouching slightly with Saltuk right on his heels, he could smell the warm stench of rot from the long-trapped air. Young stepped down off the ladder reverently, savoring the moment of entry, as his beam struck the remains of a body laid out in state on a thick pile of colorfully dyed textiles inside what was left of a log coffin.

Feeling his theory about to be affirmed, Young turned his flashlight about in search of the treasures of a king that would invariably be buried with him. The beam swept one way, then the other. Then back again.

"Well, Professor?"

Young could only turn back to Karem Saltuk in utter surprise and dismay. Other than the coffin, the tomb before them was empty

"Wait," Saltuk said suddenly, "what's that?"

Young spotted a lockbox on the dirt floor. Feeling his hope briefly renewed, he brushed the dirt and debris away and inspected it gingerly.

"It's empty," Young reported, hope sinking again, "the lock smashed open the same time the tomb was plundered."

Saltuk crouched, gazing over his shoulder. "All Mita's treasure left in the open, except for whatever was inside this. I wonder what . . ."

"I don't know," Young said, dejection creeping into his voice. "And I never will."

CALTAGIRONE, SICILY, 1975

I don't want to die, the boy thought.

His skin felt clammy and the hay in which he was hidden scratched at his arms and legs, making them feel itchy. His right hand clamped on to the gold medallion through his shirt, clung to it like some magical talisman that could wish away the gunshots and the killers behind them.

I don't want to die. . . .

* * *

Just minutes before, seven-year-old Michael Nunziato had planted his pitchfork in the thick pile of hay and lifted the gold medallion from his shirt. He let it dangle low, past his thin chest almost to his stomach. He was frail for his age and tired easily, much happier with a book than a chore.

If only he had one to read now beneath the warm spring sunlight streaming in through the windows and gaps in the barn's wooden slat walls. The rays reflected blindingly off the medallion's raised design, which he loved running his fingers over. Michael could not read the language in which the simple words *Somnia, Aude, Vince* forming a motto were written, but he had committed their translation from Latin to memory.

Dream . . . Dare . . . Win . . .

His father, Vito Nunziato, kept the medallion in his top dresser drawer tucked between his work socks and "church" socks, as he called them. Michael knew because he had found it there on enough occasions, always sneaking a gaze over his shoulder on the chance his father would appear in the doorway. For that reason as much as any other, he had always resisted the temptation to raise the medallion from between the socks and loop it over his head.

Until today.

His father had taken the medallion out of the drawer occasionally when Michael was younger, always at night before coming to sit at his son's bedside to tell him the story of how he had come into possession of it. Vito Nunziato had been little more than a boy himself, went the tale, a teenager snorkeling off Isola di Levanzo across the Mediterranean Sea from Marsala, waters rich with the ancient corpses of galleons and warships, which made the area a favorite among archaeologists. His family saved all year for that one week away from the farm, away from the chores, and Vito Nunziato took full advantage of it by searching the shallows for treasure shed from the hulls of the innumerable shipwrecks lost in these waters.

His father had been snorkeling just below the surface when he spotted what looked like a strange rock formation five meters down. He was an excellent diver, capable of holding his breath for upward of two minutes. So he sucked in as much air as he could and dove lower to investigate. Drawing closer he saw the object was actually a huge chunk of petrified wood crusted with barnacles and algae, the remains of a ship lost to a storm long ago.

Young Michael would listen wide-eyed, mesmerized by the tale of how his father had seen something shiny, a golden medallion, through a break in the wood and reached his hand in to grab the treasure he had always dreamed of finding. Suddenly the sea had begun to quake in a minor tremor common in that area, the bottom stirring sand and silt into a blinding haze in the same moment the wood collapsed inward, pinning Vito Nunziato's arm.

No matter how much he tried, his father would say in a tale Michael never tired of hearing, he could not free his arm. He began to feel light-headed, the air he had sucked into his lungs expended and the world growing darker than the coughed-up sea bottom around him. Then, suddenly, his hand closed on something round and hard beneath the collapsed pile of petrified wood and dragged it up toward him.

The next thing he remembered, the story went, was waking up on the Isola di Levanzo shore. His father claimed to have no recollection of how he had managed to free himself or how he had swum back to the surface. When he opened his right hand, though, he found the golden medallion he had spotted amid the wood clutched in his palm, the golden chain to which it was attached wrapped around his wrist. From that day on, that medallion and chain became Vito Nunziato's most prized possession. And his father would always end the story by making Michael promise that no matter what happened, once the medallion became his, he would never part with it until the day came to pass it on to his own son.

Never.

But Michael had been watching a few weeks back when his father, dressed in his church clothes, had lifted the medallion from the drawer and wrapped it carefully in black cloth before stuffing it into his pocket. He left the farm that morning and did not return until late that night, Michael rejoicing to find the medallion back in the drawer when he sneaked into his parents' room to check the next morning.

His father had been sullen that day and with each passing day seemed to grow worse, as if the life were seeping out of him. Eventually he became so distant and distracted that Michael felt emboldened enough that morning to creep into his parents' room after his father headed out to the farm's citrus fields and remove the medallion from the drawer.

He held his breath as he lifted the chain over his head and felt the weight of the medallion against his chest. He tucked it inside his shirt and pulled up his collar to hide the chain.

Suddenly Michael felt different. In that moment the entire world beyond this farm he so longed to see felt much smaller, no longer something only to be glimpsed in books but to control like the pieces of a board game. Suddenly all his dreams of a bigger and better life far away from Caltagirone felt close enough to take in his hand and hold, more visions of an inevitable future than fantasies of an unlikely one.

Distinctly uneasy, out of guilt, he thought, Michael flirted with the notion of returning the medallion to his father's drawer. But he didn't, unable to dismiss the odd feeling that once draped over his neck, he would never shed the medallion again.

Michael shook off the strange sensation and headed off to the barn, where his stall-cleaning chores awaited. He began his work in earnest, finding himself standing still on more than one occasion with strange thoughts, like dreams dancing through his mind. He pulled the medallion from beneath his shirt, comforted by its touch.

"Why aren't you working?"

His father's stern voice forced him to cough out his breath, nearly gagging. Michael quickly stuffed the medallion back inside his shirt and swung to face his father, who stood silhouetted in the doorway of the barn, his bulk blocking out the light.

"I, I was taking a break," Michael stammered.

"You've been daydreaming again."

"No, I—"

"The world's no place for dreamers. I've told you that."

"I wasn't dreaming."

"You weren't doing your chores either."

Michael gulped down some air. Vito Nunziato took two more steps forward, and Michael saw the old *lupara* shotgun that always hung over the fireplace mantel held in the crook of his arm. His father glared at him, and for a moment, just a moment, Michael felt certain he was going to notice the medallion dangling from his son's neck.

Michael lowered his chin toward his chest, hoping it might help conceal the gold chain.

His father shifted the *lupara* from one arm to the other and continued to glare at him. "Did you throw out those travel books and crazy business journals?"

Michael could smell the sweet scent of fresh oranges from the family's groves rising off his father, a scent that rekindled his earliest childhood memories, reassuring even now. After lunch he would sit with his mother and tiny sister, Rosina, in the shade of the oak trees and play jacks, or just feel the cool breeze as he snuggled against his mother. With eighteen-month-old Rosina demanding ever more attention, such moments with his mother were rare and he had come to cherish them deeply.

"Yesterday, like you told me," Michael said. He left out the fact that he awoke this morning to find his books, pamphlets, and journals back safely under his mattress, returned there by his mother. As always, the two of them would never speak of their ongoing conspiracy against his father's efforts to turn Michael into something he could never be.

"America and business is no place for you. You understand that now?"

"Sì, Papà," Michael lied.

Vito Nunziato shrugged his thick shoulders, suddenly aware his son's eyes were rooted on the *lupara*. He drew his free hand over the barrel, as if to hide it.

"We're having lunch early today," he announced, voice gruff from the packs of cigarettes he smoked each day. "Finish your chores and join us."

Michael dragged in some breath and held it until Vito Nunziato turned and retraced his steps from the barn. Then he moved to the doorway and watched his father stride toward the adjacent farmhouse. Located in the clearing that also contained the corral for the horses and grazing area for livestock, the house had been built by Michael's great-grandfather. His grandfather, who had died just days before he was born, had rebuilt it after a lightning strike set the roof on fire. Michael could see his mother setting the table on the porch, adorning it with plates of sliced fresh oranges picked from the groves that very morning, as Rosina looked on from her perch on the floor.

Then something else claimed his eye.

He saw a man tucked into the thick stretch of grove that rimmed the clearing between the horse corral and grazing area. His shape was made briefly visible by the breeze shifting the dense, drooping branches. Then, just as quickly, he was gone, but not before Michael glimpsed him holding something that looked like the kind of old hunting rifle his father had tried to teach him to shoot without success.

Probably just one of the farm's hired hands, wielding a shovel instead, the rifle conjured up by the imagination his father so loathed.

Michael spotted Stefano and Ercole, two of the farmhands, emerging from the groves mopping their brows with the sweaty kerchiefs tied around their necks. Then the ear-wrenching whine of the tractor with bad belts driven by the ancient, white-haired Attilio Cecchini, the third farmhand, poured forth, just as the ancient machine appeared in a slit between rows of crops.

Michael swung toward the position of the man with the gun, real or imagined. Couldn't find it or him.

Imagined then, Michael thought, feeling his heart begin to slow. Perhaps his father was right; he resolved to stop seeing things that weren't there, part of the same youthful folly as the dreamy visions conjured up by long nights studying his American travel books and trying to understand his business journals by flashlight.

He turned toward the tractor as it roared deafeningly into the clearing, caught the sight of Attilio smiling at him and tipping his sweat-stained hat from high in the driver's seat. Atillio was far more than just a farmhand to the Nunziatos; he was like a member of the family. His granddaughter Daniela lived with him and was a frequent playmate of Rosina.

Attilio was still smiling when his face exploded, the old man's teeth vanishing in a burst of gore from his ruptured skull. The tractor continued forward on its own, the hands of its faceless driver still clinging to the wheel.

Michael shrank back into the shadows of the barn. He wanted to scream, wanted to cry out a warning as he rushed toward the screen porch where his father had just taken a seat at the bare wooden table. But Michael froze, the words lost between breaths, his legs suddenly leaden.

pffffft . . . pffffft . . . pffffft . . .

The clacking sounded like sodden firecrackers, the bullets that spawned them taking Ercole and Stefano down in their tracks in the middle of the grazing area. The sight of them falling drew his father's attention. Michael saw Vito Nunziato lurch up from the table and lunge for the *lupara* he had propped up in the corner where screen and wall met.

pffffft . . . pffffft . . . pffffft . . .

The bullets ripped through the screen, spun his father around before he could reach the shotgun, and slammed him backward against the wall. Michael's mother reappeared in the doorway in that moment, dropping the pair of plates she was carrying to the porch's plank floor. Michael thought she may have screamed, but the sounds of the plates shattering drowned out everything else.

He watched three figures dart out from the brush into the clearing between the corral and the grazing area. Badly spooked, the horses rushed about as if searching for a break in the fence, while the cows barely looked up from their grazing. Two of the men wielded rifles with magazines jutting down from their stocks, while the third, the one Michael had glimpsed earlier, held a longer, bolt-action rifle with a sight mounted atop its housing.

Michael's mother spun back into the doorway.

The three guns began to clack.

He saw his mother thrown forward inside the house as his father, dragging blood against the old paint, threw himself futilely sideways to shield her.

The guns blared again, shredding the screen, pocking even the mended spots with fresh holes. Vito Nunziato disappeared in the torrent of fire. Michael heard high-pitched screams, Rosina's, no doubt, as the three men swarmed toward the house, leveled rifles silenced but smoking.

In his mind, Michael saw himself rushing to Rosina's rescue, the way so many American heroes who had monuments forged in their image would have. But his feet, his legs, must not have heard the same stories; they backpedaled, pushing him farther into the haven promised by the barn.

pffffft . . . pffffft . . . pff—

Michael covered his ears, reached the haystack, and started to grab for the pitchfork. A weapon, something he could thrust into the killers when they came for him. But his fingers slid off the wooden handle as quickly as they found it, and he burrowed into the hay pile instead.

His skin felt hot and cold at the same time. Michele's right hand grasped the gold medallion tighter through his shirt, squeezing the blood from his fingers. There he waited for the footsteps to come ahead of the hands that would strip him from the hay.

A final high-pitched scream pierced the day, echoed in the breeze.

A single gunshot rang out.

I don't want to die, Michael thought.

And then there was nothing.

PART ONE

TO DREAM

LAS VEGAS, THE PRESENT

There is nothing like dreams to create the future.
—Victor Hugo, *Les Misérables*

ONE

McCarran Airport, Las Vegas

"You want the cab or not, mister?"

The voice startled Gianfranco Ferelli, and he switched his briefcase protectively from one hand to the other.

"Yes. I'm sorry," he said in broken English and climbed into the cab's backseat, instantly grateful for the relief the cool air brought after even such a brief exposure to the scorching desert heat. The setting of the sun two hours before had clearly provided no respite, and Ferelli mopped his stringy hair back into place atop his scalp. "Seven Sins Casino and Resort," he told the driver and felt the car lurch forward into traffic.

The flight from Rome to JFK had been smooth and quiet. But the next leg out of New York to McCarran Airport in Las Vegas was packed with loud and boisterous tourists who drank and gabbed away the hours. Even in first class, Ferelli was left to sit anxiously with the briefcase held protectively in his lap out of fear one of the drunken, soon-to-be-gambling revelers might make off with it if he dared sleep.

A few times he cracked open the case and peered at the photograph of Michael Tiranno, born Michele Nunziato, resting atop the stack of manila folders and envelopes. Captured in black and white, the man's face looked to have been drained of all fat as well as emotion. Lean in shape and sparse in feeling.

But Ferelli knew enough about Michael Tiranno, things that few men did, to realize quite the opposite was true. Tiranno might not have shared his passion, or worn it on the exterior. Yet that passion had been the calling card of a rise from orphaned farmboy to fabulously wealthy casino mogul. Along the way, those who had crossed Michael Tiranno had inevitably lived to regret it, and those who had aided him inevitably prospered as a result. It was said he interviewed all of his employees personally and could greet each and every one by name, offering a hundred-dollar, on-the-spot bonus anytime he failed to do so.

Ferelli had been in the company of royalty before; he'd been in the company of fame. But something about Michael Tiranno, captured even in a photograph, transcended both. Something about his eyes, the way he held his smile. Stare at the picture long enough and the eyes seemed to rotate until they locked on to Ferelli's gaze, at which point they would not let go. And that made the task before him all the more daunting because he could not imagine what it would be like to meet Michael Tiranno in person, much less how he might react to what Ferelli had to say.

Because the information contained in his briefcase would change Michael Tiranno's life forever.

Ferelli had spent the bulk of the flight from New York rehearsing lines in his head to explain his discovery. The circumstantial evidence that defied reason. The truth discerned from a terrible lie. Tiranno had never heard of him, and Ferelli was headed to the Seven Sins without benefit of an appointment.

Just give me five minutes, five minutes, I beg you. . . .

From there, a glimpse into the briefcase would be enough to guarantee all the time Gianfranco Ferelli needed.

Ferelli felt cold sweat soaking through his shirt and asked the cabdriver to turn up the air-conditioning. Thankfully, he had made it this far without incident and had full confidence Michael Tiranno would greatly value him coming all this way to share the secrets contained in his briefcase.

Gianfranco Ferelli knew he had nothing to fear, as his cab fell in behind four virtually identical sedans on Tropicana Avenue.

TWO

The four sedans clung to the speed limit, McCarran Airport shrinking in the distance behind them. The cars had been left in four different long-term lots the day before, the parking stubs tucked beneath the driver's-side visors. The cars had been chosen for their innocuousness, typical rentals that cruised the Vegas Strip with frequently flashing brake lights as their occupants took in the glitz and glamour they had come to sample.

But the sedans weren't rentals. Rentals might have aroused suspicion. Instead they had been purchased from used car dealerships, where the possibility of a sale dwarfed all other concerns. Even then, added precautions had been taken. The dealers were hundreds of miles apart and none less than five hundred miles from Las Vegas itself. In each instance the buyers were trained to barter before agreeing on a price, then to return the next day with a cashier's check for the agreed-upon amount.

At that point the cars were driven to four designated load points where their trunks were packed with chemical fertilizers stockpiled over a six-month period and dynamite smuggled in through Mexico. The drivers then headed for McCarran Airport and boarded four different flights out of the city during peak travel time.

The four men currently driving the cars had flown in today, arriving within ninety minutes of each other from four separate airports chosen for the least likelihood of delays. The weather had cooperated brilliantly and each of the flights had landed on time.

The drivers were now right on schedule, the lights of Las Vegas twinkling before them in the night.

THREE

"Mr. Trumbull," Naomi Burns greeted the man seated in a hand-carved chair in the lobby of the Seven Sins Casino and Resort.

"Sorry I'm late," Lars Trumbull told her, rising to his feet. He was tall and gangly, dressed in jeans with designer tears and a loose black Dolce & Gabbana shirt that hung shapelessly over his belt. He was younger than Naomi Burns had expected.

"Actually," she said, "you were an hour early. I imagine you've seen everything the lobby has to offer."

Trumbull's expression tightened a little. His face was thin, showcasing cheekbones that looked like ridges layered into his face. "I'm impressed. Keeping track of your enemies, Ms. Burns?"

"That depends, doesn't it?" As an attorney, Naomi was well versed in answering one question with another. And, as the corporate attorney for both Michael Tiranno and King Midas World, she was equally adept at deciding who would be allowed to meet her employer and who would not. Her attractiveness—dark wavy hair always perfectly coiffed, a tall, shapely frame, and a wardrobe made up of the finest designer names—helped by giving men like Trumbull a false ease. Naomi's graceful manner could be, and often was, misconstrued as weakness, and she enjoyed nothing more than turning the tables on those who took her lightly.

Her navy blue Chanel suit, the same color as Trumbull's jeans, fit the lines of her taut frame elegantly. She wore her hair short, just grazing her collar, a style that complemented a face she had always thought too narrow, further exaggerating her deep-set eyes. A soft, powdery scent, something trusted like Bijan or Samsara, melded into the air around her, refreshing it, in stark contrast to Trumbull's drugstore cologne. Brut, she thought.

"I'm a journalist," Trumbull told her. "I'm only here because of certain information about Michael Tiranno that has recently come to my attention."

"I know what you are."

After wandering about the lobby and retail area for the past hour, Trumbull had phoned her from this chair set just beyond the hotel's entrance of glass doors inlaid between golden archways. The desired effect was one of stepping from the mundane present into a majestic and ancient past offering the spirit of adventure. A forest of golden ionic columns stretched upward from a black marble lobby floor adorned with live exotic flowers, from the radiant golden iris to rare red poppies. Remnants of ropes of amber from Baltic lands, ostrich eggs from Nubia, and a silver stag from Asia Minor covered by a delicate shower of gold rosettes posed amid golden masks, belts, discs, and shields. The lighting, adjusted automatically throughout the day to account for the sun, was soft and easy on the eye: plenty to read by but lacking the overbright glitz of the gaudy. The air, meanwhile, had a fresh rose scent to it, courtesy of carefully concealed automated fragrance releasers.

"Old news, Mr. Trumbull," Naomi told him. "The Nevada Gaming Commission investigated the same allegations and dismissed them as baseless."

"The Gaming Commission doesn't have my sources, Ms. Burns. You'd be wise to keep that in mind."

"Michael Tiranno doesn't take kindly to threats."

"And I thought that's how you must have gotten the job as his corporate counsel. Why else would he hire someone fresh off an embezzlement charge at her prestigious New York law firm?"

"So your article's about me, then."

"You're a part of it, specifically how the charges mysteriously went away after the debt was mysteriously paid. What have you to say about that, Ms. Burns?"

"It all sounds very mysterious to me," Naomi said simply, unflustered.

"Michael Tiranno swooped in and rescued you. Saved your proverbial ass and your career in the process."

"You spoke to my former partners, then."

"It wasn't necessary."

"Of course. Why bother looking for facts when rumors will suffice?"

Trumbull sniffed hard, swallowing mucous. Perhaps he was allergic to some of the exotic flora that adorned the lobby of the Seven Sins.

"Allergies, Mr. Trumbull?"

"Nothing that'll kill me."

"Not yet," Naomi said. Neither moved his or her eyes from the other until a tourist bumped into Trumbull, turning him around into the path of another guest who smacked into him and pushed him backward.

"Your guests always this rude, Ms. Burns?"

"They're always in a hurry to check in, as you can see."

True to Naomi's word, the check-in line behind the eighteen-station marble reception counter wound through an elaborate maze of stanchions strung together by velvet rope. The casino's best customers, identified by a gold medallion, used a separate, lavish VIP room where all their needs were handled. Many of them would be staying in the high-roller suites erected six floors beneath ground level, with one entire wall offering a view into the world's largest self-contained marine environment, prowled by the only great white sharks ever in captivity. Those suites not held back for returning regulars were booked two years in advance at the rate of two thousand dollars per night. One section of the lobby floor was glass as well, allowing strollers a clear view of marine life captured in a perfectly re-created ocean habitat and, if they were patient, a glimpse of a thirty-foot great white.

"Can we cut the bullshit, Ms. Burns?" Trumbull snapped suddenly. "Am I going to get to see Michael Tiranno or not?"

"He asked me to see you first, give him my opinion."

"Have I impressed you so far?"

"Yes, as a hack, a journalistic hatchet man."

"Behaving like a lawyer, in other words."

"Bad lawyers can be disbarred. Bad writers end up in rehab. So," Naomi continued, after a brief pause, "can I get you a drink?"

"What exactly am I doing here?" Trumbull asked, recovering his bravado. "Why grant me an interview with Michael Tiranno if you had all these suspicions?"

"I granted you an interview with me, not Michael Tiranno."

"You said—"

"I said Mr. Tiranno was appreciative of your interest in him and expressed a desire to make sure you had all the facts straight."

"Which means you've already made up your mind."

"That doesn't mean you can't still prove me wrong, Mr. Trumbull. Mr. Tiranno has asked that I give you a tour of the casino," Naomi told him. "Who knows, you might actually like what you see."

FOUR

THE SEVEN SINS, THE PRESENT

"Roller's out. New roller up, please."

Edward Sosa accepted the dice from the stickman and moved what was left of his chips about the pass line at the no-limit craps table. The last five disastrous rolls had nearly exhausted his two-million-dollar line of credit.

"I need another million," Sosa said to the boxman before rolling.

"Sir, your credit line—"

"Fuck my credit line. Do you know who I am?"

"Sir, I'm not authorized—"

"Then find someone who is."

The boxman rose from his chair and approached a pit boss who was already speaking softly into a wireless, handheld microphone, his eyes fixed on a security camera mounted on the ceiling.

"Eddie," Jeannie, the luscious and willowy blond showgirl who was Sosa's companion for the night, said softly, looping an arm around his thick bicep, "why don't we just go back to the room?"

"Because I'm losing my fucking shirt here," Sosa snapped, rolling the bulky shoulders his former days as a bodybuilder had gained him. He had never once expended his entire line of credit, at the Seven Sins or any other casino, and he wasn't about to tonight. With the roll having finally come round to him, this was his chance.

"Eddie," Jeannie started again.

Sosa jerked his arm from Jeannie's grasp. "Stop calling me that!"

"But—"

He wheeled and backhanded her face. Blood trickling down her nose, Jeannie lurched backward into the arms of one of Sosa's two hulking bodyguards.

"Keep her the fuck out of my sight," Sosa ordered, swinging back to the table to find one of its two dealers glaring at him. "What the fuck you looking at?"

Before the dealer could respond, the pit boss slid in between him and Sosa. "Your line's been increased, sir," he announced, "an additional one million dollars as requested."

Sosa seemed to relax a bit, enough, anyway, to accept another one million dollars in chips, half of which he began to disperse about the table. Why not? He'd never gone this long without a winning roll. Now, when it came, he'd walk away with his original stake and then some.

"New dice," he ordered the stickman, who proceeded to peel the plastic off a fresh package. Sosa accepted the assortment of dice from him and selected a pair that felt right in his grasp.

He ran a hand through his thick, gelled hair and shook the red squares in his closed hand, listening to the reassuring plastic clack, willing them to be kind to him. Then he looked up at the same hidden camera toward which the pit boss had turned.

"You just made the biggest mistake of your fucking life," he said to the man on the other end.

Sosa snapped his hand open and flung the dice. They skimmed across the felt, banged up against the bumper on the opposite side of the table, and skittered to a halt.

Sosa saw a four and, he thought, a three. Seven, a winner!

"Six," said the stickman, "the point is six."

It was a two, not a three, his eyes having deceived him. No matter. Six was an easy point to make and, once he did, the payoff would be even greater.

Sosa took the retrieved dice from the stickman and squeezed them. He could have played the table conservatively to cover himself, but felt his luck about to change, a winner coming on, and decided to press. When his next three rolls failed to produce the point, he had his entire one point two million remaining on the table, eight hundred thousand on the numbers, and another four hundred behind the line. Make the point now and he'd be even. Not a bad night's work, considering how much he'd been down.

Sosa rattled the dice about in his hand, snapped open his fingers, and launched his toss.

"Seven," the stickman announced.

Sosa gazed down in disbelief, his throat heavy, something sharp churning in his stomach, as the dealers collected all his chips and slid them away.

"Roller's out," the stickman continued. "New roller up, please."

For a long moment Sosa didn't move at all. Then he stormed away from the table toward the private elevators located in the far rear corner of the floor, trailed by his bodyguards and knocking anyone close to him from his path.

Jeannie snuggled up against Sosa in a show of comfort once they were inside the first compartment to arrive.

"Get off me," he snapped.

"Eddie—"

"I told you *not to call me that*!" Sosa flung her off him the way he had flung the dice across the green felt table. "It's *Edward*."

Jeannie hit the wall hard and bounced off right into Sosa's hand crashing against her face. He felt her nose compress on impact, the cartilage absorbing the brunt of the blow. She slumped to the floor, teary-eyed and belching blood from both nostrils.

"Clean her up and get her away from me," Sosa ordered his

bodyguards. He looked at the blood running onto Jeannie's gold silk blouse. "She's bad luck."

It took both bodyguards to hold the whimpering Jeannie up while Sosa slid his key card into the door of his Daring Sea suite. Entering the most exclusive lodging in all of Las Vegas, if not the world, promised to make his losses almost palatable.

The light above the lock flashed green. Sosa started to push the door inward.

This suite, and all the others composing the hotel's underwater levels, featured a twenty-four-foot glass wall that offered a view so clear into the waters beyond that it seemed high-roller guests like Sosa shared the Daring Sea with the various sea creatures roaming it. The wall extended across the width of the suite's living room area all the way into the bathroom and exposed glass shower. When staying here, Sosa especially enjoyed lingering in the shower in hopes of spotting one of the Seven Sins' great white sharks, preferably the largest, while wet himself, to magnify the power of the experience.

Sosa felt the latch jerked from his grasp, the door rocketing inward as a figure burst out. Motion flashed, everything a blur mixed with grunts and moans. Sosa pinned against the wall, trying to register what his eyes showed him, made sense out of the impossible, as a hand locked on to his throat and began to squeeze. Then a voice in his ear, muted, disembodied, detached: "You just made the biggest mistake of your fucking life."

FIVE

THE SEVEN SINS, THE PRESENT

"This is where all VIP tours begin."

Naomi Burns had escorted Trumbull to a quieter section of the lobby directly below the rope-covered catwalk bridges connecting the various sections of the casino on the floor above. Here only guests strolling about in search of a glimpse of the great whites through the glass confines of the Daring Sea would pose a distraction. But thus far the first such creatures to ever survive in captivity had yet to show themselves.

"I guess three billion dollars doesn't buy what it used to."

"Three point two billion," Naomi corrected, gazing down through the glass alongside Trumbull.

"All that money, your star attractions should come when you whistle."

Naomi's gaze narrowed. "Depends how hungry they are." She stopped, but spoke again right away. "We call the largest Assassino, 'assassin' in Italian, a fitting name considering what he did to the fishermen hired to catch him."

Trumbull continued to stare downward. "There are three great whites, right?"

"Yes. The other two are females. Mr. Tiranno didn't want Assassino to be lonely."

"So your most prized guests can witness the mating rituals of the great white shark."

"Actually, Mr. Trumbull, sharks are known to eat their young, just like some journalists."

Trumbull sniffled again. "Does anyone actually gamble here, Ms. Burns?"

"Should have done your research. Barely half of those who come to Vegas play the tables or slots these days. The Seven Sins is a casino that offers its guests an experience they can't get anywhere else."

"I already watched your promotional video," Trumbull sneered.

"We left feeding time for the great whites off. Once a day, the equivalent of four entire cows are dropped into the tank for them to shred mercilessly. Something I'm sure you can relate to."

"Along with the thousands of visitors they draw to the Seven Sins."

"Indeed."

"A few of them probably stay to gamble," Trumbull said curtly.

"Gold Medallion–level guests are able to scuba dive inside the tank, under the guidance of marine biologists, of course. I'm told the experience is every bit the equal of the real Pacific Ocean."

"Does your insurance policy cover accidental ingestion?" Trumbull smirked.

"No, but it does cover missing guests and reporters who attempt to discredit Mr. Tiranno and besmirch his character. Mr. Tiranno has his share of enemies here in Las Vegas. And when they failed to stop him from gaining his gaming license, they began using people like you to lend credence to unfounded rumors put to rest long ago."

"Like Mr. Tiranno once being part of the Sicilian Mafia."

"Mr. Tiranno's family is from Rome, not Sicily. He was raised in an orphanage there following the deaths of both his parents in a traffic accident, as confirmed in his U.S. immigration and citizenship papers."

"I've read the press kit, remember?" Trumbull said smugly. "A penniless orphan builds the most successful casino in the history of Las Vegas. The ultimate rags-to-riches story."

"Perhaps that's the article you should consider writing."

"I prefer the version of the story that has your client being raised by a Mafia godfather in Sicily and later taking the name Tiranno, because it's Italian for 'the Tyrant,' the nickname he earned thanks to his reputation for ruthlessness while serving the Scaglione crime family."

Naomi took a step closer to him, Trumbull backpedaling until a golden railing stopped his progress. "The people I asked about you must have been wrong."

"Really?"

"I asked if you were a hack. They said you once had some talent."

"I'm sorry if the truth hurts, Ms. Burns."

"Only the kind of truth you read in gossip rags in the supermarket checkout line. What's next after Michael Tiranno? The woman who gave birth to twin alien babies or a dog with three heads that had trouble making up its mind?"

Trumbull held his ground as best he could. "Very funny."

"I'm not laughing. And neither will Mr. Tiranno when he learns what you've been saying about him."

"Should I be scared?"

Naomi shook her head. "Not at all. Michael Tiranno's never hurt anyone. Why should you be the first?"

SIX

The Seven Sins, the present

"You can open your eyes now, Mr. Sosa."

Edward Sosa had not realized they were closed, had thought he was dreaming. He opened them to find himself seated in a high-back leather chair looking up into the darkest pair of eyes he had ever seen. Liquid black, set back deep in an angular face with prominent cheekbones.

"My name is Michael Tiranno."

Sosa's head was cloudy, and his temples throbbed. He felt an achy pressure on his throat and touched it to feel swelling just beneath his jaw.

"I don't usually invite guests into my office, Mr. Sosa, but in your case I made an exception."

The large, circular office was dimly lit with a greenish hue. And when Sosa finally glanced about he saw why: the dome-like structure forming Michael Tiranno's office was composed entirely of thick, waterproof glass located at the bottom of the giant, hundred-foot-deep swath of re-created ocean spiraling through the lower levels of the Seven Sins Resort and Casino. The dome was perfectly spherical, not a single bracket or brace in evidence anywhere. Sosa could also tell that the glass was deeply tinted, allowing a clear view out but no view in, and thus rendering the dome invisible both from above and from within the suites that rimmed the Daring Sea.

Sosa shifted his wrists, as if to reassure himself they were not bound to the chair's arms. He continued to shift his gaze about Michael Tiranno's undersea office until it locked on a tall, powerful-looking figure with close-cropped hair and eyes that seemed not to blink. A coiled menace of a man whom Sosa could see was gazing directly at him from behind a stare that turned his insides to ice.

He remembered opening the door to his Daring Sea suite, and the shape that had burst from within. Remembered a blurred flurry of blows and the sickening sound of bones cracking as his massive bodyguards were downed effortlessly without even managing to retaliate. Then the shape had lunged at him, Sosa powerless to do anything but stand there.

Seated in the high-back chair, he stretched a hand again to his aching throat, recalling the man's iron grasp closing upon it before the world went black.

"I think you've already met Alexander, Mr. Sosa. You should know that your bodyguards are receiving medical attention." Michael lifted a thick cigar from an ashtray atop a black marble desk next to a tall glass of fresh-squeezed orange juice. "The woman you struck too. She's being treated in our infirmary right now. Insists on not being taken to a hospital, still very frightened of you."

The smoke from the cigar drifted up into the air, sucked toward the air-conditioning vents responsible for continuously recirculating the room's air.

"I told her she was under my protection and has nothing to fear, Mr. Sosa. You have a problem with that?"

"Hey, fuck the bitch silly for all I care."

Michael took a step closer, the room's ambient lighting casting dark shadows over his face. His olive complexion was smooth, his brow unmarred by wrinkles beneath a shock of black hair slicked back behind his ears. His shoulders were broad and six-foot-frame lithe, courtesy of light weight lifting and jogging religiously five days a week. He wore a dark blue Versace suit that looked molded to his silhouette.

"Is that what you did?" he asked Sosa.

"My girl. My business."

"But it's my casino."

"I don't give a shit. I don't care who you are; you don't
want to fuck with me. You hear what I'm saying?"

"I hear you."

"Do you know who I am?"

"I know what you do."

"I'm connected, you pretty-boy twat. Mess with me and the
wrath of God gets unleashed."

Michael calmly crouched so he was face-to-face with Sosa.
"Let's watch, shall we?"

With that, he pressed a button on a remote control he was
holding and instantly a bank of twelve television monitors oc-
cupying one of the glass walls filled with an identical overview
of the casino's Greed section, reserved for the Seven Sins'
highest of rollers, where Sosa had lost three million dollars
earlier that night. The glow off those screens caught the dull
gray shape of the thirty-foot great white shark cruising past the
glass office.

"It took six months and ten million dollars for the expedition
I chartered to find Assassino. He was hooked off the California
coast between Santa Barbara and Catalina Island. That was the
easy part," Tiranno continued. "The hard part was transporting
him. You can't put him in a tank; he'd die. You can't sedate him;
he'd die." He checked his watch. "As a matter of fact, here's
something I think you'll enjoy watching live. . . ."

Michael Tiranno worked the remote control again, and the
bank of twelve screens filled with a shot of a throng of spectators packed shoulder to shoulder in the hotel's retail area
around an "island" in the Daring Sea. Many stood on the four
bridges connecting the island to the retail area. Others watched
from the railings above or from the underwater viewing tunnel
that swept round the expanse of the Daring Sea below. Many
had held their cherished spots for hours in anticipation of what
was to come.

The spectators jockeyed for position as six sides of beef
atop a dolly were wheeled into place onto the island. Then the

hotel's full-time marine biologist poured four twenty-gallon drums of blood-rich chum into the Daring Sea, creating the "Red Water" for which the immensely popular daily event was named. Spectators crowded forward in anticipation of the sharks', especially Assassino's, appearance.

Suddenly the sharks' sleek gray frames, led by Assassino's, broke the surface, spreading the red froth of chum in all directions. Taking that as their cue, the marine biologist's two assistants dropped the sides of beef into the Daring Sea one at a time. The beef sank quickly, though not before the spectators were greeted by the sight of Assassino soaring through the water to take an entire side in his massive jaws. His eyes rolled back as his teeth clamped down, shearing the side of beef in two while keeping both halves trapped in his gaping mouth, much to the delight of the thrilled spectators, who roared their approval.

Assassino then disappeared back below the surface, the remaining great whites and smaller sharks creating a bubbling, murky swell of red-churned water as they disposed of the beef. The spectators, though continuing to applaud with delight, stood in their tracks in the hope that Assassino might reappear.

A hundred feet below, meanwhile, Edward Sosa looked up through the office's clear ceiling to see the bloody chum floating down toward the glass in frothy red sheets. The chum touched the glass, stuck only long enough to cast Sosa's reflection in red, and then dissipated into the dark waters beyond.

"Magnificent. Wouldn't you say, Mr. Sosa?" Michael asked. He touched another button on the remote and this time the twelve monitors finally settled on Sosa losing the roll that had put him down almost two million dollars. Michael wandered to the desk, took a sip of his orange juice, and tapped the ashes from his cigar into an ashtray featuring a drawing of the medallion that served as the casino's symbol.

"The tank was constructed and filled before I'd caught the shark," Michael said, picking up his earlier train of thought. "Do you know why I'm telling you this, Mr. Sosa?"

"Should I care?"

Tiranno ignored the question. "Because my casino wouldn't

have been complete without a great white. That meant I'd do whatever it took to capture one, just as I do whatever it takes to make sure certain things never happen at the Seven Sins."

On the twelve monitor screens filling out the glass wall before him, Sosa slapped Jeannie across the face, forcing her backward into the grasp of one of the bodyguards.

"Do you like hitting women, Mr. Sosa?"

"She's my woman."

"But it wasn't your face. And it happened in my hotel." Remote in hand, Michael drew within Sosa's striking range. "Maybe you'd like to hit me too."

Sosa cocked his gaze back toward Alexander.

"I can ask Alexander to leave us alone," Michael offered.

Sosa shook his head. "You haven't done anything to me."

"Neither did the girl."

Michael touched the remote again and the twelve screens changed to a picture recorded later inside the elevator: Sosa striking Jeannie hard enough to send twin geysers of blood bursting from her nose.

Michael froze the picture and retrieved his glass of orange juice from the desk. He lifted the cigar from the ashtray and tapped the ashes before taking a deep drag to make the end glow orange.

"But her younger brother owes you a hundred and sixty-five thousand dollars, a debt you knew was going to go bad. Explains why a woman as beautiful as Jeannie Vega would be seen with an ugly thug like you."

Sosa grasped the chair arms tighter. "Who the fuck you think you are?"

"Michael Tiranno. Any other questions?"

SEVEN

TROPICANA AVENUE, THE PRESENT

The four cars cruised through the sweltering night heat of Tropicana Avenue, clinging to the right-hand lane. The brilliant lights of the Las Vegas Strip blazed before them, their radiant incandescence cutting the dark sky into separate swatches. The names of the casinos burned the brightest of all, the letters easily distinguishable even from this distance.

Until today the four men had never actually met one another. They had come to the United States at different times, under different guises, and had been residents for different durations. All had encountered surprisingly little difficulty in gaining access with Saudi Arabian passports and student visas in spite of the fact that they were closer to thirty than twenty. Like the explosives they carried in their trunks, those who wanted quicker access to the country now simply entered through Mexican drug tunnels that smelled of rancid air, unwashed bodies, and marijuana.

The men knew this land had been empty desert in the time of their grandfathers and took quiet comfort in the irony that it would soon be a wasteland again. Occasional nestings of palm trees dotted their route down Tropicana Avenue, but for the most part the road was lined with commercial buildings and strip malls often hidden by gaudy billboards advertising the entertainers and shows currently playing at the hotels.

The men took great pride in their mission because they obsessively believed they were doing the world a favor by removing the temptations that bred avarice and contempt. It was a city forged in sin that flaunted the very values they cherished and further propagated the moral decline that dominated the Western world they so loathed.

Since both alcohol and gambling were forbidden by their religion, none of the men had ever set foot inside a casino and none of them would tonight, not technically, anyway.

A sea of bright, flashing, color-rich letters begging for attention grew brighter as they approached the MGM Grand. There, the drivers would turn right onto Las Vegas Boulevard at the symbolic start of the famed Strip and begin to focus on their specific targets: the Venetian, Treasure Island, the Mirage, and the newest and most glamorous casino of them all:

The Seven Sins.

EIGHT

The Seven Sins, the present

Trumbull's expression spread into a grin. "What about Max Price? You remember him, don't you? Former client of yours and owner of the Maximus Casino until it blew up on the eve of its opening."

"Gas leak, I believe."

"Is that what you call it?"

"It's what the FBI called it in their final report."

"And the fact that Michael Tiranno profited handsomely from the Maximus's destruction and Price's death. What would you call that, coincidence?"

"Foresight and good business sense."

Trumbull let his gaze drift across the lobby toward the Gold Medallion VIP room, where unaccompanied males were escorted out by ravishingly beautiful women charged with taking the guests to their suites and then personally assuring that their stay at the Seven Sins was a pleasant one. Naomi Burns watched him smile smugly yet again.

"I'm sure you're aware, Ms. Burns, that a hotel employee engaging in sex-for-payment activity is a serious violation of Nevada Gaming Commission rules and is grounds for a casino's gaming license to be suspended."

"The Seven Sins' personal concierges are just what the name implies, Mr. Trumbull."

"That's not what I heard."

"Yes, it is," Naomi Burns said, extracting a sheet of paper from her pocket and extending it toward Trumbull, flipping it open as she did. "The names and billing information of three men I'm told are connected to you."

"I don't know what—"

"Their rooms were all prepaid on a corporate credit card traced back to you. The Seven Sins prides itself on understanding our guests so we may be better able to serve their needs."

Trumbull left the piece of paper suspended between them, eyeing other scantily clad beautiful women, the so-called Tyrant Girls, moving about the lobby.

"Our concierges and personal hosts," Naomi continued, following his gaze, "are selected by a most reputable casting agency with access to the most beautiful models and actresses in the world. Each is interviewed personally by Mr. Tiranno before being hired."

"I don't suppose you're prepared to tell me precisely what these interviews consist of."

"Michael Tiranno loves beauty of all kinds, Mr. Trumbull. But that beauty must come with an understanding of what makes the Seven Sins exotic and unique, and not all candidates can communicate that sense to our guests. Because the Seven Sins is all about offering an experience that can't be had anywhere else."

"Which is of no interest to me."

"But Michael Tiranno is."

"Obviously."

"Then you need to understand all parts of his casino to understand the man. So let's continue the tour," Naomi told him. "I hope you don't mind if I serve as your escort."

NINE

The Seven Sins, the present

"Go ahead," Sosa taunted, growing suddenly more brazen. "What are you gonna do? Torture me? Beat me up? Have me killed? All 'cause I smacked around a dime-a-dozen bitch?"

Michael edged deliberately back toward Sosa, his shoes clacking against the tile floor. "You owe me three million dollars, Mr. Sosa. Be hard to pay off your debt dead."

The picture on the twelve screens remained frozen on Jeannie slumped against the elevator wall, blood pouring from both nostrils.

Sosa seemed unmoved. "I don't think you understand who you're dealing with here. I can change your life, Mr. Tiranno, and not for the better."

"You've changed a number of women's lives, haven't you? Not just Jeannie's and not just at the Seven Sins. You've developed quite a reputation around town."

"So let me go and we can forget this ever happened."

"Until it happens again, you mean. And when it does I'll be an accomplice, because I could have stopped it and didn't."

Sosa bounced up from the chair and looked into the black eyes before him. "You can't stop shit. You know what? Fuck you. I don't need this crap." He looked to his right and saw the man named Alexander had silently closed the gap between them. "Back your man off, Tiranno."

"Or what, Mr. Sosa? You'll slap me in the face hard enough to break my nose? Sic your bodyguards on me? Sit down."

Sosa held his ground.

"Axelrod," Michael said.

Sosa stiffened.

"That's the password for your computer, isn't it?"

Sosa sat down.

"There's something else you need to see."

Michael worked the remote control again and all twelve screens filled with a picture of a lavish Spanish-style home set amid beautiful, sprawling grounds. "This is your house in Bel Air, Mr. Sosa." He pressed another key, and the exterior shot switched to interior, rotating every second or so to a different room like a slide show. "I like the decor. I admire your taste."

"Wait a fucking minute—"

"I'm not finished yet." Michael clicked a button and a rustic three-story wood villa encased by snow replaced the mansion on the twelve screens. "Your chateau in Vail."

Click . . .

"Your condo in South Beach."

Click . . .

"The Ferrari you took from a business associate when he was late with his loan payment."

Michael worked the remote control again and this time long sequences of numbers, followed by the names of banks and investment companies, scrolled down the twelve screens.

"These are your bank and investment accounts, both known and unknown. As you can see, I've included your access codes."

Sosa grabbed hold of the chair arms again and squeezed.

"You won't be returning to Vegas, Mr. Sosa, and you'll never gamble here again in *any* casino. Ever. If you do, I'll know it. You'll never strike a woman again. If you do, I'll know it." Michael edged closer to Sosa, glaring down without blinking. "Because I know where you live."

Sosa swallowed hard.

"And I'll expect your debt to the Seven Sins to be paid up within fourteen business days, minus the one hundred and sixty-five dollars Jeannie Vega's brother owes you. Call it compensation for her medical bills. I'll have a release sent to you promptly for your signature. You can return to the lobby now. Your bags have already been packed."

Sosa rose sluggishly and started for the elevator, trailed like a shadow by Alexander. He stepped inside the glass elevator built to blend perfectly with the Daring Sea beyond and looked back at Alexander and then at Michael.

"This isn't finished, Tiranno."

"No," Michael said, holding Sosa's gaze as the compartment doors started to close, "but you are."

The elevator started upward and he looked back toward Alexander to see him touching a hand to a wireless communicator tucked into his ear.

"There's a problem in the casino, Michael."

TEN

THE STRIP, THE PRESENT

The cars glided to a halt at a snarl of traffic even with the MGM Grand at the corner of Tropicana Avenue and Las Vegas Boulevard. Headlights burned through the night, unneeded with the glowing lights of the Las Vegas Strip creating a near-daytime brilliance.

The drivers cringed, yet rejoiced in the properness of their mandate. Here was everything decadent to be loathed and avoided, clustered within a ten-square-mile area that at any time might boast tens of thousands of corrupt inhabitants. A vast stinking cesspool of debauchery that sucked the weak in from far and wide, only to release them back into the world where they could spread the decease.

The drivers knew that destroying the West was not about bombs or germs. It was about fear, fear that order and control could be snatched from its dying domain in the blink of an eye. Attitude was a far greater weapon than the ones packed into the trunks of their cars, and in a few short minutes the attitude of the world the drivers loathed above everything they loved would be changed forever.

But not soon enough—the traffic moving in maddening stops and starts, as they finally turned right onto Las Vegas Boulevard, saw to that. It was all the drivers could do not to trigger their backup switches here and now. They resisted because that would be a violation of the sworn duty they had been chosen to fulfill.

The drivers had seen themselves barreling down the road known as the Strip, picking up the speed of ancient chariots of fire as they roared toward their targets. Now that dream would have to be altered, though not the end result. As their cars inched along at a pace beaten by pedestrians on the sidewalks, the drivers kept their calm by focusing on the marquees of the four chosen casinos that rose like beacons in the night begging for their fates.

ELEVEN

THE SEVEN SINS, THE PRESENT

"Mr. Tiranno wanted to change the gaming experience," Naomi explained when she and Trumbull reached the casino level directly above the lobby. "He believes it to be much more than just a simple roll of the dice, flip of the cards, or spin of the slot machine. For Mr. Tiranno, gambling is a lifestyle concept he wants patrons of the Seven Sins to savor. Big risks for even bigger rewards, that's the pure message of life we're expressing here."

"But the message here is really all about sin."

"Are you a religious person, Mr. Trumbull?"

"Hell, no."

"That explains your interpretation."

"Save the sales pitch, Ms. Burns." Trumbull frowned. His shoulders straightened inside his oversized shirt. "I'm interested in the *real* Michael Tiranno, not the one you created behind all this glitz and glamour."

"You gambled on getting an interview with him."

"Was that a question?"

"No, a point, the point being that we gamble every day of our lives without realizing it. Betting that our subway car or airplane won't crash, that our job will still be there when we get to work, that our children will come home safely from school.

Casino gambling reduces that concept to its purest level, a microcosm that becomes a moment. It's why forty-three million people come to Vegas every year. And when they come to the Seven Sins, the experience will leave them understanding just how far their dreams can take them."

"And what does Michael Tiranno dream of, his real life or his fake one?"

"We can end the tour now if you like."

"And miss out on the chance to visit the seven sins of Michael Tiranno? Please, let's go on."

"What's your favorite sin, Mr. Trumbull?"

"The story's not about me."

"I was just trying to decide which section of the casino to show you first."

"Right," Trumbull droned, feigning boredom. "Seven sections, one for each sin."

"Each with its own theme and atmosphere connected by these catwalks."

Trumbull glanced down at the lobby level from their perch between the Envy and Wrath sections. "Has anyone ever fallen?"

"Not yet," Naomi said, continuing on toward the casino's Envy section. This was the most dramatically lit and furnished of the seven, outfitted with lavish displays of precious jewels, gold, and authentic artifacts. Palatial in scope and decadent in design, although Trumbull seemed to take it all in with varying degrees of disinterest.

"Players in this section are rewarded with small gifts of jewelry earned both through play and point accumulation," Naomi explained. "The difference is that one in fifty of these trinkets is actually an authentic diamond. The models you see walking about, mixing with the customers, are showcasing the latest lines from top designers. The tables in Envy may tend to be lower in stakes, but Mr. Tiranno wants all his guests to have an opportunity to experience the opulence of another class of wealth as they enjoy the chance, anyway, of gaining riches. It's all about the dream, Mr. Trumbull."

"Save the cheap slogans for the customers, Ms. Burns."

" 'To Dream, to Dare, to Win' isn't a cheap slogan. It's a way of life Mr. Tiranno offers every guest who enters the Seven Sins."

Trumbull frowned again, clearly unimpressed. Naomi Burns wanted to ask him if he understood what drew people here, to Vegas, when they could have gone to the Bahamas or any other resort. Wanted to tell him that what made Michael Tiranno different was he possessed that precise understanding in a way no other casino owner ever had before, drawn from his own past. Wanted to tell him but knew it would make no difference.

From Envy, Naomi led Trumbull across the catwalk to the Wrath section, where interactive slot machines held often goading conversations with the players behind them. She watched Trumbull's gaze linger on the Wall of Fire, which flamed high and bright every time a guest hit a jackpot, then pulled him aside just before one of the combatants in the floor-mounted Greco-Roman wrestling ring was tossed out of bounds, much to the delight of the patrons who had bet on his opponent.

In Sloth, sleek beds and sofas tempted less active gamblers to stretch out and be pampered spa-style while playing hand-held games. Typically, Trumbull appeared disinterested until a woman, painted in gold and wearing a golden mask, seemed to float down from the ceiling directly in the path of a young couple and handed each $500 in casino money.

"Trying to impress me?" Trumbull asked, an instant ahead of a sardonic smile.

"You flatter yourself," Naomi Burns told him. "The idea, the entire philosophy, is that luck is all about being in the right place at the right time. Just like that couple was and someone else will be a few minutes from now. You never know when something good is going to happen."

"Or bad."

"Depends who's pulling the strings."

Naomi proceeded to point out the Plexiglas medallions, replicas of the casino's symbol, that dotted the floor, lighting up randomly to denote the guests fortunate enough to be standing upon them the winners of cash or some other amenity.

"Patrons of the Seven Sins, Mr. Trumbull, need not even be gambling to win; they only have to walk through the door."

Next Naomi escorted him to the Gluttony section of the casino, laid out like a scene from ancient Rome with players surrounded by tables filled with boundless delicacies and sumptuous food displays. Drinks were served in crystal goblets by waitresses garbed in the white dresses with sash belts of Roman slaves, and entertainers costumed in exotic, sensual garments served players from gold and silver platters.

"The more active the player, of course," Naomi explained to Trumbull, "the more attentive the service."

From there, she led him into the Lust section, where beautiful models of both sexes and celebrity look-alikes roamed the floor, offering themselves as companions to the highest bidder via silent auctions.

"For obvious reasons," Naomi said, "the models aren't permitted to leave the floor with their patrons. And no subsequent contact outside the casino level is permitted under any circumstances."

Inside the Pride section of the casino, she directed Trumbull's attention to a stage above the floor where a dance troupe was performing. As he watched the latest show, a chime rang, signaling the appearance of a dozen Tyrant Girls offering envelopes to everyone they passed and surrounding the latest big winners in a clearly scripted fashion.

"The envelopes contain cash, gifts, and vouchers for future stays at the Seven Sins," Naomi said, directing Trumbull out of Pride toward the Greed section of the Seven Sins. "I've saved the best for last. This is the one section reserved for members of Gold Medallion status with the highest minimum stakes in the casino. Only those with the Seven Sins keepsake are granted entry by a door guard holding a special light to confirm each medallion's authenticity."

Once inside, Naomi explained, guests were permitted to exchange their signature medallion for one identical in all respects except that on occasion it turned out to be 24-carat gold inlaid with real diamonds worth one hundred thousand dollars.

No one outside Michael Tiranno's inner circle knew how often the occasion actually came up, or if the solid gold medallions were bestowed at random. Guests permitted entry to the Greed section didn't seem to care, more interested in the mountainous display of gold bars that adorned the floor's center and the different rules that applied here.

"At any moment," Naomi said, "flames can ignite from invisible fiery fountains, signaling a five-minute period in which table games increase customer odds, slot machine payouts double, and patrons race the clock to maximize their winnings before the fires, literally, burn out."

"Is there a reason why you're telling me this?" Trumbull challenged her.

"I thought you'd be interested, considering you're such an expert on greed yourself."

"I don't get paid nearly as much as you think I do for my stories, Ms. Burns."

"Which explains why you've invented quite a side business for yourself."

"I don't think I follow you."

"Yes, you do. We have sources who've confirmed you like to offer the subjects of your 'profiles' the ability to opt out— for a price."

"You offering me a bribe?"

"What's the going rate these days?"

Trumbull's expression remained flat. "I think you're afraid of the truth, Ms. Burns."

"Depends who's inventing it, Mr. Trumbull."

Trumbull was about to respond when the doorway to the nearby Lust section of the casino suddenly jammed with guests rushing to exit.

"You stage this for me?" Trumbull asked curtly.

Naomi glimpsed Michael striding across the casino floor with Alexander by his side. "Absolutely," she said. "So you could watch Michael Tiranno work."

TWELVE

The Seven Sins, the present

"Let me handle this, Stolarchos," Alexander pleaded, using the Greek term meaning "king of kings," as he and Michael Tiranno headed through Lust. "I beg you."

Ten years before Michael had saved Alexander's life in Zaire during the final days of the Mobutu regime. A veteran first of the Camorra crime syndicate and then the French Foreign Legion, Alexander had since become his personal protector, a position to which he brought not only his well-honed deadly skills but also a reputation sufficient to ensure he wouldn't need to use them. Enemies both old and new who might have otherwise contemplated action against Michael Tiranno now did so with the knowledge that they would be unleashing Alexander's wrath, a formidable preemptive indeed for those wise enough to look into his past.

"It's my casino, Alexander," Michael said softly but firmly. "That makes it my problem."

"The kind of problem you pay me to handle."

"I pay you to handle professionals, not disturbed guests with a complaint about one of the tables."

"This disturbed guest grabbed a gun from a security guard and is holding an entire blackjack table hostage. I'd say that qualifies as a bit more than a complaint."

Michael laid his arm on Alexander's powerful shoulder. "Then let's find out what's bothering him."

"Deal! I said deal!" an angry voice rang out.

Michael and Alexander continued toward a single blackjack table occupied by six terrified players and a seventh waving a gun before the dealer. Seven Sins security guards steadied their own pistols on him from the modest areas of cover in view of the table.

"Deal!"

The frightened dealer nervously fanned cards from the six-deck shoe and spread them in place before the players.

"Come on," the gunman said, "I want a winner this time."

It was then that Michael noticed he was the only player with no stack of chips before him. The man, dressed in a windbreaker and Sansabelt slacks, wore his hair too shaggy and long. His eyes blinked rapidly and patches of perspiration had soaked through his denim shirt. He looked up, saw Michael coming, and moved the pistol from the dealer on to him.

"No! Table's full. Sorry. Find a seat somewhere else."

Michael signaled Alexander to hold his ground while he maintained his approach, hands where the gunman could see them, not breaking stride. "I'm not a player. I own the casino."

Recognition flashed in the gunman's face, his shifting eyes becoming even more fearful and tentative. "Michael Tiranno . . ."

Michael nodded.

"I don't believe you."

Michael stopped under a thin shaft of light radiating from recessed bulbs in the high ceiling. "Do you believe me now?"

"I haven't been here for a while."

"Why?"

"What's it matter to you?"

"You wouldn't have brought it up if it didn't matter to *you*. That's what's important here."

"Hard times. Bad luck. You wouldn't understand."

"You'd be surprised."

The gunman turned back to the dealer. "Keep playing!"

Michael recognized the dealer as Jimmy Tate, married with two kids. Worked his way up from bartender and had just started in Lust two weeks before. He dispensed second cards to the rest of the frightened players, fanning a five on top of the gunman's queen.

"Wouldn't you fucking know it?" he said both to Michael and no one in particular. "That's the way my night's been going."

"How much are you down?" Michael asked.

"Seventy-five thousand, give or take. My last seventy-five thousand. Give or take."

"I'll make you a deal," Michael told him. "Let these people go and I'll play you for it."

The man tightened his gaze and turned his head slightly to the side, as if not understanding.

"You heard me."

"I don't believe you."

"You didn't believe I was Michael Tiranno either. But since you now know I am, you also know I'm a man of my word. And right now I'm giving you my word that if you let these people go, I'll give you a chance to win all your money back."

Interest flickered in the gunman's eyes, his attention claimed. "How?"

"Let the players go first."

The gunman waved away the others at the table, but aimed the pistol at Jimmy Tate when he tried to follow. Michael could feel Alexander starting forward and stilled him with a quick thrust of his hand. Then he continued on to the table and took a seat directly opposite the gunman.

"How can I win my money back?"

"Sit down first. Tell me your name."

Holding his gun tight, the man sat down. "Kevin Desjardin."

"One card, Kevin, one card for each of us. If yours is higher than mine, you get your money back. If mine is higher than yours, you lay your gun down and go with my security guards. Fifty-fifty chance."

"I don't believe you."

"I told you, Kevin, I'm giving you my word." Then, to Jimmy Tate, "Count out seventy-five thousand dollars in chips."

Jimmy did so quickly and stacked them neatly in the center of the table.

"How do I know you'll keep your word?" Kevin challenged from the other side of the table.

"Who am I, Kevin?"

"Michael Tiranno."

"That answers your question." Michael angled his gaze toward the dealer. "Jimmy."

Kevin flashed his gun again. "No! I want a fresh deck, dealt from the top not the shoe."

Jimmy tore the wrapping from a box, lifted the cards out, and shuffled the deck adroitly between nimble fingers. When he was done, he offered the deck to Desjardin, who cut it halfway down and slid it back across the brushed felt. Moving his fingers deliberately, Jimmy peeled off the top card toward Kevin Desjardin's side of the table and the next card toward Michael's, both facedown.

Desjardin took a deep breath, lifted the edge of the card, and then flipped it over to reveal the King of Diamonds. His expression changed, turning hopeful. He left the pistol resting next to his card, just close enough to his hand.

Michael kept his eyes steeled forward as he flipped his card. Could sense what it was from the collective breath let out by the guards even before Desjardin's expression sank, sucking out his hope.

The card was the Ace of Clubs.

Still trembling, Kevin Desjardin backed away from the table and didn't resist when Seven Sins security guards took him into custody and escorted him past Naomi Burns and Trumbull, who were standing in the doorway.

Alexander came up to the table and stood next to the still-seated Michael. "Would you really have given the man his money back if you'd lost?"

"I wasn't going to lose," he replied.

THIRTEEN

The Strip, the present

The traffic grew lighter as the cars crawled farther down the Strip. Their targets were clustered just ahead, but traffic lights left two of the cars lagging behind the others and then split these two as well.

The impact of four simultaneous blasts would be lost, which disappointed the drivers immensely. That, combined with the fact that dramatic crashes through lobby glass had already been lost to the endless snarl of traffic, left the drivers with a hollow foreboding feeling where excitement had reigned just minutes before. All of the omens up until this point had been positive, and they tried not to give this final difficulty more weight than it deserved.

From his stalled position at the traffic light, the fourth driver glimpsed the two lead cars peeling off to make their approaches toward the Mirage and Treasure Island, where a booming performance atop pirate ships had just begun beneath the glow of spotlights. The smoke from theatrical cannon fire drifted upward in the air, making the fourth driver grin at the thought of the faux blasts being replaced by ground-shattering real ones. The crowd clustered tightly along the sidewalk would be in no position to applaud that.

Of course, neither would he, the fourth driver thought, as the third joined the long line of traffic waiting to enter the Venetian's front drive. Before him the traffic light turned red yet again, and the wait to finally proceed through it on a direct path for the Seven Sins on the opposite side of the Strip became interminable, now that he was effectively alone. He grasped the plunger-style trigger in his right hand for comfort and turned his attention to the targets themselves to replenish his resolve.

Treasure Island with its absurd booming-buccaneer theme, played out at regular intervals by scantily clad young men and women nearly indistinguishable from one another. The Mirage with its facade of sparkling waterfalls and statues of dolphins. The Venetian with its gaudy re-creation of Venice, complete with an actual inlet roamed by gondolas and a fake cloud-rich sky roof that could shut out the heat but not the reality about to come crashing down.

The driver opened his window, as much to distract himself now as anything else, letting in a hot rush of air. The stench of car exhaust mixed with baked tar turned his stomach even before a symphony of voices, cackling laughter, and reverberating roars from Treasure Island filled him with a hatred so deep his head began to pound. The overly bright lights on both sides that turned the Las Vegas Strip into a tunnel made his eyes actually ache.

A pair of women clad in tight, low-rise shorts and leather boots that climbed past their knees approached his car, smiling seductively. The man closed the window again but the vile stench of their perfume had already permeated the interior.

If there had been any doubt, hesitation, it was gone. The light turned green and he accelerated through it, swinging left toward the Seven Sins.

"You said the Seven Sins, right?" the driver asked.

"Yes," Gianfranco Ferelli told him, lowering the briefcase from his lap and leaning forward, as the majestic, palatial facade of Michael Tiranno's casino came into view.

"It's crazy in there," the driver said, cocking a gaze backward. "Never seen anything like it in all the years I been in Vegas. And the women, man, wait until you see the women! You getting excited?"

"Starting to," said Ferelli, as the cabdriver swung around the median, honking to make the sedan before him pick up speed.

The fourth driver's hand was dry, but his brow was sweaty. The horn honking behind him made his heart jump, and he started forward again, sliding over to enter the Seven Sins drive. In his rearview mirror he watched the third car disappear into the Venetian's covered entry an instant before the first two explosions sent curtains of flame and glass into the night.

Michael had just emerged from the Lust section of the casino when the two blasts hit. He felt Alexander move to cover him, while outside the hotel's multimillion-dollar security system sprang into action.

From the gardens adorning the majestic entrance of the Seven Sins a dozen steel barriers rose, closing off the semicircular front drive and underground parking garage. In the same instant, gray Kevlar hurricane shutters capable of withstanding a grenade blast lowered over the lobby windows and all exposed glass on the hotel's first three floors. The sophis-

ticated system was triggered by active sonar constantly scan-
ning for seismic alterations within a narrow grid. The shock
wave generated by a single blast, much less two or three, would
have been sufficient to activate it. Alexander, meanwhile, dispatched the Seven Sins' best-trained armed guards to various
points of access.

"The Mirage and Treasure Island," he informed Michael
outside the casino's Lust section, hand held to his ear.

"We should get you somewhere safe," advised Naomi Burns,
having drawn even with Michael.

Michael eased her protectively behind him. "I already am,"
he said, continuing on toward the ornate stairway that wound
toward the lobby, when a third blast shattered the night beyond and the jam-packed crowd below rushed for any cover
they could find.

The fourth driver saw the steel barriers just as he swung his
car toward the Seven Sins. They had risen from nowhere, the
gray wall forming an impenetrable barrier to any vehicle.

For a moment the driver considered aborting his mission, so
much of the intended result forfeited now. But the sight of desperate and screaming hordes surging through the smoke and
flames spouting on both sides of the street made him think
again. He opened his window to a hot breeze of dry desert heat
carrying anguished screams to his ears. The sound recharged
him. He felt a flush of heat hotter than the air beyond fill him
with fresh purpose. The crawling traffic of the Strip had become a frozen mass of twisted metal and smashed cars that left
him sealed in on all sides except one, which was all he needed.

The fourth driver took a deep breath and twisted his steer-
ing wheel to the left. He jammed the gas pedal downward and
tore sideways onto the sidewalk, smashing two fleeing pedestrians aside en route to the steel barriers before him and crying
out as he depressed the button on the cylindrical detonator
squeezed in his hand, *"Allahu Akbar!"*

The blast ruffled the hurricane shutters drawn down from floor
to ceiling, the percussion alone enough to shatter much of the

lobby glass and send it crackling to the floor. Instinctively, Michael wrapped Naomi in a protective embrace and felt Alexander take them both down. Michael heard the shriek of the Seven Sins' alarms, intermixed with screams loud enough to penetrate the thick steel of the shutters from the streets beyond.

He climbed back to his feet and helped Naomi to hers. Alexander hovered protectively between them as the casino's elite force of security guards swept across the lobby, herding stunned guests away from the entrance as if expecting a breach at any moment. Sirens screamed through the night from all directions, mixing with the cries coming from the Strip beyond.

Michael wrapped an arm around the trembling shoulders of Naomi Burns, following Alexander's rapid exchanges over his combination cell phone/walkie-talkie.

"The Strip's been sealed," he reported. "McCarran's already closed. Estimates of casualties are heavy at Treasure Island, the Mirage, and the Venetian."

"Offer our grounds for triage and dispatch our medical teams to help as soon as all our guests have been tended to."

"Both done. The attacks have stopped, Stolarchos. It's over."

Michael Tiranno's dark eyes seemed to bleed liquid black onto the whites. "Only for now."

Among the victims was a middle-aged man in the back of a yellow cab who had the misfortune of being wedged in traffic before the Seven Sins Hotel when the fourth car exploded. The cab had been caught in the center of the blast wave, the steel literally incinerated in a breath's-length flash.

Gianfranco Ferelli was actually dead before his mind had time to process the flash. His remains would be found amid the rubble clinging to the handle of a charred briefcase that remained unaccounted for.

FOURTEEN

The following afternoon Michael and Alexander walked slowly down Las Vegas Boulevard, approaching the yellow crime scene tape that flapped in the hot breeze to shut off all access to the front of the Venetian. The facade of that hotel and casino had suffered the worst, its majestic, regent entryway now replaced by a patchwork assortment of boarded-up glass fronts and jagged husks of steel and concrete.

It could have been the Seven Sins.

His hotel had been saved by a combination of the blast barriers and protective shutters, activated by the three other hotels being hit before it.

"This feels familiar," Michael said suddenly.

Alexander turned in silence, waiting for him to continue.

"I've felt like this before, as a little boy, cowering in the barn while my family was murdered."

Standing there in the center of the shut-down strip, the man and boy seemed to merge, joined by equally cataclysmic events with virtually identical effects. Helpless in the barn as that world was destroyed. Helpless inside the fortified Seven Sins as the peace of another world was pierced.

"Why was the damage at the Venetian so much worse?" Michael asked Alexander, suddenly changing the subject.

"The overhang at the hotel's entrance, Stolarchos. Because the car bomb was detonated directly beneath it, the blast's percussion was magnified many times, the shock waves powerful enough to even damage the stores along the Grand Canal shops."

Michael and Alexander continued to the south side of Las Vegas Boulevard between the Mirage and Treasure Island. A combination of sawhorses and Jersey barriers cut the Strip off from traffic that was virtually nonexistent anyway, aside from an occasional taxi with passengers tucked low in the backseat.

Michael gazed over at the Mirage, where the damage done by the blast was substantially less. "Much different than the Venetian."

"The pools of water fronting the buildings worked to cushion the blast."

Michael turned to look at Alexander. "I heard some of those watching the pirate extravaganza at Treasure Island thought at first the real blasts were part of the show."

"You can feel a real blast in the pit of your stomach, almost like an earthquake. That's the difference."

"Makes me think about the reasons people come to this town. And the reasons they might never come back."

Las Vegas had emptied in a single day, leaving it eerily quiet at a time it would have normally been bustling with energy and activity. Michael could not remember a quieter time, even when jogging the Strip in the predawn hours when the city paused briefly to catch its breath.

Only four years earlier in the aftermath of the sudden and unexpected implosion of Maximus Hotel and Casino, which had also claimed the life of Vegas legend and wunderkind Max Price, had Michael seen the Strip even remotely like this. But authorities had swiftly attributed that tragedy to a major gas leak, not terrorism, and subsequently, King Midas World bought out all assets of Price World Resorts in order that the Seven Sins could rise from the rubble.

Michael could feel heat building behind his cheeks, hotter than any jog-induced flushing he had experienced, even when the predawn temperatures stretched into the nineties. The Strip was never quiet. Las Vegas never closed.

The Strip was quiet.

Las Vegas might as well have been closed.

Michael thought of the exodus from his own casino, nothing he could do to quell the fears of the guests of the Seven Sins. They had left in droves, waiting in endless lines for taxis and shuttle buses, some opting to walk to McCarran with luggage shouldered or wheeled along the sidewalk. The airport had reopened to an overflow of standby passengers it could not handle, who were content to sleep atop their bags for as long as it took to flee the besieged city.

"What do you smell, Alexander?"

"Dirt, concrete, sulfur . . ."

"I sniff the air and I smell farm manure and orange groves."

Alexander drew closer. "This isn't Caltagirone and you're not Michele Nunziato anymore."

"No, I just feel like him today."

FIFTEEN

Caltagirone, 1975

Michael held his breath when he heard the barn doors thrust open, not because he tried to, but because he couldn't suck in any air. He had lost track of how much time had passed since the last gunshots had sounded and could only assume the killers had ventured to the barn after a search of the house failed to turn up the one surviving Nunziato.

When powerful hands began to pull away the straw concealing him, Michael could only sit curled up at the bottom of the pile shaking, breathless, and stinking of his own urine. But the faces attached to the powerful hands were not those of his family's killers. These were big men with creased faces and callused hands like his father's. One fetched a blanket to cover his shoulders and still his shaking, while another made him drink water from a canteen that was tepid but welcome. They carried *lupara* shotguns slung from their shoulders and had wedged pistols into their belts, a picture out of history books, as if they had dropped in from another time to rescue him.

The men placed Michael in the back of a flatbed truck and kept vigil over him during the drive that ended at a house inside a stone fence guarded by more men who might have been brothers of his rescuers. He was lowered down from the truck under the watchful eye of a pair of heavyset boys several years older than he, twirling slingshots in their hands. Twins, Michael guessed, not quite identical but twins all the same. As one of the men led him toward the house, one of the twins loaded a marble into his slingshot and felled a bird soaring from a tree.

Inside Michael was taken to a room he judged to be an office where he met a man older than his father without being . . . old. Big-boned with thick forearms, wearing suspenders over a white shirt and smelling of olives and oranges. His hair was slicked from halfway down one side of his scalp all the way across the other.

"I am Don Luciano Scaglione," the man said, coming to kneel on one knee before the chair in which Michael was seated. His big hands touched Michael's shoulders and lingered there. "I am very sorry for the loss you suffered today. I sent my men as soon as a loyal neighbor called after hearing the shots. I am sorry they arrived too late."

He stopped, as if waiting for Michael to say something, and lifted his hands off the boy's shoulders.

"Do you know who I am, *picciriddu'*?" Don Luciano resumed when Michael remained silent, using the Sicilian word for "young boy." "Your father did. We knew each other for many years. Never did business, so to speak, but I held him in high esteem and liked to think of us as friends. He never turned away from me in fear, or asked me to do bidding that would have left him in my debt, and for both of those reasons he had my respect."

Don Luciano rose and took a deep breath. "The men who did this, did you see them, get a look at their faces?"

Michael shrugged, only then remembering his father's cherished medallion and clutching for his chest to make sure it was still there.

"What's your name, *picciriddu'*?"

"Michele."

"I'm going to tell you something, Michele," Don Luciano said, "even if you are not old enough to fully understand it. Your father lived under my protection, and an attack on him and his home must be treated as an attack on my own. That means you have become my responsibility. That means I will never let you down and never let anything bad happen to you again."

Don Luciano knelt down again, easing a notebook from one of his pants pockets. The notebook was covered in well-worn brown leather faded in patches. Inside, the edges of the pages had yellowed with age and featured tabs separating equal-sized clumps into sections, seven of them.

"Do you know what sin is, Michele?"

"Something bad you get punished for," Michael heard himself reply.

Don Luciano regarded Michael warmly, making him feel safe for the first time since the shots rang out. "There are seven deadly sins and most men have committed more than their share of them, me more than most," he said with some regret in his voice. Don Luciano fanned through the pages with a single hand, skirting over a number of entries to reveal plenty of blank pages waiting for more. "I keep a record of all my sins in this book—in my own special code, of course, that no one else can read. I file my sins away in the appropriate place, careful to note when and where each occurred and, on occasion, against whom. Do you know why I do this, *picciriddu'*?"

Michael noticed there was writing on all seven of the tabs, dull and faded now, just legible enough to make out the words *greed, envy, wrath, sloth, lust, gluttony,* and *pride*.

"No, sir," he said.

"To remind myself of how many acts of goodness I must perform to atone for them. A man must achieve his own balance in life. This is how I keep mine." He stood up and re-pocketed the notebook. "Where I failed your father, Michele, I will not fail you. My men tell me you have no other family. They tell me you are a good student in school and a hard worker. You have earned a better lot than you have received, and my responsibility is to make the best of it as we can. So you will live here on my estate, enjoy my hospitality and protection for as long as you wish."

Don Luciano laid a powerful hand on Michael's shoulder.

Michael grasped the back of the hand and held firm until Don
Luciano eased away, smiling behind his orange- and olive-
scented breath.

"Sei un bravo bambino, Michele," he said warmly, patting
Michael's head. "You've got a very good future ahead of you."

Michael shared a room with a slightly older boy named Carlo
whose father, Giovanni, was one of the estate's groundskeep-
ers. Their modest home was located at the rim of the woods
within sight of the main house. Giovanni reminded Michael of
Attilio, the old man whose granddaughter Daniela played with
his sister, the old man whose face Michael had seen shot off
as he rode toward him on the tractor. The memories hurt.
Michael tried to push them aside.

Carlo told him that the heavyset boys he had glimpsed outside of Luciano Scaglione's house were the Don's twin sons,
Francesco and Vittorio. They went to school with the other children on the property, holding even the older students at their
beck and call through fear and intimidation. The Scaglione
name alone afforded them a large degree of respect, and they
earned the rest on their own, challenging older and bigger boys
to fights and never losing.

There was no boy at the school immune to their wrath or
control. The twins ruled with fear and intimidation, even over
the teachers, who never intervened in their bullying escapades.
They left Michael alone through his early days living on the
family grounds. But their taunts grew more and more caustic
until Michael knew he was about to become their latest target.

They would wait for him on the road, as they waited for all
their other victims, where they would strip him of the coins in
his pocket and anything else he held of value.

My medallion, Michael thought fearfully.

He could walk off in the opposite direction, circle back to
the estate through the woods, and plead with Don Luciano for
refuge. That, though, would only earn him a worse beating the
next day or the day after. And he wouldn't be able to hide his
medallion from the twins forever.

Besides, the mere thought of going to Don Luciano for help

rekindled memories of hiding in the barn while his parents and sister were killed. He feared he was a coward; only a coward runs to others to fight their battles for them.

So he would fight this one against Francesco and Vittorio himself, his own way.

Outside the school building that afternoon, he tore his shirt, rubbed dirt all over his face, and used a jagged fingernail to dig a painful gash down his cheek before heading off down the road.

"What happened to you?" Francesco asked, looking at Michael as if distressed over the beating suffered at someone else's hands.

"Luca and his gang," Michael muttered, referring to a boy who had been arrested twice since dropping out of school in the sixth grade.

"What about him?" Vittorio asked.

"He tried to beat me up."

"Why?"

"Because I said the two of you were stronger than him and his *fetusi,*" Michael said, sniffling as fake tears welled up in his eyes.

Francesco laid a hand on Michael's shoulder. Michael flinched beneath it, but the touch was fond, protective instead of threatening.

"You said that?"

Michael nodded.

"Where?"

"Outside the school. Then they dragged me into the woods," Michael said, referring to the spot where Luca smoked cigarettes daily with the two or three boys he had enlisted in his gang.

Francesco and Vittorio looked at each other and nodded resolutely. Leaving Michael standing there, they started back up the road toward the school.

That night they found Michael sitting on Giovanni's porch. His hand moved protectively to the medallion hidden inside his shirt at their approach. The twins took a seat on the step on either side of him, each laying a hand on his shoulder.

"Luca won't be bothering you anymore," Vittorio said.

"We took care of him for you," Francesco added. "And brought you this."

Vittorio handed Michael a bloody tooth, the twins flashing full grins of their own.

"No one will ever bother you again while we're around," Vittorio promised.

Michael slid the tooth into his pocket. "Someday," he said to the twins, hand positioned to hide the bulge of the medallion through his shirt, "I'll protect you too."

SIXTEEN

THE STRIP, THE PRESENT

Michael fingered the medallion through his shirt, as he rotated his gaze from one side of the Strip to the other. His skin felt gritty from the dust clouds rising from the damaged hotels, kicked up by front loaders clearing away the rubble. His throat felt dry and chalky.

"I never want to be that boy hiding in the barn again, Alexander."

"That boy could have done nothing against men with guns."

"I can't remember their faces anymore. I try, but I can't." Michael turned toward Alexander. "The men who did this have no faces either."

"And no souls."

"I thought I was safe."

"You are."

Michael seemed to ignore him. "I thought I was safe thirty years ago too."

"There's nothing you could have done then. There's nothing else you can do now."

Michael just looked at him, seething silently when his cell

phone rang, and he waited several rings before raising it to his ear.

"Michael?" a soft female voice greeted after he answered.

"Miranda."

"When I heard what happened, I had to call," said Miranda Alvarez. "Are you all right? Please tell me you're all right."

"I'm fine."

"When they said the Seven Sins was one of the targets, I feared the worst. I didn't want to call. I was afraid what would happen if you didn't answer."

"Everything's okay."

Silence filled the line.

"Michael?"

"I'm still here, Miranda."

"How long has it been since we talked?"

"I don't know. A year, a little more, maybe."

"I used to call on my sons' birthdays, twice a year. I don't know why I stopped."

"You left a message the last time. I never returned it." Michael could feel the tension through the line, the metal of the cell phone hot against his palm. "How are the boys?"

"Growing up. Thanks to you, Michael. That's why when I saw the news I had to call, even though it's not either of their birthdays."

"I always forget their names."

"Fernando and Luis. Michael, is there anything I can do?"

"You've already done it, Miranda: you called."

More silence followed before they said their good-byes, shocking Michael back to the present amid the bitter stench of scorched concrete and steel.

"Let's go back to the Seven Sins," he told Alexander.

Michael's first stop upon returning to the hotel was at the infirmary to see Jeannie Vega. Her eyes were still black and blue and her jaw temporarily wired shut from Edward Sosa's blows. Seeing her like that made him wonder if he had treated Sosa too kindly.

"Don't try to talk," he said, taking her hand gently in his. "I know who you are, you know. I used to come watch your show at Caesar's all the time."

She blinked, twisted her lips into a sad smile.

"You have every right to be scared," Michael continued, "and you can stay here as long as you like. But you have nothing to fear from Edward Sosa, not ever again."

The sadness slipped away for what passed as a smile. Jeannie squeezed Michael's hand back.

"I know a plastic surgeon, a personal friend of mine who's coming to see you tomorrow. And you don't have to worry about his bill; the Seven Sins is picking it up."

A tear slid down Jeannie's left cheek, and then her right.

"You'll be dancing at Caesar's again in no time and I'll be there your first night back—if you can comp me a ticket, that is."

"Front row," Jeannie mumbled through the wire holding her jaw shut.

"Deal," Michael said, joining his other hand atop hers.

"Michael," Alexander called from the doorway, "you need to get up to the Forum. CNN has received a tape."

SEVENTEEN

The Seven Sins, the present

The tape had been delivered to CNN an hour earlier and had already been played repeatedly by the time Michael followed by Alexander, entered the Forum, King Midas World's corporate conference room, to find Naomi Burns standing before the wide-screen monitor.

"They're just about to play it again," she said, without turning away from the television.

Alexander closed the door behind them a moment before a grainy picture of a bearded man kneeling with his white robes flared out to the sides filled the screen. The man had a ruddy complexion and a glass eye distinguishable by the fact that too little white surrounded an overly large eight-ball-shaped pupil. The man held his hands coiled on his lap before a white matte screen. His expression looked trapped between a snarl and a grin when he began to speak in Arabic, accompanied by a simultaneous English translation.

"I am Jafir Sari Bayrak, the voice of Al Altar. Yesterday America paid for its sins in the city where sin is flaunted before the eyes of God. But God will stand silent no longer. We are His messengers, His servants, and His soldiers, chosen to bring forth His will into the world. The time of passive tolerance ended when America invaded Iraq and even now seeks to spread its poison beyond the borders of that ravaged country.

"People of America, the soldiers of Al Altar did not start this war. We are merely fighting one already begun. Our two ways of life can live side by side in peace if we stay to our worlds, but your government's intrusion into the Middle East has rendered this impossible. You have brought the battle to us, leaving us no choice other than to bring the battle to you.

"We are sad civilians must be punished, but in this war there are no civilians because your government and its soldiers act on your behalf. So the responsibility, and the burden, of change fall upon you. We cry for the sons and daughters you have lost, just as we cry for our own lost children, and pray the actions of your government will make further loss unnecessary.

"That same government can end this horror in a show of good faith by releasing all the prisoners currently held at the prison in Guantánamo Bay within thirteen days time. Do this, and only this, and you will be spared our wrath. Do this so that our peoples can find a way to live apart in worlds of our own making. Ignore this warning and know that the next attack on the City of Sin is coming, one far greater than the blessed one of last night. For I am your fate. I hold the key to your destiny, and I alone have been chosen by the Holy God to unleash our punishment upon you. If our demands are not met, know that the City of Sin and all within it will be swept away in a wave of vengeance that will return it to the desert from which it came. *Assalaamu alaykum*."

Michael continued to stare at the television after the tape had ended and commentary from correspondents and so-called experts began again. Their faces rotated upon one side of the screen while the other broadcast the carnage from the night before from varying angles. Then the carnage was replaced by the face of Jafir Sari Bayrak in still frame.

For I am your fate. I hold the key to your destiny. . . .

"We'll see about that, asshole," Michael said.

EIGHTEEN

WASHINGTON, D.C., THE PRESENT

"Sorry for intruding, Mr. Grasmanis," Michael greeted Deputy Undersecretary of State Paul Grasmanis as he entered his apartment in the Watergate Building just after dusk, "but I thought it best not to bother you at work in the State Department."

Grasmanis started to turn back for the door, stopping when Alexander closed it behind him.

"I work in Las Vegas," Michael continued. "You know Vegas, don't you?"

Grasmanis swallowed hard, said nothing.

"Sure you do, especially my casino, the Seven Sins, where you've run up a considerable tab on your brother-in-law's marker. Good thing too. Imagine what your superiors might think if they knew about the debt. I assume you know who I am."

Grasmanis mopped the fashionably long hair from his brow and nodded, eyes reluctant to leave Alexander.

"Too bad we couldn't have met under better circumstances," Michael continued. "Before Vegas was struck by terrorists maybe. You have friends in Vegas, don't you? Besides me, I mean."

"Not really."

"No? That's odd."

With that, Michael picked up the remote control and switched on a wide-screen television nestled within an entertainment center. Instantly a tape he had already cued began playing. Grasmanis's eyes widened as his own naked form gyrating atop a woman filled the screen.

"Seen enough?" Michael asked him.

"She's not really a friend. How did you get this?"

"The tape? From the girl, where else? You should really be more discreet, Mr. Undersecretary. At least choose call girls who don't videotape their clients for future use. Don't worry; I bought this from her on your behalf. Can't have it circulating, can we, not with prostitution being illegal in Clark County. I added the cost to your debt."

Grasmanis swallowed hard. "What do you want?"

"For starters, I want you to sit down." Michael waited until Grasmanis had sat down on the couch set before the chair in which he himself was seated. "Second, I want to erase your debt and destroy the tape."

Grasmanis glanced back at Alexander. "You must want something in return."

Michael slid his chair slightly closer. "Just information. About a group called Al Altar and a man named Jafir Sari Bayrak."

"I can't tell you anything you don't already know."

"Can't or won't?"

"The information's classified."

Michael restarted the tape, kept it running again for a few seconds until Grasmanis finally said, "Stop."

Michael hit the stop button. "Be a shame if that's what happened to your career. I've been reading up on you."

"You have?"

"And I've got to tell you, I'm impressed. You advocated diplomacy in the Iraq war when no one else dared go against the company line. They reassigned you to the Far East desk, but you waited the bastards out until ultimately you were proven right and they had no choice other than to call you back. I like a man who stands up for what he believes, puts his money—and his career—where his mouth is."

"Thank you, Mr. Tiranno."

Michael moved to the couch and sat down next to Grasmanis. "Don't thank me, *help* me."

Grasmanis nodded. "Al Altar is a hybrid of several different terrorist groups. Hamas, Islamic Jihad, the Muslim Brotherhood out of Egypt, Al Qaeda in Iraq. We've been watching them for some time, but they're difficult to get a handle on because each individual cell functions independently."

"But all under the control of this Bayrak."

"We don't believe that to be the case, no."

Michael leaned back. "Then tell me what is the case."

"That Bayrak is just an underling to someone else actually pulling the strings."

"Bin Laden?"

"If bin Laden surfaced to scratch his ass, we'd know it, Mr. Tiranno," Grasmanis said, emboldened now. "No, this is someone different, someone who doesn't crave the limelight. But whoever it is, they're trying to consolidate power in the terrorist world. Al Altar is just one of the groups they seem to be controlling."

"How?"

"Money. Bayrak and his terrorist brothers have a new source of funding we can't track. It's all transpired in the last six months or so since this new force we've yet to identify appeared on the scene. Such a coordinated strike on Vegas never would have been possible without it."

"So this threat about a second, more devastating attack?"

Grasmanis gulped down some air. "We believe it's authentic, Mr. Tiranno."

"Call me Michael."

"Michael."

"Obviously you can't give in to Bayrak's demands to release the prisoners from Guantánamo. So, Paul, why not just kill him?"

"You think we haven't tried?"

"What stopped you from succeeding?"

"We can't find him, not so long as he's hiding in the Pushtun region of Pakistan just over the border with Afghanistan, the one place in the world our people can't operate."

"It's good to see my tax dollars are being put to such good use."

"Those tax dollars can't change the fact that we're talking about an operating theater roughly the size of Maine. Men like Bayrak live in caves, stay on the move constantly. Every time we get a tip, they're gone by the time we get there. But we're getting closer and it's only a matter of time before we get him and all the others."

"The next attack on Vegas could come as early as thirteen days from now. Is that time enough for you?"

"Probably not," Grasmanis conceded.

"Probably?"

"Definitely."

"What brought you to Vegas, Mr. Grasmanis, besides the girl?"

"Money."

"So where did Al Altar get its money before this new source of funding appeared?"

"Primarily by running supply lines of heroin into Asia and Indonesia, dealing with the same Afghani warlords we do to keep that country from imploding."

"Nice company our country keeps."

"The rules change by the day. It's a fluid situation."

"Fluid situation . . . operating theater . . . Do you use terms like that when you explain things to the families of the dead?"

"We'll get Bayrak, Mr. Tiranno," Grasmanis said, trying to sound confident. "It's just a matter of time."

"Las Vegas doesn't have the time," Michael said, rising, "and neither do I."

NINETEEN

WASHINGTON, D.C., THE PRESENT

Jafir Sari Bayrak . . .

Michael memorized his face, studied it as if it might yield answers to questions he hadn't yet posed. He fingered the gold medallion through his shirt, wishing he could put faces to the murderers of his parents as well.

From the ashes of that day, he had forged the life he had always dreamed of from the times he sneaked glimpses of pictures of the great cities of America beneath his sheets by flashlight so his father wouldn't catch him. Nor did his father ever know about his free hours spent in the local library, mostly in a section of books devoted to biographies known only to adults. He didn't understand all he was reading, of course, but understood enough to be transfixed by tales of the great conquerors and leaders of their time, separated from all others by the fact that they would not be denied their dreams.

Now Michael's dream had been threatened, the sanctity of his world violated again. But this time he had a name, a face, and now a location.

From the Watergate complex, he and Alexander drove back to the airfield where King Midas World's private jet, a Gulfstream IV, waited for them on the runway.

"Tell me about the Seven Sins," Michael said to Naomi Burns over the phone as soon as he was on board.

"We're at fifteen percent capacity, the casino's empty, and bookings are nonexistent. It's the same for all the Vegas hotels, even the ones off the Strip and downtown. We're hemorrhaging, Michael. If this goes on much longer, which it very likely will, we're going to have to consider massive layoffs. Fifty percent of our workforce for starters. There's no other choice."

Michael knew Naomi was right. The Seven Sins was steeply leveraged in debt, a fact easily ignored when the opening eighteen months had exceeded all projections and expectations.

"And I think we should consider postponing the opening of the Seven Sins Magnum Arena," Naomi continued.

"Not yet. There's still time."

"You think Bayrak's choice of date for the second attack was coincidence, Michael? We need to give the boxing promoters time to find a new venue for their three title fights."

"The Magnum Arena will open as planned, Naomi."

"To an empty house?"

"It won't be empty. I won't let that happen."

"You don't have a choice."

"Yes," Michael said, "I do."

Part Two

TO DARE

There is nothing more difficult to take in hand, more perilous to conduct, or more uncertain in its success, than to take the lead in the introduction of a new order of things.

—Machiavelli, *The Prince*

TWENTY

The Aegean Sea, the present

"We've got no choice. Rules of the sea," Dennis Overbay told his wife.

Mackie Overbay fixed her eyes on the abandoned sailboat dwarfed by the shadow of the yacht *Quartermaine*. The waters around them off the coast of Turkey in the Aegean Sea were calm and empty, neither land nor other ships as far as the eye could see. Until the sailboat had strayed into their path, Mackie Overbay couldn't have imagined a more idyllic scene or a more fitting way to christen the yacht paid for with the handsome profits gleaned from an especially lucrative hedge fund. The Overbays knew virtually nothing about the sea, but with a full-time, professional crew of nine, they didn't have to.

Mackie Overbay took her eyes off the sailboat long enough to regard Dennis derisively. "Bullshit."

Dennis Overbay's glance turned toward the bridge of the 155-foot custom-made *Quartermaine*, named after the adventurer of lore. "It's the captain's call."

"It's our yacht."

"Somebody might need help on that boat. Have a heart, Mackie."

Mackie Overbay frowned. "I'd rather have a drink."

Custom-made in Italy, by the luxury yacht manufacturer Baglietto, the 6,500-square-foot, fifty-meter *Quartermaine* had been outfitted with a sprawling, view-rich master suite and six staterooms that allowed it to sleep upward of twenty guests. It was decorated in dark cherrywood and beige marble with leather-upholstered furniture, white carpeting, and walls covered in mauve silk. It featured a screening room, an eight-person whirlpool tub, a boardroom, a gymnasium, two Riva speedboats, and an impressive array of diving gear the Overbays wanted the option of using. The yacht's massive twin-diesel engines and twelve-thousand-gallon gas tank were capable of putting out twenty-eight knots even in rough seas.

Mackie Overbay returned her gaze to the sailboat, a forty-foot schooner, before swinging back toward her husband. "Thirty million can buy a handcrafted ship, but it can't buy balls, I guess. Look, for God's sake, she's dead in the water. And if there's anyone on board they're dead now too. I just don't see why we have to interrupt our vacation to get involved, that's all."

"Why don't you go check on the kids?"

"Don't worry, Denny. They're still passed out from the bottle you gave them last night," Mackie Overbay snapped, her gaze back on her husband. "For the love of Christ, what were you thinking?"

Dennis Overbay shrugged, not exactly sure himself. He could feel the *Quartermaine* slowing as they drew amidships of the stalled boat. She rocked listlessly beneath them, drifting in the mild currents of the Aegean Sea.

"I see something," Mackie said, leaning over the rail to better view the stranded boat's deck. "Oh Christ, I think it's a body, a woman . . ."

Lyle joined Mackie in gazing down at a woman lying on her right side, partially submerged in water. Her eyes were closed and her mouth was dangerously close to sinking into the pool. Her long blond hair had snaked up and around her face so only the tips were soaked. She was dressed in khaki shorts with a halter top, barefoot with no life jacket in sight. Her skin looked sunburned.

"God," Mackie continued, "you think she's dead?"

"I don't know," Dennis muttered.

"I told you we shouldn't have bothered."

By then Ravelle Harvey, captain of the *Quartermaine,* had joined them against the rail, a ship's mate on either side of him.

"We'll lower down and take her in tow," Captain Harvey said. "See what we can do."

"Shit," said Mackie.

With the *Quartermaine*'s hull nudged up against the sailboat to keep her in place, the captain ordered the yacht's lifeboat lowered with three ship's mates on board. Dennis and Mackie Overbay watched it motor around to the sailboat, settling close enough astern for the first mate to step onto her deck. The first mate's black sneakers sank into the accumulated water as he moved agilely toward the woman, kneeling down to check her pulse. Feeling a surprisingly strong one, he started to gently turn her over.

Something hard jammed into his stomach and the first mate looked down to see a pistol wedged there, attached to the hand that had been pinned beneath the woman's supine frame. Before the other crew members could respond, the cabin door burst open and three men surged out, assault rifles held ahead of them.

"Beautiful ship you've got there, boys," the woman said, rising to her feet. "She's ours now."

They left Dennis and Mackie Overbay, their children, Captain Harvey, and the ship's mates on board the sailboat with no radio or gas. The woman's final gesture was to toss down bottles of bourbon, scotch, and vodka from the main deck. She then saluted Captain Harvey as the *Quartermaine*'s engines engaged and the ship motored away.

"Will someone tell me what just happened, who the hell they were?" demanded an outraged Mackie Overbay.

"Pirates," Captain Harvey told her, baling water, the *Quartermaine* already shrinking in the distance. "They were pirates, ma'am."

TWENTY-ONE

"We're going after Bayrak," Michael had told Naomi Burns over his satellite phone before he and Alexander left the country. It was the same kind of phone used by CIA operatives in the field, equipped with encrypted microchips that continuously bounced the signal off different transmission sources, rendering all calls untraceable.

"I don't think you'll find him in the mountains of Sicily, Michael."

"No, but I will find Luciano Scaglione."

"Michael—"

"I know what you're going to say, Naomi."

"No, Michael, I don't think you do. I helped you build King Midas World, and the Seven Sins, because you promised me that part of your life was over."

"It is."

"No, it isn't. Not if you're going back to Sicily. I've dedicated my career to watching your back, protecting you from the enemies who would just as soon see you destroyed. You're making me feel like all my work's been for nothing, like the person I should be protecting you from is yourself."

"It's Vegas that needs to be protected, Naomi, from Bayrak's second attack."

"Michael, the Scagliones have been waiting for their chance to kill you for ten years and you're going to give it to them. Is Vegas really worth sacrificing your life for?"

"If Vegas dies, I die with it."

"Even assuming Don Luciano is willing to help, what then? What's your next stop? Afghanistan? *Pakistan*?"

"Alexander will handle things from that point."

"You've got other problems to consider," Naomi told him. "That reporter Trumbull knew things about you no one else has ever uncovered. Someone fed him the information, someone with a reason to bring you down."

"A very long list, Naomi."

"He knew about the Scagliones, Honduras, Zaire."

"A short list, then."

"You don't seem worried."

"Oh, I'm worried, all right. Just not about Trumbull right now."

"You should be." Naomi paused, hoping her point would sink in. "There are no blast barriers I know of that can keep information out. Whoever's behind Trumbull can do as much damage with a briefcase as a car bomb."

From Washington, he and Alexander had flown straight to Rome, where Michael purportedly had urgent business. For anyone who might have been watching, they boarded a black Mercedes S600 that took them to the Excelsior Hotel. Once inside, Michael was personally escorted by the hotel manager to the front of the reception line to be checked in. Suitcases packed with bed linens for weight were taken up from the bell stand to his suite, Michael remaining only long enough to shower and change into one of the new outfits ordered en route from the Versace couture store on Via Borgognona, which had his measurements and tastes on file. From there, he and Alexander made their way to a service exit where a smaller Mercedes was parked outside waiting for them.

Night bled into morning quickly after they took to the road. Michael tried to rest, managing to close his eyes repeatedly to no avail. Hours into their journey, he recognized the Autostrate Del Sole, meaning they were almost to Calabria. Once there, they'd drive the Mercedes onto a ferry for the trip to Sicily across the Strait of Messina. Sleep finally came to Michael with the realization that he was almost home.

TWENTY-TWO

Michael awoke from a nightmare, feeling himself to see if he'd been shot. Behind the wheel of the Mercedes, Alexander barely noticed him stir.

Michael steadied himself with several deep breaths. In the nightmare he was a seven-year-old boy again, standing in the barn with his father's medallion dangling from his neck. He rushed to the main house to find his mother incredibly still alive, preparing lunch just as she had in the last moments before the gunmen came.

"What's wrong, Michele?" she asked when, trembling, he hugged her tight and wouldn't let go.

"They're coming."

"Who?"

"Killers." He grabbed her hand and tried to pull her toward the door. "Please."

At that point in the nightmare, Michael's eighteen-month-old sister Rosina rushed in sobbing from a cut finger, and his mother separated herself from him to tend to her.

"Why won't you listen to me?"

He realized he was a man now in the nightmare, only his mother and sister were gone, replaced by Luciano Scaglione standing before him with a gun.

"I told you I'd kill you if you ever came back to Sicily, Michele," the Don said. "You leave me with no choice."

Don Luciano fired again and again, Michael standing there watching the muzzle flashes until he floated away and snapped awake in the front seat of the car.

Approaching Sicily, he realized he faced the very real possibility that he could be joining his family soon. Following their split, Don Luciano Scaglione had sworn to kill him if he ever set foot in his homeland again; it had been one of the old

man's conditions and Michael never expected there would be
reason to break it.

But now he had no choice. As much as he feared his own
death, he feared more doing nothing to prevent the second
attack on Las Vegas. Because allowing the second attack to
happen, just as he had let his family die a second time in the
nightmare, would leave him a broken man. And he would
rather be a dead man than a broken one.

The old saying that it was better to live a short life as a lion
than a long one as a sheep never seemed more relevant, Michael
thought, as the ferry dock appeared before the Mercedes.

Once the ferry dropped them in Sicily on the other side of the
Strait of Messina, Michael took the wheel and followed the
growing shape of Mount San Calogero towering over the sea.
The sight set his stomach fluttering, even as the smell of the
salty air mixed with the rich scents of the lush vegetation that
dominated the countryside. He took the freeway from Messina
to Catania, reaching the outskirts of Caltagirone with a lump in
his throat and heaviness in his heart.

Michael continued on through the center of Caltagirone. The
light wood and stone buildings were uniformly ancient, most
dating back hundreds of years and many remaining frozen in
time. Like much of Italy, the village claimed churches as its
most cherished landmarks, along, in this case, with a centuries-
old town hall in the Piazza Municipio that was registered among
official Italian landmarks.

His heart hammering, Michael realized the town center was
now behind him, shrinking in the rearview mirror as it had
shrunk in his memories. Before him lay soft rolling hills that
featured cattle, as well as sheep and goat farms. Layered amid
the hills were the many graveyards from which Caltagirone—
derived from the Arab term Qalat-Jerun, meaning "Castle of
the Burial Grounds"—had taken its name.

Oranges, he realized, *I can smell oranges.*

In that moment he was a boy again, a boy before his life
was cut down in the same hail of bullets that killed his family.

The smell made him feel safe, as it had many a night when the breeze brought it through his open window. That safety had proven as fleeting then as it did now.

Michael held his breath as he neared his family's farm, his stomach sinking at the sight of ten years' accumulation of rot and decay. He had purchased the land years before from the bank that had repossessed it with the first profits earned from his work for the Scagliones, to make sure it remained unchanged, just the way he remembered it. Michael harbored no nostalgic, whimsical thoughts of someday returning to live in his boyhood home, especially when the memories he carried were neither nostalgic nor whimsical. No, he bought the land simply so no one else would.

Only in his dealings with the bank back then had Michael learned the true extent of his father's financial problems. The farm had been teetering on the brink of foreclosure in the weeks before the massacre, his father having tried every means at his disposal to stave off the inevitable. *Or had he?* Michael thought, recalling the day his father had lifted the medallion from its hiding place and tucked it into his pocket for a trip. To Rome? Michael imagined him going there to test its value, perhaps selling it in order to obtain the funds required to keep the farm afloat. But in the end Vito Nunziato had been unable to part with his most cherished possession, no matter its potential value, even if it meant losing the farm.

Michael strolled about the property, hand feeling for the medallion beneath his shirt. Missing was the sweet smell of citrus he had gone to sleep by and awoke to during harvesting season, replaced by the tart stench of weeds and fetid soil. With the fields dead and overgrown, certainly Michael had known it would be long gone, but he still harbored a distant hope that the soothing scent had somehow clung to the air. But that, like everything else here, was a relic of a vanquished past. Someone had boarded up the windows and screens on the main house, denying him passage inside.

Why was my family murdered?

The question had haunted Michael since that day, the source of first tearful and then sleepless nights. Don Luciano had told him that someone must have made a mistake, confused the Nunziatos for someone else associated with Cosa Nostra. The lack of an answer, the Don explained, was an answer in itself.

As if in search of a better answer, Michael ventured back into the barn through a jagged opening where the door had been. Then, with the sun sneaking in where slats had given way and pock holes dug through wood, he stood in the very spot where he had hidden all those years ago, letting his mind drift. . . .

TWENTY-THREE

CALTAGIRONE, 1981

Even with Vittorio and Francesco Scaglione won over as allies, Michael was left to consider what would've happened had they not fallen for his ruse about Luca and his gang. He was skinny for his age, always shying away from physical labors in favor of mental ones. Instead of working himself strong in the fields of the Nunziato farm, he had preferred the company of the books he kept hidden in his room, especially travel books of the United States promising a bigger and better life.

For now, though, he needed to grow stronger. So he began running deep into the woods, always early in the evening just before sunset so he would have to race back just as fast in order to be out before night fell, when the lush foliage turned ominous, filling him with foreboding. He worked himself up to four miles, two in and back. And when that became easy, he added push-ups over the soft ground and pull-ups with his hands holding fast to low-hanging branches overhead.

Michael was walking past the main house just after his twelfth birthday when Don Luciano summoned him to his table on the veranda. In the shadows cast by fig trees behind him stood a square-jawed man with a scar running through his upper lip. The twins had told Michael this was Marco, the

Don's personal bodyguard and the one man of whom both
Francesco and Vittorio professed to be frightened. Michael
had never met Marco, never even seen him move, but took the
twins at their word.

"I've been watching you, Michele," Scaglione greeted him.
"You've grown up into quite a young man."

"I've been working very hard, Don Luciano."

"So I've heard. I have received regular reports from your
teachers about how well your studies are going. I also understand you have taught yourself to read English."

Michael didn't know what to say, unsure whether or not
Don Luciano was pleased with that.

"Relax, Michele, I'm proud of you for it. English is the language of the world and I consider America my second home,
even though my visits there have been regrettably brief. Do
you understand what I'm saying?"

Michael shrugged.

"In America, there is no limit to how far a man can go, the
heights he can reach if he is willing to believe that anything is
possible." Don Luciano smiled warmly and leaned forward
over the table. "I've watched you with Francesco and Vittorio,
Michele, never seen them show such deference to anyone who
could not best them in a fight. You beat them with your brains
instead of your fists. You are strong where it truly counts."

"Thank you, Don Luciano."

"Perhaps someday it is I who'll be thanking you, eh? I am a
powerful man, Michele, and a powerful man must always sur-
round himself with those he can trust and rely upon. If not from
family, where is he to find such men so beholdened to him that
their loyalty would never come into question?" Don Luciano
reached across the table and squeezed Michael's shoulder af-
fectionately. "Are you going to be such a man, Michele?"

"I owe you a great debt, Don Luciano."

"I don't want your loyalty out of debt, I want it out of respect. You are part of my family now."

Don Luciano pulled his worn leather notebook from his
pocket. Michael recognized the plastic tabs protruding from

the pages, one for each of the seven sins, the notebook look-ing unchanged.

"It's been five years now since I showed you this for the first time," he resumed. "Many more sins committed, many more notations in my secret code added. Pride is in the lead now. I haven't made an entry under Greed for some time, maybe a year now. I point this out because I want you to think how a man can commit so many sins and still live with himself. Remember how I explained to you that in my case I try to do something good for each entry? Like taking you in after you were orphaned. But sometimes goodness pays dividends. That's the way it's going to be with us." Scaglione tucked his book of the seven sins back into his pocket. "Do you know why we're having this conversation?"

Michael shook his head.

"Because I believe you have the potential for great, great things. I feel that in my heart."

With that, the old man ducked down in his chair and came back up holding a hefty stack of books, magazines, and news-papers he set down before Michael on the table. Michael rec-ognized one of the newspapers as *24ORE* from his trips to the local library before he came to live here.

"These are all about business, some in English to help you practice your new skills. Not our kind of business, you under-stand, but it must become our kind of business if the Scaglione family is to survive. These are the weapons of our future," Scaglione said, tapping the stack of books and periodicals. "And you are the one who must wield them, as ruthless and knowledgeable in the world of business as we are in Cosa Nos-tra. I am counting on you, Michele. I believe what you see for yourself is the same as what I see for you." Don Luciano sat back comfortably and tore two small strips of paper from a page in his notebook. "Here, we'll each write a word down that best describes your future. See how close we come."

Don Luciano slid one of the jagged strips of paper across the table along with a pencil. Michael hesitated briefly before taking the pencil in hand and printing out a word. When he looked up, Don Luciano had already finished writing, his strip of paper held before him.

"Now we exchange."

Michael pushed his strip forward, accepted the Don's in return.

"Read mine out loud, Michele."

"Power," said Michael.

"Power," followed Don Luciano, laughing. "A bright future indeed."

TWENTY-FOUR

CALTAGIRONE, THE PRESENT

The sound of footsteps snapped Michael abruptly back to the present. He stood before the graves of his parents and sister now, arms crossed over his chest, tugging at the gold medallion beneath his shirt with one hand. He wore a turtleneck and light jacket atop corduroy pants. He had grown so accustomed to wearing suits every day that the casual attire produced the reverse effect it should have had, making him less instead of more comfortable. Not that anything could make him feel comfortable now.

"Leave your hands where we can see them," the voice of Francesco Scaglione ordered.

"And don't move a muscle," followed Vittorio.

Michael turned the twins' way slowly, seeing them as enlarged versions of the boys with whom he had grown up. Their features remained surprisingly unchanged, though they carried substantial bulk, more fat than muscle now. Francesco was the taller, Vittorio the slightly broader of the two. Besides a single gravedigger at work on a hilly slope layered with headstones, the three of them were alone in the cemetery.

"The channels you used said you wanted to talk," said Francesco.

Vittorio looked about, certain Michael wouldn't have come alone. "We could kill you right now, you know."

"Then you'd never know why I risked coming back."

Vittorio stopped gazing about. "You're assuming we care."

"I'd already be dead if you didn't," Michael said and rotated his gaze between the two of them.

"Why *are* you here, Michele Nunziato?"

"My name is Michael Tiranno."

"Not to us."

"The only reason we haven't killed you yet is our father wants to see you first."

Keeping his hands in plain view, Michael walked right past the twins. "Then what are we waiting for?"

From the hill, the gravedigger watched Michael Tiranno walk off with two men he identified as the twin sons of Don Luciano Scaglione, suspected of being the most respected and powerful crime lord of the Sicilian underworld. Surreptitiously, he snapped off a few more pictures with the digital camera concealed in his hand.

The task was difficult from this angle without actually focusing the lens. But the gravedigger was much practiced, with a skill further facilitated by the Canon digital landscape camera, formatted specifically for long-distance shooting. Even then, the telescoping lens protruded only slightly from his grasp, undetectable from this distance.

The gravedigger kept firing off some more shots of Michael Tiranno, then lingered briefly with shovel in hand before heading back to his vehicle to transmit the pictures.

TWENTY-FIVE

Michael sat atop a pair of burlap seed sacks inside a dark storage shed. It had probably been abandoned in favor of newer structures dotting the property, the seed sacks long forgotten. Francesco and Vittorio had escorted him to the Scaglione estate and deposited him in here, locking the door behind them. The heat in the unventilated shed was stifling. The stench of manure permeated the shed's air, so thick it had washed into his clothes and hair.

According to his watch, two hours had now passed and Michael was certain Scaglione family soldiers had spent them scouring the woods and surrounding grounds for Alexander, just as he was certain they wouldn't find him.

When he had first come here, Don Luciano barely ever left his Caltagirone estate. The days of Mafia dominance in the Sicilian countryside and beyond were waning. Many of the Don's contemporaries were already in jail and far more were to follow. It was a fate he seemed to accept, as inevitable as the blood he had spilled to perpetuate his power.

But Michael had changed all that and, thanks to him, today Don Luciano enjoyed vast holdings that had him dividing his time between Geneva and London. He also spent substantial time in Rome, maintaining his hold on state-sponsored contracts for his construction company, Société de Construction Européenne, based in Lugano, Switzerland. The location was chosen not only for its proximity to the northern Italian border, but also the city's reputation for discretion when it came to financial matters. It was said more secrets were kept in Lugano than money and that was good enough for Don Luciano. The contrast between the mobster resigned to his eventual incarceration over thirty years ago and the businessman beyond the reach of the law today was striking.

Again, thanks to Michael.

He heard footsteps approaching the shed, followed by the sound of a key jangling in the lock outside. The door jerked open, flooding the shed with sunlight that blinded Michael.

"So, Michele, you have come home."

He recognized the voice of Don Luciano a moment before his vision cleared to the sight of the old man standing before his twin sons and a trio of men, each of whom held a raised pistol directly on him.

Michael rose to his feet. "Don Luciano," he greeted, bowing slightly.

Scaglione's expression wrinkled in displeasure. He looked shorter than Michael remembered, his frame substantially withered and his mouth looking too small for jowls that appeared as if he were holding his breath.

"So respectful after all this time. So meaningless in view of the circumstances of our parting." The old man took another step forward, silhouetted by the sunlight now partially blocked by his frame. "Let me ask a question in your preferred language of English: *What the fuck are you doing here?*"

"Maybe I was homesick."

"You must have forgotten the conditions of our truce."

"Remember the first day you brought me here?"

"What about it?"

"You said you'd never let me down."

"I agreed not to have you killed ten years ago. That's close enough."

"You called me *picciriddu',*" Michael continued. "Said you'd make sure nothing bad ever happened to me again."

"So?"

"It happened. That's why I'm here. I need your help, Don Luciano."

The old man seemed taken aback. "*My* help? Surely a man as rich and powerful as you has many sources for help closer to his new home."

"Not in this matter."

Michael watched the Don angle his gaze back on the three men holding pistols. "You like gambling, eh, Michele?"

"Only when I own the house. That way, you can't lose."

"Ah, but you've become quite the gambler in life. I've heard many stories of 'the Tyrant,' as they call you. Tell me, is the reputation well earned?"

"As a gambler or a tyrant?"

"Both."

"Ask my enemies."

"You want my help."

"I *need* your help."

"Are you willing to risk your life to receive it?"

"I wouldn't have come back if I wasn't."

The old man nodded. "Fine." He stepped to the side, enough so the three gunmen each had clear shots at Michael. "One of these guns is loaded. Two are not. You must choose the one to be fired. Choose properly and I'll hear your request. Choose wrong and you'll be speaking to angels in the afterlife."

"I'll take that as a compliment."

"Men like us are the product of our ends, Michele, not our means."

"The odds are two to one in my favor, better than I'm used to," Michael said and pointed to the gunman in the center. Don Luciano nodded impassively, holding his gaze on Michael as the gunman cocked the trigger and eased his hand forward.

Michael's breath froze. His heart lurched for his throat. Time stood still.

Click.

Michael exhaled.

Don Luciano nodded smugly, satisfied. *"Puzzi di merda, Michele,"* he said. "You smell like shit. Get yourself cleaned up and then we will talk."

TWENTY-SIX

SCAGLIONE ESTATE, THE PRESENT

Michael showered and changed into clothes laid out for him in the room beyond. Francesco and Vittorio met him outside the door and escorted him to his accustomed chair at the shaded table on the veranda.

Don Luciano was already seated, struggling to maneuver a knife through an apple before his gnarled fingers rebelled and he abandoned the effort. The bodyguard he recognized as Marco stood statue stiff in the same shadows Michael last remembered seeing him. Michael noticed pistols resting atop the table on either side of Don Luciano, recognizing them as the ones the other two men in the shed had been holding.

"One of these is still loaded," the Don explained. "I'll keep them close in case I change my mind. You think your ghost watching us from the woods could stop me? Shall we find out?"

"Only if you want to join me in the afterlife."

"Are we bound for heaven or hell, Michele?"

"What's the difference?"

Don Luciano's lips moved slightly in the semblance of a grin. For just a moment, a younger man's gleam flashed in his eyes. Then it was gone, as if he had forgotten how to hold it. His frame was hunched, his hair thinner and grayer, his suspenders tighter over his expansive girth. Even his blue eyes had lost their piercing brightness, one partially covered by a cataract.

Michael watched as the Don extended a knobby hand to the spine of the old leather notebook that rested before him between the two pistols.

"What sin will I be guilty of today, Michele?"

"That depends on whether you help me or not."

Scaglione seemed to consider that briefly. "In asking for my help, you ask also that the past be put behind us."

"I'd rather speak of the present."

"Difficult to separate the two in our case, under the circumstances. We both made mistakes, did we not?"

Michael grinned.

"What are you smiling about, Michele?"

"It's the first time I ever heard you admit that."

The old man flapped his leather notebook in the air. "What do you call this?"

"What you always told me it was: a ledger of transgressions so you'd know how many acts of goodness were required of you."

"My point exactly."

"Mine too."

"Huh?"

"It's time for both of us to make up for the last meeting between us."

"Here, wasn't it?"

"It was."

The old man sat back and sighed.

Michael wanted to gaze across the table and feel nothing for him, the passage of time having widened the gulf between them. Instead, though, it seemed to have narrowed that gulf. Sitting across from him today, Michael Tiranno felt much the same awe and respect as the seven-year-old boy ushered into Luciano Scaglione's house on the day of his family's murder to learn the most important lesson the Don would ever teach him: that life went on.

"The place is no different than when you left it," Scaglione said, as if reading his mind. "I'm speaking of the land, of course." The Don took a deep breath. "I am spending more time here now. An old man growing nostalgic and reflective."

"Bullshit."

The old man frowned. "I have never been good at lying but the financial world has made me better at it. And I have you to thank for that, don't I, Michele?"

"Business or lying?"

"I didn't know there was a difference."

Michael watched as Scaglione ran a hand along the cover of his leather notebook.

"Nothing changes, I suppose," Don Luciano resumed. "Even my sins continue, though I've been a bit short on lust these last few years."

The brown hide of the notebook was even more faded, cracked in places from the strain of the years. The pages inside were thick with writing in the Don's special code and stained yellow at the edges.

Scaglione took a bite of his apple and chewed it slowly. "This help you need, does it have something to do with the lawyer who's been looking into your past?"

"What lawyer?" Michael asked, taken aback by the change in their conversation's direction.

"A man named Ferelli, Gianfranco Ferelli. He's been asking questions about you and your family all around Calta-girone."

"The Scaglione family?"

"The family of Michele Nunziato. I understand he's even been pestering the carabinieri at the post in Fontanarossa about the killers of your parents and sister, whether or not they were ever captured. He also spent time at the *commune*, city hall, there."

"Someone who wants to harm me, you think?" Michael asked, thinking of Naomi Burns's suspicions about the journalist Trumbull's sources.

"I'm not sure. Our sources describe him as very nervous, agitated. Some of the locals tell us he asked them questions about the workers who lived in those shacks on your farm, especially one named Attilio Cecchini. Do you remember him? Who was he?"

Michael turned toward the tractor as it roared deafeningly into the clearing, caught the sight of Attilio smiling at him and tipping his sweat-stained hat from high in the driver's seat. He was still smiling when his face exploded, the old man's teeth vanishing in a burst of gore from his ruptured skull. The tractor continued forward on its own, the hands of its faceless driver still clinging to the wheel.

"A worker on our farm," Michael said. "He used to let me sit in his lap and drive the tractor."

"Ferelli told the state authorities that Cecchini had a grand-daughter who lived with him on your farm."

Michael hadn't thought of her in a very long time. "Daniela. She was about the same age as my sister. They played together. But why would a lawyer care?"

"Perhaps Atillio was a *mascalzone* from the old days, hiding out from the authorities with a bag of cash stuffed in his mattress, eh?"

"He couldn't even afford new teeth when his dentures broke."

"Our sources say that Ferelli was very interested in death certificates," Don Luciano continued. "But little attention was paid to such things all those years ago. People lived. People died. Simpler."

"I always thought Daniela was killed that day with everyone else."

Don Luciano Scaglione shrugged. "Perhaps not. Perhaps she saw something Ferelli wanted to know more about. Information he may have wanted to use against you." He leaned forward. "So if not this lawyer, tell me what is worth risking your life over, Michele?"

"The future, Don Luciano."

TWENTY-SEVEN

SCAGLIONE ESTATE, THE PRESENT

"We have a common enemy hurting our common interests," Michael continued.

"There was a time when all our enemies and interests were the same, Michele."

"This one has brought Las Vegas to a standstill."

Don Luciano chuckled. "I sold off my interests in the casinos there while you were still in diapers."

"They attacked my casino, Don Luciano."

"*Your* casino, Michele." Scaglione took another bite of his apple. "I'm still waiting to hear where my interest in this lies."

"Because there's a good chance I'd die going after the terrorists."

"You think that's what I want?" Don Luciano started to reach his hands across the table, as if to lay them atop Michael's as he had years before, but pulled them back well before they got there. "I suggested the deal that let you keep your life."

"You left me no choice."

"Honor over business, was it as simple as that for you?"

"You tell me—you're the one I learned from."

"Then I would have said it was inevitable all along."

"And I would have agreed."

"But different times, those."

"And different times, these," Michael said. "And different enemies. It wasn't only my business the terrorists attacked. You still receive millions of dollars a year from interest in your investments in a half dozen nightclubs and strip clubs across town. Your American puppet affiliates control the city's three largest construction companies. I'd say you've been damaged too. And you risk lots more if the terrorists make good on their threat to strike the city again in twelve days."

Don Luciano eyed Michael Tiranno sternly. "Cut the bullshit and tell me what it is you want."

"The terrorist behind the attack on Las Vegas funds his killing by selling Afghan heroin through Asia and Indonesia. The warlords who control the poppy fields are the only ones who know where he is, the same warlords beholdened to the crime families of Sicily for the heroin trade in Western Europe and parts of the United States."

"These days, matters like this must be brought before the Commission to be acted upon."

"I'm sure your support still carries great weight, since the Commission members' investments in your legitimate holdings now total several hundred millions of dollars."

Don Luciano remained impassive. "So you want the Commission to request that these warlords help you find this terrorist."

"Or risk losing the Commission's business."

"That won't be an easy sell."

"I have great faith in your persuasive abilities."

Don Luciano leaned forward and studied Michael with a gaze that, for the time, had lost its indifference. "Killing this *fetuso* won't bring your family back to life, Michele."

"That has nothing to do with it."

"Ah, so you're just a greedy businessman out to save his ass. Is that it?"

"Your ass too."

The old man studied him from across the table, his smile thinning. "You haven't changed at all, have you, Michele?"

"Does anyone?"

"I suppose not. I used to take men's lives. Now I take their money." He shrugged. "What's the difference?"

"Blood."

"Don't play games with me, Michele, because we are two of a kind. We both made each other into the men we are today. I have not forgotten that." Don Luciano stopped, resuming in a softer voice, "Even though I have sometimes tried to." He touched the apple on the plate before him. "I think I'll finish my snack first, Michele. Then we'll see what we can do with the Commission. In the meantime, you and your ghost can go back to Rome and wait for my call."

Michael studied Don Luciano, framed by the two pistols across the table. "So tell me, Don Luciano, which of the guns was loaded?"

With great effort, the old man lifted both pistols from the table and raised them into the air, curling gnarled fingers round their triggers. Michael expected two harmless clicks to sound when a pair of resounding *pops!* made him recoil against the chair's back.

Don Luciano laid both guns, their barrels still smoking, upon the table again and took another bite of his apple. "See? You always had the luck, Michele."

TWENTY-EIGHT

The Black Sea, the present

Captain Henri Lebut stood on the bridge of the freighter *Miramar,* binoculars held uneasily at his eyes to better see through the misty, cool night before him. Around him, his senior crew members were understandably nervous, given the captain's sudden orders to change course and head to the Port of Odessa in the Ukraine and then south through the Black Sea. Nervous and frightened, since their stop in Odessa had seen the boarding of a half dozen well-armed men in conjunction with whatever new orders had been received.

As far as the crew knew, the *Miramar* was hauling no more than scrap metal to salvage yards in Varna on the Bulgarian coastline. What they didn't know was that the boarding of the six armed men had coincided with the loading of another piece of cargo. Captain Henri Lebut couldn't say what rested inside the large strongbox he had been ordered to store in the ship's safe; that didn't concern him nearly as much as the punishment he would face if the strongbox did not reach the Port of Sudan on the Red Sea in a timely manner. From the Black Sea, the *Miramar* would head through the Bosporus Strait to the Aegean and Mediterranean seas en route to the Suez Canal, making no stops whatsoever until she reached Sudan.

"Captain, radar's picked up something!"

"Range?" Lebut demanded through the clog that had lodged in his throat.

"Two miles and closing fast, directly astern."

Lebut twisted his binoculars in that direction, able to make nothing out through the misty night. Last time he checked, just a few minutes ago, they were still a hundred miles north of Istanbul.

"It's a small craft, Captain," the radar operator reported, tightening his fix. "No more than seven meters in length."

"This far out? That's impossible."

"Not at all," came a voice from behind the captain against the far bridge wall. He turned to meet the chilling gaze of the tall, nameless man who had brought the strongbox on board, along with the guards to protect it, in Odessa.

Lebut couldn't pin down the man's accent, as if years of moving among cultures had blurred it akin to the way a chameleon changes colors to better blend into the jungle. He didn't know the man's name, knew only he was effectively in charge of the ship until the *Miramar* reached the Port of Sudan, where her latest piece of cargo, and passengers, were to be offloaded.

"Captain," the man continued, "I want no alterations in course, nothing to alert them that we're on to their presence."

"Who's out there?" Lebut asked him. "Is there anything I should tell my—"

"I'll need the precise coordinates," the man said to the radar operator.

"One mile and closing!"

The radar operator's call echoed in his ear, as Henri Lebut watched the tall man place his guards in a tight cluster across the stern. In addition to Kalashnikov assault rifles, Lebut saw two of them were wielding grenade launchers, all weapons aimed directly at the fast-approaching craft's coordinates.

Like all captains, Lebut had been briefed countless times on the dangers of piracy at sea. No cargo or crew was safe these days, although open waters in the Black Sea offered innumerable disadvantages for the renegade pirate gangs more used to trolling the Malaccan Strait beyond Kuala Lumpur, the Panama Canal, or the Straits of Gibraltar. That's why an attack this far out seemed inconceivable, unless . . .

Lebut let his thought drift, the contents of the strongbox taken aboard in Odessa having clearly changed the rules. His hand dipped reflexively to the pistol he had wedged into his belt before descending from the bridge.

"Two thousand feet and closing!"

Lebut heard the soft hum of an engine an instant before a

speck of motion flared against the misty backdrop on the sea beyond.

"Fire!" the tall man ordered.

The resulting cacophony of fire deafened Lebut and sent him scurrying across to the port side of the ship with hands pressed over his ears. The blasts continued to resound as he sank to his knees, noticing a strange protrusion on the port gunwale. His vision sharpened enough to recognize it as a grappling hook in the same moment he spotted other identical hooks wedged in comparable positions across the deck; having been hurled up over the side, no doubt, from a *second* boat below.

Lebut tried to shout out a warning, but in that moment the craft speeding toward the *Miramar* exploded in a fiery blast that coughed flames high in the air. The next moment found fresh gunfire erupting, from everywhere on deck, it seemed, focused on the concentration of guards whose attention was rooted astern.

They tried to turn, twisting their weapons around futilely as bullets from the unseen force tore them apart. The most fortunate of the mysterious guards who had boarded the *Miramar* at the Port of Odessa was pitched over the side in the initial barrage. Lebut watched the heads of two of the less fortunate explode like melons under the relentless onslaught. Two others tried to find cover, only to have a hail of fire blast blood, bone, and entrails across the transom, some of the gore striking Lebut with what felt like the force of a bullet. The leader of the group went last, firing wildly out of reflex as bullets pushed him back against the gunwale and left him propped there with pools of near-black blood soaking the deck at his feet.

Forgetting about his own pistol, Lebut pressed his back against an exhaust manifold, then ducked through a bulkhead door and clamored down metal stairs into the bowels of the ship. He took them fast, clinging to the railings, realizing that the second pirate boat must have approached in the shadow of the *Miramar*'s radar, the now flaming craft nothing more than a decoy, a distraction.

Gunfire continued to reverberate on the deck above, mixed

with orders being shouted at his crew. Lebut could hear the echoes of ricocheting shells, the hollow ping of bullets lodging in the ship's steel. His goal now was to secure the strongbox, but not in the ship's safe, where the pirates would expect to find it.

Lebut knew the price he would pay should his precious cargo, whatever it was, be stolen, so he had come up with his own plans to secure it. He fit his captain's key into a rusty door and twisted it with a trembling hand, then shouldered his way into the ship's storeroom. After switching on a single dangling bulb, he rummaged amid the boxes of toilet paper, plastic utensils, and coffee filters until he found the strongbox he had moved here from the ship's safe.

"I'll take that, if you please."

It was a female voice, which shocked Lebut as much as hearing it in the first place. He turned slowly toward the figure of a woman armed with a semiautomatic pistol. A mask covered her face and matted her hair into a tight bulge beneath it.

Lebut held his ground and glanced at the pistol tucked into his belt.

"Touch that and you're dead," the woman warned. "Hand over the strongbox and you live."

Lebut hesitated, then extended the strongbox before him. He felt like a fool; in the process of trying to safeguard his secret cargo, he had led the enemy straight to it.

"There's no reason for anyone else to die, Captain," the woman continued. Her accent was difficult to pin down. Turkish, Lebut thought, with a strong hint of British thrown in. "Just place the strongbox down before you and toss your gun toward me. Then kneel down, facing the far wall."

Lebut laid the strongbox on the floor, flung his pistol aside, and knelt fearfully in anticipation of his own death. He held his breath as long as he could before turning slowly around to plead for his life. "Please, I—"

Lebut stopped. The woman was already gone.

TWENTY-NINE

Michael and Alexander returned to the Excelsior Hotel's Presidential Suite to await Don Luciano's phone call. Two anxiety-riddled days passed with no communication. Then Michael's satellite phone finally rang, an underling on the other end of the line providing instructions to meet Don Luciano the following morning at the Vatican Bank.

Michael and Alexander entered the Vatican Bank lobby at precisely ten o'clock. A Swiss guardsmen stood vigilantly inside the door, eyeing them cautiously as they walked to a reception desk occupied by a single man in civilian clothes. The man found Michael's name on a list before him and summoned a young man garbed in the black robes of a neophyte to escort them. The neophyte led Michael and Alexander up an ornate staircase to the third floor, which housed the bank's private offices, available to its most generous donors and patrons.

The Vatican Bank was a common name given to the Istituto per le Opere di Religione (IOR), or Institute for Religious Works, the central bank for the Roman Catholic Church located in Vatican City. Administered by the Roman Curia, the bank did business all over the world from this single location situated in the tower Nicholas V had built onto the pope's palazzo. The Vatican Bank did not issue loans or even its own checks. Its depositors were dioceses, parishes, religious orders, as well as agencies or businesses with religious purposes, and its aims centered almost exclusively on investing the proceeds from charitable efforts. The closest thing to traditional banking was an ATM machine placed in the lobby that allowed transactions to be completed in Latin.

The private offices were all named for past popes, and the neophyte led Michael and Alexander to the one marked ALOYSIUS, where Don Luciano's longtime bodyguard and chauffeur,

Marco, stood vigilantly at his post. Marco eased open the door as soon as the neophyte had taken his leave.

Michael followed Alexander inside a beautifully furnished loungelike room complete with shelves of elegantly bound books and brown leather furniture set atop a priceless Oriental carpet. The room was paneled in a rich wood the same color as the parquet floor.

"Amazing what twelve million a year given to Catholic charities gets you, eh, Michele?" Don Luciano Scaglione greeted him from the depths of a plush leather chair as Michael approached.

"I couldn't agree more," he said, taking the chair next to the old man.

The Don's gaze fell on Alexander standing before the now sealed door. "So your ghost has a face, after all. I could still use such a man in my employ. Then again, a man like this doesn't kill for money, does he?"

Alexander's expression didn't even flicker.

"He kills for sport," Scaglione continued, "to prove he's better than everybody else."

"Just like us, you mean, Don Luciano."

The old man moved his eyes back to Michael and smiled. "My teeth are going bad. Dentists tell me there's nothing they can do. With all that I've amassed, the best they can offer me is dentures."

"Men like us are prone to holding on to things we've already lost."

"Our romantic sides, then."

"A balance, Don Luciano, just like you taught me."

"A difficult lesson to learn, all the same, Michele. It's why I'm glad the Commission agreed to cooperate. There is enough in life for us to battle without each other."

"I quite agree."

Don Luciano uttered a deep sigh. "I can remember the days when the heads of all the families would meet for a meal, toast to our good health while we wished each other dead," he reminisced, smiling. "Now it's too dangerous to meet at all. Everything's conducted through intermediaries, never face-to-face. Days lost where it used to be hours."

"You've come to understand the business world better than I ever imagined."

"I guess you taught me as well as I taught you, Michele."

"Your contributions to the politicians of Rome, Catania, and Palermo haven't hurt either."

"Don't forget the Vatican. Helps keep the authorities from looking too closely at my affairs. The Boss of Bosses, Provenzano, hid for twenty years and they still found him, living with a donkey, no less. Thanks to you, Michele, I don't have to hide at all." Don Luciano paused and shifted about in his chair, as if the words made him uncomfortable. "In any case, the meeting of the Commission did not begin well. The families from Catania demanded a percentage of your casino holdings in return for their cooperation. Expecting such a request, I instructed our representative to remind the Commission of their substantial investments in my construction and financial subsidiaries in Europe as well as America, including our interests in Las Vegas. I believe that drove home the point."

"*Gràzie,* Don Luciano."

"It is I who should be thanking *you,* Michele." The old man's expression sank slightly. "But the cooperation of the Commission comes with one condition."

"I'm listening."

"That you make the contact in Afghanistan yourself as their representative."

THIRTY

ROME, THE PRESENT

The Vatican jet was scheduled to leave from Rome for Kabul that evening. Michael and Alexander were provided with diplomatic visas under false names on the pretext of researching potential charities for Luciano Scaglione to fund through his annual gift to the Church. Vittorio and Francesco, who would be accompanying them as another of the Don's conditions, required no such documentation since their name rendered their business on behalf of the Church legitimate.

"These friends of yours from the French Foreign Legion we'll be meeting in Kabul," Michael said to Alexander while they waited on board for the twins to arrive from Caltagirone.

"Hired previously to provide security for President Karsi's top staff," he explained. "They decided to stay on in the country after their tours were up to market their skills in the private sector. I've served with all of them before. They're good and they know the territory."

"Tell me more about the warlord we'll be meeting."

"His name is Dotson, former commander of the Northern Alliance that helped topple the Taliban. His influence has broadened immeasurably since Afghanistan's warlords have seized more control over the country's day-to-day affairs."

"How's he been able to avoid assassination?"

"Mostly by mending fences with the Taliban," Alexander explained. "That's enabled him to consolidate his power by coordinating poppy shipments through Taliban members to the terrorists."

"A marriage of convenience, then. This Dotson must be a survivor, kind of man I like doing business with."

"Don't be fooled. He controls upward of thirty percent of the country's estimated sixty-one hundred metric tons of opium harvested last year, far more than any other individual warlord."

"All the more reason to believe we speak the same language."

"You need to understand something, Stolarchos," Alexander said firmly. "Once we reach Kabul I'm in charge. When this plane takes off, we leave your world and enter mine."

Michael didn't argue.

Once on board, Francesco and Vittorio Scaglione held their eyes on Alexander for a long moment before finally taking their seats. For his part, Alexander seemed to have no interest in the twins, regarding them only briefly before returning his gaze to the maps of Afghanistan and the border region with Pakistan.

Michael could not help but be amazed by the man, his total commitment and confidence in his ability to pull off what others would deem impossible. Michael had heard many legends, and met some of the figures behind them, but Alexander was the only one who lived up to everything that had been said about him.

His background with the French Foreign Legion, which operated like no other fighting force in the world, was much to blame here. The Legion culled a portion of its core membership from dark, dank prison cells the world over, the most deadly men on the planet accepted into their ranks in exchange for a second chance. Since the missions the Legion undertook were usually dangerous, if not suicidal, that second chance was often short-lived. But those who accept it were paid well for their efforts, and the duration of their service, if they survived, was always considerably shorter than the long, often life terms to which they had been sentenced.

Alexander Koursaris was Greek by birth, born in the city of Sparta. Proud of his heritage, he proceeded to learn everything he could about his ancestors, whose society and entire lifestyle were based on war and battle, culminating in the famed battle of Thermopylae when three hundred Spartans held back a million-strong Persian army long enough for the Spartan army to regroup and gain victory. For Alexander, this tale was far more than a legend, becoming a mantra for how he planned to live his life.

But poverty led him to join gangs practicing petty street crime on the streets of Athens, where he saved the life of an old man during a brutal beating at the hands of a rival gang. The old man's name was Eugenios, a slovenly recluse who'd long lived on the fringes of the Athens underworld.

"Now, I'm going to save *your* life," Eugenios promised with a smile, as if Alexander had just passed a test he'd been given.

In the months that followed, the old man taught Alexander the ancient Greek martial art of Pankration, combining deadly techniques that utilized every part of the body as a potential weapon, the primary objective to kill an opponent with a single blow. Derived from Spartan warriors and dating back to the time of Alexander the Great, Pankration did more than save Alexander's life; it *gave* him a life. Alexander used his newfound skills to enter the world of high-stakes, bare-knuckle brawling in which the fight was almost always to the death. He built a considerable nest egg by betting on himself, while at the same time building a reputation that attracted the notice of the Camorra crime syndicate out of Naples.

Drained of personnel by massive police sweeps in Italy, the Camorra recruited Alexander into their employ. One of the most violent and bloody criminal organizations to this day, the Camorra's primary vehicle to raise money for its various activities was cigarette smuggling. Alexander took charge of security surrounding the transport of *contrabbando* cargoes of cigarettes from Marseilles and Athens to Naples.

His primary duties revolved around the Camorra's fleet of powerful speedboats used to offload crates from vessels stopped in international waters for prearranged rendezvous. They were then distributed out of Naples without the burden of taxes, which amounted to 75 percent of the sale price.

Alexander's success in this regard brought him to the attention of Raffaele Cutolo, the king of the Camorra. His rise through the various levels of the organization was incredibly swift, derailed finally when Cutolo and his top lieutenants were jailed. Alexander was arrested in Marseilles by Interpol and had been sentenced to ten years in prison in France for smuggling when the French Foreign Legion offered him a way out: his freedom after the same ten years in its service, if he managed to survive that long.

The training he endured at the Legion's camps on the French island of Corsica was the hardest physical regimen he had ever experienced. Six months of eighteen-hour days that claimed half the class by attrition and another quarter by death left him an expert killer with any weapon or firearm imaginable. Hand-to-hand combat was taught by former Israeli commandos expert in the deadly art of Krav Maga, a style swiftly mastered by Alexander thanks to its similarities to Pankration. As he deftly outfought his Israeli instructors, Alexander imagined he could almost feel Eugenios smiling at him once again and embraced his training with the understanding that he wasn't learning how to fight so much as to kill—and not just kill, either, but kill with as few blows as possible.

That training became crucial to Alexander's surviving ten years in the Foreign Legion's elite Rapid Insertion Force, the *Force D'Intervention Rapide,* a capacity in which he was deployed numerous times against terrorist strongholds and staging grounds. There were also a number of hostage rescue scenarios, never garnering the kind of publicity that would have forced the Legion to forfeit the especially brutal methods Alexander welcomed. Survival mattered to him only to the extent that it allowed him to become the absolute best at what he did: killing. It became more than that, though, as those years progressed and Alexander found himself mixing the various skills he had learned into his own form of combat that made him as deadly as he was unmerciful. Fiercely loyal to his cause and without conscience, he became known among the Legion's ranks as the Achilles of modern times.

Upon surviving the stretch that cemented his legend, Alexander was recruited by the Zaire embassy in Paris to become personal bodyguard to Mobutu Sese Seko, president of that country. He twice personally foiled rebel assassination attempts launched by Laurent-Désiré Kabila and his Alliance des Forces Démocratiques Pour la Libération du Congo-Zaire, the second incident coming just before Michael met Alexander for the first time. This earned him the ire of the murderous Kabila himself.

It was not an exaggeration to say that the Seven Sins Resort and Casino might never have come to be if it wasn't for the bond Michael later formed with Alexander. The deadly man who had sworn lifetime allegiance became first the facilitator of his dream and then the protector of it. Anyone who dared make a move on Michael Tiranno, after all, risked evoking the legendary Alexander's skills, skills Michael would need more than ever in the coming days.

THIRTY-ONE

"Are you asking me what I think, Michael?" Naomi Burns challenged, after Michael called her on his satellite phone from the rear of the cabin once the Vatican jet was airborne.

"No, because I already know."

"Then why bother calling me?"

"You needed to hear it from me."

"Just as you need to be back here running your company."

"I've read my e-mail, Naomi. Morgan Stanley and Credit Suisse have downgraded King Midas World's bond ratings, now trading at eighty-five cents on the dollar. And our stock price is down thirty percent in the last forty-eight hours. Our CFO's been fielding calls from CIBC World Markets and Deutsche Bank. Business articles are predicting that King Midas World will default on its payments within ninety days."

"Our problems are external as well as internal. Everyone wants reassurance, and there's nobody here to give it to them. We've got wolves at our door and they can't be kept at bay forever."

"That's why I want you to get them on the phone."

"Who?"

"Everyone that matters. Tell them you're scheduling a conference call."

"For when?"

"Now."

It took Naomi two hours to make the necessary contacts and arrange the call for 11:00 A.M. eastern time in the United States.

"All right, Michael," she said from the Forum, "in addition to Kenneth Cohan, you are on the line with the CFO from King Midas World, COO of the Seven Sins, securities and bond analysts from CIBC World Markets and Credit Suisse, and money managers from the major institutional funds I detailed earlier."

"Hello, everyone," Michael greeted them through his satellite phone. "Sorry for the short notice."

"Picked a fine time to leave the country," came the gruff response of one of the institutional investors, Franklin Marks, representing Bank of America Securities.

"It's a business trip."

"Business trip? Losing three million dollars a day with all the problems facing us?" Marks shot back.

"I'm working on solving them."

"Michael," came the much calmer voice of Kenneth Cohan, manager of the hedge fund that had invested more cash in the Seven Sins than any other, "nobody blames you for what's happened. But the fact remains that the Seven Sins is a standalone property that won't be able to manage the crisis as well as your bigger and better-capitalized rivals on the Strip."

"What he's saying," Franklin Marks picked up, "is that the ship's sinking and we can only plug the holes for so long."

"And if I was still in Vegas, I'd be sticking my fingers in the same dam. Might buy us some time, but not enough. So I decided to pursue a longer-lasting solution."

"Just what is that exactly?" came the heavily accented voice of Stephan Beauvais from Credit Suisse.

"You trusted me with your money four years ago, Stephan. I ask you to trust me now."

"Now is considerably different."

"That's right, because thanks to all of you, King Midas World built the greatest casino property the world has ever seen. That was true before the attack and it's still true now."

"Except hotel capacity is down to ten percent. Action at table games is nonexistent. Win per day per slot is down from three hundred fifty dollars to forty dollars," Marks noted. "The Seven Sins is dying."

"But you all believed in the vision that conceived it, didn't you? *My* vision. You didn't just trust a business plan with all its projections and debt ratios, you trusted me. Just like you trusted me when our first year of operation doubled those projections, and just like you trusted me up until ten o'clock last Saturday night when Las Vegas was hit."

"Things have changed, Michael," another voice reminded him.

"But I haven't. And all of you have gotten rich watching me deliver on everything I promise."

"What are you promising now?" asked Kenneth Cohan, his tone more conciliatory than the others'.

"That things are going to get better soon."

"When is soon?" a voice asked. "And how exactly are we going to turn things around?"

"Not we—me."

"With all due respect, Michael," came Franklin Marks's sharp response, "I don't believe in miracles."

"Me either. Just wait."

"What are you suggesting?"

"It's not a suggestion, it's a promise."

"Promises, miracles," droned Marks slowly. "What's next, prayer?"

"No, a plan that may include new sources of capital to cover our mounting losses until the situation improves," Michael lied.

"Ah, so now you're a magician, making funds appear for Vegas out of nowhere."

"He's right, Michael," Kenneth Cohan said. "You can't pull a rabbit out of your hat this time."

"Just sit tight for now. And keep trusting me."

THIRTY-TWO

VATICAN JET, THE PRESENT

"Well?" Michael asked Naomi, after the call was finished.

"You bought yourself time," she told him, "so long as you're alive to use it."

"I already promised Alexander I wouldn't participate in the raid."

"Just like you were going to come straight home after your

meeting in Sicily. Who am I talking to here? Please tell me, because I'd like to know."

"You already do."

"That's what I'm afraid of. You think your enemies wouldn't love to let the SEC or the Nevada Gaming Commission know what you're up to? My God, Michael, after all we've been through, all we've fought for."

"We're still fighting, Naomi. Forget that and none of what we've accomplished matters."

Silence filled the line before Naomi Burns finally spoke again. "Scaglione could be setting you up. Please tell me you've considered that, at least."

"He's not."

"So now you're a miracle worker and a psychic too."

"No," Michael told her, "just a prophet."

"There's something else," Michael continued, holding Gianfranco Ferelli's business card, given to him by Don Luciano. "I want you to contact this lawyer in Rome. He's been digging into my past."

"All the more reason to get back in your plane and come home," Naomi said, even though she knew it was futile. "Which part of your past?"

"Michele Nunziato's, all the way back to the massacre, apparently. I'd like to know what he's so interested in."

"I'll make contact immediately," Naomi Burns promised.

Michael placed another call on the satellite phone as soon as the connection was broken, the number committed to memory long ago but never once dialed.

"Michael," Miranda Alvarez greeted him.

"How'd you know it was me?"

"A feeling, I guess."

"I wanted to thank you for calling the other day."

"Is that why you're calling me now?"

"I called to say I'm sorry, Miranda."

"For what?"

"For not calling before. For waiting so many years."

"I never expected you to. You're not in Vegas, are you?"

"No." He stopped, started again after briefly collecting his thoughts. "Ten years ago, you know I had no choice. It was the only way to ensure your safety and the boys'."

"Has something changed, Michael?"

Michael ran his teeth over his lower lip. "I'm sorry about your husband. I'm not sure if I ever apologized for that."

"You didn't have to then and you don't now."

"It changed a lot of things."

Michael could hear Miranda's breathing on the other end of the line through the silence.

"That's why you're calling me now, isn't it?" she asked him suddenly. "You've gone back."

"I had no choice."

"But why call me, Michael? Why now?"

"Because I needed to hear your voice. Because I needed to know I'm still the same man."

"No one ever changes."

"I hope you're right, Miranda."

Silence filled the air between them again, Michael searching for something to say when Miranda spoke.

"Can we see each other, Michael?"

"I was thinking about that too. When all this is over."

"I guess people do change, after all."

"Not really," Michael told her.

THIRTY-THREE

KABUL, THE PRESENT

The Vatican jet landed in Afghanistan six hours later at a private airstrip five miles from the main airport in Kabul, huge plumes of dust rising into the dry, sun-baked air on either side of the jet as it taxied. After being cleared through customs, Michael, Alexander, and the Scagliones were escorted to a holding area where the veterans of the French Foreign Legion whom Alexander had contacted were waiting. He referred to them as the Koruf, Greek for "the very best," since he claimed these were the finest fighters he had ever seen.

The Koruf did not introduce themselves by name and their handshakes were uniformly firm; they didn't need to prove anything by squeezing harder. There were eight of them in all, and Michael saw in their eyes the same thing he saw in Alexander's. They were being paid upward of twenty thousand dollars per month by private contractors for their work in Afghanistan, a sum Michael had agreed to double for this one mission.

A trio of black armored SUVs with bulletproof glass waited for them outside. Tailgates were raised and cargo hatches opened to reveal duffel bags containing the weapons Michael hoped they were going to need. The scents of gunmetal and oil were heavy on the air until the duffels were zipped closed and the cargo hatches sealed again.

The convoy headed west from the airstrip to the InterContinental Hotel, taking a slightly longer route to bypass the inevitable midday traffic congestion that dominated the ravaged portions of western Kabul. Located on the outskirts of the city, the hotel had become host to a number of international conferences, as well as home for many journalists, diplomats, and Afghan government ministers. Accordingly, security was tight even before Alexander's added precautions.

Once at the InterContinental, Alexander left two guards with Michael and the Scagliones and headed inside with the rest of the Koruf to ensure the hotel was secure. He returned alone some twenty minutes later, having left his men posted at strategic points on the floor where the meeting was to take place. This time Alexander bypassed the lobby in favor of an unmarked side entrance used by dignitaries with a need and a desire not to be seen. A single elevator inaccessible to ordinary guests took them to the hotel's fifth floor. Another of the Koruf waited there to escort them to the suite where the Afghan warlord known only as Dotson was waiting.

Michael moved to the front of the pack when they reached the door guarded by one of Dotson's plainclothes bodyguards.

Noting his approach, the bodyguard stepped respectfully aside as he eased the door open for Michael to enter along with Alexander and the Scaglione twins, leaving the Koruf to their posts along the floor.

Inside, Dotson rose from an easy chair relocated to be in direct view of the door. He was a wide-shouldered man who still wore the military uniforms that had been his trademark when he commanded the Northern Alliance forces that rolled south on the United States's behalf after the Taliban fell. His hair was silvery and thick, his appearance Western in all respects. The distinctly American army camouflage fatigues he wore bagged slightly, making him seem even huskier.

Dotson smiled broadly at Michael's approach, showcasing twin rows of glistening white teeth. He had similarly dismissed all of his guards, save for three, to match the number of men he knew Michael would be bringing into the room.

Michael extended his hand toward the warlord but Dotson swallowed him in a hearty hug instead.

"This must be the man I have to thank for much of my riches." Dotson beamed, holding Michael by the shoulders at arm's distance now, his slate blue eyes full and wide.

"Only indirectly, General," Michael replied, addressing Dotson by his chosen title. "Since I've never had anything to do with this part of the business."

"The route does not matter to Dotson, only the money." The warlord grinned. "I agreed to meet with you out of courtesy, but if this is about a renegotiation . . ."

"The terms of your arrangement are fine as they are," Michael told him. "In fact, the members of the Commission look forward to many, even more profitable years, considering Cosa Nostra is your biggest trading partner. But we have a problem."

"Let us sit as friends," Dotson said, offering Michael a simple armchair next to his larger one. The display was meant to demonstrate who was in charge, and Michael let it go out of deference to the man whose help he badly needed.

"Now, my new friend," the warlord began, "Dotson is listening."

THIRTY-FOUR

"The recent attacks on Las Vegas have complicated the supply chain between you, General, and the Commission of Cosa Nostra," Michael started, getting right to the point.

The warlord crossed his legs, then uncrossed them as if afraid of disturbing the perfect creases in the pants of his uniform. "Dotson does not understand what one has to do with the other."

"The issue," Michael explained, "is the source for your product. I'm afraid the Commission finds itself no longer able to do business with anyone who does business with Jafir Sari Bayrak and Al Altar."

The smile slipped from Dotson's face. The three guards who'd remained in the room with him tensed visibly.

"We do not deal directly with him or his organization. We are simply a conduit."

"Yes, for the Taliban."

Dotson stiffened, bristling at what he might have taken as an offense to his honor, had Michael not elaborated.

"Business mandates such unsavory alliances, General. None of us are immune, not Cosa Nostra, not even me, so we can live with that. But the profits reaped from selling your product helped fund the strike on Las Vegas, and that we cannot live with."

Dotson weighed the portent of Michael's assertion. "You speak of a considerable percentage of our business," the warlord said.

"Our estimates put the number at twelve percent, fifteen at most," Michael said, cocking his gaze back toward the twins. "Is that correct?"

Vittorio and Francesco nodded in unison, taking their cue.

"As Dotson said, considerable."

"The Commission is willing to increase the level of their own distribution to make up for your loss," Michael told him.

The warlord waved a finger before his face. "Dotson does not see the issue as that simple."

"It isn't, which is why Jafir Sari Bayrak must also be eliminated, General."

Dotson caught the look in Michael's eyes and smiled again. "You mean, you're planning to . . ." His voice tailed off, as he realized the reason for Michael Tiranno's visit. "You want Dotson to tell you where he is."

"And lead my men to him."

The warlord flashed a smile that lingered only until his eyes fixed briefly on Alexander. "You and Dotson are much alike, my new friend."

"I take that as a great compliment."

"But you ask a lot of Dotson."

"I am authorized to tell you that the Commission cannot accept doing business with anyone who does business with Jafir Sari Bayrak," Michael repeated.

"Is that an ultimatum?"

"A necessity."

Dotson studied Michael again. "Yours was one of the casinos hit?"

"Yes, General."

"I understand your business, but I'm not sure if you understand mine."

"There is ample product available from other sources."

Dotson snickered at the mere possibility. "All shit."

"Worse than shit."

"You are offering Dotson a choice."

"The Commission is offering the choice: Cosa Nostra or the terrorists," Michael confirmed.

"At considerable risk to Dotson, definitely worth a premium."

"There will be no premium. But, as I said, the Commission is willing to increase distribution to compensate for any lost business."

Dotson's face looked chiseled in stone, emotionless for the

first time. "We are both businessmen, yes? So I must ask you, as a businessman, would you accept such terms?"

"Under the circumstances, yes, because in the long run it will be better for your business." Michael began to speak again before Dotson had a chance to respond. "Especially, General, if you wish to stay in business."

Dotson's eyes widened in surprise. Vittorio and Francesco Scaglione exchanged a nervous glance. Francesco started forward, only to feel Vittorio restrain him.

"We are sitting like friends and this is how you speak to me?" the warlord said to Michael, sounding more hurt than enraged.

"The Commission is not about to take no for an answer. Not only will you not be able to sell your product to us, you will not be able to sell it to anyone. Cosa Nostra will enforce an embargo on distribution of your product to all sources outside this region. You should also be aware that the Commission has secured the cooperation of the 'Ndrangheta syndicate out of Calabria. I believe they're big clients of yours too." Michael paused to let his point better sink in. "You have many others beholdened to you who won't like that, General, and they will not appreciate the fact that you've become a pariah no one wants to do business with. Am I making myself clear?"

Out of the corner of his eye, Michael could see the Scaglione twins standing dumbfounded and flabbergasted. But things had progressed too far for them to intervene without the substantial risk of losing face and sacrificing the respect their father commanded. They were left to hold their ground tautly, seething inside.

Dotson's breathing, meanwhile, had become louder and more rapid as his gaze remained on Michael. The stillness in his nearly unblinking eyes betrayed none of his intentions.

"I will need time to consider your . . . proposal."

Michael rose deliberately. "I don't have much of it to waste, General," he said and started for the door.

THIRTY-FIVE

KABUL, THE PRESENT

"Don't ever try anything like that again," Francesco Scaglione threatened, inches away from Michael's face, as soon as Alexander had finished electronically sweeping the suite to which they had adjourned. "You risked the honor of my family."

Alexander moved to within a single lunge of both brothers, waiting for Michael's cue.

"You think your father would not have approved?"

"Not when a man pretends to speak with the voice of the Commission."

"He'd understand I had no choice. He knew this was the way it was going to be from the beginning."

The bravado slipped from Francesco's features. "He said this to you?"

"He didn't have to. He gave me his blessing; that was enough."

"But we did not give you our blessing, did we?" Vittorio challenged.

"Then you have a choice, don't you? Either you let this go, and we part for good when Bayrak is dead. Or you hold a grudge and we remain sworn enemies long after. Which do you think your father would choose?"

Francesco Scaglione backed off, silent and red-faced, brushing aside a hand of comfort from his brother. "And what happens if Dotson turns you down anyway?"

"The way I put it to him, I'm betting he won't."

"And what if you lose?"

"I never lose," Michael said, smiling tightly.

THIRTY-SIX

Caltagirone, 1987

"You can't accept failing, can you, Michele?" Don Luciano reflected while they sat in their customary chairs at the veranda table to celebrate Michael's graduation from high school.

"It's the only thing that scares me."

"Everyone fails. A man learns from it and moves on, and once he succeeds, it feels all the better. And you are destined for success, Michele, of that I am sure."

They had been occasionally conversing in English for years already, even though the Don's was rusty at best. Michael had now mastered the language through a combination of his studies and a steady diet of American films along with daily viewings of CNN. Once his homework was done, he would read books on American history for hours on end, fascinated by the place of the United States in the world economy and the creation of the free market. He not only taught himself to speak English flawlessly, but also to think in his new language.

"So what is it you wanted to talk to me about?" Don Luciano asked him after a pause.

"I want to attend the International University in Monaco."

Scaglione's eyebrows twitched. Located in Fontvielle on the French Riviera, the International University was regarded as one of the finest business schools in Europe.

"You wish to study business, Michele?"

"Remember what you told me years ago, Don Luciano?"

"I told you many things."

"You said my strengths were different, that my future lay with helping you change the way the Scaglione family did business."

"So?"

"The means to accomplish that is what I want to study."

Michael regularly scrutinized the financial papers and journals, leaving him with a fascination for trade in soft commodities like coffee, cane sugar, and cocoa. He was keenly aware of

Don Luciano's wariness over the Italian authorities' and Interpol's recent crackdowns on illegal activities and their dogged pursuit of any number of his contemporaries. The old ways were dying and it seemed only a matter of time before Luciano Scaglione would suffer the same fate.

More than anything else, Michael wanted to prevent that from happening. But he had not told Don Luciano he had chosen International University for another reason, that its rolls were filled with children of the ultrarich and powerful of Europe. Jet-setting spoiled youths who yearned for excess and perpetuated it with their unlimited expense accounts. They figured prominently in Michael's grand, but still hazy, plan.

And there could be no better place in which to enact it. The Principality of Monaco, which encompassed Monte Carlo as well, enjoyed a long history of manipulation and struggle, beginning in 1297 when François Grimaldi successfully led a small army into the fortress that controlled the strategic port. The Grimaldi family ruled until the French Revolution led to Monaco's annexation to France, only to have their power restored with the abdication of Napoléon in 1814.

It was another Grimaldi descendant, Prince Charles III, who laid the groundwork for modern-day Monaco by establishing the Société des Bains de Mer. The company started out as a handful of hotels, a theater, and a single casino, which would soon flourish and form the foundation of the now famed district of Monte Carlo. In later years, the efforts of Prince Rainier III further expanded this vision, building Monaco into a haven for the rich and powerful, thanks in large part to the privacy, and confidentiality, it offered its residents.

For his high school graduation present, Don Luciano bought Michael an Alfa Romeo Spider, which was waiting for him when he arrived in Monte Carlo just shy of his nineteenth birthday. Then, to cover his tuition and living expenses at the university, the Don's people opened a special account for Michael known as a *compte courant* at Compagnie Monegasque des Banque. He was issued a Carte Bleue Internationale Visa card from which he was able to draw funds up to twenty-five thousand dollars. He utilized the funds sparingly, paying just enough bar tabs and buying just enough meals to ingratiate himself with the jet-setters of which he needed to be a part.

Michael knew he could not match his schoolmates in money. And yet gaining their graces was crucial to achieving what had brought him to Monte Carlo. From the day he had managed to escape the wrath of the Scaglione twins as a young boy, Michael had learned the ease with which people could be manipulated. The trick was to make them do what they wanted to already, work within their nature instead of trying to change it.

The schoolmates to whom he needed to ingratiate himself were young men, like him, some of whom were not even currently enrolled. And the quickest way to win them over was to win over the young women with whom they wanted to be seen. Michael began frequenting the Café des Paris in the main plaza, where some of the women he was interested in loitered away many an afternoon. He always sat by himself, drawing their attention by appearing to pay no attention to them.

One day a pair of young men began harassing the girls, speaking crudely to them. Michael approached, fresh double espresso held casually in hand.

"You're being rude," he told them in English, then repeated the words in French and Italian.

The larger of the two men snickered in his chair. "Think you're smart?" he asked Michael in French.

"Not really," Michael said, and poured his scalding-hot double espresso onto the man's crotch.

The man rushed away screaming, as the hot liquid soaked through his jeans, followed closely by his friend.

For his part, Michael simply smiled at the girls and walked off, depositing his empty cup in a trash can.

"You did well," Michael told the young man whose jeans were still sodden five minutes later and two streets away. He counted out five hundred French francs and handed it to him.

The young man grimaced. "If I had known it was going to hurt this much, I would have asked for more."

"You're lucky it wasn't a triple."

The next day the girls joined him at his table, approaching tentatively.

"Not going to throw coffee on us, are you?" one of them asked.

Michael tipped his cup upside down to show it was empty. A second girl smiled and ordered him a refill.

He had never entirely shed the earthy nature that came, first, with being raised on a farm and, later, being among the workers on Don Luciano's estate. So he decided to use that to his advantage by buying his way into the upper crust's favorite haunts dressed in jeans and simple T-shirts, the distinction adding to a mystique that was rapidly developing into legend.

Upon meeting him, girls like those from the coffee bar quickly learned that his fashionably simple garb was complemented by a level of sophistication rare for someone his age. Similarly, the young men who might otherwise have been jealous of the many advances made toward him found Michael as interesting and unique as the women did. The ease with which he graced their presence was balanced by the distance he always kept, just far enough away to make them work for his attention. Michael always knew when to draw close or pull back, forging an enigmatic persona that heightened his mystique.

He pretended to snort the lines of powdery cocaine and smoke rich hashish with them. At bars, the straight vodka he was known to fancy was actually water and nothing more. The capacity for excess of these trust fund children repulsed Michael, and he found himself unimpressed with a status they had achieved based solely on the accomplishments of their families. But their acceptance brought him into the rarefied world he was determined to enter.

He would stroll with his "friends" about the luxurious shops on Avenue Grimaldi, interested not so much in the merchandise as the shoppers: the rich and powerful, those who had risen to the top of their respective worlds, achieved their dreams. Michael was envious not of their wealth, but of their standing, individuals who had beaten back all challenges, vanquished the competition. Avenue Grimaldi was their playground, their personal souvenir stand.

One of the students Michael befriended was a young Arab man who boasted of never attending a single class during his three years at the university, while passing all his courses with flying colors. Samar Pharaon preferred to go by Sam, but it was his surname that interested Michael more.

Sam was the son of Amir Pharaon, considered to be the richest man in the world, who owned the *Atlantis,* a 450-foot, $130-million yacht complete with a helicopter that was docked in the Port of Monaco. Many a night when his thoughts and dreams kept him from sleep, Michael would drive over to the port just to stare at the *Atlantis,* imagining himself one day possessing the kind of wealth required to live such an exorbitant lifestyle. In moments like this, he realized that his true future lay beyond the Scaglione family in a world he would make on his own, remaking himself in the process. For now, though, his goals continued to center around finding the means to legitimize the Scagliones' vast fortune, and in the process launch his career in the business world.

He continued to focus on the soft commodities market, seeing them as potentially holding the means to this end. Coffee, cane sugar, and cocoa were not greatly regulated at their origins; quite the opposite, they were often controlled by dictators and governments in corrupt regimes, located mostly in Africa and South America, seldom held accountable for their actions. These commodities were also extremely liquid and easy to sell, the demand for them insatiable in markets all over the world, in any economic conditions. Michael willed himself to remain patient and not force the issue, knowing he'd get only one shot to enact his plan and prove himself to Don Luciano.

That shot finally came when he was still a junior at the university, excelling in his studies while continuing to carouse with his newfound friends till all hours of the night and morning. He was shopping with a few of them in the exclusive Metropole Palace shopping mall, when he saw a tall black man enter a jewelry store enclosed by a half dozen bodyguards and a strikingly beautiful black woman. Michael followed them inside and trolled the display cases, trying to discern as much as he could before a portly, prematurely balding jeweler in his early thirties escorted the group into a private room.

After the entourage had departed, Michael selected a ten-thousand-dollar Cartier watch to purchase and made sure the portly jeweler waited on him. Small talk revealed him to be Charles Devereaux, son of the store's owner. In the additional conversation that followed, a prod from Michele led Charles to boast of his many powerful clients, including the woman Michael had just glimpsed: Bobi Ladawa, wife of the president of Zaire. He invited Charles to a party he was giving the following night, which, of course, he hadn't planned yet.

At that party, after finishing a bottle of champagne Michael provided, Charles told him the tall black man who had accompanied Bobi Ladawa into his store was Kananga, the country's ambassador to France. And, after spending the night with two beautiful prostitutes hired by Michael to pretend to be lustful coeds, Charles helped arrange a meeting for him with Kananga at Zaire's embassy in Paris. Hopelessly addicted to beautiful women otherwise unattainable to him, Charles agreed to vouch for Michael, telling the ambassador he was interested in investing substantial assets from a trust fund provided him by his wealthy parents.

Michael purchased a Canali suit and flew to Paris from Nice-Côte d'Azur International Airport. He'd hoped Kananga would have a car meet him and was a bit apprehensive when he ended up taking a cab to the embassy instead. Nonetheless, the ambassador proved hospitable and affable, listening intently to Michael's explanation of his interests in the vast coffee reserves exported yearly from Zaire. Michael made it clear that a recent riff had left him estranged from his family and he wanted nothing more than to prove himself by attaining a fortune even greater than theirs, starting in Zaire through a trading company he had founded called World Trade Agricola. Kananga informed Michael that a fellow Italian named Antonio Carpacci already controlled the vast majority of the country's export quota. But, intrigued and impressed by this wealthy and ambitious young man, Kananga offered to set up a meeting for Michael with Carpacci in Zaire.

"I owe you a great debt, Ambassador," Michael said grate-
fully.

"So long as I am not wasting both our times."

"Ambassador?"

"I hope you understand this isn't going to be easy,"
Kananga said, suddenly sounding skeptical. "After all, it's not
your world."

"Not yet," Michael told him.

THIRTY-SEVEN

ZAIRE, 1989

Michael flew from Nice into the capital of Kinshasa the following week on Swissair through Geneva, using the last reserves of his Visa card to purchase a business-class ticket and
book himself a junior suite at the Hotel InterContinental. He
then gave instructions to Carpacci's office to have a car pick
him up, knowing they would have checked up on him to confirm his validity and that such a man would inevitably expect
to be taken care of in that manner.

The car, a Bentley, arrived right on time the next morning
and drove across dirty, unpaved roads to a simple, one-story
building on the city's outskirts. The unmarked building was
surrounded by an electrified fence and guarded by a brigade
of armed men. Inside, Michael was ushered to a waiting room
where he sat with upward of twenty black men, their shirts
wet with jungle sweat, speaking loudly in Swahili, while three
more guards armed with machine guns looked on.

Michael guessed the men were all farmers here to exchange
their receipts for harvested coffee beans, already deposited in
Carpacci's vast warehouses, for cash. Michael took a seat in
the corner and almost smiled; the process was exactly as he
pictured it and would suit the needs of the Scaglione family
perfectly. He fully imagined that in a country as riddled with

corruption as Zaire, nothing happened without the blessing of President Mobutu himself. Therefore, Carpacci must have been paying dearly for control of such a huge portion of Zaire's coffee quota. And, while that may have boded poorly for Michael in the short term, it held great prospects in the long.

He was escorted into Carpacci's office ahead of others, drawing a host of angry snarls and recriminations, barked at him in Swahili. The dapper and perfectly coiffed Carpacci sat behind a desk with another two guards armed with assault rifles flanking him.

"So what can I do for you, my young friend?" Carpacci asked, not rising to accept Michael's outstretched hand.

"I have a business called World Trade Agricola," Michael told him, referring to the corporation he had founded, on paper anyway, in Geneva.

"Never heard of it."

"The truth is my associates and I have never heard of you either." Michael watched Carpacci bristle. "But we are extremely liquid and would like to move some of our assets into coffee trading."

"Well, if you're here for my blessing, I wish you luck. If you're here to make a deal, I'm afraid my crops are already spoken for."

Michael had anticipated as much, aware that Zaire's Mobutu government had assigned nearly 90 percent of their international quota to Carpacci. Carpacci, in turn, had huge deals in place with multinational companies like Cargil and Sucre et Denrées, which already had paid vast sums of cash to Carpacci's organization for reserved crops and future shipments.

"I believe I can offer you more favorable terms," Michael said, producing an envelope that contained his business plan.

He handed it across the desk to Carpacci, who discarded it indifferently.

"I'll read your memo and get back to you," Carpacci said. He held his gaze on Michael, undistracted for the first time. "Don't expect much. My contracts are long-term and I'm a man of my word. How much were you looking for?"

"World Trade Agricola can move twenty thousand tons per month."

Carpacci looked taken aback. His expression changed. "My entire quota. Who do you think you are?"

"Someone with whom it would be in your best interest to do business."

Carpacci almost laughed. "A fucking kid?"

"Money knows no age, Signore Carpacci."

"You've got a long line ahead of you, my young friend; our robusta crops are among the most wanted all over the world." Carpacci paused, continuing to gaze at Michael as if unsure exactly what he was seeing. "I'll tell you what. Out of respect for Ambassador Kananga, I think I can manage five hundred tons."

"Per month?"

"Total."

"For now," Michael said, aware Carpacci was effectively brushing him off.

"Have your bank forward us evidence of funds, and financial references, and if acceptable we will contact you to provide the necessary instructions," Carpacci said, returning his attention to the papers before him while a pair of armed guards moved to escort Michael from the room.

The meeting had gone pretty much as expected, Michael reflected on the flight back to Monaco. He had learned those parts of the business that had eluded him before. His next step would require an audience with Don Luciano to convince the old man to back his plan of creating a totally legitimate business enterprise to remove the family's vast reserves of cash from the scrutiny of the authorities and put them to good use through aboveboard investments. He was considering how precisely he might manage this, when he opened the door to his apartment in Monte Carlo to find the Don himself sitting next to Marco, his ever-present bodyguard.

"We need to talk, Michele," Scaglione said sternly.

THIRTY-EIGHT

"I received notice that your Carte Bleue Internationale Visa card is over its limit by five thousand dollars," Don Luciano continued. "I assume you have an explanation."

"You already know my explanation."

"Then please refresh my memory."

"I'm doing what I came here to do, Don Luciano."

"I thought you came here to learn."

"A means to an end."

For the first time ever, Scaglione regarded Michael harshly. "And do these means include all this partying I understand you've been doing? I must tell you, Michele, I'm very surprised."

"You didn't let me answer, Don Luciano: yes, all the partying is part of my plan to save the Scaglione family."

"I wasn't aware it needed saving."

"It will."

The old man gazed at Marco before responding. "You know, I wasn't going to come at first. Thought I'd send Vittorio and Francesco to bring you back to Caltagirone, where you could work off the money you owe me. But I wanted to see for myself. Tell me, Michele, what am I seeing?"

"A great opportunity, Don Luciano."

"Escusé? Is that what you call being out all hours of the night at clubs, chasing girls like a Casanova with these rich *spacconi*? I'm disappointed, Michele. For the first time, you have disappointed me and I'm pissed."

"You won't be after I explain."

"I doubt it," Scaglione said, as Michael retrieved a set of the incorporation documents from his desk with the new business cards he had printed and handed them to him.

"World Trade Agricola," Don Luciano noted, paging through the documents. "I suppose you can explain what all these charges you've been ringing up, like this trip to Zaire, have to do with this."

Out of respect, Michael remained standing as he began explaining his intentions. Although the inner workings of the family's illicit businesses remained a mystery, Don Luciano had shared enough with him for Michael to know that the only chance for the Scagliones, and Don Luciano himself, to avoid prosecution was to conventionalize their assets. Essentially the vast sums of cash procured from their trading in gambling, drugs, and prostitution, just to name a few, needed to be not merely laundered, but reinvested to create a totally legitimate business enterprise.

"So this trip you took to Zaire was about business," Scaglione concluded, once Michael had finished.

"*Your* business, Don Luciano. Third World countries like Zaire have treasure buried in their soil in the form of coffee, cane sugar, and cocoa. The farms are usually small, decentralized. In Zaire the farmers carry their harvested crops to market in pickup trucks, atop mules, sometimes even on their own backs."

Scaglione glanced at the incorporation papers for World Trade Agricola again. "I'm still listening, Michele."

"The farmers receive what the states, all run by corrupt governments—"

"Like Mobutu's."

"—like Mobutu's choose to pay. The governments then allow their quota of crops to be sold through their designated exporters, which is where World Trade Agricola comes in."

"And where would we sell all this coffee?"

"To roasters or traders across the world who need to cover their positions in the futures exchange, or importers who need to supply their buyers. Coffee is fast and easy to sell. All you need is access to the crops, which in countries like Zaire are available only to a qualified few at undervalued prices. In Zaire a man named Antonio Carpacci controls most of the country's coffee trade. I approached him about partnering with WTA."

"Was he receptive?"

"He agreed to sell me five hundred tons of robusta coffee beans."

"Meaning he wasn't receptive."

"I can sell the first cargo myself with a phone call and samples to an importer based in Le Havre. But for future purposes, as we expand, we'll need to hire professional traders and open offices, starting in Kinshasa with our main branch in Geneva."

"You've thought everything out."

"As you predicted I would."

Scaglione ran a hand over his face, pinching the tip of his nose. "And what would you need from me to do this?"

"Three million dollars wired to Carpacci's account at Crédit Lyonnaise in Kinshasa with another two million available to take delivery of the initial shipment."

"This Carpacci, do you trust him?"

"I trust that in World Trade Agricola he sees an opportunity to reap rewards of his own down the line, so long as he can keep us under his control."

Michael waited for Don Luciano's reaction, to see if he was ready to nip at the bait.

"Then he is bound to be disappointed, isn't he?"

Michele nodded, hiding his satisfaction at Don Luciano's response.

"All the same, you're asking a lot of me, Michele."

"I wouldn't if I wasn't sure of the results."

"When did you become so cocky?"

"Not cocky—prepared. Your initial three-million-dollar investment will be wired to Carpacci's organization and converted to Zaire currency to pay the farmers. The remainder makes up Carpacci's expenses and profits."

"And what about *our* profits?"

"Once the coffee is sold, both your original investment and all profits will be returned to WTA in American dollars you'll no longer need to stash in the family's accounts in the Caymans."

"I see." Don Luciano nodded, grasping the brilliant simplicity of Michael's scheme. "The money goes in dirty, comes out clean. But still, five million dollars represents a substantial risk."

"The money is useless to the family now, Don Luciano, just

gathering dust as potential evidence to be used against you someday."

"And where did you tell Carpacci this money would be coming from?"

"My trust fund. He thinks I'm just another rich brat, like the ones I've been partying with. He would never do business with anyone he considered a risk."

"Like me."

"The others who come after him as well. In order for WTA to succeed, on paper I need to own the company and you and the family need to stay as far away as possible."

"Mustn't let your business partners think for one moment they're doing business with criminals, eh, Michele?" Scaglione sighed, a bit disenchanted.

"They're the criminals, Don Luciano. They just don't know it and that's how we will beat them: by taking advantage of their greed."

"Ah, one of my favorite sins. Perhaps we should get this Carpacci a notebook like mine, eh, Michele?" Scaglione slapped his thighs, perking back up. "Then let's call this a trial. See if your plan is truly worth pursuing."

"It will be," Michael said.

"Save me the assurances, Michele." Scaglione's knees cracked as he struggled to his feet. "Just don't fuck this up."

"Not a chance, Don Luciano."

THIRTY-NINE

KABUL, THE PRESENT

One hour passed before one of Dotson's soldiers returned to escort Michael back to the warlord's suite. Francesco and Vittorio were clearly anxious, wondering where this might lead if Dotson felt he had no choice other than to respond violently to the ultimatum Michael had laid down.

For their part, Michael and Alexander relaxed as soon as they saw the warlord still seated comfortably in his chair, certain he would never have remained present if an ambush or attack were in the offing. Even better, they saw Michael's smaller chair had been pushed aside and another one, matching Dotson's, slid into its place.

"Don't worry, my new friend," the warlord began, after Michael had sat down. "I was just testing you, to see how truly important this was to the Commission." He slid his chair closer to Michael's. "You know, I once fought for my life against the same men who brought the twin buildings to the ground."

"Very bravely, I'm told."

Dotson accepted the compliment with a grateful nod. "Sometimes business makes us do things we regret. A good thing, then, not to be doing business with men like this, now that you have guaranteed me enough additional distribution to compensate for my losses."

"I quite agree."

"How many soldiers will you require to accompany your men?"

"None. Your cooperation is all I came for."

"I would like to do more, to show my good faith toward my Sicilian friends. Please, tell me what I can do for you."

"A guide who can lead my men to Jafir Sari Bayrak's exact position is all I require."

Dotson regarded Alexander with a long gaze again. "You will need Pushtun locals once your men cross the border into Pakistan. Don't worry, there are several beholdened to me."

"How beholdened?"

"They owe me their lives." The warlord reached out and clamped both hands down on Michael's forearm, pinning it gently to the chair arm. "It is a good thing we do, Dotson and Tiranno."

"Dotson and the Commission," Michael corrected.

The warlord smiled again, letting it linger this time. "Whatever you say, my new friend. One problem remains: I can help your men in but getting them out . . ."

"Already arranged once they reach their destination," Michael told him.

Dotson thought for a moment, the look in his bright eyes turning sad. "In the attack, you lost a loved one?"

"No," Michael told him.

"I lost a son to the Taliban, was there when the great Massoud fell to their bomb, listened to him take his last breath." The warlord's expression hardened again, turning firm and resolute. "It will feel good to spit in their faces. Tell them to go fuck themselves in hell."

"I agree, General."

"But this meeting never took place. You understand what I'm saying, yes?"

Michael nodded.

"Then I have your pledge."

"You do."

"One more thing, my new friend. This Bayrak is a very dangerous man. He lives to kill and nothing more—that is his true religion. I have killed many men like him over the years, and they never die easily."

Michael sneaked a glance toward Alexander. "You let us worry about that."

Vehicles would only be able to get Alexander and the Koruf as far as three miles from the Pakistani border. From there they would have to travel on horseback down a treacherous mountain pass, the same route used by Jafir Sari Bayrak's Al Altar soldiers coming in and out of Afghanistan. Dotson provided a rendezvous point where they would meet their Pushtun escorts at ten o'clock that night. A five-mile trek through the toughest terrain in the world lugging all their gear would follow.

Michael studied Alexander's impassive features as the logistics were laid out. The daunting nature of the task he was about to undertake seemed not to faze him at all. If anything, he seemed invigorated by the prospects.

Alexander arranged to have Michael and the Scaglione twins stay in side-by-side rooms in the InterContinental while he was gone, Michael's door to be guarded by two members of the Koruf whom Alexander elected to leave behind. If all went as planned, they would rendezvous at the airstrip early the following morning to make their way home.

"Bayrak's body, Alexander."

"I know what to do, Stolarchos."

"The world has to know he and his lieutenants are dead. Otherwise, this was all pointless. And don't forget to leave the note."

"The world will know. And I won't forget."

"Then good luck," Michael said, feeling anxious and uneasy.

"The only kind I know." Alexander smiled.

FORTY

Pakistan, the present

Alexander kept the binoculars pinned to his eyes, cataloging the scene before him around the cave mouth on the flat stretch of land above. Midnight had passed now, and the clouds that had swept in to cover the moon were a blessing he had not counted on but was nonetheless thankful for.

Hours before, more of Dotson's men had been waiting at the beginning of the pass into Pakistan with enough horses to carry both men and equipment. The bright half-moon proved a godsend here, keeping the trail ahead visible. Four miles in, the team abandoned the horses for the final stretch. Before starting off again, they and the guides they had met just over the border ate processed meals mixed with cold water that were stale and dry. Building a fire to boil water would have improved the taste and texture immeasurably, but they didn't dare risk the attention it might draw.

The terrain was rugged to the point of being nearly impassable, one patch of rocks and mountain face indistinguishable from the next. No wonder American forces had continually failed to find their long-sought quarries in these hills. It was an angry world that forgave only those with an intimate knowledge of its landscape. Without Dotson's help, they could have searched for months and never found Bayrak's lair.

But that familiarity could become a detriment as well. In the case of Jafir Sari Bayrak, overconfidence in his command of the region had led him to remain in one place long enough to be identified by couriers beholdened to men like Dotson. And, true to the warlord's word, the group finally reached a ridge above which lay a smooth track of land enclosing a large cave mouth.

"Eight guards placed outside the cave," Alexander said softly to the men clustered tightly around him, as he lowered his binoculars. "The two you see in front are just decoys to distract invaders from the presence of the others hidden in the hills. I'm also guessing there are separate lines of booby traps between us and the cave entrance. The two of you will move to higher ground to serve as snipers," he continued, indicating the men as he fixed a short-range wireless headset into place. "Once you're in position, the rest of us will move toward the cave mouth."

"What about the choppers?" another man asked him.

"Twenty minutes flying time from us on the other side of the border."

"We'll be cutting close."

"Nothing new," said Alexander.

FORTY-ONE

PAKISTAN, THE PRESENT

Inside the cave that had become his home, Jafir Sari Bayrak tightened his grasp on the satellite phone.

"I am very proud of the work you have done," the voice on the other end of the line, metallic and dull-sounding due to alteration, said in Arabic.

"Thank you, *sayin*," Bayrak said, addressing the man reverently. He spoke with his head bowed slightly, half convinced the man could see as well as hear him through the phone. His free hand swirled about his bearded face, fingers dipping into the acne scars that deeply pockmarked both cheeks. "I praise God for your words."

"The next phase is fully prepared?"

"Inevitable as God wills."

"Then I want you to do something for me," the metallic voice told Bayrak. "You must depart for safer quarters."

"I do not understand, *sayin*."

"You don't have to."

"Is this about Tiranno? You think we have something to fear from a man who so goes against the ways of God?"

"This has nothing to do with fear," the voice said firmly. "This is about fate. There is more to Tiranno than you think, and he is my problem now."

"Your words confuse me, *sayin*."

"Then heed them and be done with it." The voice was sterner now, impatient, even sounding a bit ruffled for the first time Bayrak could recall.

"I will do as you wish."

"Go with God."

Jafir Sari Bayrak hesitated long enough to study the technological marvel constructed over the course of the past few months, thanks to his new benefactor. His other hideouts contained nothing that even approached this.

"I must make the recording first, to celebrate the moment of our greatest victory."

"By all means. Just be quick about it. Then be on your way."

FORTY-TWO

A loud thump stirred Michael from his uneasy slumber atop
the couch in his room at the InterContinental in Kabul He
groped for the satellite phone, thinking it might be Alexander
calling him with an update, but saw the LED screen was dark
and quickly gathered his senses.

Where had the sound come from?

He gazed about his hotel room, satisfying himself that
everything was in order. As he stood, something nonetheless
gnawed at him. He tried to replay the sound in his head, esti-
mate its origin, then moved to the door to see if perhaps the
two Koruf Alexander had left to guard him knew the source.

Michael was about to open the door when he remembered
Alexander's instruction to always check the peephole first.
Pressing his eye against it, he expected to see the guards
whose posts required them always to be visible from this vantage point.

Nothing. The guards were gone.

Michael eased his head away, refocused, and moved his eye
in again.

Same result.

His heart began to pound against his chest. He considered
any number of possible explanations, rejecting all of them over
the fact that these men would never have abandoned their posts
in direct violation of Alexander's orders.

Michael slid back from the door, slowly and cautiously so as
not to alert anyone beyond to motion in the room. He picked
up the hotel phone to call Vittorio and Francesco Scaglione in
the room next door.

The line was busy.

Who could they be talking to?

Michael dialed the front desk. The phone rang and rang, went
unanswered.

Again, any number of possible explanations surged through Michael's mind. This was Afghanistan, after all. Hotel service could generally be expected to be unreliable. Who knew if the front desk was even manned at such a late hour?

He returned to the door, flirting briefly with the notion of opening it until Alexander's second instruction, as well as his own common sense, ended the consideration.

Michael thought he heard shuffling in the hallway and peered out through the peephole again.

Nothing.

An unsettling sense of discomfort struck him anew, almost palpable in its intensity. Michael backpedaled toward the room's rear, turning when he reached the drawn blinds in order to peer out through a crack at the balcony beyond to find it empty.

Another thought struck him and he unfastened the lock, slid the door softly open, and stepped out into the inky darkness of the night. Vittorio and Francesco's balcony was right next to his, separated by only three or four feet. He had hoped their door might be open but could see it was closed, with the blinds covering it just as they had his.

Michael resealed his door to study the lock, then moved to the railing closest to the twins' balcony and hoisted himself atop it, five stories up. His stomach fluttered and he leaned against the hotel's exterior wall for support. The distance between the two balconies was closer to four feet than three, a leap more than a stride, a simple enough task if not for the fifty-foot drop a misstep would cause.

Michael bent his knees and pushed off before he could consider the prospects of that further. He cleared the railing on the twins' balcony, but landed awkwardly, with much more noise than he had intended. He regained his footing and rapped on the glass lightly, then louder when neither Vittorio nor Francesco appeared to part the blinds.

After no amount of rapping stirred them, Michael went to work on the lock. It was a simple mechanism, not to pick so much as to jostle into place by working the door on its runner until the tumbler snapped home with a distinctive click.

Michael slid the door open, pulled the blinds back slightly, and entered the twins' room.

He saw Vittorio first, lying with only his head on a ruffled set of bedcovers, soaked in blood. Michael drew closer through the room's murky half-light, realizing something was terribly wrong even before the sight of Vittorio confirmed the worst: both of his eyeballs had been gouged out and placed atop his closed, empty sockets. A glimpse of the rest of Vittorio's frame angled awkwardly on the rug confirmed his neck had been snapped, his head twisted a hundred and eighty degrees in the wrong direction.

Michael stepped over Vittorio's legs and spotted Francesco's feet sticking out from the far side of the room's second bed. Peering downward, Michael saw what he already suspected. Francesco's neck too had been broken, his eyeballs left in identical fashion to his brother's. His body lay in a pool of blood atop the phone that must have spilled off the night table in the struggle.

Michael thought of the raw-boned strength of the twins. They were thugs, yes, but also ruthless men whose brutish skills had served them well for more years than Michael chose to count. But someone had slain both Francesco and Vittorio with nary a weapon, someone not just the equal of the two, but their collective better. Michael would not have thought such a thing possible, if not for the sight before him.

He needed a weapon.

But Alexander had refused to let either of the twins carry one, and Michael himself had not seen the need to have a pistol himself, not with two men guarding his door. He thought fast, considering his options, reducing them to one.

Escape. Weaponless, what other choice did he have?

But he could not escape whoever had done this to the twins and the Koruf guards who'd been posted in the hallway, at least not alone.

A thought struck him and Michael yanked open the closet door, saw the full-length prayer robes that hung in the rooms of all upscale hotels in Muslim countries like bathrobes, available if custom and practice required. He pulled the prayer robes over his clothes, added a tight-fitting cap that clamped down his hair, and scanned the room quickly.

Smoking was prohibited at the InterContinental, but not surprisingly, the twins had turned a minibar glass into an ashtray for their cigarettes. A box of matches rested next to the ash-laden glass and Michael fished a piece of hotel stationery from a bureau drawer before taking the box in hand and standing atop the bed.

Once in range of the room's smoke detector, he lit the piece of stationery on fire and held it up. It had burned down almost to his fingers when the hotel fire alarm began to shriek and the room's sprinkler activated, dousing him with water.

He leaped down from the bed and pressed his ear against the door, waiting for the sounds of guests flooding the hallways to evacuate the hotel when the glass patio door shattered behind him. Michael swung to see the drawn blinds blowing inward as a huge figure surged into the room.

FORTY-THREE

PAKISTAN, THE PRESENT

Jafir Sari Bayrak positioned himself in front of the camera, kneeling to exaggerate the width of his shoulders and making sure the assault rifle was in view, propped against the stark wall behind him. Fleeing this stronghold in favor of another, more primitive one meant the recording had to be made now in order that the plan stay on schedule. He cared nothing for the motivation of the man he knew only as a voice on the other end of the satellite phone, Bayrak was interested only in the vast funding and logistical support the man had supplied.

Bayrak felt his glass eye roll upward in its socket and eased it back into position so that the quarter-sized pupil was facing the lens. With his good eye, he watched the green light begin to burn on the camera before him and began to speak.

* * *

As Alexander expected, there were three layers of booby traps set before the cave, each separated by several yards. Two were formed by trip wires strung beneath a light layer of rocks and dirt, undoubtedly attached to Claymores or the Soviet version of Bouncing Betties buried deeper underground. The wires were undetectable to anyone who did not know how to read the land, creating a slight discoloration and ropelike line too straight to be anything but man-made.

The third booby trap was simpler, with the potential to be infinitely more effective: mercury switches set beneath rocks that triggered pressure sensitive grenades if the rock was jostled. To stop a stiff wind from setting them off, the rocks had to be of sufficient size to hold their ground, so only the jar of a misplaced boot could trigger a blast. The oversized rocks stood out enough to warn off any man cognizant of their potential purpose.

That left Alexander only twenty yards from the cave. His snipers were already in position to take out the guards Bayrak had positioned in the surrounding hills. Once the booby traps were disabled, Alexander had signaled the Koruf to await his command and then slid forward atop the ground alone. Skills learned long ago in the Foreign Legion came back to him as if he'd been using them every day. Alexander had his knife based on the Gerber MK-2 American Special Forces fifteen-inch killing blade, but custom-made for him by the world's greatest crafter of knives, J. W. Randall—out by the time he finally rose at the side of the cave entrance. From that point, surprise and quickness would serve as his greatest allies.

Alexander clicked his communicator twice to signal his snipers, then spun into the cave mouth with blade leading. He lashed out at the motion flaring before him, relying on instinct with no time to fully focus on his two targets. There was no sense of impact, just gurgling sounds and the warm spray of arterial blood against him, as he finished his work just as the snipers finished theirs.

He entered the cave moments later, crawling on his stomach with his elbows for thrust to make sure no video surveillance or additional booby traps were in place. He expected neither. Men who hid in places like this uniformly believed a combination of the unforgiving terrain, their constantly shifting hideouts, and the insular nature of the surrounding tribal people rendered them safe from anything but an overt attack. And that form of strike inevitably provided the warning they needed to escape through the labyrinth of tunnels within.

The grade of the cave dipped sharply a few yards in, and Alexander called for his men to join him there. A hundred feet down, the ground leveled out and the air warmed suddenly, telling Alexander that Jafir Sari Bayrak's lair was equipped with air recirculators powered by the same generators that likely allowed him to maintain contact with the outside world. He doubted they would encounter any more guards until they were inside the lair itself, when the fury of the Koruf's fire would negate anything they'd be able to do.

Surprise was nothing without the skill to back it up, and tonight Alexander could only hope he had been blessed with both.

FORTY-FOUR

KABUL, THE PRESENT

Michael yanked open the door to the Scaglione twins' room, as the figure who'd crashed through the glass swept aside the drapes. He caught a glimpse of a massive, bald figure, nearly as tall as the seven-foot-high balcony door. Michael slammed the door behind him and joined the uneasy flow of guests heading toward the stairwell exit.

Fortunately, the InterContinental catered almost exclusively to men and, just as fortunately, many of them were dressed in traditional burkas, as Michael was now. His escape must have coincided with late-evening prayers.

Michael felt the crowd jostle slightly and resisted the urge to peer back to see if the huge bald shape he had glimpsed moments before was behind him. If he swung round nervously, he would almost certainly be spotted, especially in his wet robes.

The crowd spilled onto the stairwell and began an orderly flow down the five flights to ground level. His thoughts again turned to Vittorio and Francesco, slain in seemingly effortless fashion along with Michael's Kofur guards by the huge figure that was pursuing him now. His heart raced. Perspiration soaked his skin, mixing with his sodden robes to make him feel clammy.

Think!

If the stairwell spilled into the lobby, he would move with the flow outside and keep walking. If the stairwell spilled directly outside, he would pick up the pace as soon as he was out the door.

A propped-open door at the foot of the stairwell revealed the lobby beyond. Sirens screamed through the night, announcing the timely arrival of fire engines. Michael moved with the crowd into the wave of chilly, air-conditioned air from the lobby, where hotel security guards acted as traffic cops herding guests through the glass entry doors.

The warm night instantly wiped away the clamminess that had claimed Michael from head to toe. He veered for cover behind the first fire truck to arrive. Once there he picked up his pace, skirting hastily parked cars and moving into the main street beyond.

Surprisingly, traffic was still fairly heavy, plenty of cabs available if he simply raised his hand in the air. But Michael bypassed them out of concern, again, of drawing attention until he was safely away from the hotel. He swung round a corner and picked up his pace to a light jog, finally chancing a glance to his rear.

No one was there.

Slightly reassured, Michael continued on and joined a crowd lined up along the chipped sidewalk at a bus stop. They were all men, mixed evenly between those garbed in Western attire and those, like Michael, who wore burkas. A glance down the street revealed a bus angling toward the curb, and he slithered deeper into the crowd pretending to be joining a friend. He kept his knees crimped to disguise his height and better hide himself. While his eyes had revealed no one offering pursuit, his instincts, his senses, told him otherwise.

The bus ground to a halt. Its creaky doors opened with a hissing sound.

Michael felt the crowd jostle him, the scent of stale body odor mixed with cheap cologne pungent enough to make him hold his breath. He was fortunately among the first to board and took a seat near the front, keeping his face angled from the window as the bus pulled back into traffic.

FORTY-FIVE

PAKISTAN, THE PRESENT

Jafir Sari Bayrak had felt the warm rush building in him as he completed the recording and switched off the camera. He ejected the DVD and moved to a computer console, where he fed the disc into the slot tailored for it. The contents of that disc would now be downloaded onto the computer's hard drive to be sent automatically via satellite to news organizations across the globe at a prearranged time.

Bayrak grinned at the thought of American troops and spy satellites scouring the mountains in search of couriers riding donkeys carrying such messages in their rucksacks. A pointless exercise in an age where technology could trump virtually anything.

At least, Bayrak mused to himself as the disc began feeding his message onto the computer, the West had been good for something.

Alexander had his team slow to stalking speed at the first sign of voices: muffled at first, intermixed with laughter, the sound of men with no fear for their safety. Being safe too long in these mountains had made them turn away from the kind of precautions that might have otherwise alerted them to a pending attack.

Alexander led his team on, not a single one of their steps as much as disturbing or roiling the ground. It was a skill learned from much practice with bare feet crossing floors layered with shards of broken glass. Each draw of blood represented a kicked stone, strewn pebbles, or dirt disturbed in a telltale cloud. Soon the need for subtlety would end. The lack of hostages within, along with the nature of their mission, called for a strafing approach: as many bullets fired as quickly as possible.

With that in mind, Alexander and his men burst into the lair of Jafir Sari Bayrak in a spread formation. They fired where their bullets took them, the streams never crossing, and with no more sound than muffled *pffffts*, thanks to the sound suppressors affixed to the barrels of the Koruf's assault rifles.

As the first men fell and others cheated the barrage long enough to at least reach for their weapons, Alexander had time to record the fact that the lair was amazingly high-tech, lined with tables full of computers and monitors and satellite relays. This meant there might have been time to get off a distress call, a fact he distantly recorded as LED screens were blown out in a smoky haze and paper flew into the air like confetti.

The initial barrages of gunfire sent Jafir Sari Bayrak scurrying back around the corner to the recording and transmission equipment. He rushed straight for the wall, angling for the screen before which he had recorded his messages for the world to see and hear. Grabbing the assault rifle still propped in place, Bayrak crashed through the screen's flimsy material and into a narrow tunnel promising escape to the other side of the ridge.

Alexander saw the figure at the last moment, his mind freezing the face long enough to recognize Jafir Sari Bayrak from the picture he'd committed to memory and had kept tucked in his pocket through the entire trip. By the time Alexander could right his machine gun, Bayrak had disappeared down a tunnel.

Unperturbed, he followed the terrorist through a jagged tear in a white screen into the darkness.

Jafir Sari Bayrak swung at the last moment, spraying the tunnel with automatic fire. He snapped a fresh clip home and continued on, satisfied the pursuer he had sensed behind him had been stopped in his tracks.

Bayrak knew every step, every drop and rise, of this tunnel by heart. He had practiced the route often enough to recognize the subtle signs on the ground and shifts in the feeling of the walls around him. Once inside, escape was assured.

Gravel crackled beneath heavy feet behind Bayrak to the right. He unleashed a fresh burst of fire, shocked that someone had made it this far. Someone very good, he thought, his mind closing on an obvious contradiction: someone that good would not suddenly reveal his presence in such clumsy fashion.

Bayrak felt for his rifle's trigger again, prepared to widen the spray when a shape whistled through the darkness. A shadow—that's what it looked like—a shadow somehow shed from its owner. But this shadow had a grip of iron that closed on him before he could fire. A pain first searing hot and then horribly cold jolted his belly, as he felt a warm river pouring out from inside him.

Alexander dragged Bayrak's body through the tunnel back into his underground lair. He gazed about, amazed at the amount and level of technology with which Bayrak had managed to outfit his hideout. Alexander noticed even a video recording station set against a nearby wall and moved toward it, attracted by the mechanical whir of a disc humming in a nearby computer's hard drive. He hit the eject button and felt the disc pop out into his grasp.

The Koruf choppers, unable to land on the uneven terrain, were forced to hover unsteadily in the air. Boarding them meant climbing rope ladders dangling precariously from the choppers' rear holds one at a time. Alexander would ride alone in the first one and be taken straight to the airstrip to meet Michael Tiranno. The Koruf would ride in the second, taking with them the bodies of Jafir Sari Bayak and two top lieutenants to be delivered tomorrow morning to the United States embassy in Kabul.

Alexander loaded that chopper first so he could help his men on board. The last moments were the most tense, Alexander certain he could hear voices rising through the mountains over the rotor wash and bracing for expected gunfire. But it never came and the first chopper quickly reclaimed the air, carving a path through the night back toward Afghanistan.

Alexander climbed the ladder onto the trailing chopper in uneventful fashion, remembering the disc salvaged from Jafir Sari Bayrak's underground hideout only after he was safely airborne. He waited until they had crossed back into Afghan airspace, on a direct course for the airstrip to board the Vatican jet flying under diplomatic cover, before switching on his satellite phone and dialing a number.

"Alexander," Michael Tiranno greeted him.

"It's done, Stolarchos."

"We've got another problem."

FORTY-SIX

KABUL, THE PRESENT

The car had been following the bus for several blocks now.

"You're sure?" Alexander asked him.

Michael gazed back through the bus's rear door again. The black sedan, a make and model he didn't recognize, was still there, hanging discreetly back in traffic.

"Very. How far away are you?"

"Ninety minutes. We need a rendezvous point."

"First, I need someplace to hide."

"Where are you?"

"Western Kabul. Riding the number sixteen bus, letter *C*. The nearest cross street is Maiwand. Wait, I can see signs for the Kabul Zoo."

"Excellent. Now stay on the line for a moment." Michael could hear Alexander exchanging words with the Koruf pilot, who was familiar with Kabul, their conversation too muffled to discern. "Okay," he resumed, "two stops from now is Darulaman Palace."

"I can see it up ahead."

"Good. Exit there and make your way to the Kabul Museum, which will be directly across the block."

"Great. Always wanted to see Kabul Museum."

"Just make sure you do it in the dark."

West Kabul had once been home to a huge residential area with a grand avenue leading to the Darulaman Palace and Kabul Museum, until rival mujahiddeen factions had rained shells at each other across the avenues from their strategic positions in the surrounding hills. As a result of that sustained shelling, the area was reduced to rubble and dust. While determined rebuilding efforts had led to the construction of several apartment houses, the palace and museum remained the final standing relics of the city's ancient past.

Michael could see the palace approaching through the bus's windows, and directly before it, the museum. The building looked shuttered, closed for renovations that were made sporadically when funds, and priorities, allowed. He exited the bus at the stop just as Alexander had instructed, regretting he had shed his wet prayer robes while still inside. Being dressed as a Westerner would clearly make him stand out, all the occupants of the black sedan needed to pick him out amid a crowd.

Michael stayed hidden among the six or so passengers who climbed out with him, then broke away from them when they crossed the street in the opposite direction from the museum.

A fence enclosed the site, but he saw a broken gate swaying in the night breeze and pushed his way through it. He found similarly swift access to the building itself through a chasm around the far side where a boarded-up window had been.

The museum's interior smelled of mold and sawdust, though Michael could see no visible evidence of ongoing renovations. Instead, where antique treasures collected over many centuries had rested, there was nothing at all. Just dust-covered floors and empty shells of display cases.

Michael took cover amid several of these toppled and splintered cases near a functioning exit door, further concealing himself with additional debris. Almost as soon as he had finished, he heard footsteps echoing lightly in a nearby exhibit hall followed by soft whispers. Both the footsteps and whispers grew louder as his pursuers entered the hall in which he was hiding.

Michael held his breath, convinced his heartbeat would give him away. Flashlight beams sliced into his hiding place. Seconds later their wielders approached his position and he prepared himself to lunge at them at the first sign of the debris over him being ruffled. But they moved on without noticing anything amiss in the pile of clutter.

Thirty minutes later, Michael's satellite phone flashed with an incoming text message.

WE'RE COMING UP ON YOUR POSITION NOW. COME OUTSIDE AS SOON AS YOU SEE OUR LIGHTS.

Michael texted back, GOT COMPANY.

EXPECTED, came Alexander's reply.

Wop-wop-wop . . .

Michael parted enough of the debris covering him to see through a nearby window a black helicopter angling its descent for the museum's blast-riddled parking lot. He knew his pursuers, if still in the building, would have heard it too, giving him little time to escape. With none to waste, he flung the remainder of the debris from him and burst through the exit door, emerging just as the chopper began its slow drop over the parking lot.

Wop-wop-wop . . .

Michael rushed toward it, feeling the rotor wash kicking up debris and spraying it into him. Halfway there, orange flashes lit up the night, the soft pops of gunfire struggling to be heard over the sounds of the helicopter. Michael glanced behind him to see three dark shapes converging on him from the museum. He turned back toward the chopper just as Alexander leaned out the open side with assault rifle in hand. He fired a few precise shots, rotating the barrel along the arc of the onrushing gunmen, as the chopper's landing pod settled on a flat section of concrete.

Michael watched fissures of blood and bone spray into the air with each impact, the three gunmen downed as if the ground had been yanked out from under them.

"Michael!"

Alexander's call came an instant before fresh gunfire resounded from inside the museum, coming from a window this time. Michael remembered to duck below the rotor's reach as he dashed the final distance and accepted Alexander's free hand to pull him inside. The pilot lifted off before he was all the way settled. He thought he might slide back out when Alexander fastened a powerful grasp on to his belt and dragged him to safety, just averting the final spray of bullets.

"Goddamnit, Michael!" was all he said, barely breathing hard. "That was too close!"

Michael told him everything on the flight to the diplomatic airstrip where the Vatican jet had been prepped to leave at 6:00 A.M., the pilots clearly wondering what had happened to the Scaglione twins but not daring to ask. Inside Alexander plopped down into the seat across the aisle from him but didn't relax, or take his gaze from the windows, until they were safely airborne.

"The twins," Michael said, remembering the one thing he had forgotten to tell Alexander about their murders. "Whoever killed them gouged out their eyes, left them resting on the empty sockets."

Something changed in Alexander's expression, not fear so much as recognition and trepidation.

"What now?" Michael asked him. "That means something to you. Go on, tell me."

Alexander removed the disc he had ejected from Jafir Sari Bayrak's computer from his pocket. "We should watch this first, Stolarchos."

FORTY-SEVEN

ISTANBUL, THE PRESENT

Raven Khan saw the older man, cane in hand, as soon as she started up the private dock in the Port of Istanbul, the cigarette boats moored in the slip behind her with the rest of her team. The early morning sky was showing its first light, making his pale features stand out even more.

"I could have taken a cab, Adnan," she greeted him, forcing a smile on to her face as she tucked her leather bag farther behind her broad shoulders. Raven normally wore loose-fitting clothes to disguise the lithe, athletic frame that made her seem even taller than her five feet eight inches. Her face was smooth and olive-toned. She never wore, nor needed, makeup, preferring the perpetually tanned look her dark shading created. Her unique combination of grace, strength, and beauty led to the stares of men being constantly cast her way. Raven always pretended she didn't notice, never meeting their gazes with her emerald green eyes she had once been told could pierce any man's very soul.

"I happened to be in town," he told her, leaning heavily on his cane as he shifted his weight gingerly to help Raven up onto the pier.

"You never *happen* to be anywhere."

Adnan Talu shrugged. "True enough, I suppose." His eyes strayed to the strap supporting her shoulder bag. "A successful trip?"

"Quite so."

Talu smiled warmly. "Come now," he said, sensing her tension, "what's wrong with an old friend greeting you upon your happy return?"

"Why don't you tell me?"

"How about, it's been too long since I last saw you," Talu said instead.

Two years, six months, and fourteen days, give or take one or two, Raven thought to herself. They'd had lunch inside the Hotel Princess Ortaköy here in Istanbul. She had ordered a salad that had come with a tart cucumber dressing. Adnan Talu had left most of his crepe dish uneaten, complaining it was too thick.

Raven possessed an uncanny memory, capable of recalling people, places, and dates long after they would have normally faded. She thought it to be more the result of practiced skill than gift of birth, gained from lonely hours spent in the orphanage where her earliest memories were based. A survival skill, then. Something to take away the misery she always felt but never shared.

"How about," Raven returned, "I don't believe you."

"Come," Talu told her, gesturing toward a waiting car, his driver behind the wheel, "let's go into the city. Perhaps get an early breakfast."

Raven hesitated briefly before accompanying him, adjusting her pace to match his lumbering gait. Talu's limp, from a shattered leg in a boyhood accident at sea, had noticeably worsened with age. As a young girl, Raven had little recollection of him even using a cane and it saddened her to see how badly his infirmity now hobbled him. Talu was the closest thing to a parent Raven had, and she still remembered the day he plucked her from the orphanage to be raised as his daughter.

He sent her off first to a boarding school in England and then a college in the United States where she studied fine arts and antiquities in preparation for her following in his footsteps as a leader of the modern-day criminal organization that had grown out of the Cilician pirates whose legacy dated back over two thousand years. In fact, he had been preparing her from, the first day they'd met. Thousands of children of the organization's members to choose from, and yet he had selected her.

"Why me?" Raven had asked him once years later. "Why not choose a big, strapping boy?"

"Because none of their eyes had the fire yours did," Talu had replied, leaving it at that.

"I love what you've done with your hair," Talu said when they were inside his car with the door closed behind them.

Raven ran a hand through the blond locks that tumbled casually past her shoulders. It was the first time she had ever changed them from the black color that had provided her name, and she looked forward to changing them back. She was conscious of her beauty, but not enamored by it. Sometimes she would accept the overtures of the right man, always turning him submissive, invited into her bed but not her life, which for good reason was an emotional vault.

"I needed a disguise," she told Adnan Talu, as the car pulled away from the curb.

"To steal that yacht, no doubt. I understand you were able to unload it for eleven million dollars."

"We were filling an order. Our contact at the shipyard was kind enough to furnish the specifications."

Talu nodded. "Taking piracy into the twenty-first century."

"Internet piracy is the twenty-first century. We netted six million in identity theft last month alone. We control cyberspace the way Cilician pirates used to control the Aegean."

"We still pass cars in Italy stolen by the Camorra crime organization and ship more of them to the Middle East than Mercedes and BMW combined," Talu reminded. "We smuggle speedboats and weapons to the Corsican Mafia in France and supply small propeller planes to the drug lords in South America."

Raven nodded. Talu made it all sound simple when, in fact, it was anything but. Managing the fake documentation and forged bills of sale, not to mention physically altering the registration numbers was precarious at best.

Talu shook his head fondly. "When I think of how our great

tradition started, our predecessors chasing corn ships through the same waters we virtually still own today . . ."

"Too bad they didn't have the advantage of GPS transponders that make yachts like the *Quartermaine* easy to track. All you need is the signal code, readily available to any decent computer hacker or from an employee of the manufacturer with a gambling habit."

"Not the same with the big transport ships, though," Talu noted.

"Just slightly. Transport ships are outfitted with a kind of homing beacon that automatically broadcasts their positions on a regular basis, usually hourly. That way the company knows exactly where their goods are located twenty-four hours a day."

"And so do you."

But her ability, and that of the entire pirate organization, to steal oil and SUVs had been hampered most recently by the presence of on-board security forces. The shipping companies were wising up, especially in the West Indies, Jakarta, Singapore, and on the South American coast. Continuing to target their cargoes required more sophisticated weaponry and better-trained forces. Further, crews weren't surrendering as easily as they used to, and the last thing the pirates wanted was the kind of deadly assault that would draw undue attention to their work.

Talu stiffened slightly. "Not everything has changed, Raven. You'd be wise to remember that."

"Is that what you've come here to discuss?"

"You didn't come straight back to Istanbul after taking the yacht," Adnan Talu noted curtly.

"Something else came up."

Once again Talu's gaze drifted to the leather shoulder bag Raven clutched in her lap. "I applaud your ambition, but only so long as the risk matches the rewards."

As always he chose his words carefully, leaving Raven to wonder how much he knew and how much he assumed.

"A risk well worth it this time, I assure you," she told him. "A financial windfall."

"Is that all, Raven?"

"Isn't it enough?"

They fell into silence. Talu's gaze drifted out the darkly tinted window to the brightening sky. "It's going to be a beautiful day."

"How can you tell?"

"I can't. Dawn holds its truths close in secret. Like you."

"You're no more sure about the weather than you are about me."

"My point exactly, Raven. There is too much at stake here for you to be pursuing unworthy distractions."

Raven followed his gaze to the shoulder bag she had brought back with her from the *Miramar* in the Black Sea. "You don't even know what's inside."

"I don't need to. These risks you keep taking have become an unnecessary liability."

"The assets I obtained this time more than justify it."

Talu slid closer to her on the bench seat, eyes darting between Raven and the leather bag. "And what exactly are these assets, Raven? What is so important that you'd risk everything you've accomplished, including your status as a leader continuing the Cilician tradition today? Tell me, please."

"I'd rather show you," she told Adnan Talu, "as soon as we reach the gallery."

FORTY-EIGHT

VATICAN JET, THE PRESENT

Alexander inserted the disc into the Vatican jet's DVD player. The television sprang instantly to life, Jafir Sari Bayrak's face and frame stretched slightly to fill out the wide screen. He began to speak and Michael could see the recording included a convenient translation at the bottom, as if Bayrak wanted to make sure his words were understood properly.

"People of America, you have awoken today to find your

world a much different place than it was yesterday. You would seek to blame me for this when your government is the true culprit for failing to agree to the terms I laid out and heed the warning I provided in service to the one all-merciful God who has blessed this action from heaven itself.

"You have awoken today to know the pain and heartache my people have known since the time of their ancestors. In the light of the full moon, your world has run red with the blood from a fear you will never vanquish again and will know as I have known it. You fear for your safety in your own land. You realize your home is not safe, that it can be violated at any time. Your government has made you believe you were immune to this, that they could protect you.

"People of America, as you have seen now they cannot. Their lies have forced us to strike a crippling blow to the heart of your world. The city of sin, of debauchery, of decadence has been reduced to ash beneath a river of fire. This symbol of immorality lives no more, giving you the opportunity to renounce your old ways and to demand that your government renounces theirs. For otherwise we will strike at you again and again and again in great rage and with impunity granted by Allah himself. *Assalaamu alaykum.*"

Michael had remained silent for several long moments after the tape ended, Alexander leaving him to his thoughts.

"The message isn't another warning, it's an announcement to be sent after the next attack, after Vegas is swept away," he said finally. "That means everything's already in place."

" 'In the light of the full moon, your world runs red with the blood from a fear you will never vanquish again,' " Alexander recited. "The full moon is six days from now."

"The night the Seven Sins Magnum Arena is scheduled to open." Michael's voice was grim, detached. "We stopped nothing."

FORTY-NINE

Adnan Talu gazed about the antiques that fought for space amid the gallery's neatly cluttered confines. He rested his weight heavily on his hardwood cane, the day's exertion already taking its toll on him.

"I love what you've done with the place," he told Raven Khan.

"I've kept things just as you left them."

"Except the contents." The old man's face flirted with a grin, as he came to a section of apparently simple trifles. "Da Vinci?" he asked, lifting an exquisitely intricate spring trap device from a shelf.

"He invented this in total secrecy. No drawings or schematics of it have ever been found among his other plans."

"How did you come by it exactly?" Talu asked, returning the spring trap to its place on the shelf.

"The Paris museum job," Raven nodded.

"Ah, the fake bomb threat."

"Stealing a page from your book, Adnan."

"In my book it was a fake fire, was it not?"

"I improvised."

Talu returned the device to the shelf. "Hiding your plunder in plain sight . . . you're a true professional."

Belas, the antique store and art gallery belonging to their secret organization since the turn of the century, was located in Ortaköy Square overlooking the Bosporus within sight of the famed hotel where he'd last dined with Raven Khan. The view through the store's plate-glass window, even in the early light, included the vast Feriye palaces from Byzantine times and the great columns of the Bosphorus Bridge. In centuries past the network of canals winding back and forth to the strait had been the only way to travel among the villages that lined it. Though connecting roads had long since been added, the character of this famed section of Istanbul still relied on the waterway that had once been cluttered with boats carrying both people and merchandise, the lifeline of a city for which water was like blood.

Raven slid the leather bag from her shoulder and held it by her side. "You didn't come all this way to relive old times."

The fatherly warmth disappeared from Talu's expression. His eyes dipped to the bag clutched in Raven's right hand. "What is it this time?"

"You came here to ask me that?"

"I came because there are concerns about how you are utilizing our resources."

"*Our?*"

"Risks, Raven. Your recent escapade in the Black Sea should never have happened."

"Well worth it, I assure you."

The old man shrugged, running a hand through his shock of thick white hair. "Your assurances no longer hold much weight. There are those among us who feel your bravado is becoming an unnecessary distraction."

"I got that from you."

"Only my efforts never risked exposing our existence to the authorities. Stealth is the greatest weapon we have in our arsenal, greater even than all our other resources and contacts."

Raven thought for a moment. "There's something here you should see before passing judgment, Adnan."

"I used to run this place. I've seen everything."

"Not yet," she said.

Raven led Adnan Talu to the rear of the gallery where she drew back a curtain exposing a wood-paneled wall finished with ornate molding. As Talu watched, she peeled back a section of that molding to reveal a keypad. Raven entered a numerical code, and a hidden door before her clicked open. Then she flipped a switch, illuminating a staircase.

Talu gazed down it tentatively. "I don't recall a second entrance to the basement."

"A separate subbasement built in World War Two to hide

Jews," Raven explained. "I found it myself by accident, put it to good use."

"You should have told me."

"For permission?"

"Advice," Talu said, concern clear in his voice.

Raven shrugged and led the way down the steep steps, keeping a slow pace so the hobbled Talu could keep up while using both the rickety railing and his cane to support himself. When they reached the bottom, fluorescent lighting snapped on automatically, illuminating what looked to be an extension of the store above in the form of a smaller gallery. The air felt cooler, clearly processed and dehumidified, to protect priceless paintings and various pieces of artwork on display while they awaited a buyer.

Raven lay her leather bag down upon an empty table and eased a section of wall sideways to reveal a hidden safe. She entered the combination into a digital keypad and the pressurized safe hissed open. Then Raven removed the four identical softball-sized objects stolen off the *Miramar* from her bag cautiously, placing them inside the safe one at a time. The identical objects consisted of a dull steel casing wrapped with inlaid bands of reinforced titanium that seemed to divide each object into separate sections.

"Krypton nuclear triggers," she explained to Adnan Talu.

Talu backpedaled, forgetting his infirmity for a moment. "I know what they are."

"Then you should know they're stable. Neutron initiators emit no radiation themselves. But they do generate the electrical charge needed to jump-start the chain reaction leading to nuclear fission. Along with the nuclear fuel and the delivery system, triggers like these are the most essential components of an atomic bomb."

Talu kept his distance. "And just how did you come by them?"

"We learned a rogue Ukranian official responsible for overseeing destruction and maintenance of his country's nuclear stockpile was selling the triggers."

"To whom?"

"Does it matter?"

"If that party decides to come after us to retrieve their property, yes."

"They're in no condition to do that, and they have no idea who we are. Trust me," Raven said and closed the safe behind her.

"I assume you already have a buyer."

"The CIA. Paying top dollar for objects they intend to destroy. Several million in cash."

"The sale was prearranged, then."

"Necessary high-level contacts were established."

"With the CIA?" Talu shook his head derisively. "When are you going to learn, Raven, that this isn't a game? The CIA doesn't do business with pirates. Your actions risk leading them straight to us. You're playing with fire."

"I'm not playing at all. Everything was conducted through intermediaries."

Talu shook his head again and wandered to a glass display case set in the center of the basement room. "Something seems to be missing here."

"An object you know all too well, Adnan. Something the Cilicians had in their possession once only to lose it."

"Captain Ali-san Kubivaros," Talu said, almost too softly for Raven to hear.

"The last known object of the treasure he surrendered to Caesar," she nodded. "A gold medallion."

FIFTY

ISTANBUL, THE PRESENT

In place of that medallion, the display case contained an enlarged, crystal-clear picture of a gold medallion along with several press clippings. True to Raven's word, the medallion was eminently familiar to Adnan Talu.

"This is what I was afraid of," he said stiffly. "I've warned you repeatedly in the past, Raven. You must not pursue this medallion."

"It's the one object I'm after that actually belonged to the Cilicians once and so it will again."

Talu made himself turn away from the case before studying the rest of its contents. "The medallion's gone. Forever."

"What if it's not? Imagine what the last surviving piece of one of the greatest treasures in history might fetch. . . ."

"Only if you were willing to sell it."

"We can't sell what we don't have. Yet."

"Yet?"

Raven moved to the case, dragging Talu's eyes back to a *New York Times* story displayed inside. "A year ago Michael Tiranno's casino called the Seven Sins opened in Las Vegas," she continued, indicating the picture of Tiranno wearing a striped designer suit with black shirt opened enough to afford a clear glimpse of his medallion. "He made that medallion the trademark for his casino and parent company."

The old man did not respond right away, trying hard to disguise the brief tremor that coursed through him. "King Midas World," he said finally, leaning more heavily on his cane.

"You *knew* and yet you came here out of concern for my priorities?"

"I came *because* I knew. Because this can't be the same medallion."

"So, what, calling his company King Midas World was just a coincidence?"

"That makes more sense than believing Tiranno knows the medallion's origins lie with the real King Midas, Raven. It's a well-known legend, after all."

"Tiranno never takes the medallion off, Adnan. I'd say it's more than a legend to him."

"I admit to certain bizarre similarities, but trust me when I tell you that this is not the same medallion that passed from Cilician hands to those of Caesar."

"Vito Nunziato's son apparently survived the massacre," Raven persisted. "You told me that yourself."

"What's the difference?"

"Michael Tiranno is the difference. If Michele Nunziato was alive today, they'd be almost the same age. So I hired a lawyer in Rome to backtrack, find the truth using all means available."

"The truth?"

"That *Michele* Nunziato in all probability grew up to become *Michael* Tiranno. The lawyer was about to confirm that much before . . ."

"What?"

"He disappeared."

"The lawyer didn't disappear. He was killed in the terrorist attack on Las Vegas, in a cab outside the Seven Sins Casino, where he was going to meet, presumably, with your Michael Tiranno."

Raven Khan looked flabbergasted.

"Did you hire him to do that as well, Raven?"

"You've been watching me."

"I've been protecting you."

"From what?" she demanded, boring her stare into Talu's in the hope of seeing something she hadn't yet.

"Yourself," he answered flatly. "Michael Tiranno is known as 'the Tyrant' for good reason. Do I need to say anything more?"

"What is it you're not telling me?"

"I've told you everything you need to hear," Talu said evasively.

"Then let me tell you something, Adnan: the medallion belongs to us."

"You must let this go, Raven."

"I can't, any more than you could thirty-three years ago. You were close; I'm closer."

"I think you're chasing another myth, another legend."

"All myths, legends, have some basis in truth. Your pursuit of the medallion was rooted in money, mine in pride, necessity. And money," she added.

"Because you are a pirate at heart, not a crusader. Dollars are your currency, not convictions, and if a buyer with sufficient interest and resources came along . . ." Talu turned back to the display case. "In the case of the medallion, I'd say tens of millions."

"Now imagine that price if the legends about the medallion's power are true."

Talu's eyes widened. "You're saying you *believe* the tales associated with it?"

"I believe history proves at least the possibility that the medallion's mystical power may well be real when in the hands of the right man."

"Or woman?"

"I have no desire to be Caesar, Adnan." Raven Khan looked back toward the display case, where a series of shots of Michael Tiranno snapped off while he stood by the graves of his parents and sister rested against the glass. "Those were taken a few days ago in Caltagirone. Tiranno came home. Something brought him back."

"Leave it alone, Raven."

"Give me a reason."

"What about an order?"

Raven continued to stare at him.

Talu sighed deeply. "Have I not always looked out after you, have I not always had your best interests at heart?"

Raven Khan thought back to the first day she had met Adnan Talu when he came to get her at the orphanage. "Of course."

"Then you must trust my judgment and stay away from Michael Tiranno."

"There's far more at stake here."

"What, you think he wants to take over the world?"

"Don't mock me, Adnan."

"I'm mocking the absurdity of what you're suggesting."

"Thirty years ago, you believed the same thing about the medallion's history that I do now. Legend, myth, monetary worth, historical value—call it whatever you want, but that medallion is meant to be ours. As it has been ever since our ancestor Ali-san Kubivaros found it amidst the treasures of King Mita's grave."

"Which means taking the medallion out of Michael Tiranno's hands, and that is something I don't think we can let you attempt."

"I don't think you have a choice, Adnan," Raven Khan told him.

FIFTY-ONE

Vatican jet, the present

Michael had sat for several long minutes in silence before remembering he had neglected to call Naomi Burns.

"Damnit, Michael, goddamnit!" she snapped after he had finished his tale.

"I thought you'd be glad to hear I was alive."

"Alexander was right: it was too close this time."

"Have you learned anything about the lawyer, Gianfranco Ferelli?" Michael asked, grateful to change the subject.

"He came to Vegas, but he didn't stay long; his remains were identified among the blast victims inside a taxi just outside the Seven Sins."

"Any idea where his interest in me lay?"

"According to his firm in Rome, he's been on vacation for the past three weeks and they have no idea where he went or was. I did manage to track down a flight attendant on his plane from New York to Las Vegas. He didn't eat or drink a thing—she remembered that specifically because he held a briefcase in his lap for almost the entire duration of the flight."

"I don't suppose his firm knew what was inside, or would have any reason to cooperate with us even if they did."

"That's why I tracked down Ferelli's personal assistant, who was laid off in the wake of his death. I thought there might be copies somewhere in the office," Naomi Burns told him. "There wasn't much of use she could tell me, except for the fact that Ferelli was seeking an exhumation request from the local court, *il tribunale,* of Catania."

"For whom?"

"The name wasn't filled in."

"Ferelli was probably just another fortune hunter on the trail of the late Michele Nunziato," Michael said and cleared his throat.

"So long as you don't join him.

"What you saw in that hotel room, Stolarchos," Alexander said suddenly, moments after Michael's conversation with Naomi was finished.

"The twins," Michael picked up, looking at him. "Francesco and Vittorio."

Alexander spoke softly in an almost dull monotone. "Removing their eyes prevents them from finding the path to the afterlife—an Arab legend associated with the Hashishin, an order of assassins that dates back a thousand years. The Hashishin were Ismaili Muslims themselves from the Nizari subsect. They called themselves *al-da'wa al-jadida,* translated roughly as the 'new doctrine.' "

"Even then, Alexander, there was nothing new about assassination."

"But the Hashishin turned it into an art form. Under the leadership of a man named Hassan-i-Sabbah, they terrorized the entire Muslim world. The word *fedayeen* originated with them, meaning one who is ready to sacrifice their life for a cause."

"And what was their cause?"

"Killing. Terror. Some say the word *assassin* is derived from their name."

"Rightfully so, from what I saw."

Alexander turned away, as if looking at something only he could see. "Marco Polo was the first to bring word of their exploits to the West. According to him they were drugged, often with materials such as hashish, then spirited away to a garden stocked with attractive and compliant women and fountains of wine. If you believe Marco Polo's account, at that time they were awakened and it was explained to them that such was their reward for their deeds, convincing them that Hassan-i-Sabbah could open the gates to Paradise."

"And what do you believe?"

Alexander turned back toward Michael. "What history says. That for centuries beginning just before the first Crusade, the Hashishin held the Muslim world in the grip of fear. From his mountain keep, the master, as Hassan was called by his murderous devotees, the *fidai,* directed campaigns of holy terror chiefly against his Turkish and Persian neighbors. The great Saladin himself survived at least three attacks, and at times supposedly traveled in an armored wooden box for protection. Yet no Muslim force was ever able to eliminate the threat entirely."

Michael tried to make sense of Alexander's words. "Terror for its own sake."

"The most dangerous rationale of all."

"A legend didn't kill Vittorio and Francesco Scaglione and the Koruf guards, Alexander. A man did."

"You saw him?"

Alexander listened impassively as Michael described the huge man he had glimpsed crashing through the balcony door in Kabul. He remained silent for a few long moments when Michael finished, finally speaking in a distant, almost reserved tone.

"When I was a young boy in Greece, I heard tales of the *drakos,* a deadly, shape-shifting creature capable of appearing as a serpent or an ogre in human form. No man, according to the tales, has ever defeated the *drakos* in battle."

"This was a man, not a monster."

"Sometimes they're the same thing, Stolarchos. From the first time I heard the story, I imagined I would be the first man to slay the *drakos.* Now I know I'm going to finally get that chance."

"I've never heard you talk like this before."

"Because we've never faced an enemy like this before. Removal of the eyeballs was one of the Hashishin's best-known traditions, assuring their victims would roam Purgatory forever, a fate worse than death itself."

Michael thought for a moment. "Remember what Grasmanis said?"

"A force above and beyond Jafir Sari Bayrak, pulling the strings but remaining in the background."

Michael pressed his fingers against his chest and felt for the medallion beneath his shirt. "I want to know if the Hashishin have somehow returned or not."

"There are sources I can contact in the Middle East who might know something."

"Whoever they are, they've also made an enemy of Cosa Nostra."

"If this is the Hashishin we're facing, that won't matter."

"Tell that to Don Luciano."

FIFTY-TWO

CALTAGIRONE, 1990

Just short of graduation at the age of twenty-two, Michael took a leave of absence from the International University in order to devote his efforts fully to building World Trade Agricola, starting with the five hundred tons of robusta coffee Don Luciano agreed to buy from Antonio Carpacci. In the end, Michael was pleased with the meager $100,000 profit, amounting to 2 percent of the Don's original investment, and so was Scaglione himself. There was actually another $58,000 in profit, but that had been negated by the shipping costs. And Don Luciano allowed Michael to use an additional $25,000 to cover his credit card debt.

"We'll call that your commission, eh, Michele?" he chided, Michael sitting across from Scaglione in his office on the estate that day. "Thanks to you, we now have five million clean dollars deposited in the accounts of World Trade Agricola. So our profit is not two percent, it's *one hundred and two* percent, ready to be reinvested in your legitimate enterprises."

"I've already filed papers to register a corporation in Lichtenstein," Michael explained, "that would effectively give it a controlling interest in WTA."

"Why, Michele?"

"To further the legitimization of Scaglione assets by guaranteeing the necessary bank loans to WTA through the newly formed company. The loans can be secured by funds currently on deposit in your Cayman Island accounts. And we're not going to stop with Zaire either. I'm already exploring expansion into Cameroon, Honduras, Cuba, Angola, Rwanda, and the Ivory Coast—countries joined by both vast commodity resources and the kind of turmoil that makes them open to doing business in an unconventional manner."

"Lots of risk. Cuts down on the competition."

"Exactly."

Don Luciano smiled broadly.

"What is it?" Michael asked him.

"I'm proud of you, Michele. That's all. You've become everything I envisioned from the first day I laid eyes upon you."

Michael saw that moment as the opportunity he'd been waiting for. "But there's a problem, Don Luciano."

"What?"

"Zaire offers us everything we need to assure our expansion. But, unfortunately, Antonio Carpacci has nothing to gain by enlisting WTA as a potential partner and we can't prove our business model there without his approval."

"So in Zaire, this Carpacci is a *pezzo novanta,* eh?"

"Making him a potentially insurmountable obstacle in our path."

Don Luciano smiled thinly this time.

Michael smiled back. To him, Carpacci was just another piece in a chess game he had become exceptionally adept at playing. The only way he could possibly expand WTA's interests in Zaire, and thus elsewhere, was to remove Carpacci from the board. The key in such matters, he had learned, was to utilize others to make the desired moves for him.

"Of course," Michael said, "thanks to the relationship I've built with Ambassador Kananga, World Trade Agricola is positioned to move in should the Mobutu government elect to do business with someone other than Carpacci."

Scaglione stroked his chin. "Something you see as unlikely."

"Carpacci has spent a decade consolidating his power, Don Luciano."

The old man frowned. "It would take considerably less time than that for him to lose it, Michele."

MONTE CARLO, 1990

Three weeks later Michael had reenrolled at the International University when Ambassador Kananga once again escorted Mobutu's wife, Bobi Ladawa, to Monaco. He asked Michael to meet him in a private room of the Louise XV restaurant inside the famed Hôtel de Paris.

"Antonio Carpacci was killed in a helicopter crash two days ago," Kananga informed him as soon as the door closed behind them.

"An accident?" Michael asked, keeping his smile down. Don Luciano had acted even faster than he had expected.

"It does not matter, my young friend. What matters is that a vacuum now exists in an area very important to our country. Our trade minister does not trust Carpacci's would-be successors and is interested in exploring other options."

"WTA has already proven itself a potential worthy successor, Ambassador."

"Yes, but on a much smaller scale. Our trade minister is interested in considering new partners with very deep pockets."

"And a willingness to gamble everything on your government's ability to keep the rebels from cutting off supply from the East and disrupting shipments from Mombasa. I doubt conventional companies would take that risk, meaning you need someone who can see past it."

"You?"

"I have very keen vision, Ambassador."

"All the same, as a start-up, it is doubtful World Trade

Agricola would be able to guarantee the funds required to ease my government's fears and concerns."

"How much are we talking about to ensure the quota is met?"

"I imagine tens of millions. Up front."

Michael made himself look concerned. "That would require me to take out additional loans from banks that will want assurances my connections in Zaire are second to none."

Kananga considered his words. "What if I could schedule a meeting for you with the minister of agriculture?"

"Not good enough. I'll need to meet President Mobotu himself. That's where the buck stops."

"I can't promise anything, but I shall certainly try."

Michael saw another piece tipping over on his chessboard and suppressed a smile. "And, of course, any man who helps close such a favorable deal for Zaire would find himself high in the president's esteem as well, Ambassador."

"That goes without saying." Kananga smiled.

FIFTY-THREE

Zaire, 1990

One week later, upon official invitation of the Zaire government through its embassy in Paris, Michael returned to the InterContinental Hotel in Kinshasa and checked into the Presidential Suite, permanent visa in hand. After breakfast the next morning, the same black Mercedes that had picked Michael up at the airport arrived to take him to the presidential palace. A tall man who seemed to look right through Michael when his gaze fell upon him climbed out. He apologized for the need to pat him down and proceeded to do so gently with fingers that felt like coiled bands of steel.

"Michele Nunziato," Michael said, extending a hand when he was finished.

"Alexander." The man introduced himself with a viselike grasp of Michael's hand. "President Mobutu's personal body-guard."

"Very likely the only white man assigned to the palace."

Alexander looked at him quizzically.

"You must be very good at what you do," Michael continued.

"As you must be. Otherwise, President Mobutu wouldn't be seeing you."

Michael climbed into the backseat with Alexander, grateful to be out of the stifling heat, the air so thick and stagnant it was difficult to breathe. The Mercedes headed toward the heart of the city amid traffic composed of old battered Peugots and Renaults inching their way along the ruddy, unpaved streets. The sides of the roads were littered with natives of Zaire too poor to afford any other form of transport. Few of their shoes were whole, their clothes mostly rags draped over their emaciated frames. Michael had never seen such poverty before, knew it did not bode well for a country full of natural resources in quest of a prosperous future.

Closer to the center of the Kinshasa, many of the pedestrians had stopped to gawk at something ahead. Michael followed their eyes to a trio of men dressed as soldiers hanging from a makeshift gallows suspended across the road within sight of the presidential palace itself.

The palace, fronted by majestic fountains, was beyond anything he could ever have imagined. The only comparable structure Michael had ever seen was Versailles in Paris. Mobutu's personal home and headquarters for his government was similarly furnished with priceless antiques and hand-made furniture that were distinctly Western in design. To call it lavish would have been an understatement; no expense spared in any quarter, which pleased Michael no end since it confirmed everything he had learned about the president himself.

Michael was searched again and then ushered by the presidential guards into a reception area where he waited alone for an hour before one of Mobutu's assistants appeared to say the president was ready to see him. The assistant escorted Michael to a museum-quality art gallery that might have doubled as a ballroom. A long table of polished mahogany with an inlaid marble top and ivory legs, rimmed by at least fifty hand-burnished matching chairs, dominated the center of the room. Leopard-skin throw rugs dotted the floor, and the fixtures, to a one, were of rich, shiny gold.

He heard the clack of footsteps and turned to see a smiling Mobutu striding into the room, wearing a Savile Row suit and his ever-present smile, trailed by the man named Alexander. Mobutu was shorter than Michael had expected but radiated a charisma that commanded instant respect and familiarity. He continued forward into the room, while Alexander took up a post by the door.

"It is a true pleasure to meet you, Mr. President."

In shaking the dictator's hand warmly for the first time, Michael felt they had known each other for years instead of moments.

"A very ambitious young man, you." Mobutu beamed, refusing to release his grasp.

"Sir?"

Mobutu squeezed Michael's hand a bit tighter. "Mr. Carpacci's tragic passing has created an opportunity for one bold and capable enough to seize it." He paused. "Financially capable, that is."

"Mr. Carpacci cared about making money for himself and only himself."

Mobutu smiled and turned toward Alexander. "You may leave us now," he said, and then waited for the door to close behind him before resuming. "The truth and without hesitation: I'm impressed. Of those who lie to me, most leave quickly and some never leave at all."

Mobutu clamped a hand lightly on Michael's shoulder, the gesture composed without quite being arrogant. His French, Zaire's language of choice since it was a former colony of Belgium, was excellent, which suited Michael just fine, since he had mastered the language in his studies in Monaco.

"So tell me, my ambitious young friend, what do you think of the city I have built for my people?"

"Impressive. That was the second thing that struck me."

"What was the first?"

"The reception committee."

The dictator laughed heartily. "You speak of today's bodies, of course. We make sure to hang fresh ones every day for sanitary reasons. All of them members of Laurent-Désiré Kabila's Alliance des Forces Démocratiques Pour la Libération du Congo-Zaire. As if Zaire needs liberating from anything. We display them there as a warning to others who may be foolish enough to heed Kabila's calls." Mobutu caught the look in Michael's eyes. "Something disturbs you about this?"

"About the rebels? Yes."

The dictator pulled his hand back and stiffened. "Go on. Speak then."

"Their boots."

"Boots?"

"The men I saw today were wearing new ones."

"And that is what you find disturbing?"

"As you should too, because if Kabila's rebels have the resources to equip themselves this well, you're going to need a lot more rope."

"There have always been rebels in Zaire, my young friend. And as such, my government must ensure we have the funds required to keep them from intruding on the freedom and lives of our people. Do you feel your World Trade Agricola can do better than Carpacci in this regard?"

"No doubt in my mind, Mr. President."

"I leave the specifics of such negotiations to subordinates. You understand that."

"Of course, sir."

"In this case, that subordinate is Maurice Quanga, minister of agriculture. You will find that Minister Quanga speaks for me at every turn and enjoys my fullest confidence." Mobutu flashed his bright, confident smile. "As I expect you will too, my young friend."

"Thank you, Mr. President."

"My first responsibility is to the people of Zaire, making sure their interests are respected. For that reason you must understand that on behalf of the people of Zaire I will always do business with those who seem best able to fulfill their needs and prevent our country from falling into the hands of terrorists like Kabila."

"I understand perfectly, sir."

Mobutu flashed a glistening smile and extended his hand. "Just one question, my ambitious friend: How does such a young man find himself with such impressive financial resources?"

Michael looked Mobutu in the eye, smiling too. "I keep the right company."

Michael knew WTA's assets, as well as his own credibility, would be thoroughly vetted over the course of the next seventy-two hours. If either failed to pass muster, he doubted his meeting with Minister of Agriculture Maurice Quanga would ever take place.

He received the highly anticipated call three days later at the InterContinental that Minister Quanga was prepared to see him. Based on his knowledge of the country's coffee trade, he estimated that Carpacci was likely paying a 6 to 8 percent kickback to the government and expected Quanga would probably insist on between 12 and 15 from WTA. At the meeting Michael held firm on 10 percent and arranged for $32 million to be deposited into WTA's account at Chase Manhattan Bank in Kinshasa within two weeks to provide proof of WTA's financial capacity and commitment to do business in Zaire. It was further agreed World Trade Agricola would initially be granted control of only one-third of the country's coffee quota for exports with the opportunity to increase the amount to 70 percent over a two-year period. That condition actually suited Michael just fine, since it freed up funds to allow WTA to invest in other countries utilizing the same model.

He remained in Zaire long enough to open offices in Kinshasa and begin hiring the personnel required to handle his operation. Michael culled younger, ambitious underlings from Carpacci's organization, but avoided his predecessor's more

seasoned employees out of certainty that their loyalties would
be divided.

He returned to Monte Carlo confident that the success of
World Trade Agricola was now assured and began preparing a
detailed confidential report for Don Luciano toward that end.
Michael's cell phone rang when he was halfway through it and
he almost didn't answer the call. Curiosity prevailed, though, ultimately providing him with yet another opportunity for which
he had been hoping.

FIFTY-FOUR

MONTE CARLO, 1990

The call was from Sam Pharaon, insisting that Michael join
him at the upscale Jimmy's Nightclub at the Sporting Club in
Monte Carlo. Sam's speech was slurred, his words barely in-
telligible. Michael got there just as Sam was being carried from
the men's room, where he had passed out after urinating and
vomiting all over himself. Paramedics, who arrived just after
Michael, found Sam Pharaon's blood pressure dropping and
heart rate soaring past two hundred beats per minute. He was
rushed to the hospital in critical condition, Michael following
in Sam's Mercedes SL-500, retrieved by the valet, and leaving
his own Alfa Romeo behind in the process.

"You are good to do this," a nurse told him once Sam was
admitted.

At the hospital, Michael paid off the ambulance and registration personnel to list Sam as an "unidentified male" to ensure
the Pharaon name would not suffer any unnecessary tarnishing.
He then stood vigil outside Sam's private room to fend off any
eager reporters who may have caught wind of a potential scandal unfolding in the hospital's hallways. He made sure to pay
the orderlies and nurses an amount greater than any they could

have received by contacting any sources in the media. And the next day, when Sam was released, Michael escorted him out a side door and drove him back to his apartment in his Mercedes.

A week later Michael responded to the knock he had been expecting on his door to find Amir Pharaon's chauffeur standing there. Michael was driven to Monaco's heliport, where he was ushered into a waiting helicopter and flown out to sea to Pharaon's yacht. To him, the 450-foot, one-of-a-kind *Atlantis* looked more like a floating city. Michael had never seen such opulence and excess before. A submersible, a virtual personal submarine, was mounted on the aft deck along with a speedboat attached to a mechanical winch. The wooden deck slats were made of polished mahogany and the rails running between them were plated in 24-carat gold.

Waterproof, if nothing else, Michael mused to himself.

He noted a half dozen female guests swimming in the top deck pool and at least that many bodyguards posted strategically about. Michael was escorted down to the main deck, where a table had been set with Lenox china and sterling silver utensils around a tray of caviar and toast tips, along with two bottles of Dom Pérignon.

"So this is Michele Nunziato."

He turned to see Amir Pharaon descending another set of stairs toward him. The wealthiest man in the world walked straight up to Michael and hugged him tight.

"For what you have done, I am forever in your debt," he said, still holding Michele's shoulders tenderly. Pharaon wore white linen trousers with a matching shirt and seemed discomfited by the breeze blowing his thinning hair about. He was a short man, but of so much global stature he actually seemed taller. "Please, you must let me do something to repay you."

"Thank you," Michael said, feeling horribly underdressed, wishing his escort had given him a chance to change before leaving his apartment. His youthful appearance, though, likely proved fortuitous in keeping Pharaon's thoughts from straying from his son and all Michael had done on Samar's behalf. "But there's no need."

"At least what it must have cost you to pay off the workers at the hospital and the nightclub to keep them quiet."

"Sam's my friend. He would have done the same for me."

"No, he wouldn't. I know my son."

Michael didn't bother to argue and spent the entire day on board the *Atlantis,* entertained by Pharaon's colorful tales of outrunning government gunboats in the waters of Southeast Asia in his early days as an arms dealer. His contacts had been established thanks to his family's relationship with the royal family of Saudi Arabia, giving birth to a whole new set of stories. Pharaon had a pleasant wit and humility for a man more used to dining with heads of state. He seemed transfixed by Michael's fabricated tale of his work founding WTA, which carefully left out all mention of his connection to the Scaglione family.

"Please," Pharaon pleaded just before Michael was ready to board the helicopter back to Monte Carlo, "there must be something I can do for you."

"Actually, there's something I may be able to do for you."

Michael proceeded to outline briefly his work in Zaire and his relationship with President Mobutu. Since Pharaon made no secret over the fact he was by far the world's largest private arms dealer, Michael saw an opportunity to bring the men together to serve both their needs, and his, at the same time. The introduction resulted in a deal for Pharaon to sell the additional armaments Mobutu required to fend off Kabila's forces' increasingly concerted efforts to disrupt his rule. For the introduction, Michael received a 1 percent cash fee equal to four hundred thousand dollars that he immediately deposited into an account at the Chase Manhattan Bank in New York, the first step in his grand plan to make his mark in America.

"So young a man to have made so many important connections," Pharaon said over dinner to celebrate the closing of the deal.

"I've been lucky."

"Nonsense. Just like this story you tell of being just another trust fund brat." Pharaon leaned forward and touched Michael's

shoulder as his father might have. "Believe me, I know that kind
and you're not one of them."

Michael held his gaze. "Maybe I used to be."

"And maybe I used to be a donkey," Pharaon followed, shooting him a look that said everything and nothing at the same
time. "Enough of this talk. Let us celebrate our good fortune."

Instead of marking the culmination of their relationship, the
deal served to further it. Michael found himself spending more
and more time with the fabulously wealthy Pharaon, enamored
and even seduced by the man's lavish lifestyle. Pharaon wanted
for absolutely nothing. Though Pharaon was still married to
Sam's mother, Michael normally counted at least three beautiful women sunning themselves on the decks of the *Atlantis*.
During subsequent visits, Pharaon would take him to the Hôtel
de Paris casino, where he enjoyed a $20 million line of credit
granted directly by the Société des Bains de Mer, the government entity that formally owned Monte Carlo's casinos. Michael
was both impressed and shocked to watch Pharaon gambling
millions, once losing four million at the roulette table in the
blink of an eye. The billionaire remained unfazed, not because
he was certain he would win it back as much as for the pleasure
the experience had brought him.

The world of gambling fascinated Michael, all those at the
tables rendered equal in their own minds, the only difference
being the stakes they were playing for. Everything was relative
in that respect. All came to the casino with big dreams, and
amid the rickety spin of the roulette wheel, clacking of dice at
craps, or blurred turn of the slot machines, anything seemed
possible. Gambling, he thought, was a matter of luck and timing, just as business and life were. And cash was its bloodline,
offering the casino's owners instant and continual control over
affairs not subject to the whims of the stock market or investment fads.

Somni . . . Audi . . . Vici . . .

For the first time, he began to see the medallion as more
than a valued keepsake, as if his entire life, from the time he
first donned it on the day of his family's massacre, had been
building to this. His father had insisted the medallion was

inexplicably responsible for saving his life the day he had found it in the waters off Isola di Levanzo. Perhaps, in the end, that had been much more than a bedtime story. Perhaps it had been a harbinger for the path Michael's own life had taken and the lessons that had come with it.

Everything, he had learned, starts from the point of setting one's sights on a goal and not stopping until it is achieved. But that achievement requires luck as well as skill; after all, only Sam Pharaon's accidental drug overdose had won Michael the esteem and good graces of his father, even though Michael had known just what to do with the opportunity.

He fell in love with the sounds and the smells of the casino. Those who won just a small amount by the standards of many celebrated with hoots and hugs, leaving better than when they had come. Even those who lost, for the most part, left energized, recharged by the opportunity to reach for a greatness they'd have no chance of touching otherwise. A vast treasure so real they could feel it in their hands even after it had slipped out of their grasp. Viewed like that, gambling was not merely entertainment, but part of a lifestyle concept that could reap a fortune for the man innovative enough to define it.

To Dream . . . to Dare . . . to Win . . .

The English translation of his medallion's motto sent a chill up his spine, affording him a glimpse into his own future.

FIFTY-FIVE

SICILY, THE PRESENT

Michael could have called Luciano Scaglione from the Vatican jet, but decided that the news of his sons' murders should be delivered in person; he owed the Don that much.

Michael ordered the pilots to bypass Rome this time in favor of landing at Filippo Eredia Airport in Fontanarossa, Catania, where the diplomatic visas and fake identifications he and

Alexander still possessed made for swift passage past the on-duty carabinieri guards.

Dawn had just broken in the silent countryside when the car Alexander had arranged to be waiting for them at the airstrip reached the outskirts of the Scaglione estate fifty miles away in Caltagirone. Alexander slowed when they approached the security gate that fronted the property, the dense fields and foliage looking especially rich in the rising sun.

"Wait, there's no guard," Michael noted tensely. "There's always been a guard, for as long as I can remember."

Alexander brought their car to a halt and climbed out, not bothering to tell Michael to remain inside. Michael saw the Sig Sauer nine-millimeter pistol flash in his hand, held low by the hip so as to be invisible to anyone watching.

They checked the guardhouse and surrounding area to no avail. Michael lifted the intercom phone hung from the guardhouse wall and hit the button next to the switch hook.

"Nothing," he said, returning it.

Alexander remained silent as he wiped Michael's fingerprints from the phone with his handkerchief. "We should continue on," he said finally.

"What did you see?"

"Nothing, and that's what bothers me."

Alexander unhitched the gate and eased it all the way open. Michael climbed back into the car with him.

"Don't bother telling me to wait behind," he told Alexander.

"You'll be safer with me, Stolarchos."

They drove on through the property, greeted by nothing other than the rising sun. Alexander brought their car to a sudden halt where the road narrowed slightly within view of the main house where Luciano Scaglione had lived for the better part of his life. Offering no comment, he climbed out and headed for a thick nest of brush that rimmed the driver's side of the private road.

Michael followed, drawing even just as Alexander crouched over what at first glance looked like a clump of leaves but at second was clearly a body.

"Shot once in the head, and then dragged in here." Alexander touched the dead man's forehead, then his stomach. "One hour ago, no more."

Alexander moved farther into the brush and then out again, his eyes taking in everything. He continued down the road past their car, veering to the right this time where the body of a second man, a hideous look frozen forever on his face, lay hidden in the shadows of an ancient well, a river of blood spread out around it.

"His throat was cut from behind," Alexander reported, looking up at Michael while careful to avoid the soaked patch of dark ground.

Michael barely heard him, the acrid stench of blood taking him back to his family's massacre. Somehow he must have smelled the blood that day too, drifting on the breeze all the way from the house or perhaps carried on the bodies of the men who had looked inside the barn but never entered. Perhaps the ruthless killers who had come to the estate had been leaving him a message.

"A fucking ambush, then," Michael heard himself saying.

"More like a coordinated attack." Alexander climbed to his feet. "We should leave now, before the authorities arrive."

Michael turned his gaze on Luciano Scaglione's house. "In there first."

They approached the main house tentatively, Michael careful to cling to Alexander's shadow without having to be told. The screen door at the main house's entrance flapped against the frame, the heavy door behind it open, confirming what they already suspected was inevitable.

Pistol in one hand and knife grasped in the other, Alexander led the way into the house, stepping over or past four bodies that lay in heaps just inside.

"Only two of the men were killed here," he explained. "The other two were carried in after they were dead."

Michael didn't bother asking Alexander how he could be sure of such a thing. His heart hammered against his chest, thinking only of Don Luciano even though his fate was obvious now. His ever-present bodyguard, Marco, sat slumped against the wall outside the Don's office study, the hilt of a knife protruding from his throat, the blade driven all the way into the wall behind his neck.

They found the old man inside his second favorite place on the property after the shaded veranda where he and Michael had spoken so many times. He lay facedown atop his desk, arms spread out before him as if to reach for the drying pool of blood that had soaked through the blotter to the wood beneath it.

Michael lifted his head up slowly, gently, revealing the single bullet hole centered almost directly between a pair of empty eye sockets. He noticed Don Luciano's ancient leather notebook resting on the desk, splattered with blood. He took it in his hands protectively, as if afraid it might break. He wondered what the Don's final entry might have been, under which of the seven sins it had fallen, something he would never learn since Scaglione's code was known only to him.

"We need to get out, Michael," Alexander said, laying a hand gently on his shoulder.

Michael had trouble focusing as Alexander carefully erased all traces of their presence and then cautiously led him back to their car. Once he was in the passenger seat, the ringing of his satellite phone snapped Michael out of his near trance. He saw the caller was Naomi Burns and answered.

"Where are you?" she asked him.

"Back in Caltagirone," he replied, not about to say more at this point.

"You need to come home, Michael. The lawyer, Gianfranco Ferelli—they found his briefcase."

FIFTY-SIX

The hot breeze ruffled the man's hair as he stood within the parapet of the ancient French fort. Located nearly two hundred miles southwest of Khartoum, the fort was part of a network of encampments instrumental to the rapid success French colonialists enjoyed in conquering Sudan in the seventeenth century. Inside the now crumbling walls, French troops had been able to rearm and resupply while easily fending off the attacks of natives ill-prepared to mount any meaningful resistance.

The main buildings, including the storehouses and barracks, were gone now. Just jagged piles of rubble remained to reveal the fort's once imposing footprint. The exterior walls were still intact, for the most part, outlasting the elements to preserve the blood and memories forged here.

The man had laid his plans to come here years before, bribing corrupt Sudanese officials in Khartoum to look the other way while his construction crews erected a palace amid the cisterns, storage dumps, and escape tunnels that lay beneath the main structure. The crews, composed almost entirely of natives, had completed their work just a few months before. In the weeks since, all had met with untimely fates, as had the corrupt officials and anyone else aware of the fort's elaborate and inexplicable renovation. Money would have kept them quiet for a time, but the man preferred a more permanent solution.

The man had gone by another name years ago, but had shed it along with all of his past on the occasion of his second birth, defined as the moment he grasped his true purpose and identity in life. He actually had little memory of the years occupied by his former self; even his childhood was trapped in a milky haze he had no desire to penetrate.

The past, filled with lost memories of hatred and jealousy, was dead to him. The future, the future of his new self, pulsed with life.

That new self had been conceived in the Al Qaeda terrorist training camps of Afghanistan at the virtual beginning of the new millennium. The man appreciated the symbolism; a new age had dawned for him at the same time it had for all of humanity.

The war that followed the attacks on America on September 11 found him trapped with other loyal soldiers in the treacherous mountains of Tora Bora. The collapse of a cave to an American bunker-buster bomb had left him in a coma for weeks, carried by similar faithful over the border with Pakistan. When he finally awoke with shrapnel a permanent part of his skull, a new purpose had dawned in him to replace the memories partial amnesia had left as vague shadows in his mind. He embraced his fresh beginning, welcomed it with a sense that the many days that had come before were better forgotten. And yet even then the simplest of all questions plagued him.

Who am I? What am I doing here?

The answers came to him while reading the Koran around modest fires at night while it was still safe to burn them. An identity salvaged from the tales of Arab legends from the distant past told to maintain the faithful's hope against an all-powerful and merciless enemy. Most of these tales, recited time and time again, held only a passing interest for him. But there was one that set him trembling with gooseflesh, sending tremors down his spine. The story of the man whose legacy he was destined to restore.

Hassan-i-Sabbah . . .

Founder of the Hashishin, the greatest and most feared assassins who had ever lived. The similarities between them were too striking to be anything but fated, forming a bond that transcended time. They were both fedayeen, willing to sacrifice their lives for a cause in which they believed. They were both leaders to whom others flocked with deference and unyielding loyalty, men who had not sought their mantles but did not shy away from the responsibility they brought either.

The man came to understand the source of the pain and weakness that had dominated his old life: he had been purged of that identity by another that lay dormant within him, waiting for its time to surface. Finally, he found a history book that featured a portrait of Hassan-i-Sabbah.

They were both tall with gaunt, angular faces, their beards jet black. But it was their piercing eyes he thought were most similar.

His choice, then, was easy. He had learned if not who he was, who he should become:

Hassan-i-Sabbah.

His namesake had built a small army that struck terror at the heart of the Muslim world ten centuries before. Rulers, generals, prime ministers, all could be struck down at any moment not just by a hidden assailant, but by a beggar or holy man on the street, even a trusted member of their own households. When captured, the attackers were contemptuous of death, resisting severe torture without betraying their comrades—sometimes even naming innocent people as their supporters, causing their deaths as well.

Hassan of today believed his predecessor had used such force and power to unite the various factions of the Arab world behind him. Whether true or not, he had accepted that mantle, his goal to organize the radical Islamic world into an unstoppable force capable of vanquishing those who impeded the inevitable. The weapon he would use would be the same as that employed by his predecessor: terror.

The original Hassan's search for a base from which to launch his holy missions ended when he found a castle called Alamut, more a fort, actually, that stood at the entrance to a valley in the Rudbar area in 1088. It took two years to take the fort, and for the next thirty-five the original Hassan-i-Sabbah seldom ventured beyond its walls. He spent his days reading the Koran and dispatching his loyal *fidai* to strike terror through the Muslim world if his will was not followed.

Despite vigorous efforts, the fortress of Alamut was never retaken, nor did the fear Hassan struck in the hearts of his enemies ever abate. In deference to that as well as reverence, his namesake had chosen this fort amid the plushest of Sudan's landscape, halfway to Darfur, as his home. Though his underground base lacked impregnability, no one outside his inner circle knew of its existence.

From within those walls, Hassan had planned the attack on the United States that would be the harbinger of doom struck throughout the world by armies unleashed by him. A dagger was about to strike into the heart of the West with his hand on the hilt, bringing terror as it had never been brought before.

Hassan looked up to skies that seemed even with the parapet to see a falcon soaring directly overhead. A sign surely sent by Allah, voicing His approval and support for Hassan's own unfinished holy mission.

"*Sayin,*" came the voice of a subordinate from behind him in the parapet.

"What is it?" Hassan demanded harshly. "I told you I was not to be disturbed."

The subordinate swallowed hard. "There is news, *sayin,* about the . . . shipment you were expecting from the Black Sea."

"What news?"

The falcon vanished as the subordinate began to explain, taking the day's positive omen with it.

FIFTY-SEVEN

The Gulfstream, the present

Exhausted, Michael had hoped to find sleep on the long flight home from Rome but could barely close his eyes. Every time he tried, the thoughts and memories came flooding back, and he found himself passing the time absently flipping through the weathered pages of the ancient leather notebook filled with indecipherable patterns of letters and numbers.

While it was true that Don Luciano had left him no choice ten years ago when they had parted ways, it was equally true there was no person to whom Michael was more indebted. The Don had turned him from a helpless boy into Tiranno, the Tyrant. And in return, Michael kept him from the scrutiny of the authorities, and out of jail, by building him a legitimate empire.

The growth of their relationship had left Michael melancholy with mixed emotions. While he loved the warm father figure who had saved him from an orphanage, he loathed the violent thug who had never grown out of the old ways of running a criminal enterprise. He could not endear himself to the men who gave the orders any more than those who carried them out. Michael had grown so far removed from the paradoxes of Mafia life that it was difficult to fathom the crucial role it had played in his development.

Michael hated leaving Don Luciano's body as he and Alexander had found it. But there was no choice. A mass murder at the home of a man suspected to be the leader of the Sicilian underworld and reputed to be the most powerful man in Sicily? In no way could Michael let himself be drawn into such a calamitous event, certain to draw attention the world over.

The Vatican jet took them back to Rome, where they would board Michael's Gulfstream for the trip home.

"You need to have a talk with the pilots," he told Alexander "They never saw us. We were never on this plane. Make sure they get the message."

"Understood, Stolarchos. I'll take care of it."

His suitcases had already been loaded, and for anyone obsessive enough to seek further confirmation of his presence, phone calls and room service orders gave every indication he had been at the Excelsior the whole time.

He tried to keep his thoughts on what the salvaged contents of Gianfranco Ferelli's briefcase might reveal. But they quickly strayed to whatever force was behind Jafir Sari Bayrak's attack on Las Vegas. By now the corpses of Bayrak and his cohorts would have been found before the blast barriers that enclosed the heavily fortified U.S. Embassy in Kabul, having been deposited there by the Koruf. The elaborate security had thwarted Michael's plans to leave the bodies right on the embassy's front steps, a disappointment more than made up for by an anonymous tip assuring CNN would be on the scene to report the story to the world.

But Michael took only minor solace in this, since it did not mark the expected end, only a new beginning. The death of Bayrak was supposed to restore the peace of mind required to bring people back to Vegas while preempting a second, even more devastating attack. Now the disc Alexander had salvaged from the terrorist's lair could mean quite the opposite was going to happen.

Five days to the next attack . . .

Michael squeezed Don Luciano's bloodstained leather notebook tighter, the weight of his father's gold medallion heavy against his chest. Two talismans, each salvaged from tragedy, one the symbol of his casino and the other the source of its name.

I file my sins away in the appropriate place, careful to note when and where each occurred and, on occasion, against whom. Do you know why I do this, picciriddu'?

No, sir.

To remind myself of how many acts of goodness I must perform to atone for them. A man must achieve his own balance in life. This is how I keep mine.

That had been part of his first conversation with the Don, and Michael thought now of how much that credo had come to define him. Don Luciano understood this in a way even Michael himself could not. Holding that notebook now, he found himself smiling sadly at the irony of the Don's blood staining the detailed listing of his sins, his having finally paid the ultimate price for them.

The Gulfstream flew into the morning, Michael overcome by a sense of great relief when it reached American airspace even as memories continued to vex him. Those memories represented decisions he had made that had collectively carved him into the man he was today. He had never regretted a single one, even the ones that resulted in setbacks since failure, he had learned, was inevitable on the road to success. It was perhaps the greatest lesson Don Luciano had taught him: that dreaming and daring were rewards in themselves. If the winning did not come this time, it would come the next or the one after that, as it had for him beginning in Zaire.

FIFTY-EIGHT

ZAIRE, 1991

After reaching agreement with Maurice Quanga, the country's minister of agriculture, Michael returned to Zaire to formally install World Trade Agricola to replace Antonio Carpacci as the country's leading coffee exporter. Upon his arrival, President Mobutu assigned his bodyguard Alexander to be Michael's personal escort and protector, guaranteeing access to the country's most powerful coffee growers with the blessing of the president himself. Michael returned the president's good graces by convincing Amir Pharaon to lend Mobuto one of his older yachts for Mobutu to use when he traveled to the south of France. The gesture further solidified their burgeoning business relationship and, ultimately, Pharaon became the largest supplier of weapons to Zaire.

Michael flew from Geneva into Kinshasa to personally oversee the first major shipment of coffee, again under Alexander's escort and protection. Michael embraced the sight of trucks packed with sixty-kilo bags of freshly harvested robusta and arabica beans ready to be transported to another facility where sophisticated machinery would clean, select, and separate the crops. His gaze then wandered to long lines of farmers waiting to unload their coffee into World Trade Agricola's warehouses, the two sights becoming the first visual confirmation of his success. The transactions were overseen by armed guards, there more to intimidate the farmers than protect them. All the same, Michael knew it was important for him to make sure those farmers were compensated fairly and in cash, just as it was crucial to make all his shipments on time in spite of the increasing efforts of Kabila's Alliance rebels to disrupt the country's trade.

After the first six months of aggressive growth in Zaire's coffee trade and export, WTA had netted nearly $24 million in profit, on top of laundering the initial investment of Scaglione assets.

"So, Michele," Don Luciano asked, "where do we go next?"

"Cuba," Michael answered without hesitation.

HAVANA, 1992

Don Luciano enthusiastically approved Michael's proposed plans for WTA's expansion into the cane sugar trade and to further increase the amount of funds guaranteeing the company's bank loans through Lichtenstein. Then, acting upon Michael's request, Ambassador Kanaga agreed to arrange an introduction for him to the Cuban ambassador in Paris. Shortly after that, Michael flew to Havana for a series of meetings with officials of Cuba Azucar, the government agency responsible for all sugar exports. Now that WTA had a working business model, Michael offered the Cuban government the same formula, applied to sugar instead of coffee. He also provided Havana an additional incentive in the form of agreeing to finance crops up to two years in advance of delivery, a great boon to an otherwise cash-starved nation.

American multinationals, after all, were prohibited from doing business with the Castro regime, and most outside the U.S. shied away from risking investment in what they perceived to be a poor Communist country. So World Trade Agricola stepped into the void by infusing much needed funds at the risk of bad weather and, Michael said, with great faith in the integrity of the Cuban people.

After two years of success exceeding even that achieved in Zaire, Michael was finally invited to meet Castro himself. Over dinner that night, he smoked his first cigar, and never lost his taste for Cohibas Edicion Limitada, although he limited his smoking to three cigars per week in order to maintain peak physical condition. And no matter where he was, he made sure to jog five times a week, keeping up the ritual begun as a boy growing up on the sprawling Scaglione estate.

GENEVA, 1994

Michael's success in Cuba provided further respect and credibility, soldifying WTA's status as a major player in the soft commodities market. So much so that back in Geneva, Michael was contacted by Father Clemente Roberto, an emissary from the Vatican.

"We're most impressed with your success and the success of your company. We congratulate you. Most impressive, Signor Nunziato."

"'We,' Father?"

"Signor Nunziato—"

"Michele, please."

"Michele. Given your . . . heritage, we were hoping you would like to share some of that success with those in need."

"A donation?"

Father Roberto seemed to bristle at the word. "We prefer the word *contribution*. It is so less crass."

"On two conditions."

"Please."

"First, my *contribution* is to be totally anonymous. No one anywhere can know anything about my involvement, including your associates in the Vatican. My donation will come from me personally and not from WTA. Not substantial at first, but certain to grow in time. Of that, I promise you."

"Agreed. And second?"

"That the funds be used exclusively for children in need."

Father Roberto didn't bother to hide his exuberance. "We have several missionary villages in Latin and South America that would fit that bill perfectly. In fact, an American doctor named Anthony Lazarra has established a home for destitute ill children in Peru called Hogar San Francisco de Asis, where they are treated free of charge. I believe his foundation, Villa la Paz, is the kind you would like to support."

"Let's make it happen, then," said Michael.

HONDURAS, 1994

Subsequently, upon Michael's request, officials at Cuba Azucar and the Cuban ambassador to Honduras arranged for him to meet the Honduran minister of agriculture, Alejandro Alvarez. A car from the ministry picked him up at the airport in the country's capital of Tegucigalpa and drove him to the Caserio Valuz outside the city in the town of Zambrano, where he was given the hotel's finest room offering a brilliant mountainside view. Michael was invited to dine that night at the Alvarez home, where he met Alejandro's wife, Miranda, for the first time.

She was closer to Michael's age than Alvarez's and had given birth to the sons he desperately wanted and constantly doted on. Michael wouldn't describe her as beautiful, even at first glance. But she projected a radiance that transcended beauty. She wore no makeup and let her dark wavy hair tumble gracefully past her shoulders. Her smile was full and natural and Michael caught the scent of lilacs from across the table. She had the look of someone who would never age, forever in control of years inevitably used to controlling others. Michael felt he had known her all his life and found himself very much wanting to know her better.

That night Alejandro Alvarez endeavored to discuss business over dinner, but Michael was totally distracted by Miranda's presence at the table. Each time their eyes met, she cast a soft smile his way and he found himself entranced with the powdery lilac scent that rose from her skin. He couldn't get her out of his mind even after she finally took her leave to put her sons to bed.

Michael left the house that night with his stomach in knots, wondering if he had fallen in love for the first time. While there had been women in his life before—mostly older, some younger—none of them had given him cause for anything beyond base physical attraction that ended when the sex did. Always one time and one time only and never, never, did he let them spend the night. Love was something in which he held no interest, viewed as an inconvenience, a distraction in the straight path he had drawn for himself.

Miranda Alvarez changed all that. He had thought himself immune to love because he had found a replacement for the security it provided in the pursuit of wealth and power. Now Michael realized it was more a matter of being afraid. He had witnessed the brutal murders of the only three people in the world he'd ever truly loved, terrified that the same fate awaited anyone he dared love in the future. Keeping himself detached was a much better option to spare him the pain of loss again. Love was too unpredictable, the one thing he couldn't control and, accordingly, didn't fit into his master plan.

His feelings for Miranda Alvarez confirmed that much, forcing Michael to confront the passion he'd up to then been able to channel entirely into his pursuit of power. But it didn't matter, for so long as she was the wife of another man, he would never consider her anything more than a passing acquaintance. There were also her children to consider, and regardless of how much he tried, he was never able to remember their names.

Still, no matter how busy Michael was, no matter how far his travels took him as the business of World Trade Agricola expanded across the globe, he always made time to return to Honduras as frequently as possible, usually arriving a day or two early for his scheduled meeting with Alejandro Alvarez, if for no other reason than to recharge his memories of, and unrequited feelings for, Miranda. She made him feel alive in a way no one and nothing else did.

Apart from her, there was no distraction from the remarkable success World Trade Agricola had achieved. Using the commodities trade to legitimize and expand the Scaglione family business had taken him beyond anything he could ever have possibly imagined. But much of that began to change the day Don

Luciano summoned him from WTA's main office in Geneva to Caltagirone for a meeting about the family's cane sugar interests in Honduras.

"Michele," he began from his customary seat at the table on the veranda, "you're spending a lot of time in Honduras. Is there anything you'd like to tell me, anything I should know?"

"Nothing at all, Don Luciano," Michael told him.

FIFTY-NINE

THE GULFSTREAM, THE PRESENT

"Michael, you should watch this."

Alexander's voice roused Michael from his daydream and he snapped alert to a CNN breaking news bulletin on the wide-screen television in the front of the Gulfstream's cabin.

"American officials have confirmed that the three corpses found in body bags just outside the grounds of the U.S. embassy compound in Kabul, Afghanistan, have been identified as Jafir Sari Bayrak and his top two terrorist lieutenants, Hussein Musawai and Mahmoud Talid," announced a female anchor, while footage of a body bag being carted away filled the other side of the split screen. "Bayrak's group Al Altar, which had previously taken credit for the recent strike in Las Vegas that claimed over two hundred lives, was believed to have been hiding in Pakistan. A note found on Bayrak's corpse indicates he may have been executed by a rival terrorist faction, denouncing the initial attack and assuring there would be no follow-up. Thus far, the same American officials have denied all involvement in the terrorist's death, as do American forces in the region, while expressing their satisfaction that justice was done. The White House had no comment, but the president will be holding a press conference this afternoon to address the terrorist's death and what it means for the United

States. However, interviews with representatives for a number of leading Internet travel sites report a spike in Las Vegas bookings. While not yet approaching levels tracked prior to the attack on four casinos, this upturn is clearly great news for the city."

Michael felt a strange melancholy course through him as the report droned on. He should have been celebrating now. Instead, Bayrak's final recorded message left him filled with an even worse sense of foreboding.

Suddenly a shot of the exterior of the Scaglione estate took over the television above the headline BREAKING NEWS.

"In other international news," the anchor droned, "CNN has just learned that Luciano Scaglione, long reputed to be the most powerful organized crime figure in the Sicilian underworld, was found murdered earlier today on his estate in Caltagirone."

Michael's attention was again riveted to the screen, while the anchor continued.

"The body of Scaglione, the suspected *capo di tutti i capi,* or 'Boss of Bosses,' was discovered along with the bodies of a dozen bodyguards in what local authorities are calling an execution-style massacre, confirming those authorities' long-held suspicions. Those same authorities did not speculate further on the circumstances of the murders, but suspicions are clearly aimed at a long-simmering Mob feud.

"Frustrated Italian and Interpol officials recently revealed that an eight-year-long undercover investigation into the late Luciano Scaglione's affairs revealed only a legitimate business empire he indirectly controlled valued at some three billion dollars that included vast holdings and investments in construction, real estate, and commodities trading focused mostly on agricultural exports from Third World countries. Those same officials have thus far offered no comment on his murder. CNN has also learned that Scaglione's twin sons, Francesco and Vittorio, were not on the property at the time and are being sought for questioning. Meanwhile, in—"

Alexander used the remote to switch off the television, his gaze back on Michael. "I'm sorry."

"Forget that. Whoever's behind this knows everything about me, my past with Don Luciano—everything."

"With good reason," Alexander told him. "This was never about Vegas, it was about you, Stolarchos. You were the target all along."

SIXTY

Las Vegas, the present

Naomi Burns was waiting when Michael and Alexander entered the terminal at McCarran reserved for private aircraft.

"Bookings are up considerably this morning," she reported. "It's the same across all of Vegas. We're not out of the woods yet, but things are improving and fast. I guess you can count your trip a success, Michael."

Michael accepted her warm hug without enthusiasm, producing the disc Alexander had salvaged from Bayrak's lair. "We need to get this to CNN."

"What is it?" Naomi asked, taking it.

"A final message from Bayrak. This may not be over, after all."

Naomi clutched the disc tightly. "I'll make sure it arrives at the network via an anonymous source. Nothing that can possibly be linked back to us."

"Good. Now tell me about this briefcase."

"It isn't a lot," Naomi told him in the back of the limousine. "The contents were too badly damaged for even our contacts at the Las Vegas Police Department to uncover much in their crime lab."

"But something."

"Words, phrases, a few handwritten notes captured cryptically. Nothing that makes any sense at first glance."

"I want to see everything. But first I want to see the Strip."

* * *

The famed Strip along Las Vegas Boulevard had been totally reopened. Traffic, although not back to normal levels, buzzed north and south, perhaps grateful for the temporary swift passage through the normally maddening traffic lights. The Mirage had already reopened for business and Treasure Island was scheduled to within a few days, though with services curtailed and primary entrances still shuttered at both. Only the Venetian, which had suffered considerably more damage, remained closed, though the indoor shopping mall attached to it was again fully functional.

The presence of construction equipment in the form of heavy cranes and freight helicopters, meanwhile, was nothing new on the Strip, especially with the eight-billion-dollar City Center project inching along. So too the fresh placement of concrete road barriers required among the targeted hotels, while inconvenient, was only moderately disruptive.

When they passed the Seven Sins en route to the freeway for the thirty-minute ride to his house on Lake Las Vegas, Michael noticed a heightened level of security in the form of additional guards and a checkpoint at which all approaching vehicles were required to stop before proceeding on to the entrance of the casino and resort. He imagined similar precautions were in place at every hotel in Vegas, certain to be scaled back with the passage of time now that the perpetrator of the initial attacks had been killed.

Alexander had also arranged for additional security around Michael's gated seventeen-acre estate on Lake Las Vegas, called Roma Vetus, Latin for "the Old Rome." All of it was focused on the periphery of the property, though, since the grounds inside the twelve-foot-high iron speared fence were patrolled by Michael's collection of big cats. His seven tigers and five lions had free reign on thirteen acres Michael had named the Serengeti. He had hired a big-game expert he'd met in Zaire as caretaker and handler of his animals, amazed at the man's ability to walk safely among them, to supervise their care and feeding along with a veterinarian who lived on the premises in one of the guesthouses.

The rickety cobblestone drive forced those entering to keep their pace slow, on the chance that one of the big cats strayed into their path. The four-acre area surrounding Michael's palatial but relatively modest nine-thousand-square-foot house was accessible by a second gate opening into a valet area and enclosed with an electronic fence to keep the big cats from wandering inside.

The house's interior was laid out akin to a Roman imperial palace, starting with a marble statue of Caesar in the foyer. Fitting, since it was the kind of residence someone like Caesar would've had constructed in the provinces or countryside, lined with marble floors, authentic moldings, and archways constructed in Italy. The foyer floor before the statue of Caesar was graced with the words *Ad Honorem Roboris et Potestatis,* or "In Honor of Strength and Power," carved in gold letters. The walls beyond featured portraits of other historical figures Michael admired, including Alexander the Great and Leonidas, the king who led three hundred Spartans against the Persian army in the famed battle of Thermopylae. Nearby original works by Caravaggio, Cézanne, and Botticelli were centered over a marble bust of Napoléon set atop a pedestal fashioned in 24-carat gold.

The first floor's rear wall was comprised entirely of extra-thick glass that looked out over the vast Roman pool outside, just up from the lakeshore. Since the Serengeti's lush, thick vegetation was visible from this vantage point, Michael often reveled in watching his big cats frolicking in the flora he'd imported to more accurately replicate a junglelike environment.

Once inside Roma Vetus, Naomi spread the contents of Gianfranco Ferelli's briefcase that the local crime lab had been able to salvage atop the coffee table in Michael's living room, finished exquisitely in the Greco-Roman fixtures and art that made him feel most at home. The dominant tones were light gray and white, the built-in ash bookshelves lined with often long-sought editions of the books Michael had studied as a boy in the Caltagirone library. Several shelves were reserved for his extensive collection of biographies and six different editions of Machiavelli's *The Prince.*

Michael slid a chair close to the coffee table, with ivory legs he'd commissioned in Florence, to study the random words and phrases, looking at them like a puzzle to be rearranged in search of answers.

... STE ...

A fragment of a word.

NUN ...

And on another page: *ATO ...*

Fragments of *Tiranno* appeared in a number of places, as well as *Seven,* capitalized to indicate it likely referred to the Seven Sins Casino. Studying the rest of the salvaged contents of Ferelli's briefcase yielded obscure clues that could only be references to Michael's life. True to what Don Luciano had indicated, though, the clues also confirmed the lawyer Gianfranco Ferelli's interest in the Nunziato family, starting with the massacre in 1975.

What had Ferelli uncovered that was worth a clandestine trip to see Michael in Vegas?

There were two reasonably decipherable clues, the first being *Cesare Battisti 76,* followed by *Mes.*

"It's a street address," Michael noted. "In Messina."

"What about this?" Naomi asked him, pointing to the words *Agostino Pàtria.* "Ever heard that name?"

"Never," Michael said, frustrated by the confused jumble before him. "I want a meeting with the FBI agent in charge of the investigation into the attack on Vegas tonight."

"You may want to reconsider that," said Naomi.

"Why?"

"Because the agent in charge is your old friend Dell Slocumb."

Michael exchanged a wary glance with Alexander. "All the better. There's something to be said for familiarity."

"It also breeds contempt, Michael."

Five hours after Naomi and Alexander left the house, the doorbell rang just before 10:00 P.M. A barely awake Michael finally answered the videophone after several annoying rings, wondering why his security staff had not responded. He opened the front door in his bathrobe, still annoyed.

"Hope I'm not disturbing you," said Jeannie Vega, her jaws no longer wired shut.

"Not at all," Michael said, amazed at how much better she looked than just nine days before in the Seven Sins' infirmary. Her eyes were still puffy, but most of the swelling was gone from her face and the soft wavy hair tumbling to her shoulders cloaked the rest of it. Her shapely figure, meanwhile, was everything Michael remembered from her show at Caesar's, which he'd left each time thinking she was the most beautiful woman in all of Vegas.

Jeannie entered and he closed the door behind her.

"The tall man dropped me off," she said, referring to Alexander.

"That explains it." Michael grinned. "I like what I see."

"Thanks to you."

"Bring my tickets to your comeback show at Caesar's?"

Jeannie tapped her head dramatically, smiling. "I knew I forgot something." She strolled about the living room, admiring Michael's vast collection of art. "Interesting."

"What?"

"All your paintings are portraits."

Michael moved his gaze to follow hers. "I never thought of it before."

"I'm still impressed."

"With me or my art?"

"Both." Jeannie smiled.

"Would you like a drink?"

"Sure. Whatever you're having."

"Orange juice?"

"That's fine."

Jeannie sat down on the sofa, as Michael moved to the wet bar in the living room. He studied her in the mirror, remembering the showgirl who had so captivated him at Caesar's. She looked even more striking in person, the skin of her crossed legs radiantly tan. She wore a skirt that rode high on her thighs, revealing no panties beneath.

Michael had started to pour two glasses of fresh-squeezed orange juice when he caught Jeannie approaching in the mirror, drawing close enough for him to feel her breath when he turned.

"They told me what you did for my brother."

"I did it for you."

Jeannie's hand reached for the sash holding his bathrobe closed and Michael stopped it.

"But you don't owe me anything," he continued. "You don't need to do this."

"I know."

Michael pulled his hand back, letting her come away with the sash. She dropped it to the floor and then joined her other hand to the robe to hold it open.

"I like what I see," Jeannie told him, looking at his body.

"Thanks to you."

Michael took her in his arms and kissed her, feeling himself melt away in her grasp. His mind stopped working. Jeannie was in his arms. Then she was on her knees and finally they were on the couch.

Michael let go of the world. Afghanistan and Caltagirone vanished from his memory. Thoughts of the future of the Seven Sins and Las Vegas were suspended, at least for the moments he was inside her. His motions were graceful, tender, Michael cognizant even then of the trauma she had suffered and how hard being this close to someone so soon afterward might have been for her. It was like being in the midst of a dream he didn't want to wake from, reality meaningless for as long as it lasted.

It ended atop Michael's hand-stitched carpet with their arms and legs intertwined; just lying there listening to the ticking of a clock in the hope time might stop for good.

SIXTY-ONE

Raven Khan watched the tall woman emerge from the arrivals level at Kennedy Airport's international terminal. According to the woman's itinerary, she was returning from a trip that had taken her to Singapore and Macao before a month full of meetings in London squeezed into a week. She had no meeting scheduled here in her home base of New York City over the next forty-eight hours prior to heading out on the next leg of her trip.

Raven watched the woman approach a limousine driver holding a white card with her name printed boldly upon it. The driver smiled, accepted her carry-on bag, and led her out to the curb, where the woman's limousine was waiting. As always, the woman had shipped her luggage ahead via private carrier to save time and the inevitable inconvenience.

Raven remained inside the terminal while the woman climbed into the limousine's rear seat, PDA already in hand as if she had gone as long as she could without consulting it. The driver closed the door behind her and climbed back behind the wheel. An instant later the car pulled away from the curb and disappeared into the sea of vehicles forever enclosing the airport.

Raven Khan's cell phone rang twenty minutes later, a bit ahead of schedule.

"It's done," said the voice on the other end. "I'm on my way back with the woman's passport."

Raven flipped her phone closed, and slid off to book her own flight to Las Vegas.

SIXTY-TWO

Special Agent Dell Slocumb was already waiting in the bar lounge of the Riviera Hotel and Casino when Michael arrived.

"You're late, Mr. Tiranno."

"Something came up," Michael said, taking the chair across from him at the table. "Sorry."

"You take all your meetings here?" Slocumb asked, pressing out his cigarette in a cracked ashtray and lighting up another.

"Only the ones I'd rather not have."

"Yeah, that's funny." Then noting, "You came alone."

"Surprised?"

"I expected you to bring that gorilla babysitter of yours. At least your lawyer, like our last conversation."

"That was different."

"Why?"

"I was being interrogated."

"Your babysitter being elsewhere, what's to stop you from tripping and cracking your head open?"

"You want to trip me and find out?"

"Nope," Agent Slocumb said with no hesitation. "You're not worth fucking up my career over."

"Didn't know you'd been promoted since the last time we talked."

Michael knew this was a particular bone of contention for Slocumb, given his ambitions to advance his career at Bureau headquarters in Washington. But those plans had been derailed several years before, thanks in part to Slocumb's inability to pin the death of Max Price, and implosion of his Maximus Hotel and Casino, on Michael.

As a result, Slocumb's features grew tight enough to exaggerate the patchwork of wrinkles forming around his eyes and the furrows in his brow. He blew smoke from his mouth in a long straight line. A marine who served in Desert Storm, Slocumb had a protruding chin at the bottom of a square, angular face and still wore his now graying hair in a close-cropped military style.

"Ten years with the Las Vegas branch, and this is the first time I ever been inside this dump," Slocumb said, wiping up the condensation that had formed around his rocks glass with a thin napkin.

"The CEO's a friend of mine."

"Yeah, your kind sticks together."

"You're right: none of us wants to see Vegas ruined. Did you see the tape CNN's been playing all day?"

"You mean Bayrak's curtain call? About a hundred times. Anonymously delivered, by the way."

Michael ignored any insinuation Slocumb might have been making. "And?"

"And what?"

"What does the FBI intend to do about it?"

Slocumb blew some smoke in Michael's direction. "Man who made it is dead, supposedly killed by his fellow radical nutjobs who basically said everything's cool. But I guess you heard about that."

"Good news for the city, if it's true."

"I guess your business suffered."

"Not just mine."

"But you were the only casino owner who left the country."

A waitress came and set a fresh drink down in front of Slocumb.

"Drinking on the job?" Michael asked, waving the waitress off.

"I've been off the clock since you were an hour late. How was Rome, by the way?"

"Sunny and beautiful as always. I didn't see much of it this time."

"Spent most of your time inside the Excelsior Hotel, I suppose."

"Still keeping tabs on me, huh?"

"As the saying goes, keep your friends close and your enemies closer."

"Are we enemies, you and I, Agent Slocumb?"

"We're not friends, Mr. Tiranno."

"But we have the same enemies, don't we? And something made you agree to meet me here at one o'clock in the morning."

"I've been here since eleven thirty, remember? Maybe I should've tried the slots instead."

"Tightest ones in town."

"Yeah, much looser ones at the Seven Sins, or was it the Maximus? That's right, it *was*," Slocumb said, and took a hefty sip from his drink. "You remember the Maximus, don't you?"

"Not really. I didn't find it very memorable."

"Stood in the same spot as the Seven Sins until it got itself blown the hell up."

"Gas main went, according to the FBI report. You've heard of them, right, the FBI?"

"Oh, that's right. Phillip McBane, site manager for Cassini Building Company, got the blame. You knew Mr. McBane, didn't you?"

"Never met him, never heard of him, never knew he existed."

"Then let me enlighten you. Max Price took his nineteen-year-old daughter's virginity five years ago, and when McBane confronted the asshole, Price fired him."

"Sounds to me like you've got your man."

"Except he disappeared. Nowhere to be found."

"You check the rubble?"

"We've got McBane on tape at a truck stop on I-15 North an hour after the blast. Real convenient, right? And how does one of the country's largest general contractors fuck up at this level?"

"People fuck up more often than you think."

Slocumb blew out some more smoke. "What about Max Price, the owner of the Maximus? Remember him, the famous casino mogul?"

"Sure, poor guy died in the blast."

"Right, only no body was ever found, just an arm and a leg.

I thought the rest of Mr. Price might have turned up while you were building the Seven Sins on the very same spot. Lucky thing, you shorting stock in Price's company in the weeks prior, especially after that falling-out you had with him that was no secret around town."

"Not lucky at all. Anyone who looked close enough could see his business plan was flawed and that the Maximus was overly leveraged, overbuilt, and, most importantly, overrated. Inevitable that Price World Resorts would have ended up a losing money machine."

"Takes pretty good vision to see its centerpiece casino would start the process."

"Not really. Price's worst enemy was his ego. He thought with his dick more than his brain. Built a resort aimed at catering to the very rich. Ended up spending too much money on marble bathrooms and plasma televisions. But that's not the Vegas of the present. And the bottom line for the Vegas of the present is offering a one-of-a-kind experience to get people to stay at the tables longer, or for the nongamblers to try their luck."

"You mean like watching a thirty-foot great white shark eat dinner? Guess that's what makes the Seven Sins so family friendly. What is it you call feeding time, Red Sea or something?"

"Red Water. You should stop by and see it sometime, Agent Slocumb. I'll get you a front-row seat, right up against the rail. Better watch your step, though." Michael grinned.

Slocumb held his cigarette in his hand, studying Michael in between glances at two showgirls who had just entered the room, having finished their "Crazy Girls" performance upstairs. Recognition flashed in their eyes when they glimpsed Michael.

"Hope I'm not distracting you," Michael said.

"Know what distracted me? The Securities and Exchange Commission's report. I reread it before I came over here. Refresh my memory on the particulars of your good fortune."

Michael focused on his glass. "Were you having a drink at the time?"

"You making a point?"

"Alcohol clouds the judgment. Probably explains why you forgot that the report failed to recommend any charges against me."

Slocumb drained the rest of his drink and slapped the glass back down on the table. "Didn't exactly exonerate you either. And, as I understand it, the file's still open. Can't blame them, can you? Hey, it's not every day a man clears near eight hundred mil on a single investment in two, three weeks."

"Ancient history."

"Sure, like you being unable to break into Vegas's tight little boys' club. Then Max Price conveniently dies, his casino implodes, and, low and behold, you become a mogul virtually overnight by buying his company for fifteen cents on the dollar, making a fortune on Price's ashes." Slocumb waved his glass at the waitress, signaling for another. "That what happens to people who mess with Michael Tiranno?"

Michael fixed his gaze on Slocumb's glass. "No, some of them just drink themselves to death."

"Everyone in town knows Price screwed you."

"Business is business."

"What is it people call you behind your back, the Tyrant?"

"In Italian, Tiranno means 'tyrant,' Agent Slocumb. I'm not ashamed of my name."

"Or of the fortune you built on top of Price's makeshift grave. So what are you worth now? A billion, two, maybe?"

"Sorry for not spending it on booze and cigarettes."

"You forgot women."

Michael followed Slocumb's gaze through the thick haze of smoke to the showgirls seated at the bar. "Guess we have different tastes."

Slocumb took a deep drag of the Marlboro and held the smoke in this time. "You know what *conchita* is, Mr. Tiranno?"

"Afraid I don't."

"Claylike stuff that looks like orange-colored dirt on the surface," Slocumb continued, smoke following his words out like a vapor trail. "But when you dig down, trying to plant some shrubs or bushes, you find it's harder than concrete. The further you dig down, the harder it gets, making it impossible to grow anything. Like it's sucking the land dry to make itself stronger."

The waitress set another drink down in front of Slocumb.

"Can't leave anything dry, can we, Agent Slocumb?"

"Put this one on Mr. Tiranno's tab," Slocumb said, already raising his fresh drink as the waitress took her leave.

"We don't water them down at the Seven Sins."

"I'll remember that when I come to arrest you there someday."

"Don't bet on it." Michael leaned closer. "Just tell me what the Bureau's planning to do about this latest threat."

"Bayrak's dead."

"Tape indicates maybe his plan's still alive. Maybe everything's not so cool, after all."

"You want us to evacuate the city, shut Vegas down?"

"I was thinking more along the lines of taking the threat seriously."

"Maybe we don't have to do anything."

"You don't buy that, I hope."

Slocumb's eyes widened, seeming to further square off his already rectangular face. His eyes darted back and forth between Michael and the two Crazy Girls at the bar. "No, I don't. But that doesn't mean I'm in a position to do anything more about it than we've already done and are doing."

"I'm sure the forty-four million people who come to Las Vegas every year will feel better with you watching their backs."

Slocumb's face twitched. "We've got five hundred agents still in the city. The next step is the National Guard. Tanks and Humvees in the streets. That what you want?"

Michael pictured Vegas becoming a ghost town again. "I was thinking more along the lines of finding the rest of the members of the Al Altar cell here before they launch this second strike."

"Be glad to run their pictures on *America's Most Wanted*, if we had any."

"Maybe your five hundred agents are looking in the wrong places."

"Tough to convince Washington to keep looking for the body when you've already got the head." Slocumb started to raise his drink, then stopped. "You care so much, why'd you run off to Rome, Mr. Tiranno?"

"To keep my casino running, Agent Slocumb."

"So you're in the city, what, five or six days and all you see is your hotel room."

"I was born there. Makes the tourist spots a little less interesting."

"Spend any time at the Vatican?"

"My business in Rome was private and confidential."

"Any of it take you to Sicily?"

"I'm allergic to the trees there and I don't like the landscape."

"Ever been to Afghanistan, Mr. Tiranno?"

"You're kidding, right?"

"Hey, I hear the weather's nice this time of year. Their dry season or something. Maybe they got *conchita* over there too."

"I'll take your word for it, Agent Slocumb."

"What about the gorilla who usually travels in your shadow? Would he know?"

"Mr. Koursaris is head of security for the Seven Sins Resort and Casino. I'm sure he'll be happy to answer your questions himself."

Slocumb's eyes bore into Michael's, trying to stare him down; when all else fails, resort to intimidation. The futility of the effort was lost on Slocumb, who was accustomed to getting anything he wanted with a flash of his ID. Michael had been given the same stare during Slocumb's investigation of the implosion of the Maximus. He didn't break his gaze then and he didn't break it now, just waved over the showgirls from the bar. Without hesitation, they bounced down off their stools.

"On me," Michael said, moving away from the table as the girls took up positions on either side of Dell Slocumb. "Keep you on the side of Vegas you're comfortable with."

"Long as it's away from you."

Michael was halfway to the lounge exit when his PDA beeped once, signaling an incoming text message from Naomi. He eased the device from his pocket and checked the screen, feeling the breath lock up in his throat and his heartbeat freeze, as he churned the message over in his mind:

MIRANDA ALVAREZ IS DEAD.

SIXTY-THREE

LAS VEGAS, THE PRESENT

Unable to attend the funeral of Miranda Alvarez in Honduras, Michael instructed Naomi Burns to arrange for a video feed of both the church service and graveside ceremony to be transmitted via wireless broadband service from Tegucigalpa to his office in the Daring Sea. He couldn't say exactly why he had done it, especially since the technology offered him no opportunity to provide comfort to any of the bereaved even if he had known them. Michael supposed he had done it for himself, at least to provide closure to a relationship that haunted him to this day.

Miranda and two servants had been murdered two days before at her estate in Zambrano, on the same day as Luciano Scaglione. Reports from the scene he'd been able to gather indicated it had been quick and professional. Local officials were far more reticent to reveal the condition of her body, Alexander's sources unable so far to learn whether her eyeballs had been gouged out as had been the case with the twins and Don Luciano.

But Michael knew they had been.

Naomi and Alexander had kept their distance from Michael throughout the day, knowing he needed to deal with Miranda's death himself.

The unobtrusive camera focused on the front of the cortege

and the gravesite itself, making it easy for Michael to pick out Miranda's two sons, who'd be seventeen and eighteen, he thought. Orphans now, their lives spared by the assassins only because they were away at a boarding school fifty miles from home.

Even now, within the large crowd gathered for the funeral, guards dispatched by Alexander were watching vigilantly. They would keep their distance for the time being, but eventually they would approach the boys' appointed guardians with a murky explanation of the danger they were in.

Ironically, Michael had saved their lives once before, as he had Miranda's. Now she was being laid to rest in a grave alongside one reserved for her husband, Alejandro, the minister of agriculture who had coordinated World Trade Agricola's appointment as the primary buyer and exporter of the country's sizable cane sugar crop. He had granted WTA an exporting license and facilitated the company's efforts to win the quotas from the government over other exporters who controlled varying smaller percentages of the crop. This effectively gave WTA control over thousands and thousands of acres, along with a trio of sugar refineries Michael agreed to have WTA buy and upgrade, requiring a substantial additional investment.

The feed may have originated in the Honduran capital, but Miranda's funeral actually took place in a graveyard on the outskirts of the village of Zambrano, some twenty miles from Tegucigalpa on the highway toward San Pedro Sula. Michael had always looked forward to his trips to Zambrano, a small village located high in the mountains and surrounded by pine forests, where he had stayed at the Caserio Valuz from his initial visit to the country.

To this day Michael did not fully comprehend his feelings for Miranda Alvarez, especially since those feelings had never been consummated. He wondered if he would've felt better today if they had, searching his past for the answer.

SIXTY-FOUR

Tegucigalpa, 1996

Alejandro Alvarez scowled at Michael from across their iso-
lated table in Porcao, a steak house located in the capital city's
Palmira district, safely away from the ministry building. Meeting Alvarez here instead of his office had raised Michele's
suspicions even before the agriculture minister had issued his
ultimatum.

"My terms are nonnegotiable," he said, growing bolder
with each breath. "If you do not accept them, you will leave us
no choice but to entertain other offers."

Alvarez was a short, stout man with a mustache that was too
big for his face. He kept it groomed meticulously and tugged
the hairs back into place whenever he felt them slipping over
his lip. His hair was thick and dyed jet black, the base of the
hairs framing his temples showing their true gray color. He had
the look of a man once in fine shape, but whose stomach was
now beginning to stretch well over his belt.

Michael guessed his marriage to Miranda was part of an
arrangement of convenience for both parties. Her family had
no doubt been paid off handsomely, while Alvarez had been
rewarded with the sons he desperately wanted. A younger, fer-
tile wife for an older, powerful government official was often
the way of the world in South America.

"Alejandro," Michael began calmly, even though he could
feel the burn of rage heating up inside him, "I'd first like to remind you of the investment we've made in the sugar refineries, enabling Honduras to double their export ratios."

"For which you have already been well compensated."

"Not me, Alejandro: World Trade Agricola."

"That's right. You already have your trust fund to fall back
on, Señor Nunziato. So what's a few more dollars for World
Trade Agricola?"

"Why don't you tell me?"

"I just did. Thanks to me, the ministry of agriculture of the Honduran government has granted you, WTA, a fifty percent export quota. In exchange for that courtesy, I feel I deserve a quarterly fee on the order of two point five percent of the gross profit."

"A bribe, in other words."

Alvarez's stare hardened even more. "You'd be wise not to offend me, Señor Nunziato."

"And if WTA could accept, say, one point five percent?"

"WTA would be short, leaving me no choice but to dilute your quota, effective next year, when your current contract expires."

"I thought you were a man of integrity, Mr. Alvarez."

"I have a big family to support, Señor Nunziato."

"We all do," Michael said, leaving it at that.

He was well aware that Alvarez lived an exceedingly lavish lifestyle that was well above his means. A huge and beautiful home, fast cars, and, according to Michael's sources, a number of women on the side in spite of his beautiful and younger wife.

"Why be greedy, Michele? The cane sugar crop this year promises to set a record."

"Exactly. In large part because of those refineries acquired and upgraded by WTA."

"Your refineries without the quotas I control are a write-off."

"But I have one thing from you these other potential partners don't."

"And what's that?"

"Your word of honor."

Alvarez smiled broadly. "So what? Sue me." He laughed. "I don't think you realize how South America works."

Michael rose, his skin already cooling as he steadied himself. "Trust me. You don't want to do this."

"And why's that?"

"Because you have no idea who you're fucking with."

"Don't threaten me, Señor Nunziato."

"I'm not, I'm only advising you. When you're ready to be

reasonable, and honorable, you can reach me at the Caserio Valuz."

"Don't wait for my call," Alvarez said, disrespecting Michael by not rising with him. "Just read the papers when the government announces its new partners in the cane sugar trade."

Michael stood there, studying him.

"Some genius, eh?" Alvarez taunted sarcastically.

Michael left the restaurant without another word. He lingered briefly in the city to plan his next move, then returned to the Caserio Valuz, where, surprisingly, he found Vittorio and Francesco Scaglione sitting on the spacious porch smoking cigars.

"We hear things are not going very well with the agriculture minister," said Vittorio. "Quite shitty, to put it politely."

"And just where did you hear that?"

"We have our sources in Tegucigalpa," Francesco answered. "They also informed us about Alvarez's betrayal."

"Which, of course, cannot be tolerated," followed Vittorio.

"So our father dispatched us to deal with another of these *pezzi novanta* politicians."

"Pour him a bath of acid."

Michael swallowed hard, understanding that a suspicious Don Luciano had obviously hired someone behind his back to keep tabs on his affairs and report back to Caltagirone. He should have expected as much after their last meeting. Still, he felt hurt, stung by the Don's lack of confidence in him.

"What, surprised you didn't get a blank check? Nobody outside the family gets a blank check."

"I'm taking care of the problem," Michael tried to assure them, stung by Vittorio's remark. "Stay out of it."

"Too late," Francesco told him.

"Our father wants you to leave the country," Vittorio added.

"We will handle everything from here." Francesco smiled snidely.

"We'll take good care of this agriculture minister. Make sure no one ever sees him again."

"As a warning to others, the rest of his fam—"

Vittorio shot Francesco a look, cutting his words off mid-sentence. But Michael knew to what Francesco was referring.

"Get your ass to the airport," Vittorio advised. "Don't delay."

"Our father's orders."

Michael didn't bother collecting the belongings from his room, but neither did he go straight to the airport. Instead he drove frantically through the countryside, his heart pounding until Miranda Alvarez answered the door to her house when he knocked.

"Michael," she said, clearly surprised to see him since he had avoided all opportunities that might have found them alone together. "Are you here to see Alejandro? He's not here."

"I'm here to see you."

Miranda started to smile, then stopped herself when she saw the look in his eyes. "What's wrong?"

"Don't ask," he said, entering and closing the door behind him. "Just pack bags for you and the boys." He moved to the window and peered out between the drawn sheer curtains. "You won't be coming back for a while."

"You're scaring me."

"With good reason." He took Miranda gently by the arms, felt her trembling beneath his touch. "Alejandro broke his word, and too much money's at stake now. I gave him a chance to make good, but . . ." Michael let his voice trail off.

"He's my husband. He'd never do anything to—"

"It's not him I'm worried about, Miranda."

"What are you saying?"

"Already too much. There are things I never told you or him, the truth about WTA's backers. Let's just say they're the kind of people you don't double-cross."

"I don't understand."

"You don't have to. Just get the bags packed and get . . ." Michael stopped, realizing he had forgotten the names of her two sons. ". . . the boys ready to travel."

"But they're in school. I could go pick them up."

"No," Michael told her. "It's too late for that now."

"Too late for *what*?"

"Just pack the bags. And do you have a gun in the house?"

"Yes."

"Get it for me."

SIXTY-FIVE

ZAMBRANO, 1996

Thoughts rampaged through Michael's mind as he loaded the twelve-gauge shotgun. He knew what was coming, had even before Francesco had hinted as much.

Alejandro Alvarez, unknowingly and naively, had crossed the Scaglione family, and an example needed to be set. Business in this part of the world required drastic measures and Don Luciano needed to show who was in control. But Michael couldn't just walk away, not and live with himself afterward. If he let this happen, how different would he be from the killers who had murdered his family? The deaths of Miranda and her sons would be as pointless as the murders of his parents and sister. He had stood idly by then, wetting his pants as he dug himself into the hay pile. He could not stand idly by again, no matter what the costs might be.

Suddenly, all his planning, everything he had accomplished toward a much greater goal, seemed insignificant when measured against three innocent lives. Michael thought he had forever conquered his emotions the day his family had been massacred. But they had resurfaced with an intensity that overcame all else, including his loyalty to the Scaglione family. He had passed so many tests in life, most of them in his quest for power. But today he had to pass a different one that had been festering for twenty years.

"What about Alejandro?" Miranda asked him.

He closed his hands on her shoulders, felt her shaking now. "I'm sorry. It's too late."

Miranda swallowed hard, choking back tears. "I'll go up-stairs and pack the boys' things." The words nearly caught in her throat with her breath.

"Get moving. Please, Miranda."

Michael watched her disappear upstairs. His cheeks felt hot and he could feel his ever-present gold medallion stuck to his chest with sweat. Time wasn't the paramount issue here; the killers would not come until Miranda's sons were home.

Past and present swirled together. The town of Caltagirone became Zambrano. The family farm became the hilly land of Honduras. He imagined he could smell oranges faintly in the distance.

Michael stood by the window, shotgun propped against the wall alongside him. Miranda returned downstairs with three overstuffed tote bags in hand. She kept silent until the school bus rumbled to a halt and her sons climbed out at the edge of the Alvarez estate.

"I'll get them," she said, starting for the door.

Michael intercepted her on the way. "Just stay inside, and do exactly what I tell you."

He stepped out onto the porch in her place, shotgun held back behind his hip. The boys traipsed up the front walk and greeted Michael politely without noticing the shotgun. Miranda closed and locked the front door behind them.

Michael was still standing on the porch when a pickup truck, covered in dirt, rumbled down the driveway. He hoisted the shotgun before him, careful to keep the barrel angled slightly downward as he stepped off the porch and took up a position halfway between it and the end of the driveway.

The pickup snailed to a halt, and three casually dressed, square-framed men Michael had never seen before climbed out, keeping their eyes on him. They tucked their hands inside their jackets; no need to act rashly, since Michael continued to hold the shotgun in a defensive posture.

"Do you know who I am?" Michael asked, as they stood there, shocked by his presence.

The man in the center, clearly the oldest, nodded. "You should leave and let things be," the man said in Sicilian.

"I can't do that."

The three men continued to hold their ground, their confusion over how to proceed increasing by the second to Michael's advantage.

"We have our orders," the oldest man told him.

"I know. But you'll have to go through me first."

"Mr. Nunziato, you must leave for your own sake."

Michael raised the shotgun just a fraction more and pumped a round into the chamber. "I was just about to say the same thing to you."

The men tensed, slid farther apart to widen the distance among them, complicating Michael's aim.

"One of you," the oldest said. "Three of us."

"For now."

"You'll die."

"We'll see about that, won't we?"

The men looked at one another again.

"The responsibility here is mine," Michael told them. "I'm telling you this is a mistake, a miscommunication. You either have to trust me or try to kill me and risk dying yourselves. There is no third choice."

"Mr. Nunziato—"

"Choose," Michael ordered, raising the shotgun another hair.

The oldest man slid his hand back out of his jacket and backpedaled toward the pickup, passing an unspoken signal to the others to join him. No further words were exchanged, his gaze remaining locked with Michael's until the truck had turned around and headed back down the driveway.

As soon as they were gone, Michael headed into the mountains with Miranda and her sons. She had inherited a cabin there from her late grandparents, where they'd be safe until he could be sure the killers were no longer keen on pursuing her.

Michael tucked Miranda and the boys into the cabin's back room and sat out on the porch with the shotgun to stand guard. The cabin was enclosed by razor-sharp thick brush on two sides and the mountain itself at its rear. That left a direct frontal approach as the only means of access, leaving Michael confident he could manage a defensive effort in spite of his limited skills as a marksman.

Miranda made coffee and he drank it black long into a cool, silent night disrupted only when she joined him outside, sitting down next to him and laying her head on his shoulder. Michael set the shotgun down to take her in his arms, felt her trembling within his grasp as she laid down with her head across his lap.

There was so much he wanted to do, even more that he wanted to say. But before he could do either, he realized she was sleeping soundly.

Michael leaned over, easing his mouth close to her ear, whispering, "I love you, Miranda." He smoothed her hair. "No one will ever hurt you so long as I'm alive."

SIXTY-SIX

CALTAGIRONE, 1996

"What am I to do with you, Michele?" Don Luciano asked him two days later from across the shaded table upon the veranda.

"I did what I had to do, Don Luciano."

"I'm not talking about your actions in Zambrano, as foolish as they were. I'm talking about the fact that you lied to me."

"Did you bring your ledger?"

"Ledger? *Che minchia!* We aren't discussing my sins today, Michele. We're discussing yours, like sleeping with another man's wife, which clearly clouded your judgment in the Alvarez matter."

"I would never touch a married woman."

"Your actions indicate otherwise."

"Alvarez was my problem. You should've let me handle it."

"It was your problem so long as it involved business. It

became mine once things got personal. Betrayal is personal, and screwing with WTA's interests in Honduras is personal, Michele, especially when it comes at the hands of a *pezzo novanta* like this Alvarez. That's why we made him disappear. That's why no one will ever see him again."

"His wife and sons didn't betray you."

"They might as well have. This is about honor."

"No, it's about business. And murdering women and children is bad for business."

"Scaglione family business."

"Yes, the same business I built World Trade Agricola to legitimize. The future, Don Luciano, remember? And there's no place in that future for the slaughter of innocents and for ignorance. And only the ignorant would react so savagely and say they had no choice."

Incensed, Don Luciano lumbered to his feet and dismissed Michael with a flap of his hand. "I'm done talking with you. Get out of here now."

Michael remained in his chair, a clear act of defiance. "We haven't finished."

"I have."

"If you keep being stubborn about the old ways, you risk losing all the insulation from the authorities I built for you. *Errare humanum est perseverare diabolicum*."

"What, think you're smart, quoting Latin to me?"

"It means, 'Making mistakes is human, to keep making the same mistake is diabolic.'"

"Is that a threat, Michele?" Scaglione asked, wide-eyed, as if shocked by the mere possibility.

"It's a certainty. If I, if we're, to be successful, there can be no place for the old ways, the old codes."

"It was these same ways that made it possible to bankroll your World Trade Agricola. But suddenly you don't approve."

"Not suddenly. I'm not a gangster and never was."

"And you think I am?"

"Actions speak louder than words."

The Don's gray-blue eyes regarded him coldly. "In that case, Michele, am I to trust you anymore?"

"That depends."

"Does it? On what exactly?"

"Are Miranda Alvarez and her children safe?"

"That depends, Michele."

"On what?"

"On whether you ever intend to see them again."

"No," Michele said without hesitation, understanding the Don's proposition, "I don't."

"Then understand if this woman talks, the responsibility is yours and so is the punishment."

"I accept that responsibility."

The old man nodded, almost sadly. "So that's what it has come to, the two of us threatening each other."

"At least we're not hypocrites, Don Luciano."

Scaglione retook his seat, the table between them suddenly seeming very vast. "Then let us move on, Michele."

Even as Michael knew they couldn't.

SIXTY-SEVEN

LAS VEGAS, THE PRESENT

True to his word, Michael had not seen Miranda Alvarez since the night they had taken refuge at her family's mountain cabin. Miranda remained in Honduras after the mysterious disappearance of her husband, eventually returning to the family estate, but she never spoke to the authorities, protecting Michael for what he had done for her and her children.

No one will ever hurt you so long as I'm alive.

But now she was dead. Because of him.

Everyone he ever loved . . .

What was it Jeannie Vega had said to him?

All your paintings are portraits.

Perhaps that was why. Perhaps in collecting his many artistic treasures, he was painting his own future.

No one close to Michael was safe, and if Alexander's suspicions were correct, the attack on Vegas itself might have been part of the vendetta against him.

But why?

It made no sense.

After Miranda Alvarez's funeral was completed, Michael terminated the video feed and summoned Naomi and Alexander to join him in his glass office at the bottom of the Daring Sea. They took the matching chairs set before his desk, both waiting for him to speak first.

Killing this man won't bring your family back to life, Michele.

The last piece of advice Don Luciano would ever give him echoed in his mind. Michael had carried the old man's blood-stained notebook, containing a careful, coded roster of his many sins, around with him virtually every moment since he had returned to Las Vegas. Don Luciano would tell him that his life had become a matter of balancing the books as well, of overcoming his past by securing his future. The problem was, it never seemed to be enough. With a megaresort of unprecedented glitz and glamour, the world was his to take, and Michael had already turned his attention to Macao and elsewhere to expand his holdings, and implementing a vast plan for mergers and acquisitions. With the gaming business well in hand, King Midas World was seeking to branch out into other areas, making both inroads and inquiries that would position it as a multibillion-dollar global conglomerate.

At times Michael wondered if that explained his fascination with great white sharks. Stop swimming and they die. That was why it was so vital to him that Assassino, the largest and unnaturally meanest great white ever spotted, survive the journey to Las Vegas from Southern California. That was why Michael couldn't stop with the Seven Sins, even though at one point owning such a grand casino and resort had been his all-consuming passion.

"What have you learned about our asshole enemy?" he asked Alexander.

"The worst possible thing. My best sources in the Middle East tell me government officials and members of the royal families there are running scared. Security details have been doubled, even tripled. Family members are being evacuated. I'm told a mysterious new group targeting moderate governments has surfaced, capable of getting to anyone at any time."

"Assassins . . ."

"Word is the Hashishin have returned, Stolarchos."

"That's fucking great," Michael said, shaking his head. "I don't care how much it costs. Whatever it takes, no one else close to me dies. Do you hear me? No one."

"Have you made that list yet for me?" Alexander asked him.

"Yes. Except for Amir Pharaon and Kenneth Cohan, the people closest to me are right at this table," Michael said. Kenneth Cohan was the investment banker who had arranged the $1.8 billion line of credit that allowed construction of the Seven Sins to proceed. Even with the fall of the Maximus and absorption of Price World Resorts into King Midas World, without Cohan, Michael's dreams may have remained forever unrealized. "I have a call into Pharaon, but I haven't been able to reach him yet."

"I'll check on Cohan," Alexander stated.

"And I'm not too worried about us, Michael," Naomi said. "It's obvious that whoever's behind the Hashishin is after you."

"Even that's not enough for them. They want to destroy my world, my dream, everything I've created and stand for, including Las Vegas, which means we have to turn the tables on them. Just like in business."

Naomi Burns fidgeted in her chair. "How?"

"We start with the lawyer, this Gianfranco Ferelli. Someone hired him to look into my past and now that past is being used against me. And there's Trumbull, the lowlife journalist."

"He's still in Vegas," Alexander reported. "Staying at Mandalay Bay."

"The son of a bitch knew things about my past he couldn't have possibly pulled out of gossip rags and the rumor mill. That means someone was feeding him info." Michael's gaze locked on Alexander. "It's time we found out who."

Alexander flashed the thinnest of smiles.

"What about me?" asked Naomi.

"You're going to Rome."

"Why?"

"Because we won't find whatever it is Ferelli uncovered here in Vegas. The answers lie in Sicily, starting with that address in Messina. Don't worry," Michael continued before Naomi could protest. "You'll have plenty of time to pack; you're not leaving until I've had my meeting with Trumbull, because Alexander will be accompanying you."

Emotion flared across Alexander's features. "Stolarchos, you need—"

"Stop. Naomi will need your protection more than I do. I've got your entire security staff to protect me."

"Right now, that may not be enough," Alexander said grimly.

SIXTY-EIGHT

THE SEVEN SINS, THE PRESENT

Lars Trumbull awoke to the feeling of a heaviness over him and coldness below. His eyes opened to piercing bright light reflecting off a dark, shimmering surface. Confusion muddled his next thought until both his thinking and vision cleared enough for him to realize he was sitting on the edge of some form of dock. He saw that his feet were in the water, just visible below the surface, but was stymied when he tried to jerk them back up. Trumbull glanced to his rear and saw the dark shape of Michael Tiranno's bodyguard looming over him, hands clamped down on his shoulders, holding him firmly in place.

"Welcome to the Intake Center for the Daring Sea, Mr. Trumbull," Michael greeted him from a few yards away. "This is where our marine animals enter the environment and where our marine biologists treat and vaccinate them."

Trumbull glanced about him. The Intake Center was high-

tech in all respects, lined with equipment he couldn't identify. The dock on which he was seated was actually a floating
platform floor, and the black water before him was parti-
tioned into individual holding tanks that opened into the vast
Daring Sea beyond through an underwater connecting tunnel.

Trumbull returned his gaze to Michael Tiranno and noticed
three buckets of chum centered between them.

"So, Mr. Trumbull, would you still like that interview?"

According to information compiled by Naomi, Trumbull had
once been a good reporter and writer, realizing too late that
talent in his chosen profession didn't always translate to the
kind of livelihood he expected. He'd gone through the entire
advance and then some on a book deal well before the book
sold all of a tenth of its initial print run. Trumbull had watched
helplessly as the publisher pulled all the planned advertising
and dropped him as quickly as the book dropped from sight.

With an unseemly amount of debt to deal with, and the
glamour washed out of his life as quickly as once friendly bar-
tenders who no longer let him run up tabs, Trumbull invented a
lucrative new enterprise for himself. For the right price, he'd
make sure an article ran in one of the upscale financial magazines he freelanced for. He cared little about the relative merit
of the truth and in most cases required only questionable cor-
roboration.

Trumbull had remained in Vegas after the attack, his bill for
a room at Mandalay Bay handled by an unknown source.
Alexander had found Trumbull there in the top-floor nightclub, Mix, waited until he settled his bill, and followed him to
a strip club called Crazy Horse, where he intercepted Trumbull in the parking lot.

"Guess not," Michael continued when he made no reply. "Let's
try a little role reversal, then. I'll ask the questions and you'll
answer them. Don't answer, or lie, and you'll experience our
very popular attraction, Red Water, firsthand. This isn't the time
to fuck with me."

Trumbull looked down at his nearly invisible feet. "I'll tell you anything you want to know," he said finally, his voice dry and hoarse.

"Good. Let's start with the asshole who paid you to write the story on me."

"I don't know who it was."

Trumbull watched as Alexander picked up one of the chum-filled buckets and dumped a portion of its contents all over the lower half of his body.

"We don't normally use the Intake Center for feeding," Michael told him. "But I don't think it'll be too long before Assassino and his friends catch the scent."

The bloody froth pooled briefly, then spread out across the surface.

"I told you, I don't know who paid me! I was contacted by e-mail. *E-mail!* The sender told me fifty thousand dollars had already been deposited into my bank account as an advance, with another fifty thousand dollars to come once the story on you was published."

"And what was that story supposed to say?"

"The contents were all in the e-mails from an anonymous source."

"The usual lies and misrepresentations."

Trumbull swallowed hard, grimacing from the throbbing pain in his head. "I don't know."

"You mean you don't give a shit. Go back to the contents of those e-mails."

Trumbull was too busy watching for motion to answer, his gaze locked on his chum-coated legs.

"Look at me, Mr. Trumbull."

Trumbull pulled his eyes off the water before him.

This time, it was Michael who dumped a full bucket of chum into the water. "Now tell me what was in those e-mails."

"Your real name is Michele Nunziato," Trumbull said, the words racing from his mouth now. "You grew up in the Sicilian town of Caltagirone. When you were seven years old, you were the lone survivor of a massacre that claimed your family. The murders remain unsolved to this day. . . ."

Michael listened as the reporter went through the events of his life blow by blow, the facts and details almost entirely correct, from his being taken in by Don Luciano, founding World Trade Agricola, splitting from the Scaglione family, to his arrival and subsequent rise in Las Vegas. All the things that Michael, with Naomi Burns's help, had painstakingly sought either to bury or erase. It would be easily enough to draw the attention of the Gaming Control Board and instigate an investigation that could ultimately strip him of his gaming license and make him a pariah in the industry.

"Who sent you these e-mails?" Michael demanded. "Who paid you to ruin me?"

Trumbull shook his head. "I don't know. I swear to God."

Michael emptied another full bucket of chum into the waters of the Intake Center. "You're running out of time, prick."

Trumbull looked down and glimpsed a grayish shape rising slowly from below. *"I don't know! I'd tell you if I did!"*

"Prove it."

"How?"

"I want those e-mails."

"I deleted them." Trumbull glimpsed the massive, sleek shape of Assassino angling for the surface, testing the confined space. "But I printed hard copies first."

"Where are these copies?"

"In a UPS Store mailbox here in Las Vegas. I have the key with me."

Trumbull reached into his pocket and came out with a key Alexander snatched from his hand.

The surface bubbled. Trumbull saw the huge shark rising for him, its massive jaws opening in line with his legs. Michael nodded to Alexander, who yanked Trumbull backward just in time. Trumbull breathed a sigh of relief, then caught the look in Michael's eyes and held his breath.

"Have you told me everything?"

"Yes, yes, I swear I have!"

"You know what? I buy it."

Trumbull started to breathe easier, then saw the look on Michael's face hadn't changed at all.

"You're part of something that got two people very close to me killed," Michael continued. "But I'm still going to show you the kind of mercy that wasn't shown to Luciano Scaglione or Miranda Alvarez."

Trumbull swallowed hard, as Michael looked toward Alexander.

"After he's dead, don't gouge out his eyes," Michael finished and walked off.

SIXTY-NINE

SUDAN, THE PRESENT

Hassan-i-Sabbah stood in the largest room of the residence constructed for him beneath the old French fort southwest of Khartoum. He missed the outdoors, missed lingering within the still-standing parapet and gazing into the world beyond. With his major attack on the United States just days away now, though, he dared not risk being spotted by a spy satellite or Predator drone. Like his namesake, he had pledged to remain as much as possible within his self-made fortress for as long as it took him to achieve what no man before him ever could: uniting the great forces of radical Islam in the subjugation of the West and whoever else opposed them.

Hassan turned back toward the near wall where a huge shape stood just beyond the reach of the light. Hassan called him Malik, which meant "king" or "master," out of respect. He didn't know his real name since his tongue had been torn out by the Russians during the war in Afghanistan. Malik escaped, only to lose part of his face to a landmine. That part was now a patchwork of scar tissue and pocked skin from cheekbone to jawline on the left side, partially covered by a beard that grew thick on the right. He shaved his scalp clean, showing still more scars earned by shrapnel.

Hassan had met Malik during his days in an Al Qaeda

terrorist training camp, after which they had ended up together in Tora Bora and, later, in Pakistan. It had been Malik
who had practically carried the comatose Hassan across the
border. In addition to being unable to speak, the huge and brutal Malik had never learned to write. Hassan had taken it upon
himself to teach him how to read and write in at least rudi-
mentary fashion, many of their lessons taking place in fading
firelight until the fear of American air strikes banished them
to caves.

Malik was a wondrous warrior, ruthless killer, and exceptional
assassin who was amazingly quick for his six-and-a-half-foot
frame and naturally developed bulk. Of Moroccan descent, he
was especially proficient with his bare hands, a perfect specimen
to uphold the legacy of the Hashishin. Hassan now enlisted him
for only the most important missions, including the one he had
just returned from in Afghanistan.

"You must not fret, my friend," Hassan told Malik. "Michael
Tiranno was not your intended target. He was the target of other
forces and the failure is theirs."

Malik nodded and looked at him impassively.

"The news from the Black Sea is bad as well," Hassan continued "The ship carrying our nuclear triggers was hit by pirates.
To have them in my possession on the eve of our greatest victory
would have been a fine portent of many triumphs to come. Rest
assured, we will recover them to help us fulfill our holy quest,
but for now we turn our attention to the next mission. Come
here, let me show you."

Malik joined him at the table and Hassan slid sideways so
he could see the detailed structural map of the Las Vegas Strip
and downtown area spread atop the glass.

Hassan felt himself dwarfed by Malik's towering shape.
"Gaze now at the city that in the light of the next full moon
will be no more." Hassan reached up and laid his hand atop
Malik's steel-like shoulder. "I have decided to give you my
greatest gift. I have made arrangements to send you to America to finish the operation yourself. You will be the one who
secures our destiny, empowered by Allah Himself."

Malik showed no response.

"And something else, my friend," Hassan continued. "You will also have another chance to kill the man who escaped you in Kabul."

This time Malik nodded and returned to his study of the map on the table before him. Hassan knew how much he would miss Malik's prowess and loyalty, but he had no choice other than to send him to assure success, especially now that the nuclear triggers had been stolen from the ship he had dispatched to the Black Sea.

With those triggers in his possession, thanks to the great financial resources he now possessed, Hassan would have felt more empowered in his pursuit to consolidate his influence in the Arab world by standing up against the West. The destruction of Las Vegas, the city of sin that was a symbol of all the West's decadence, would serve as a catalyst that would solidify his dominance over the other disjointed radical Islamic movements. Instead of resisting his overtures, leaders of terrorist organizations would seek him out for his guidance as well as his resources. The aftermath of 9/11 had led to a substantial crackdown on their sources of funding, including the freezing of their bank accounts and arrest of their primary financiers. Hassan was now prepared to step into that void, as much to fulfill his own destiny as to reestablish the legacy of the Hashishin by launching an attack from which America would never recover.

Without the nuclear triggers, the follow-up attacks he had planned would have to be delayed. In the meantime, though, Malik's presence in Las Vegas would assure the success of the attack there and that Michael Tiranno would die, as specifically requested by Hassan's mysterious benefactor.

Three days, he thought, *just three more days before the sun rises over a much different world.*

SEVENTY

Lake Las Vegas, the present

"Nothing," Naomi Burns told Michael inside the living room of Roma Vetus, after a thorough inspection of the pages Alexander had returned with from Trumbull's mailbox. "Whoever sent Trumbull these e-mails hid his actual Web address behind dummy sites that all turned out to be dead ends."

Michael turned from the French doors overlooking the foliage of the Serengeti, where a pair of tigers romped in the brush. "Deactivated?"

"Worse: they never even existed."

"A dead end, then."

"Not entirely. I did some more research into Trumbull, specifically into his past articles. Turns out you're well acquainted with one of the subjects he inflated for pay: Amir Pharaon."

"What?"

Naomi remained silent to let her point sink in. "Would he betray you, Stolarchos?" asked Alexander

"How could he? He doesn't know shit."

"But he knew you in the days before we made sure the truth of your past was buried."

"He was my friend, Naomi. And I never told him the truth about me, the Scagliones, and World Trade Agricola—none of it."

"Don't be naive, Michael. You don't get as close as you did to a man like Pharaon without him wanting to know everything there is to know about you."

"He's an arms dealer," Alexander added. "For the right price he'd sell anything."

"Trumbull's article on Pharaon was written after he nearly went bankrupt two years ago," Naomi added. "A failed attempt to restore his reputation."

Michael looked back through the French doors, as if to look for the tigers that had disappeared into the thick jungle habitat.

"Exiling his son Samar from the family ten years ago devastated him. I don't think he ever forgave himself. Pharaon ran afoul of the Saudis, his best customers for armaments, and they made sure anyone who needed Saudi oil never did business with him again. That started the downward spiral."

"There's more," Naomi said. "The London Club publicly pursued Pharaon for several years to collect a fifteen-million-pound gambling debt he owed. That debt, I just checked, has recently been paid in full."

"So Pharaon's liquid again."

Alexander reached out and grasped Michael's forearm. "I think we should ask him where the money came from."

"But don't forget this lawyer Ferelli," Michael said. "Someone hired him to dig up everything on me dating all the way back to the massacre of my family."

"The briefcase turned out to be a dead end too, Michael," Naomi reminded him.

"Not totally. There's that address in Messina."

"You're forgetting Ferelli came to Las Vegas to see you."

"No, I'm not. Ferelli must have uncovered something that changed the rules halfway into the game. Maybe he was coming to Vegas to give up his employer. Everything the man did points to the fact that he was scared shitless."

"Of what?"

"Only way to find that out is to retrace his steps, starting with Messina, where you and Alexander will be headed this afternoon."

"My place is with you," Alexander said, his voice firm.

"Under the circumstances, I can't leave Naomi alone. And on the way back the two of you can meet me in Paris to say hello to my dear friend Amir Pharaon. See what he's got to say in person, since I can't reach him any other way."

"You remain the primary target here," Alexander persisted.

"And I've got your entire security staff to protect me, while I get back to running King Midas World. I'm trying to build an empire here, not save Gotham City." Michael looked back at Naomi Burns. "What do we have on the schedule for tomorrow?" Michael checked his watch. "I mean today."

"A meeting on expansion into Macao with an accredited investment banker from Credit Suisse specializing in the Asian markets."

"I'll take that meeting while the two of you follow the leads left by Ferelli. Business as usual."

"Except it's not," Naomi reminded him.

"It will be," Michael said, counting down the time to the grand opening of the Seven Sins Magnum Arena. "In three days when this nightmare is over. Otherwise, we're done." Michael noticed Alexander reading a text message he had just received. "What now?"

Alexander hesitated, his expression uncharacteristically grim as he returned the cell phone to his pocket. "It's on the news wire. Your friend, the banker Kenneth Cohan, was found murdered this morning."

PART THREE

TO WIN

Victory belongs to the most persevering.
—Napoléon Bonaparte

SEVENTY-ONE

Messina, the present

Naomi Burns and Alexander approached the building in the bustling yet rustic commercial center of Messina tentatively, Naomi checking the piece of paper tucked in her hand one more time.

Via Cesare Battisti 76 . . .

It was indeed the address salvaged by the Las Vegas crime lab from the contents of Gianfranco Ferelli's briefcase. The building had been entirely renovated both inside and out, with a strip mall–style ground floor housing a bakery, coffee bar, and gift shop featuring local wares, and what looked like apartments on two floors above. The original architecture had been retained, supplemented with faux gray brick, pre-aged to better blend in with the similarly old buildings around it. From other parts of the city, the citrus fields in the outlying countryside were plainly visible. But here contemporary Messina could have been mistaken for any other midsized European metropolis.

"You know what Messina is best known for?" Alexander asked, clearly unhappy to be here and anxious over leaving Michael's side. "The bubonic plague. It was brought to Europe by Sicilian traders sailing back from China's Black Sea on a ship that arrived in Messina."

"Hence the nickname 'City of Ghosts.'"

"Actually," Alexander corrected, "that comes from the Allied bombardment of 1943, forcing residents to flee to the countryside for safety." Alexander turned his focus to the coffee bar. "Could be Ferelli met someone here. That and nothing more."

Naomi remained silent, downtrodden over the possibility they had left Michael alone to fly five thousand miles for nothing more than a cannoli or a cup of espresso.

"Nothing's what it used to be."

The voice came from behind them, Alexander and Naomi turning to find an old woman selling flowers from a pushcart. She wore a shapeless black smock over her large, gelatinous frame, which seemed to have been injected with excess flesh. Her face was freckled and dappled with age spots, her hair hidden beneath a black veil wrapped tightly round her scalp. Like many of the flowers atop her cart, she seemed to be wilting.

"Are you from Messina?" Naomi asked her.

"I'm from lots of places, but this is as close to home as I have," she said in a mix of Sicilian dialect and Italian, her eyes straying to the renovated building before them. "I close my eyes and see different things, things my memories show me." The woman stopped while Alexander translated the final sentence for Naomi, who spoke only broken Italian. "Makes me happy until I open them." The woman's gaze sharpened slightly. "My name is Maddelena. Would you like to buy a flower?"

"Yes," Naomi said. "Two."

"For you and your man," Maddelena said, picking out a pair of withered carnations.

Her comment drew a grin from Alexander, who accepted his carnation after Naomi handed the old woman the proper amount of euros.

"So what brings you here?"

"Maybe a romantic getaway," Naomi replied.

Maddelena shook her head. "This is not the kind of place one should come for romance, believe me."

"What kind of place is it?" Naomi asked, after Alexander had translated the woman's words.

Maddelena started rearranging the flowers atop her cart. "A hotel once, before there was power and light. Twenty-five, maybe thirty rooms. Then a brothel when I was a little girl. After that, a mystery. I'm looking at it just like I did all those years ago, wondering what was going on inside."

Naomi slid a bit closer to the flower cart. "Now you've got

me curious," she said, trying not to seem as interested as she was.

The old woman leaned forward and glanced right and left, as if to see if anyone was in earshot. Still, she lowered her voice, her flowers looking suddenly even more wilted. *"Picciriddi'."*

"Children," Alexander repeated in English, translating the Sicilian term.

"They came and they went," Maddelena continued. "From where, to where . . ." She finished her statement with a shrug, then resumed in a whisper, "They said it was an orphanage, operated by the Church but . . ."

"You knew differently, didn't you?"

The old woman nodded again, went back to rearranging her flowers to no purpose. "The doors were always locked and no adults ever came, the way they should have."

"How long ago was this?"

"Oh, a long time. Thirty, forty years anyway."

"Nineteen seventy-five?" Naomi asked, casting a quick glance toward Alexander.

The old woman did the math in her head. "Yes, I think so. *Probabilmente.*"

"Did you ever go inside?"

"I never tried. But I know someone who did. Sister Margherita-Agnese Catina, a nun. Always thought she was better than the rest of us. She'd come bringing baskets of candy and toys. Never said a word about what she saw inside, even after she stopped coming. Kept it all to herself."

Naomi waited for Alexander's translation, then said, "Do you still speak to Sister Margherita-Agnese?"

The old woman flapped a fleshy hand before her face. "She's too busy talking to God now."

Naomi felt her hopes sink. "She's dead, then."

"Dead? No. Just rude and unfriendly. I don't even bother visiting anymore. What's the point?"

"You mean she's here in Messina?"

"That way," the old woman said, jabbing a finger to the right, "a few blocks down at the Annunziata dei Catalani church. But I stopped praying a long time ago."

SEVENTY-TWO

Shadowed by a trio of bodyguards personally selected by Alexander, Michael headed to his dinner meeting at 5:45 sharp. He detested being late but had learned over the years never to be too early, since it implied an overeagerness to close the deal. Tonight, though, it was more a matter of security dictating he not be at the dinner any longer than absolutely necessary.

The meeting with the investment banker from Credit Suisse proposing to handle the leveraged financing for King Midas World's planned expansion into Macao was scheduled for six o'clock at Zefferino's in the Grand Canal complex attached to the Venetian. In spite of the heat, Michael would've preferred to walk from the Seven Sins due to the traffic on the Strip. But Alexander had made the security arrangements before departing with Naomi for Messina, arrangements that specified Michael be picked up in the private section of the Seven Sins garage and driven the short distance to the damaged but now reopened Venetian.

Once there, he would be shadowed the whole time by three of the personnel Alexander had culled from the retirement pools of the Israeli Mossad and British SAS, among other elite sources of professional talent who specialized in discretion and vigilance. Never seen but always within reach, was the way Alexander had described them. Even with these precautions in place, Alexander would have preferred Michael postpone this meeting until his return. But the banker, a Samantha Franes, had a hard departure time that evening with a red-eye back to New York, and Michael's burgeoning interests in the Far East were too vital to risk an indefinite postponement.

Ever since coming to Vegas, the Grand Canal complex of high-end shops and restaurants had been one of his favorite places to visit. Even though the Neapolitan songs the gondoliers sang while cruising along man-made canals were utterly wrong for the reimagined Venice, this was the kind of place he would've built had it not existed already. Michael respected vision, and the highest compliment he could give a contemporary or a rival was to suggest theirs was a concept worthy of his admiration.

Such was the case with the Grand Canal, an indoor, climate-controlled environment contained beneath a manufactured blue sky built into the concave ceiling above. The illusion of walking along the traffic-free streets of Venice on a picture-perfect day was created amid two floors of luxury stores constructed of what passed as aged marble and granite.

His bodyguards shadowed Michael all the way to the entrance of Zefferino's a few minutes before his scheduled dinner and then took up posts around the exterior of the restaurant. The maître d', Ernesto, informed him Samantha Franes had already arrived and escorted Michael to his regular table on the restaurant's second floor.

As he approached the table, set in a curtained alcove in the level's rearmost corner, Michael's gaze locked on a ravishingly beautiful woman, her jet black hair tumbling past her shoulders in graceful waves. She rose at Michael's approach, revealing a tall, athletic frame silhouetted elegantly by a designer pants suit that showcased powerful thighs and a shapely waist. Drawing closer, he noticed a pair of emerald green eyes that were as alluring as they were hypnotic.

"Michael Tiranno," he greeted her, extending his hand toward her.

She took it, her grasp surprisingly firm. "Samantha Franes. A pleasure to meet you, Mr. Tiranno," said Raven Khan.

SEVENTY-THREE

Messina, the present

Alexander trailed Naomi Burns up the steep steps of the Annunziata dei Catalani church. The large double doors were
open, inviting all comers to visit one of Messina's prime attractions for residents and tourists alike.

"The building remains virtually unchanged from its construction in the twelfth century," the voice of a nun doubling
as a tour guide droned in a metallic echo from the center of
the pews. "Besides obvious updates in heating and water, the
church has undergone only one serious renovation, when the
nave was shortened and a facade added a hundred years after
its construction. But its trademarks, the magnificent cylindrical
apse and high dome emerging from an equally high tambour,
are part of the original construction, along with the architec-
turally brilliant blind arches separated by small columns along
the church's gray-stone facade I pointed out earlier."

A second nun passed Naomi and Alexander in the final stages
of her tour, guiding eight tourists with cameras and guidebooks
past them and through the door.

"Now, then," the nun greeted them, heading back their way,
"I guess it's your turn."

"Actually, we're looking for Sister Margherita-Agnese,"
Naomi said in her broken Italian.

Their would-be tour guide looked a bit disappointed. "She has
rectory duty today. It's the stone building directly next door."

"Sister Margherita-Agnese?" Naomi said to the old woman
who opened the rectory's heavy door halfway.

"Yes. Do I know you?"

"No, sister." Naomi gestured toward Alexander. "My friend
and I would like to speak to you about something that happened very long ago, if we may."

Sister Margherita-Agnese regarded them suspiciously.

"We met a friend of yours a little ways from here," Naomi continued.

"A friend of *mine*?"

Naomi nodded from the other side of the door. "She was selling flowers in front of the building located at Via Cesare Battisti 76."

"And what did this friend tell you?"

"That you used to bring toys and candy to the *bambini* who were housed there. That it was an orphanage operated by the Church. She said her name was Maddelena."

"I don't know any Maddelena. Whoever this woman is, she lied."

"You didn't bring toys and candy?"

"It wasn't an orphanage and it wasn't operated by the Church."

"Maddelena said the doors were always locked, the window shades drawn," Naomi continued, after Alexander translated the woman's words.

"I don't want to speak of this," Sister Margherita-Agnese said and started to close the door.

Alexander jammed a hand against the door to hold it in place. "Tell us about these children, sister," he said in Sicilian, menacing enough to make her eyes fill with fear.

"Who are you? Why do you care? Are you from the police? No, you couldn't be. It's been too long. What good would it do?"

"*I bambini,* sister," Alexander persisted.

"I would have done something sooner, had I known. Certainly I suspected, but I was afraid."

"Of what?"

Sister Margherita-Agnese looked past them, as if expecting someone else to be there. "You better come inside."

They continued their conversation at the kitchen table, the old nun struggling to sip from a cup of scalding tea. "These *picciriddi'* weren't orphans. They were stolen."

Naomi glanced briefly at Alexander, let the woman continue on her own without prodding.

"How do I know this? I guess I don't, never did, not for sure. But a few of them spoke to me. A few of them were old enough to remember what had happened to them, even if they couldn't understand it. So much pain. So many tears. What was I to do? I was paid to clean up after them. Tell anyone what I knew and I would be dead."

"What exactly did you know?"

"Not knew—heard, guessed. The children were never there long. I cried for each one because of where they were going." Sister Margherita-Agnese tried to pick up her teacup, but her hands were trembling too much now. *"Il mercato nero."*

"Sold on the black market," Alexander translated, when Naomi looked his way.

Naomi weighed the nun's words in her head. The lawyer Gianfranco Ferelli had clearly uncovered a child-snatching ring posing as an orphanage. But what could that possibly have to do with the research he was doing into the life of Michael Tiranno?

"Do you remember anything special or strange happening in the spring of 1975?"

The old woman shrugged, then frowned. "Another season, another year. Nothing special, no. I never asked questions. I feared for my life, you understand."

"Help me to."

"The place was protected by Cosa Nostra. Things like this could not happen here without their approval. So I kept my mouth shut. Did what I could, but never made trouble."

"Does this name mean anything to you?" Naomi asked, removing a piece of paper from her pocket and unfolding it before passing it across the table to Sister Margherita-Agnese, who took it in a trembling hand.

"Agostino Pàtria," she said out loud, as if the name was familiar to her.

"Do you know who it is?"

"It's not a who at all," Sister Margherita-Agnese said, handing the slip back to Naomi. "It's a *what*. You see there's a word missing, cut off at the end. *Camposanto.*"

Naomi seemed to freeze in midbreath. "Camposanto?"

"Yes." The old woman nodded. "Agostino Patria is a grave-yard."

"It's located in Caltagirone," Alexander told Naomi, once they were outside the rectory. "Not far from the graveyard where Michael's family is buried. We can be there in an hour."

"Not yet. First we need to speak to Maddelena again."

"For what?"

"To find the truth."

SEVENTY-FOUR

LAS VEGAS, THE PRESENT

"So why Las Vegas and the gaming industry?" Samantha Franes asked him.

It was Michael's custom to ease into business discussions, believing they always went better when there was some de-gree of familiarity between the parties. He had been making small talk when the woman across the table asked him a ques-tion he knew he could never answer truthfully. And even if he could, it would take too long to tell the tale.

In some ways Samantha Franes, international banker, re-minded Michael of Miranda Alvarez, only much stronger and clearly more independent.

So why Las Vegas?

Michael heard the question again, posed only in his mind, as he wondered how best to answer it.

ZAIRE, 1997

He never had any regrets over his actions that saved the lives of Miranda Alvarez and her two sons in the town of Zambrano.

For men like Don Luciano, though, loyalty was neither conditional nor negotiable. In standing his ground against the killers sent to execute Miranda and her sons, Michael had effectively stood against the will of Don Luciano. The indiscretion was tantamount to betrayal, cloaking the twenty years Michael had spent with the family in its shadow.

Soon after being replaced in Honduras, the twenty-eight-year-old Michael found secondary signatures required at all the banks where World Trade Agricola maintained accounts, and that he had been shut out of all direct dealings with the lawyers at WTA's headquarters in Lichtenstein. No longer was he free to transfer funds or negotiate and approve letters of credit on his own. Instead, a complex hierarchal system was put into place at WTA, aimed squarely at diminishing his power and influence. At the very least, this would threaten the relationships he had painstakingly developed over the years with World Trade Agricola's business partners, and raise questions as to who really owned the company. Don Luciano's message was clear: nobody was indispensable especially since the groundwork already laid by Michael had assured the company's success.

Michael had always known his parting from the Scagliones was inevitable. Even with all his work and efforts, Don Luciano would never fully embrace the vision he had tried to impose upon him.

The time had clearly come to move on. Michael had created World Trade Agricola partially out of debt to Don Luciano, but even more to establish a platform from which to build his own future. In his early twenties, he had proven himself capable of founding and managing what had grown into a near billion-dollar enterprise. Now in his late twenties, he wanted to be free to prepare for his long-awaited move to America and a life he could forge toward his own ends and goals instead of someone else's.

Michael's close ties with the Mobutu regime in Zaire prevented the Don from undermining him there. To supposedly guard against a bad harvest or other unforeseen catastrophe, Michael had patiently, and secretly, stockpiled 25,000 tons of robusta coffee in World Trade Agricola's warehouses there over a period of eighteen months. The revolution he had known was coming since his initial visits to Kinshasa, at the hands of Kabila and his Alliance rebels, was imminent now and, in Michael's opinion, Kabila's success inevitable. And he needed just that to happen to bring the final stages of his shrewd plan to fruition.

Unfortunately, the good news from Alexander that Kabila's rebels had begun their offensive was negated by the fact that their advance toward the capital was proceeding much faster than expected. The government's troops proved utterly unable to deter or contain the rebels, jeopardizing the resources of WTA, Cargill, *Sucre En Denrées* of France, and every other conglomerate doing business in Zaire near Kinshasa. But Michael had located his 25,000-ton stockpile of coffee in warehouses, leased to a Panamanian shell company, located in the west near the port city of Matadi to avoid such a fate, knowing the rebel forces were assembling in the southeast.

The swiftness of the rebels' advance had left Michael with no time to secure ships on which to load the sixty-kilo bags of robusta beans. He tried contacting both captains and shipowners alike while en route to gauge their interest, but none was willing to risk direct involvement, or even docking, amid the civil war that was breaking out across the country. Michael headed by private jet to Kinshasa from Geneva, where he looted the company's safes of the cash reserves in both U.S. and Zaire dollars. Then, once in the capital, he spent two days arranging to transport his coffee from WTA's warehouses to the port of Matadi, leaving by helicopter just as the rebels were taking the city.

As soon as the chopper touched down in Matadi, Michael received word from Alexander that the palace itself was besieged. Alexander informed him Mobutu had already fled the country in search of political asylum in Morocco, sending the very clear message that his government had collapsed. Not trusting the pilot enough on his own, Michael reluctantly reboarded his helicopter and soared back into the air to rescue Alexander.

When it reached the presidential palace, Alexander was on the rooftop, covered in blood, mowing down rebel troops attacking in single file with an assault rifle in either hand. Alexander had run out of ammo by the time the chopper lowered to retrieve him, reduced to making his final stand with a pistol and knife. He grabbed hold of the helicopter's landing pod as it hovered over him and climbed into the cabin with Michael's help as the chopper rose back into the air and flitted away. The pilot took a bullet in the torso but managed to dodge the remaining small-arms fire until the chopper soared out of range, leaving the bodies of fifty rebels behind on the roof and thousands more converging on the palace gates beyond.

Once they returned to Matadi, Michael provided the Zaire cash salvaged from WTA's offices to hire the men and trucks necessary to move the coffee into position. Alexander informed Michael that a Greek freighter he was supposed to meet called the *Achilles,* bearing arms resupply for the government troops, was anchored only a few miles away at sea. The captain, a criminal smuggler, was known to do anything for a price. Michael agreed in this case that price would be $1.5 million in cash, and to allow the captain to retain the weapons for which he had already been paid and would now be free to resell in Angola.

Before rebels could seize control of Matadi, Alexander supervised the convoy that brought the coffee to the port, where it was loaded onto the *Achilles* for shipment to Algiers. Michael, behind his bogus Panamanian corporation with bank accounts in Lugano, Switzerland, had already negotiated a deal with Enapal, the government organization responsible for acquiring all commodities for the country. Enapal agreed to purchase all 25,000 tons at a substantial discount, cash upon delivery in Algiers. Michael had no choice other than to accept their offer of $23 million for a shipment closer to $29 million in value, since he could provide neither documentation of ownership nor certificates of origin. Even after the freighter's captain was paid for his services, though, Michael would still be left with a sufficient nest egg to pursue his dreams and permit his split from the Scagliones.

Michael gave Alexander a suitcase packed with the captain's payment. Once on board, he would be the only thing standing between the *Achilles*'s own nefarious crew and the bags of coffee that were crucial to securing Michele's future.

The *Achilles* was still moored to a pier when the first wave of rebel forces besieged the port, seizing everything in their path. Alexander and the crew members of the *Achilles* beat them back with heavy weapons salvaged from the ship's holds, when a second, larger rebel contingent arrived and unleashed a nonstop hail of gunfire toward the deck until the *Achilles* motored beyond the bullets' range.

Michael boarded the WTA helicopter for his own escape, jostling the snoozing pilot to find him dead from the wound he had suffered in their flight from the presidential palace. He lunged out and leaped into the cab of one of the trucks that had hauled the coffee beans from WTA's warehouses and flashed enough cash to compel the driver to take him to the nearby border with the Congo.

Unfortunately, rebels driving a pilfered Zaire army jeep gave chase down the unpaved road carved out of the jungle. Michael leaned out the window, careful to avoid the sharp foliage scraping at him, and returned the jeep's fire with the nine millimeter Beretta Alexander had given him. He had never been a very good shot, but one of his bullets fortuitously found the jeep's windshield. Struck or not, the driver lost control, propelling the jeep into a wild, careening spin across the road until a tree finally ended its journey. Michael kept his eyes peeled backward in case another vehicle appeared to give chase, but thankfully, none did.

He discarded the pistol, and twenty minutes later joined the long line of refugees fleeing over the border. The final moments before his turn came at the customs station were the worst, Michael not feeling safe until he set foot on Congo territory, already planning how to meet Alexander and the *Achilles* in Algiers.

SEVENTY-FIVE

ALGIERS, 1997

The next two weeks proved among the longest of Michael's life. He had never trusted anyone before as he was forced to trust Alexander. If this man he barely knew decided to steal his money, or strike a deal with the captain to smuggle the coffee elsewhere, Michael would be ruined. There was no past into which he could recede and no future to which to look forward. His dreams, and thus his life, would be over, with little money to his name and an enraged Luciano Scaglione certain to be on his tail.

He waited day after day, watching the seas from his balcony at the Meridian Hotel at Algiers, phoning the port authorities there every two hours to see if the *Achilles* had docked after ten days had passed. He passed the time by flinging hotel pens at a map of the world he taped to the wall, in search of a destination should the *Achilles* never arrive. He couldn't resign himself to the thought of starting from scratch, agonizing over leaving himself so dependent on another man he barely knew, but in whom he had an inexplicable trust, for his own future.

How could he have been so naive? He should've known better. *Never again,* Michael vowed, *never again . . .*

Had the ship been seized at sea by ambitious or greedy African government officials on its stop in Angola? Was his coffee gone forever?

With no answers coming, he began studying weather patterns on the chance a storm had waylaid the ship at sea. But the seas and skies had been clear for a week, leaving him closer to panic with each passing hour.

Michael spent the next days lingering by the docks, walking amid them in the hope the *Achilles* would magically appear. On a rainy morning of the fourteenth day, he saw a rusted hulk of a ship tying down in Dock 7, not recognizing her until he read the barely legible letters stenciled across her bow: *Achilles.*

He stared at the name, willing it not to change as he wiped the grateful tears from his eyes. He felt he had been granted a second chance and rushed frantically onto the ship to find Alexander guarding the deck.

"Where the fuck you been?" Michael said, hugging him tight.

"Her engines are for shit and the Angolan authorities were a pain in the ass."

"What about the coffee?"

Alexander cracked the slightest of smiles. "Nobody ever got close to it."

They supervised the offloading process together with representatives from Enapal, the buyer. But the final paperwork for the transfer of the coffee was not executed until Michael received confirmation that the $23 million payment had been wired to his Panamanian company's account in Lugano. Even with that, Michael realized as he stood next to Alexander on the dock, his business was not done.

"No one, especially the Scagliones, can ever learn about this shipment," he said that night inside his suite at the Meridian. "The ship and her crew need to disappear forever. As far out to sea as possible, where the water is deepest, on her way to Greece."

"Understood, Stolarchos," Alexander replied, calling Michele that for the first time.

SEVENTY-SIX

ALGIERS, 1997

There was no need for Michael to say more. Alexander, having proven himself by making sure the coffee was delivered, was now vital to Michael's future plan and his survival. The coffee was the property of WTA, thus the Scagliones. And if Don Luciano ever learned the truth, there would be nothing

Alexander or anyone else could do to spare Michael the Don's wrath. For the second time in two weeks, he had put his life in Alexander's exceptionally capable hands, feeling much better about it this time.

Together they watched the crew of the *Achilles* celebrating their good fortune on deck before departing. And why not? Between the bounty paid by Michael to secure the ship and the funds gleaned from selling the considerable shipment of arms in Angola, this voyage had reaped a considerable profit.

Little did the crew members know that none would live long enough to enjoy it, that a creature more demon than man was about to be unleashed upon them.

Alexander secretly boarded the *Achilles* shortly before her departure from the port of Algiers that night. He climbed down into one of the ship's now empty cargo holds that still smelled of gun oil and bided his time in the near-total darkness, waiting for the *Achilles* to set back for Greece.

Night offered a number of strategic advantages, not the least of which was that the bulk of the ship's crew would be in their quarters either asleep or passed out drunk. Spending two weeks aboard the *Achilles* in her long voyage from Zaire had left him with a keen knowledge of the ship from stem to stern. Now, while waiting in the cargo hold, Alexander put that knowledge to good use by plotting every move and motion out to the letter.

Twenty-two men in the crew, all to be dead in the next few hours. . . .

Alexander rehearsed the sequence so often in his mind that it seemed over before his watch reached midnight, focusing the whole time on separating reality from conscience.

Click. Zero hour.

Time stopped. The man became monster.

He emerged stealthily from the hold and proceeded to the crew's quarters first. He killed those sleeping in their berths with silenced gunshots, without creating the slightest stir.

Eleven, half the crew's total, down inside of a minute.

Alexander dealt with the necessity of such actions by translating them into a numbers game. In this case, when the number reached twenty-two, he knew he'd be finished. His victims possessed no identity other than the order in which he killed them. And once such a process began, he felt detached from himself, his actions so planned out that final execution of them seemed more the product of his mind than his body.

His next targets were those mates posted at various areas of the ship; alone, of course, but still better taken in close with his knife to avoid any chance of them alerting others. Two of these four turned out to be asleep, their eyes bulging open as the life rushed from them with the blood from their sliced throats, spraying over Alexander's face and clothes. The other two weren't much harder, leaving only the engine room and the bridge, where more concentrated numbers had the potential to pose complications.

Alexander was sweating by the time he approached the bridge, his heart starting to pound, the taste and smell of blood coating him everywhere. Killing was easier when it came quickly, without pause for thought. He knew even the best hesitated when thinking got in the way in the moments before conscience intervened. Alexander focused instead on the fact that he'd be dead himself if it weren't for Michele Nunziato. The reality of that debt rendered all doubt moot.

The blood of his previous victims flew off Alexander as he burst through the door onto the bridge, registering five targets between breaths. He shot the captain and the men on either side of him first. The lag bought time for a hulking first mate to tear a fire ax from the wall. Alexander shot the huge man three times, once in the face, as he rushed in with the ax raised overhead. Even then, with the better part of his left cheek and jaw blown away, the man kept coming, stilled finally when Alexander thrust his knife directly into his heart. The first mate fell dead at his feet and Alexander shot a final crew member cowering in the corner before moving on to those in the engine room.

A wave of light-headedness struck Michael as he climbed on board the cabin cruiser. He felt a sudden sharp pain in his chest and wondered if he was having a heart attack. He sat down on the gunwale and fought to steady his breathing. The moment passed, leaving the scent of blood in the air; real or imagined, Michael couldn't tell. He needed to leave now in order to reach the rendezvous point with Alexander on time. But he couldn't move, no matter how much he willed himself. Sweat, cold and clammy, began to soak through his shirt.

What have I done?

Michael could only imagine what was happening on board the *Achilles,* the ship's crew being slaughtered thanks to the fury he had unleashed. He knew he'd had no choice, knew if he was to survive, these men had to die. He would have to face God for that sin one day, and no entry in a ledger book could change the responsibility he bore. In that moment he understood Luciano Scaglione better than ever. Even in the midst of their inevitable parting, the Don had taught him a lesson in the price that came with power.

Unlike Don Luciano, though, he vowed to learn from this, to make something of all his sins so none was committed for naught. After all, he thought, before he could face God, he had to face himself.

Michael finally found the strength to rise from the gunwale and pushed himself to the boat's controls. Still trembling, he started the engine and slowly reversed out of the slip, turning so the vast emptiness of the sea lay before him.

Alexander held virtually no memory of the grime-soaked mates he killed in the engine room, functioning like a preprogrammed automaton by then. With the last of the ship's crew dead, Alexander stilled the *Achilles'*s engines and set the thermal detonators he had rigged back in Algiers near the boilers and main fuel tanks. Then he opened the spigots on the auxiliary tank to drain five hundred gallons of diesel fuel onto the engine's room floor, assuring the destructive blast's optimum effects.

Alexander was safely away in one of the ship's lifeboats when the *Achilles* erupted in a violent blast that shook the ocean and lit the dark horizon with a hot orange glow that looked for several miles as if the sun had dropped from the night sky. He activated his GPS device and proceeded on through the night to the prearranged rendezvous point.

Michael was waiting when he arrived, circling the area of the designated coordinates.

"Are you all right?" Alexander asked, after climbing on board the rented cabin cruiser.

"Shouldn't it be me asking you that question?" Michele interrupted.

Alexander shrugged off his feeling of unease, then watched as Michael popped the cork off a chilled bottle of champagne and poured two glasses through the escaping foam.

"To successful ends," he toasted, touching glasses with Alexander.

"And new beginnings," Alexander returned.

"For both of us."

"A new beginning requires a new name. For you, Stolarchos," Alexander said, pausing. "Tiranno," he suggested finally.

"The Tyrant," Michael translated, nodding. "I like the way it sounds."

Alexander raised his glass again. "To Michael Tiranno, then."

"And America," Michael added, stopping just short of a smile before they drank.

SEVENTY-SEVEN

LAS VEGAS, THE PRESENT

"Why did I come to Las Vegas?" Michael said, repeating Samantha Franes's question. "To make myself and everyone who invests with me a ton of money."

"What about Asia?"

"I plan to do the same thing in Macao and elsewhere."

"Many on Wall Street question your timing, given the fact that many consider Macao to be already overbuilt."

"Are you trying to tell me my business, Ms. Franes?"

"No, I'm telling you *my* business, which is protecting the interests of Credit Suisse."

"People like you said the same thing about Vegas when there were six hotels on the Strip."

"The difference here is the questions being raised about your own liquidity in the wake of last week's attack."

"How many businesses faced the same challenge after 9/11, Ms. Franes?"

"You don't have to feel defensive."

"Not defensive, realistic. Multibillion-dollar credit lines are nothing without vision."

"But those same credit lines are needed to realize that vision, Mr. Tiranno, and you need ample resources to secure them."

"There's a long line of banks and investment companies who want to do business with King Midas World. Hesitate too long and you'll lose your place in line, since Macao still offers a wealth of untapped potential for someone willing to seize it."

"Competition is becoming more aggressive by the day. Many new casinos are already under construction there. Respectfully, I'd say King Midas World missed the train in that regard."

"Respectfully, I don't give a damn about the competition. People will always flock to the kind of experience provided by a resort on the level of the Seven Sins. Doesn't matter if it's the first casino or the hundredth."

"Macao isn't Vegas, Mr. Tiranno."

"Gambling is gambling, Ms. Franes. It's not about the locale so much as the lifestyle."

Michael watched her flash him a smile that was almost seductive in its sententiousness. Samantha Franes seemed to grow more attractive by the moment, possessed by a rare combination of natural beauty, assuredness, and, most of all . . .

What was he sensing? It was there before him but the word to describe it escaped him.

Verve, charm. That was it, or perhaps charisma was a better way of putting it.

He had done business with countless bankers, but Samantha Franes wasn't like any of the others. Didn't talk or behave in the same manner. Spoke her mind, making her points instead of letting Michael make his. His past experience with Credit Suisse had been especially amicable and less confrontational. Invariably, the company's representatives did their homework and came to meetings at least as if not better educated than he was, to a point where they could finish his own sentences.

"Did you have a chance to review King Midas World's plans we sent you for Macao?" he asked Samantha Franes abruptly.

"Most impressive," the woman told him. "I wouldn't be here otherwise."

"Strange, because we never sent you any."

The woman's expression tightened slightly.

"Who are you really?" Michael demanded.

"It doesn't matter."

"Then let me ask you another way: Who the fuck are you and what are you doing here?"

"Forgetting your manners, Mr. Tiranno?"

"Shit, no."

She toyed with a smile. "It's not advisable for men in search of multibillion-dollar financing to be rude to investment bankers."

"Why, do you know any? Because you're certainly not one," Michael said and started to stand up.

"Sit down," she ordered.

Michael kept rising.

"I'm not going to tell you again."

"Good, because I'm not listening. Whatever it is you're after, you came to the wrong place."

"And to think I heard the food here was wonderful . . ."

"The best in Vegas."

"We haven't ordered yet."

"Enjoy your dinner." Michael looked down and noticed one

of the woman's hands had ducked beneath the table in menacing fashion. "Are you fucking kidding me?"

"Neither of us is laughing. Sit back down. And make no attempt to summon your bodyguards."

Michael retook his chair, as intrigued as he was tense. He laid a hand atop his discarded napkin. "Where's Samantha Franes?"

"Still resting comfortably in New York, I'd imagine."

"If you're trying to scare me, you're doing a lousy job. No offense, but my life's been threatened by more menacing sorts than you."

"None taken. I abhor violence."

"Should have thought of that before you tried taking me hostage."

"This isn't a kidnapping, it's a robbery."

"So you're a thief, then."

"Or a pirate."

"Leave your sword and eye patch at the office?"

Her expression remained flat. "No, in my other purse."

Michael laid his wallet and watch on the table between them. "Here you go. Don't spend it all in one place."

The woman didn't even regard them. "It's not your money I'm after; it's your medallion."

Michael stiffened ever so slightly, slid his watch and wallet closer to her. "Take what you can get and get your ass out of here."

"I plan to."

"By robbing me in front of two dozen witnesses?"

"It's not robbery if you hand the medallion over willingly, without incident."

"And why would I do that?"

"Because that medallion cost your family their lives."

SEVENTY-EIGHT

LAS VEGAS, THE PRESENT

Michael suddenly felt hot, the restaurant's air-conditioning unable to stem the sudden wash of perspiration he could feel on his face and beneath his shirt. His stomach grew queasy.

"The men who killed your family left your farm without the medallion," the woman resumed. "They searched the house to no avail because you had the medallion with you that day."

"How the hell could you know that?"

"Never mind. What matters is—"

"Enough," Michael said suddenly. "This isn't the high seas and if you shoot me, my bodyguards will kill you before you take a step out of the restaurant."

"It may surprise you to hear it's not the first time somebody like you has said something like that to me either."

"Only you've never met anyone like me before. Sorry to spoil your evening," Michael said, pulling back the napkin on which his hand had rested to reveal a tiny cell phone he had hidden beneath it. "My guards are on the way."

"Why tell me?"

"So you can save your pirate ass, without incident."

"Not without that medallion."

Michael grinned. "There's nothing more sexy than a woman with a gun after something she'll never get."

"And just where does that leave us?"

Michael had heard only the start of her question. Something drew his gaze out the window offering a view of the Grand Canal complex beyond. He glimpsed a large, heavy-set bald shape amid the crowd passing below. Then, just as quickly as it appeared, the shape was gone.

His mind flashed back to the InterContinental Hotel back in Afghanistan, the huge shape that had burst through the balcony doors after he had discovered the bodies of Vittorio and

Francesco Scaglione. The same feeling he'd had then struck him again, as pungent as a hard scent.

The *drakos,* as Alexander had called him.

"What's wrong?" Raven asked him. And then, as if realizing the answer herself, "What did you see down there?"

"Someone who scares me more than you." Michael glanced down at his cell phone, calculating how long it had been since he had summoned his bodyguards. "My men are dead. Otherwise they would've already rushed in."

"Then you need my help. In exchange for the medallion."

"It'll take more than that gun you've got under the table." Michael's gaze swept about the floor in search of his friend, Zefferino's manager. "Feel free to walk out of here, thief. It's not you the killers want."

"You know who's out there, Tyrant. I saw it in your eyes."

"Killers, assassins from a secret society dating back a thousand years."

"The Hashishin," the woman uttered softly.

SEVENTY-NINE

LAS VEGAS, THE PRESENT

Michael's stare froze on her.

"Our paths crossed recently," Raven continued. "What about you?"

"They were behind the terrorist attack on Vegas and a second one to come, unless they're stopped."

"And you think you can stop them, Tyrant?"

"My name is Michael Tiranno. And I might sleep with a woman without knowing hers but not face death with one."

"Raven Khan."

"Raven as in dark."

"Not a coincidence. I love the night."

"So do I, depending on who I'm with."

"Why are you the only one who can save Las Vegas, Michael Tiranno? What about the almighty U.S. government?"

"Because it's me the terrorists, and whoever's behind them, are after." Michael finally caught the manager Ernesto's attention and summoned him to the table.

"What are you doing?"

"Getting us out of here. . . . You haven't told me who killed my family yet."

"I have no intention of leaving without that medallion."

Ernesto finally arrived at the table, his own expression tightening at the sight of the grave look framed on Michael's face. "Signore Tiranno?"

"I have a problem, Ernesto. I need your help."

"Of course. Anything."

"The lady and I need to get out of the restaurant fast, unseen. *E' questione di vita o di morte.*"

"Life or death?" Ernesto responded anxiously. "There is another way out through the kitchen. Please, follow me."

The three of them slid away from the table, not another word spoken until they were through the kitchen's rich wood swinging doors.

"This way," Ernesto said, leading them toward the rear of the kitchen. "There is a freight elevator down to the mall's service level. That's where the laundry truck makes its pickups."

They reached a trio of wheeled canvas laundry dollies containing soiled tablecloths and uniforms placed in a corner adjacent to the elevator compartment.

"One of these will accommodate both of you," Ernesto explained, wheeling one of the dollies into the elevator.

Michael nodded in agreement. "Ernesto, if anyone asks, you didn't see me leave and you don't know what happened to me. *Devi tenere la bocca chiusa. Giura sull 'onore.*"

"*Sull'onore, giuro,* Signore Tiranno! I swear on my honor."

"*Grazie,* Ernesto."

Michael heard the compartment doors slide open on the complex's service level. Then he felt Ernesto ease the dolly from the elevator and roll it to the laundry pickup area.

As soon as Zefferino's manager had taken his leave, Michael hopped agilely from the dolly and helped Raven Khan out. Then he gazed about and began a systematic check of the neighboring dollies.

"And just how are we going to get out of here, Tyrant?" Raven asked, as if testing him.

Michael's hand emerged from another of the nearby dollies holding a uniform top worn by the Grand Canal security guards.

"Wearing these," he said.

EIGHTY

MESSINA, THE PRESENT

Naomi Burns and Alexander found the old woman named Maddelena still behind her pushcart of wilting flowers.

"Come back for more?" she asked.

"Yes," Naomi told her. "More information." She turned her gaze toward the building that now housed a coffee bar, bakery, and gift shop. The windows of the top two floors held plants, wind chimes, and various forms of treatment, indicating rooms long ago converted to apartments. "Sister Margherita-Agnese told us what went on inside there."

"She doesn't know the whole story."

"But she says you do."

"She's a liar."

"I think you're the one lying."

"It wasn't my fault. I was afraid for my life," Maddelena said, staring vacantly at the building. "I sell the flowers for the souls that were lost in that place. But I will never sell enough."

"Was it Cosa Nostra?" Alexander asked her.

Maddelena shook her head. "They blessed it and supplied protection, but someone else was responsible for the *picciriddi'* who came and went."

"Sister Margherita-Agnese told us *I bambini* were stolen."

"She's right. The building that once stood here was one of many locations used to house them all over Europe, all over the world."

Naomi shuddered in revulsion at the thought. "House them until they were sold."

"The process was random at first," Maddelena confirmed. "But later, eventually, orders were filled. Toddlers and infants stolen from homes and playgrounds with deposits already down on them. They arrived, they left—often with not much time in between. A few weeks mostly, days sometimes."

"Despicable."

Maddelena met Naomi's harsh gaze. "You don't think I know that? Those years left scars on me that will never heal."

"Selling flowers here won't heal those scars either. How many *bambini* were there in total?"

Maddelena shrugged. "So many I lost count. Coming and going, every bed always full. Delivered and picked up by different men. Except for one girl. She stayed longer. Six weeks. I got to know her well, her being there as long as she was."

"What was her name?"

"I don't know." Maddelena began to sob, the guilt from those years overcoming her. "Those of us who tended to the children weren't even allowed to use their real names, a rule none of us dared break. I called this girl Bruna because of her dark hair. She was barely two when she arrived, barely even speaking yet. She looked to be in shock or something."

"Something else must have made her special."

"She arrived on my birthday: May fifteenth, 1975."

Naomi met Alexander's narrowed gaze, that particular date well known to both of them as the day Michael Tiranno's family had been massacred.

"The man who brought the girl seemed rather kind, but sad." Maddelena's eyes moistened again. "I didn't see him again until the night he came to pick up the girl. Other children were there, but she was the only one he was interested in. A few days later the carabinieri raided the house. They handcuffed me and sat me down outside on the street where I watched them take *I piccariddi'* out one at a time, all looking at me pleadingly because I was the one person they thought they could trust."

The old woman snorted, her face a picture of self-loathing.

"You went to jail."

"For ten years. Would have been less if I had told them what they wanted to know. But I didn't know anything. And even if I did, I probably wouldn't have told. There were things to fear more than going to jail."

"All those years," Naomi said, shaking her head, "all those years and you didn't leave, walk away."

"There were always the children to think of, new ones arriving every time I was ready to walk out the door when no one was looking. Who would take care of them if I left?"

"Go back to the man who brought the girl you called Bruna here. Do you remember his name?"

Maddelena shook her head. "I never knew it. But . . ."

"But what?"

"The man's leg," Maddelena said. "It was stiff, weak. I'd hear tapping and I'd know he was coming."

"Why?"

"Because he used a cane."

EIGHTY-ONE

The Strip, the present

Wearing a security guard's uniform, hair tousled to further disguise himself, Michael hailed a cab on Las Vegas Boulevard and opened the rear door for Raven Khan.

"McCarran Airport," he told the driver, closing the door behind them. "Use the private terminal entrance off Tropicana Avenue."

He leaned back to find Raven still studying his chest. "So much as reach for it and I'll break your hand."

"That medallion's caused you only pain," she told him. "Ruined your life."

"Because of the assholes that killed my family. Who were they?"

"I don't know."

"All right, but you do know why."

Before Raven could respond, a convoy of Las Vegas Police Department cruisers streamed down the Strip, converging on the Venetian. Michael's spine stiffened, aware the convergence of police could only mean the bodies of his three dead bodyguards, seasoned professionals all, had been discovered. He flipped his cell phone open and hit the preprogrammed call button for his personal assistant, Christine Goff.

"Yes, Mr. Tiranno."

"Don't talk, just listen and do exactly as I tell you, Christine. You haven't heard from me and you have no idea where I am or if I'm still alive. I need you to book an Air Royale Falcon 50 or G-4 for a flight to Paris, using King Midas World's account. Tell Air Royale it's for one of our high-roller accounts, Samantha Franes," he added, looking at the woman next to him. "Use my corporate code to guarantee payment."

"You can count on me, sir."

"Excellent. Two passengers." Michael glanced at Raven Khan, who was holding up Samantha Franes's passport with her picture inserted. "Then deliver my passport to the departure lounge in the private terminal along with some clothes, casual, in a shopping bag. Pick up clothes for a woman too: size four, athletic build. Take a cab. Clear? . . . Good. Do it now. There's no time."

Michael flipped the phone closed.

As high-roller clients of King Midas World, Michael and Raven had no trouble securing entry into the members-only lounge while awaiting his assistant's arrival to complete the paperwork for their flight to Paris. They had an entire section to themselves, complete with a television that Michael turned to a local channel with muted sound.

"Tell me more about the massacre of my family."

"All I can tell you is the reason behind it."

"This," Michael said, pulling the medallion from beneath his shirt so it dangled freely over his chest.

"Your father never told you anything about it?"

"Only how he found it. Many times."

Raven Khan hesitated, giving Michael time to study her. He had known countless ravishingly beautiful women in his life and found Raven Khan to be every bit their equal. But he couldn't say why exactly. Her angular features were strong and sensuous, her shapely frame more that of a runner than a fashion model or actress. He guessed the makeup she wore was more to fit her disguise as an investment banker, and even then the layer was thin enough not to conceal her naturally radiant olive skin. Her emerald green eyes absorbed everything like miniature camera lenses, reminding him of his mother's. He was still trying to figure out where his attraction to her lay, just as he struggled to define an odd sense of kinship between them springing from more than just the fateful encounter that had led to their sudden and uneasy alliance.

"Your medallion belonged to the Cilician pirates once before, two thousand years ago," Raven said finally. "Your company is called King Midas World."

"Get to the fucking point."

Her eyes locked on Michael's medallion again. "The origins of your medallion lie with King Midas himself."

"You mean King Mita."

"Then you know," Raven said, not bothering to hide the surprise in her voice.

"That much anyway."

"There's a lot more. King Mita ruled Phyrgia, what's now Turkey, in the eighth century. He accumulated vast stores of gold and became the wealthiest and most powerful ruler of his time. One story says that Mita somehow obtained the medallion as a young man and its possession fueled his rise to power and subsequent immeasurable wealth."

"What does that legend say about its origins?"

"Nothing. But there are other tales dating as far back as the written word about a similar medallion falling into the hands of one leader or king after another. Each, like Mita, added his mark, in which case, you might say, your medallion is as old as time itself."

Michael tucked the medallion back inside his shirt. "Keep talking."

"Upon King Mita's death, the most cherished of his treasures was buried with him in a tomb located in Gordion, the medallion in a separate lockbox."

"I guess he never learned you can't take it with you."

"The ancients believed you could. An archaeologist named Rodney Young finally discovered Mita's tomb within the Tumulous Midas Mount, about sixty miles from Ankara, in 1957. Inside the tomb, Young found Mita's skeleton lying in a cedar coffin but no gold and only an empty lockbox, seeming to rebuke the legend."

"Seeming to?"

"The gold, Mita's treasure, was missing because the tomb had been looted around 75 B.C."

"Don't tell me, by the Cilician pirates of that era."

Raven Khan nodded. "Led by Ali-san Kubivaros, the greatest captain of all Cilicians. Kubivaros and his men found the tomb and plundered it, burying their spoils on the island of Crete. Among those spoils was a golden medallion that never left Mita's neck because, according to legend, he believed it to be the source of his power and wealth," she said, gaze straying to Michael's chest again.

"Did your Captain Kubivaros know this?"

"That's unclear. What is clear is that Kubivaros and his crew were also responsible for twice kidnapping a man who would later become the most powerful in the known civilized world."

"Caesar . . . This just keeps getting better. . . ."

"You've heard the tale?"

"Only that as a young man Caesar had been kidnapped by pirates."

"Those pirates were my ancestors. The second time he swore revenge and in 74 B.C. he got it when he intercepted Kubivaros's ship and executed the captain and his entire crew.

But not before Kubivaros offered Caesar a map leading to a great treasure in exchange for sparing their lives."

"So Caesar takes the map and still wipes them out."

"That's right."

"Well done on his part."

Raven ignored his insinuation. "He brought his ships to Crete and recovered the treasure of King Mita. He used much of that treasure to help finance his ultimate rise to power in Rome, including the vast legions he used to conquer Gaul, currently France, years later. But he kept one object for himself."

Michael tapped the medallion through his shirt. "This."

"Exactly," said Raven Khan.

EIGHTY-TWO

McCarran Airport, the present

"Whether tied to his belt, hanging from his neck, or held within his robes, Caesar was never without it to the day he was murdered on the floor of the Roman senate. Hence, the motto he had inscribed upon it. *Your* motto."

"*Somnia, Aude, Vince.*" Michael nodded. "To dream, to dare, to win."

"A motto Caesar embraced as the basis of his rise to power in Rome. He secretly regarded the medallion of King Mita as a mystical talisman that had brought him his great fortune. He became so obsessed by that notion he convinced himself that should any of his enemies get hold of the medallion, he'd be destroyed. Following the conquest of Gaul, his paranoia led him to create a new, public motto acknowledged by historians, '*Veni, vidi, vici*': 'I came, I saw, I conquered.'"

"Who took the medallion after his death?"

"No one, at least no one recognized by history. The medallion became part of Caesar's riches, which were likely divided up among his enemies or salvaged by his heirs. For all intents and purposes, the medallion disappeared until it was presented as a gift to a young Charlemagne by barbarian warlords who had ultimately overrun the remnants of the Roman Empire."

"The same Charlemagne who went on to rule most of Europe."

"The medallion is clearly evident in a number of portraits of him from the era."

"And then?" Michael asked her.

"The medallion disappeared, dropped out of sight. The Cilicians, meanwhile, continued to adapt to the changing times."

"Once a thief, always a thief."

"No different from you, Tyrant."

"Why do you keep calling me that?"

"Because that's what you are, only in the world of business instead of nations."

"I didn't know there was a difference."

"Maybe that's the point." Again Raven Khan's gaze dipped to Michael's chest. "Maybe the legend is true. Maybe the medallion did make you."

"I don't believe in mystical bullshit," Michael said. But his mind recalled the reverence with which his father spoke of the medallion dating back to the incredible tale of how he had escaped potential drowning to find it clutched in his hand.

"Your father never wore the medallion, did he?" Raven asked, as if reading his mind.

"Would it have mattered?"

"In his case, no. Men like Caesar and Charlemagne—and probably you—were extraordinary leaders. Others would follow them to the ends of the earth, not even knowing why. Whatever they had, the medallion was able to focus. It turns the probable, even possible, into the inevitable, but only for a select few. And it doesn't offer immortality or even protection from harm's way, as much curse as blessing, perhaps even *more* curse than blessing. Just ask Caesar."

"Is that a warning?"

"Just a word of advice. My mentor Adnan Talu tried to recover what's left of the treasure the great Kubivaros had given up to Caesar. The vast majority of the items were in museums or private collections, the ones he could find anyway, because some had been understandably lost forever, including, Talu thought, the most important of all."

"My medallion," Michael said, running his fingers over it through the fabric of his shirt. "But what happened to it after Charlemagne?"

"No one's quite sure. Charlemagne spent much of his final years battling Viking armies. After his death in 814, there's strong indication that it ended up in their hands, stolen by a raiding party from his palace in France. But, fittingly enough, the Viking ship sank somewhere in the Mediterranean and the medallion was thought to be lost forever. Where did your father find it?"

"Off the coast of Isola di Levanzo."

"Enough said."

"And enough with the history lesson. I want to know who massacred my family."

Raven Khan hesitated briefly before resuming. "Your father was experiencing financial problems."

Michael swallowed hard, recalling his father dressing in his best clothes and donning his one fine cap after tucking the medallion, carefully wrapped in black cloth, in his pocket.

"He met with jewelers and antiques dealers in Rome to get prices, estimates of the medallion's value," Raven continued. "Some of them made inquiries. A few of these inquiries got back to Adnan Talu. He went to the farm to see about retrieving the medallion."

"Steal it, you mean."

"It doesn't matter, because your family was dead by the time he got there. He searched the house to no avail and assumed either your father had found a buyer for the medallion or the killers had made off with it. But your father couldn't sell it, any more than you could, Tyrant. Still, Talu scoured the shops of Rome in search of the medallion, eventually giving up in the belief it must have disappeared again. And, for all intents and purposes, it had."

"Until King Midas World opened the Seven Sins," Michael

added. "You found me because I made a similar medallion, a near replica, the symbol of my casino."

"The similarities were striking. So I hired a lawyer in Rome to dig into your past to find the truth."

"Gianfranco Ferelli," Michael said.

Raven Khan didn't bother to hide her surprise. "You spoke with him?"

"He died before I could, killed in the terrorist attack right in front of the Seven Sins. What did Ferelli uncover for you?"

"The story of a young boy found hiding in the family barn. His early reports, collected over months of research, uncovered your true identity and upbringing. A few weeks ago, he broke off contact. Stopped returning my calls. Then he disappeared."

"People usually do that because they're scared shitless or they're dead," Michael said pointedly.

"Not scared of me. To Ferelli I was just another client. The source of my interest in you was never made known to him. No, Ferelli disappeared because he uncovered something that changed the stakes."

"He came to Vegas because he wanted me to know whatever that was and not you. Why?"

Before Raven could respond, a breaking news bulletin appeared on the television, now featuring a shot of the Venetian rimmed by police cars and rescue wagons. Michael turned up the sound enough to hear the reporter expounding on the fact that the bodies of three men identified as security personnel at the Seven Sins Resort and Casino had been found amid the Grand Canal shops.

"I've got to make a phone call," he told Raven.

EIGHTY-THREE

SUDAN, THE PRESENT

Hassan-i-Sabbah stood over his glass conference table, eyeing the map of Las Vegas without really seeing it. Information from his operatives there indicated Michael Tiranno had not only survived Malik's execution attempt, he had escaped. The man who had paid a vast sum to ensure Tiranno's death need never learn of this most recent failure, any more than he needed to learn of the last one in Afghanistan. The man's stated preference, after all, was that Tiranno live to see Las Vegas die in the maelstrom that was coming.

But Tiranno had changed the stakes when a team he dispatched executed Bayrak and his men. Hassan took this as a personal affront. Beyond that, if Tiranno's clearly proficient sources could find and kill Bayrak, it was no stretch to think they could perhaps point the way here to his underground fortress in the Sudanese wilderness. Tiranno's escape from Malik in Kabul had seemed fortuitous at best; managing the feat a second time in Las Vegas indicated something more powerful than luck might well be involved.

That made things personal for Hassan. How could he lead the reemergence of the Hashishin and dominate the Arab world if he couldn't manage the death of a single man? With that question in mind, Hassan had begun to dig into the life and world of his new enemy: Michael Tiranno, also known as "the Tyrant" for his ruthlessness and cunning in business dealings. He stared at Tiranno's picture, his piercing black eyes, struck by his resemblance to someone from the past Hassan had almost lost to the blast in Afghanistan, which had left shrapnel in his skull to this day. Sometimes the terrible headaches brought unwelcome glimpses of the man Hassan had once been. Studying Tiranno's picture struck a distant chord of familiarity, though Hassan's memory could not frame where and how this man fit into the times mostly stricken from his memory, mere shadows now.

Perhaps this uneasy sense of familiarity was an illusion cast by Tiranno's true purpose as a test for him, a test he and the new Hashishin had to pass if true greatness was ever to be theirs.

Las Vegas was Tiranno's city, a city Hassan was about to lay siege to and destroy. Succeed in that task and Michael Tiranno, the one enemy who could stand in the way of his mission, would fall.

Hassan's past was a dark shadow trapped in his wake. His future was a beacon shining amid the blackness of Western man's soul, a beacon soon to be lit by the fires that would consume the world of Michael Tiranno.

EIGHTY-FOUR

Caltagirone, the present

"Michael's on his way to Paris," Alexander told Naomi Burns, flipping his cell phone closed.

"Pharaon?"

"Pharaon. He wants us to meet him in the city tomorrow morning."

"What the hell happened back in Vegas?" Naomi wondered, recalling the frantic calls they'd received from Seven Sins personnel in the wake of Michael's disappearance and the murder of his bodyguards.

"I don't know," Alexander said.

To Naomi Burns, the village of Caltagirone looked nothing like she had pictured from the tales told to her by Michael Tiranno of his youth. She had expected a quaint, rural village tucked into the farm-rich hills of central Sicily, realizing she was quite mistaken as soon as she and Alexander reached the town's outskirts in their rented car.

Agostino Patria Camposanto, a graveyard down the road from the one in which Michael's family was buried, was densely layered with simple headstones and aged markers. Before its historical significance made it popular as both a final resting place and tourist attraction, it had often been used by the local government to bury the indigent and destitute.

"I remember Ferelli," the caretaker, a sinewy man with two-toned skin the texture of leather, said in response to Naomi's query. "Not many men in suits come to a cemetery to ask questions, especially a lawyer from Rome."

The caretaker led Naomi and Alexander to the burial plot Ferelli had come to inquire about and then took his leave.

"Attilio Cecchini," Naomi said out loud, reading the name on the concrete marker. "The workman Michael told me was riding the tractor the day his family was murdered. Michael saw him shot."

Alexander knelt down to smooth away the weeds and brush that covered the names of any others interned below. The concrete was smooth, empty.

"Strange," he said. "Cecchini had a granddaughter who lived with him on the farm, didn't he?"

Naomi crouched next to him. "Her name was Daniela. She used to play with Michael's sister."

Alexander's gaze drifted back to the grave marker. "She's not buried here."

"Ferelli had an exhumation order," Naomi recalled, "with no name or location filled in."

"For this grave, you think?"

Naomi stood back up. "No. I think the information was never filled in because Ferelli found what he was after some other way. And whatever that was brought him to Las Vegas, to Michael."

"Where does that leave us?"

Naomi thought briefly. "Michael mentioned that Don Luciano told him that Ferelli visited the local carabinieri post that investigated the murder of his family." Her gaze moved from the burial plot to Alexander. "We do the same thing and maybe we learn whatever it is the lawyer did."

EIGHTY-FIVE

The Falcon 50, the present

Michael and Raven Khan had the Air Royale Falcon 50 all to themselves during the flight to Paris's Beauvais Airport, allowing them to sit apart from each other and for Michael to be alone with his thoughts.

"I know a great deal about you, Tyrant. . . ."

Maybe she did. But Raven Khan didn't know as much about him as she thought; no one did.

Caltagirone, 1997

With the money from his sale of the 25,000 tons of robusta coffee beans secure in Monte Carlo, Michael Tiranno returned to Caltagirone for the inevitable confrontation with an increasingly suspicious Don Luciano, who had been looking for him for nearly a month.

"I thought you were dead, Michele," Don Luciano told him from his usual seat at the veranda table, his bodyguard Marco looming ominously in the background.

"No, you didn't."

"All right, I didn't. A man of your cunning does not waste his life in a godforsaken place like Zaire."

"I was there trying to salvage WTA's coffee reserves for export. I failed. I'm sorry, but I couldn't find the trucks or ship I needed in time. It was all seized by the rebel forces."

"How much?"

"Approximately ninety-two thousand tons."

"My fucking money," Scaglione snarled. "But at least you made it out alive, Michele. That is something to be thankful for. Then again," he continued after a pause, "if the worst had happened we would've been spared the need to face this moment."

"I'm sorry."

"As am I, Michele."

"Sorry that I must leave."

"What? *Tu sei pazzo!* No one ever leaves the family. You, of all people, should know that."

"My dreams lie elsewhere."

"Not your responsibilities."

"I ask for a truce."

"But not forgiveness."

"I would not be so bold. World Trade Agricola is yours and I expect to share in none of its future enterprises."

"Very generous of you," the old man said curtly, "since I own the company."

"WTA is now worth over a billion dollars, all legitimate money. I think that's enough."

"No, never! Not in this lifetime! I just told you, nobody ever leaves the family!"

"If I was part of the family, you would've trusted me in Honduras. You left me with no choice."

"No choice? What do you mean?"

"An attorney I retained has been given all proprietary information about WTA and the family's participation in its workings. Should I die or disappear, by any means, his instructions are to transfer all that data and material to the Italian authorities and Interpol."

"I've killed men for making far less threats than that."

"It's in your best interest to make an exception this time."

The old man eyed him tautly, breathing loudly through his mouth, seething inside. "If you get out with your life, you will have more than any man has ever taken."

"That's all I ask."

"You haven't asked for any money, Michele. What am I to make of that?" Scaligione asked suspiciously. "Perhaps that you have a hidden stash of your own?"

"I made some good investments."

"Strange I did not hear of such good fortune until now."

"You never asked."

The old man hesitated, weighing how to proceed. "Understand my blessing of your offer comes with certain conditions, Michele. Your dealings with commodities trading, anything that might come into conflict with the efforts of WTA, are finished."

"Understood."

"You will never return to Sicily, not ever. Come back, and you're a dead man. And if you lie to me ever again, I'll have no choice but to forget what we've shared and treat you as I would any other *pezzo di minchia*. Take my chances with this lawyer of yours. *Capisci?*"

Michael nodded.

"Now, tell me what happened to my coffee in Zaire, Michele?" the old man asked him.

"The rebels seized it."

"I'm going to give you one last chance to tell me the truth." Scaglione leaned forward. "What happened to my coffee in Zaire?"

"It was looted and claimed by the rebels, Don Luciano."

EIGHTY-SIX

MONTE CARLO, 1997

With his split from the Scagliones finalized, Michael returned to the one other place in the world where he still truly felt safe: Monte Carlo.

Leaving Alexander behind, he ventured to the port where Amir Pharaon's yacht, the *Atlantis,* was moored. He was surprised to find it there and even more surprised to find Pharaon on board. The billionaire hugged Michael tight, his face sad.

"It's Sam, isn't it?" Michael asked, taking a chair across from him on the main deck.

Pharaon nodded.

"Was it an overdose?" Michael asked him.

"He's gone, not dead. Just gone. I had no choice. I just couldn't control him. His reckless behavior and reputation were starting to disgrace my name."

"I'm sorry," Michael said, finding a strange parallel in his and Sam Pharaon's stories.

"No, Michele, it is I who am sorry. For being a poor father. For not being there when my son needed me." Pharaon's remorseful eyes sought out Michael. "You were the only one who cared for him, and I will be eternally grateful for that. If you hadn't left, who knows, maybe . . ."

"Where is he?"

"I don't know. That's the worst thing of all. I honestly don't know. I signed the papers to release his trust fund and bid him farewell. I didn't even hug him, Michele, I didn't even hug him. You know what he said, what his last words to me were? 'Fuck off, old man.' That's what Samar said. His last words to me."

Michael remained silent.

"That's why I feel so lost; not because I'm sad he's gone but because in my heart I know I never want to see him again. To see him confronts me with all my failures as a father." Pharaon gazed across the table again, his eyes suddenly hopeful. "Have you heard from Sam, Michele? Is that why you've come?"

Michael shook his head. "I'm sorry. No."

"But you'll stay awhile, won't you? Just to keep me company like you used to. Maybe we can play chess."

Michael nodded.

He moved into a sprawling stateroom on the *Atlantis* that night and made it his home for the next week, time enough for things to cool with Don Luciano and for him to properly review the plans once again for the next phase of his life, a life Michael promised himself would be different from Scaglione's and Pharaon's, men who personified wealth and power but couldn't escape the loneliness and isolation these attributes should have helped avoid but instead contributed to. Michael reflected on them both, how they had effectively constructed prisons for themselves from the mortar of their own accomplishments. Michael would build a world for himself free of walls, constructed instead on endless possibilities.

To Dream . . . to Dare . . . to Win . . .

The translation of his medallion's Latin motto took on a whole new meaning, encapsulating the path his life had taken already and would take from here. The answer to his future, his ultimate destination, lay in the books he had hidden under his mattress, to be returned there by his mother after his father repeatedly made him throw them away. He had conjured up a world in his imagination of infinite possibilities, only to learn it really existed.

In America. The time to realize the dream of his youth had finally come, and Michael could barely contain his exuberance once the decision had been made. But that dream involved more than the United States; it now included owning a casino, and not just any casino either: the grandest and most extravagant casino ever built, which would become the cornerstone of a massive, all-encompassing conglomerate.

But first he needed to learn, to educate himself on every facet of the casino business. With that in mind, he spent the next few years visiting numerous casinos all around the world, hiring consultants in the gaming industry and commissioning business plans as well as feasibility studies defining the vision for his new brand. He also met with financial experts on Wall Street seeking the financial support he would need to realize that vision.

THE VATICAN, 1999

In between these meetings, he made a trip to Rome to meet with Father Roberto, one of the priests now responsible for coordinating the Vatican's vast charitable interests, including the children Michael had long supported.

"I'm sorry to hear that, Michele," Father Roberto said in response to the news that Michael was leaving World Trade Agricola. "If only you could see how life has changed for the children in the Peruvian village of Pacébo, thanks to your generosity. . . ."

"It will not affect my commitment to Pacébo at all, Father," Michael assured him. "In fact, I would like to expand that commitment."

Father Roberto's eyes and spirits both rose.

"Orphans, specifically," Michael continued. "And nobody need know, Father."

Father Roberto nodded. "That goes without saying." The priest thought briefly. "Perhaps I can arrange a seat for you on the board of such a charity as well, Michele, say St. Vincent de Paul, headquartered in New York City."

"I would consider that a great honor, Father."

Las Vegas, 1999

Next Michael turned his attention to Las Vegas itself. At the flashy casinos along the famed Strip, he watched and studied the patrons as much as the business, for that was where the essence of the casino world rested. The dreams those men and women brought through the door and the look on their faces as they rolled the dice in craps, took a hit in blackjack, watched the roulette wheel turn or the slot machine spin. In those moments nothing else mattered, not what they had done before entering the casino and not what they would do when they left it.

That was why he had fallen in love with the gaming business, specifically Las Vegas, a city that embodied everything in which he believed. *To Dream, to Dare, to Win* would become not only the motto of his casino, but also of the lifestyle he wanted everyone and anyone to have the opportunity to experience.

Toward that end, Michael would make a mark in Las Vegas as it had never been made before.

And that was why he needed Naomi Burns.

EIGHTY-SEVEN

NEW YORK, 1999

"What is it I can do for you, Mr. Tiranno?" Naomi Burns, a newly named partner in her law firm, asked from across the desk in her corner office overlooking midtown Manhattan.

"You're one of the most recommended mergers and acquisitions attorneys in the city."

"Some would say country. And at five hundred dollars an hour, I'd better be."

The amount caused no stir in Michael. "I'd like you to represent me."

"What kind of business interests you, Mr. Tiranno?"

"Casinos in Las Vegas."

"Which one?"

"All of them."

"That's quite a lot to acquire, Mr. Tiranno."

"Starting with one. That's our first order of business."

" 'Our,' " Naomi repeated thoughtfully. "I haven't decided to work for you yet."

"My company has decided to hire you."

"What company is that?"

"King Midas World."

Michael had chosen the name after partially solving the oldest mystery of his life. He had taken his father's gold medallion to a curator named Coyne at New York's Museum of Natural History. Coyne asked to keep it for a few days, at least overnight, but Michael steadfastly refused and the curator agreed to inspect it on the spot after Michael offered a sizable donation to help restore the Egyptian writing tablets he was preparing for exhibit.

"Ah," Coyne said, lifting his eye from the microscope. "You should see this for yourself."

Michael pressed his eye against the lens. "What am I looking at?"

"Notice the design at the top here?" Coyne asked, positioning the medallion for Michael to see. "Its etchings and brushstrokes are substantially different than the motto here on the bottom."

"What's that mean?"

"That the medallion was created in at least two phases by men from two entirely different cultures several centuries apart."

Michael looked again. "Because of the difference in language."

"Exactly. The motto is written in Latin while the design at the top is Phrygian, an ancient offshoot of Greek and Phoenician. See those two letters at the top of the pyramid?"

"Yes."

"They translate into *K* and *M* in English. I've only come across them once before. It's quite amazing."

"Why?"

"Because *KM* stands for King Mita, the historical model for King Midas."

Michael took Coyne's revelation as a sign, as well as a validation of the strange power the medallion had held over both him and his father. Suddenly his father's much-told tale of nearly dying upon discovering the medallion off the shores of Isola di Levanzo took on new meaning. Coyne asked that Michael leave the medallion with him, saying he needed more time to confirm his suspicions that, if correct, would mean it was priceless. Michael again declined, having already learned what he had come to learn.

"I require a fifty thousand dollars retainer," Naomi Burns told him from across her desk.

"Not a problem."

Naomi stared at Michael curiously. "Yes, it is."

"Really?"

"Because you agreed too readily to at least twice the price it should have been. That leaves me suspicious of your true intentions."

She watched Michael remove a Mont Blanc pen from his Versace suit jacket pocket.

"What are you doing?"

"Writing you a check," Michael said, flipping his checkbook open. "So everything we discuss will be protected by attorney-client privilege, once you give me a receipt."

"Is there something you need to protect, Mr. Tiranno?"

"Everyone has something they need to protect, Ms. Burns." Michael slid the check across Naomi Burns's desk before responding further and accepted a receipt in its place. "In my case I could use a top immigration lawyer to facilitate the green card process."

"I assume you're able to invest a million dollars in American business interests."

"Considerably more."

"The million will be sufficient to obtain a business visa for you. The normal expiration is five years, ample time to make your status permanent."

"It's in both our interests to handle that faster."

"Meaning?"

"Meaning I want a fresh start."

"Clean slate."

"That's the idea. And the immigration lawyer you retain on my behalf would need to understand that."

"Discretion."

"Necessary since I wasn't always the person I am now, Ms. Burns."

"If you have a criminal record, our business ends now."

"I don't. But I need to erase everything that connects me to my past."

"We have a few sources I can send you to. Discreet, professional, and extremely expensive—a million dollars for starters."

"On top of the million I need to invest for my business visa?"

Naomi couldn't help but smile. "There's nothing connecting myself or this firm to them, of course. If you're interested, someone will contact you. That's all."

"How good are they?"

"There'll be neighbors remembering you growing up in your boyhood home, teachers who remember disciplining you for running off into the woods with a girl during recess."

"That's what I need."

"Good. Now, a question: Why did you choose me?"

"Your reputation."

"And?"

"You're a woman. I trust women's judgment more than men's. And you're single, with no interests beyond this law firm."

Naomi Burns regarded Michael impassively, looking neither hurt nor surprised. "You're used to having your way with women, aren't you, Mr. Tiranno?"

"I can't complain."

"Then I apologize for disappointing you."

"You haven't yet."

Naomi leaned forward. "What else?"

Michael didn't hesitate. "You used to represent Max Price."

Naomi Burns ran her finger from the bridge of her nose to her hairline and back again. "Only his nongaming interests, real estate and other investments. And 'used to' being the operative phrase. Besides, Mr. Price is on record for saying he has no interest in building another casino. In fact, he's divesting his holdings in Las Vegas for over two and a half billion."

"Yes, to purchase huge tracts of land in Macao and Singapore through local shell intermediaries for a company called Price World Resorts, expected to go public in the very near future."

Naomi Burns tried very hard not to look impressed. "Apparently, I'm not the only one who's done their homework."

"I guess Max Price should have used someone more discreet and professional to hide his tracks."

"I'm not his lawyer anymore."

"No, you're mine."

"I'm flattered, Mr. Tiranno. But that doesn't change the fact that Max Price won't see you."

"Yes, he will."

"Why?"

"Because I'm the only man in the world who can give him what he wants the most."

EIGHTY-EIGHT

Caltagirone, the present

By the time Naomi Burns and Alexander reached the carabinieri post in Fontanarossa it was closed for the day, only a dispatcher and token officers present. With no way to reach Paris until the following morning, they had no choice but to spend the night.

"Everything here is connected," Naomi told Alexander over dinner at the restaurant inside the Grand Hotel Villa San Mauro, where they were staying, "and it starts in Messina. Someone was stealing and selling children. Remember what the old woman Maddelena said?"

I didn't see him again until the night he came to pick up the girl. Other children were there, but she was the only one he was interested in. A few days later the carabinieri raided the house. . . .

Alexander nodded. "This man with the cane covering his tracks," he concluded, "wiping out anything linking him to that house."

"But he didn't leave alone, Alexander. He took that girl with him, the same girl he had dropped off in May of 1975, the same day Michael's family was massacred."

"A peasant girl," Alexander said, recalling their visit to the family gravesite of Attilio Cecchini. "Granddaughter of a simple farmworker. But why would anyone care whether she lived or died?"

"Not just anyone—the lawyer Ferelli, who uncovered something he shared with no one else."

"And died before he could share it with Michael." Alexander thought for a moment. "The identity of whoever was behind the murder of his family, perhaps."

"Then why the exhumation order? Why the visit to this carabinieri post in Fontanarossa?"

Alexander shrugged. "Questions we'll have to answer later."

"The answers may be too important to wait."

"Michael needs us in Paris."

"He needs *you* in Paris," Naomi told him. "I'm staying on the trail of whatever we've picked up here."

"What should I tell Michael?"

"That I'm doing it for his own good," Naomi said, leaving it at that.

EIGHTY-NINE

PARIS, THE PRESENT

Michael had finally managed to fall into a deep sleep when he heard a knock on the bedroom door in his suite in the Plaza Athénée Hotel.

"And me thinking the Tyrant never sleeps." Raven Khan greeted him after he unlocked the door.

"I like dreaming, remember?" Michael wiped his eyes. "What time is it?"

"Just before six A.M. I need to get back to Istanbul. Adnan Talu is missing," she said hoarsely. "His men were found with their throats cut. Sound familiar?"

"Close enough. The Hashishin."

"We, *I,* stole something that had fallen into their possession." Raven's voice was more flat than bitter, but also sad, mournful. "They kidnapped Talu to get it back."

"Has there been any communication from them?"

"Not yet, but there will be."

"You feel guilty."

"I feel angry."

"I know what you mean."

"I'm an orphan too. Expect no sympathy there," she said pointedly.

"I was speaking of how I felt after the terrorists attacked Vegas."

"Like you had to do something. The way I feel now." Raven's emerald green eyes brightened slightly in the rising sun. "I have to save him."

"Casinos love your kind," he told her.

"Oh, really? Why?"

"Because you're making a bet you can't win. You can't take on the Hashishin."

"I don't have a choice." Her eyes focused on the medallion hanging outside Michael's T-shirt. "And then I'll be coming back for that."

"You're starting to piss me off again. Just when I was starting to like you . . ."

"Did Max Price piss you off too?" she asked, surprising him with mention of his name.

"Yes," Michael told her, "and he didn't listen either."

NINETY

LAS VEGAS, 2000

"You wanna see Vegas, kiddo?" Max Price asked Michael. "You can't. Know why? 'Cause it's gone. Don't exist anymore, not the way you bright-eyed entrepreneurs want it to anyway."

They were lunching in the Top of the Tower Restaurant in the Stratosphere Hotel and Casino on April 1, the view of Vegas below changing as the room rotated slowly on its axis below the amusement park–style rides above. Michael arrived to find Price in the company of a single monstrous African-American body-guard, over three hundred pounds of what looked like solid muscle, that he introduced as Bob Sapp, before dismissing him the way a man might his dog.

"I was here in the beginning, pretty close anyway. Back when a dollar and a dream were all you needed. It's a closed town now, I'm sorry to say, and if you've come here with a deal I can't turn down, it'll be the sixth one this week."

"I'm a lot different than the other five losers."

"Oh yeah? Why's that?"

"Because I've got something you'd die for."

Max Price started to laugh, then stopped. He'd been over-weight for a number of years and had lost a hundred pounds on a crash diet followed by stomach reduction surgery. As a result, his frame had a withered look to it with a spare tire of excess flesh hanging over his belt. His face had gone from flabby to gaunt, leaving angled bumps of jaw and cheek amid bands of skin that drooped, weighing down his entire expression.

"Kiddo, I made two and a half billion when I sold out to the ball-less pricks who own Vegas now. What the fuck have you got that I'd die for?"

"A plan to get back at the ball-less pricks who own Vegas now."

"A plan, eh? Here's the thing, kiddo," Price said, leaning over his salad of mixed greens and beets, "when it comes to the Club, if you're not in you're out, and you're not in."

"That's why I came to you."

Max Price pursed his lips, then puckered them, suddenly annoyed. "Look, kiddo, we're having lunch 'cause a friend who I happen to respect asked me to meet with you. I finish this rabbit food, I figure I've done my part, so say what you gotta say. I don't have all day."

"I'm going to build the greatest casino in the town's his-tory," Michael told him.

Price thrust his fork toward the window and spoke in be-tween munches, drabs of salad dressing staining both corners of his mouth. "Check the view, kiddo. Every casino you see out there went up with that very goal in mind. Know what? If they were the greatest once, it didn't last long."

"I've run the numbers on the Oasis."

Price looked out the window to catch the Oasis Casino before the Top of the Tower's rotation took it from view. "That dump?"

"Isn't that the dump you've been trying to acquire for a decade now?"

"I might've considered it before the fleas started to show, yeah. What of it?"

"It's the best stretch of property available on the Strip, Max. Fifty acres you'd kill to get your hands on."

"Not anymore. I'm out of the Vegas game, remember? And besides, those fifty acres ain't for sale."

"Not to you."

"Not to anybody."

"Except me." Michael could see Max Price twitch, his expression changing ever so slightly. "The owner of the Oasis is dying."

"Excuse me for not crying. Let me know when the miserable prick's funeral is so I can be out playing golf."

"He put the casino and the fifty acres into a trust and signed it over to the Catholic Church. Guess he wanted to buy his ticket to heaven before he died."

"Yeah, so I'll only play nine the day he croaks." Max Price leaned forward, no longer bothering to disguise his interest. "How exactly do you know this?"

"What you need to know, Max, is that I've got a ninety-day option to buy the Oasis and the fifty acres it sits on," Michael told him. "I guess the Vatican has no interest in the gaming business, just like you."

"And what if I did, kiddo?"

Michael smiled.

He had learned about the Oasis through sources in the Vatican he became acquainted with thanks to the charitable efforts he'd undertaken, most recently the spot he had filled on the board of St. Vincent de Paul. Father Roberto and his superiors arranged a series of meetings for Michael with representatives of the Curia, the minister of finance, and the Vatican bank, who wanted to move fast since the Church needed a strategy to dispose of the property as soon as possible to preserve their public image. The fact that he was known to be Catholic and a native who could converse in Italian helped Michael gain the ninety-day option, especially when he proposed that the Vatican create a charity to which 2 percent of the casino's profits would be donated should Michael be able to close on the deal.

"How much was this option?" Price asked him.

"Three million, nonrefundable, against the purchase price."

"Lot of money to lose, kiddo."

"I don't intend on losing."

"Means you've gotta come up with the balance."

"An additional hundred and ninety-seven million in ninety days."

Price chuckled. "Having the option with a down payment don't mean shit if you ain't got the resources to exercise it and the clout to make it mean something." He jabbed his fork Michael's way and swallowed some more greens. "Only one man I ever known's got the kind of balls needed to pull off something like that and he's sitting directly across from you."

"He's sitting across from you too."

Price scowled. "This is Vegas, remember?"

"Old or new?"

"Time was a wiseass like you would be carrying his teeth on the way out."

"Thanks to the boys who bankrolled your first casino?"

"You think that bothers me, kiddo? I outlasted them. Fuck, I outlasted everybody."

"Until you sold your last interests to the ball-less pricks."

"What's your point?"

"Maybe you don't have the balls for the game anymore either, Max."

Price waved a reproaching finger at Michael. "Then you'd be home picking your ass instead of here picking my brain."

Now it was Michael who leaned forward. "You sold because they wore you out, and your shareholders were holding a gun to your head. They claim you ran the company like Atilla the Hun."

"Last time I checked, kiddo, I still owned the best casino ever built on the Strip."

"You didn't own it for long. Mine will redefine the entire gaming experience. Not a sideshow, a lifestyle."

Max Price studied Michael from across the table. "Real cocky bastard, aren't you, kiddo?"

"Remind you of anyone?"

"Hey, it was an observation, not a criticism. Truth is I had you checked out, see what wheels you been greasing."

"Satisfied?" Michael asked, his heart skipping a beat over the anticipation of how well the additional etchings, forged onto his identity by the contacts to which Naomi Burns had referred him, would hold up.

"No. You're too clean. Nobody smart enough to get to me can be that clean. Hey, whatever for now. Time comes, though, I'd like to hear about the dirt. Dirt's got character. Helps me evaluate my potential partners."

Michael breathed easier. "Am I too clean for us to do a joint venture?"

Price leaned forward over his salad plate, as if forgetting it was there. "How much is the greatest casino ever gonna cost us?"

"Three billion dollars. The price includes the sticks you need to shove up the asses of the ball-less pricks who bought you out."

With that, Michael placed a leather-bound book between them on the table that included a reproduction of his gold medallion as its centerpiece.

"That the business plan for your masterpiece, kiddo?"

"Half of it."

"Normally people trying to get my interest give me the whole thing."

"I've already got your interest, Max."

Price nodded, not acknowledging the book resting between them. "You hear all the legends about the people who made this town, like Bugsy Siegel, Bill Bennett, Jay Sarno, Kirk

Kekorian. That's what they are—legends. Most of it never happened and what did wouldn't have made for the kind of press they wanted. But what they all did have was vision, kiddo, and that's what makes them different from the corporate clowns who ain't got the foresight to see past their foreskin."

Michael watched Price's eyes change. It was a subtle shift from indifferent to something akin to sad. He looked across the table past Michael to the Vegas he had helped build rotating below. Even the biggest casinos looked small from this vantage point.

"That's what chased me out of the casino business in this damn town, kiddo. I never did a deal if it meant sticking my hand in another man's pocket. But these suits, they didn't even have pockets, just their investment bankers on speed dial so they could build another piece of shit with a brighter marquee than the one next door. Truth is I been looking for the right cattle prod to stick up their ass, make 'em jump and piss themselves." Price tapped the book Michael had laid before him with an open palm, finally acknowledging it. "All this checks out, you maybe got yourself a deal."

Price rose enough to extend his hand across the table. Michael joined him on his feet and took it.

"I never lose, kiddo. Just remember that."

"Funny, Max," Michael told him, "I was just about to say the same thing to you."

NINETY-ONE

SUMMERLIN, 2000

Naomi Burns went to work immediately preparing the joint venture documents to be checked and rechecked by Max Price's army of attorneys. Changes were requested, the changes made, and the papers returned with more changes marked in red and yellow stick-its that protruded from the pages at all angles. Days turned to weeks, to one month and then two.

Max Price, meanwhile, became increasingly elusive. First there was a long-delayed vacation, then a stay in a private clinic where he was recovering from a bout of pneumonia. With only two weeks left before Michael's option expired, the documents were finally completed to everyone's satisfaction. Except Price kept making and breaking appointments to execute them, always with a different excuse. A mere seven business days remained when Price finally summoned Michael and Naomi Burns to his sprawling home in Seven Hills Country Club on the west side of the city.

Max was dressed in a bathrobe when they arrived, a bit irritable over having to cut his massage short.

"Stick around," he told a shapely Asian woman dressed in white. "This shouldn't take too long."

Michael looked toward Naomi, both of them noticing that only one of Price's lawyers was present even before Price bid them to join him at the dining room table. Atop its shimmering glass rested a single sheet of paper, held in place by a marble paperweight molded into the shape of a naked woman.

"I like you, kiddo," Price told Michael, ignoring Naomi altogether. "That's why I'm gonna treat you fair."

"I don't see our joint venture papers, Max."

"On account of we're not gonna be signing any. I'm buying you out, kiddo, lock, stock, and fucking barrel."

Michael felt heat starting to build behind his cheeks.

"See, I rethought our deal. Didn't find it fair, what with me bringing practically everything to the table. Thing is, you don't have a lot of recourse here. You haven't got the money to exercise your option on the land, and even if you did, you ain't got the wherewithal or the track record to get the financing to build this project or any other. You're a nobody, kiddo. It's a closed town, and I'm one of the ones built the wall. You're either in the Club or you're out and you were never in. That's what you needed *me* for, remember?" Spoken with a twinge of irony in his voice. "Hey, look at it this way. First time we met a few months back was April Fool's Day. Guess the joke was on you."

"And me thinking you were a man of your word."

"Business is business. We never had a signed contract."

"Our word of honor was our contract."

"What, you telling me you never done a wrong or dishonest thing in your life?"

"I never screwed anyone who didn't deserve it."

"And look where that got you. I had this made up in place of our joint venture agreement."

With that, Price lifted the heavy marble paperweight from the single sheet of paper and slid it toward Michael.

"Simple deal memo transferring hundred percent ownership of your LLC that owns the option on the Oasis to me for six million dollars. You get to double your money for your trouble."

Michael was trapped between thoughts, intentions. The thought that Price might betray him had naively never crossed his mind. The pitch and the negotiations had gone so well that he had let himself become enamored with his self-importance, a fatal mistake he vowed never to make again. For now, though, he was trapped. Price had him and both of them knew it.

"Ten million," Michael said, sliding the deal memo toward Naomi Burns without regarding it. "You want me to sign that, the price is ten million."

"You're fucking with the wrong guy. Bad idea. Make three million on the deal or lose the option and the money. Take the money and run before I change my mind. What do you say, kiddo?"

"Ten million or I walk out of here and sell the option for free to the first asshole I can find who hates your guts. Throw a stone on Las Vegas Boulevard, I'll probably hit one. What do you say, Max?"

Price smiled, thinking as he stared straight into Michael's deadpan eyes while scratching his chin. "All right, kiddo. Ten it is."

Michael realized Max Price had manipulated him the way

he had countless others, turning him into a piece in his own chess game. Price signaled his counsel to make the appropriate change in the document.

"Seven mil profit, kiddo. Not bad for three months work. Set yourself up with a Howard Johnson's on the way to Reno or Tahoe. Load the lobby with slots and eat frozen turkey to your heart's content," Price said, finally handing him a Mont Blanc pen as Naomi finished her review of the new memo.

The pen trembled in his hand as Michael accepted the document from Naomi and laid the marble paperweight atop an upper corner so it wouldn't move when he signed his name at the bottom. Then he slid it back to Max Price, who left the page lying there upon the glass.

"I owe you, kiddo. You recharged my batteries. When my new casino, the Maximus, opens, stop by for a drink. You wanna stay the night, consider yourself comped. I'll make a fortune, thanks to your cocky ass."

Michael closed his fist around the marble paperweight and drew it upward. Pictured himself bringing it down hard on Max Price's skull. Price watched him intently, smirking the whole time.

"No thanks," Michael said and tossed the paperweight Price's way.

Price fumbled for it, couldn't find purchase, and the paperweight shattered the tabletop on impact, the glass imploding inward into a river of shards atop the Oriental rug.

Max Price didn't move. "Nice doing business with you, kiddo."

"Our business isn't finished yet, Max," Michael said, already leading Naomi Burns to the door.

NINETY-TWO

Las Vegas, 2003

"I want you to use all our resources to start selling Price World Resorts stock short," Michael told Naomi Burns, who now handled legal affairs for King Midas World full-time. She had resigned from her New York firm in the wake of the embezzlement scandal from which Michael had rescued her by making all the damaged parties whole. Innocence in such cases seldom matters, and only his intervention had salvaged her career.

"I'm betting on you, Michael," she had said, when he picked her up at McCarran.

"This is Vegas," he'd told her. "You're in the right place."

It had been three and a half years since Michael's fateful meeting with Max Price. The forty-story, $3.8 billion Maximus Hotel and Casino was just seven days from opening, on December 29. After acquiring the Oasis, Price launched an IPO with Goldman Sachs taking Price World Resorts, PWR, public on the New York Stock Exchange to finance construction of the massive Maximus.

"You know something, Michael?" Naomi asked him.

"I think the Maximus is going to fail and leave Price World Resorts in the tank. His business plan is badly flawed. It's too expensive and too much of the same old thing."

"How much are we talking about here?"

"Everything we've got. And borrow as much as you can from the bank. There's no way this bastard's going to make it."

"Because he cheated you?"

"Because he's a bad businessman, Naomi."

Naomi raised her eyebrows at that. "Everything plus debt isn't good business either. That's sure to gain the attention of the SEC, no matter how much we spread out the shorts."

"Then don't bother. Leave everything open and above-board, unless you think we're breaking the law here."

"Just the laws of reason. Price World Resorts is a darling in the market right now. If Wall Street's right, we'll lose everything by the time the Maximus opens."

"Do you trust my judgment, Naomi?"

"That depends."

"On what?"

She hesitated. "I need to ask you a question, Michael. Did you have anything to do with the embezzlement charges leveled against me? Did you orchestrate the whole thing so you could swoop in and rescue me?"

"If I did," Michael replied, "it was the best favor anyone ever did for you."

Naomi Burns reluctantly did as Michael instructed, and from King Midas World's headquarters at the Howard Hughes Center he obsessively watched the final touches being put on the lavish Maximus every day. He would stand by the huge plate-glass window running from floor to ceiling in his private office that, ironically, had a direct view of the construction site. The Maximus was too gaudy and ostentatious for his tastes, since Price had built the casino of his dreams, not Michael's, after Michael's planning and preparation had made it all possible. He would even stare at the structure at night sometimes when it was visible only as a monolithic shell against the Vegas skyline. And by the end of the day the trash can would be full of crinkled pages crammed with numbers he'd been running that no one ever saw and wouldn't have understood if they did.

The day before the Maximus was to open, though, the trash can was empty.

Early on the morning of the Maximus's scheduled opening, Michael drove to a parking lot off the Howard Hughes Parkway adjoining his office building. He lit a Cohiba cigar and anxiously watched the clock of his Mercedes 600S tick ever closer to 6:00 A.M., waiting for the moment he had been craving for years to come. Time for him had never seemed to pass so slowly. The sun rising over the mountains shone against the empty monolithic structure, forcing Michael to don his Cartier sunglasses. He was staring straight through the windshield, heart hammering against his chest, when finally a rumbling he could feel at his very core like an earthquake shook the entire Strip. He felt a chill surge up his spine as the Maximus collapsed to the ground in a thundering crack that turned the air around it slate black to match the building's dominant color. Michael watched a plume of ash and grime rushing through the air, closing his eyes involuntarily as the charcoal cloud enveloped his Mercedes.

"Just business, Max." He smiled.

It was several minutes before the black cloud receded enough to reveal the scope of the disaster that had left a pile of rubble where the most expensive casino ever built had been hardly a blink before. Since the building was vacant at the time, there were remarkably few deaths and injuries, most of these resulting from falling debris. The investigation that followed quickly determined a massive gas leak, not terrorism, was to blame. Subsequently, Max Price himself was revealed to be one of the victims, having decided to spend the night in one of the hotel's exclusive penthouse suites in order to sample his own wares. DNA confirmed that much, and blood samples from severed limbs recovered from the debris revealed Price's blood alcohol level to be in excess of 2.0.

In the hours that followed the blast, the share price for Price World Resorts on the New York Stock Exchange fell from eighty-nine to fifteen dollars, and in the ensuing three days plummeted further to two dollars when the death of Max Price was announced. Since Price World Resorts' sole asset at the time was the Maximus, a single casino, his death effectively reduced the company's value to next to nil. A company like Harrah's or MGM with multiple holdings and casinos would have been able to survive such a disaster, but PWR became the perfect prey for a business-savvy predator.

Naomi Burns swung into action by leveraging Michael's short sale into a $625 million net profit and growing as the stock continued to drop.

"Now what?" she asked him, still astonished by the turn of events.

"Now we go for the jugular."

With no other choice at hand, the board of directors of Price World Resorts agreed to a buyout on King Midas World's terms, which included a tender offer at the stock's then current value plus a 10 percent premium. KMW supplemented this by acquiring the outstanding bonds for fifteen cents on the dollar, completing the absorption of Price World Resorts into King Midas World's holdings. Those holdings now included the property on which the Maximus had stood, and Michael wasted little time in enacting plans to construct the casino he had envisioned all along on the very site: the Seven Sins.

Drawn from Don Luciano Scaglione's worn leather notebook cataloging his many transgressions, the name came partly from nostalgia, but its true appropriateness stemmed from the irony of Michael's own rise to this point. How many pages would his own sins have filled? Unlike Don Luciano, he didn't keep track, comfortable in the notion that his transgressions all represented means toward a very specific end. Don Luciano might have kept his eternal log, but the truth was it made him no less cruel or mournful in taking actions he deemed necessary. Michael, on the other hand, was now free to build a resort that could offer anyone and everyone a brief sample of a lifestyle they would otherwise never experience. The Seven Sins would not only be about celebrating decadence, but also reminding all who stepped through its doors that everything in life comes with a price.

Michael and Alexander had been standing side by side at the window in Michael's office just a week before, gazing at the Maximus.

"The investigation, no matter how exhaustive, would have to deem it an accident," Michael told Alexander.

"Not a problem, Stolarchos. Casinos can implode under certain circumstances." Alexander's expression flirted with the kind of smile that chilled even Michael. "Contractors could have made a crucial mistake by using the wrong size bolts on the gas valves running into the building. All that pressure since they switched the main on could lead to a leak massive enough to fill the whole building with gas. Simple spark flares and the night becomes day. We have a tremendous opportunity with Cassini Building Company's site manager at the Maximus, a man who—"

"Stop. I don't care, I don't want to know how you do it, just get it done. And remember, the Maximus must be down by oh-six hundred sharp," Michael told him. "To coincide with Wall Street's opening bell. *Capisci?*"

Alexander grinned.

The hundreds of millions of dollars Michael had made in profit, along with King Midas World's suddenly sizable holdings, was sufficient to secure the credit line he needed to build the Seven Sins to his precise specifications, without cutting corners or compromising. Even then, Michael would never have been able to close the financing if not for his new relationship with the hedge fund manager Kenneth Cohan, who backed Michael's efforts all out with trust as the primary collateral. Thanks to Cohan's faith, the Seven Sins would include the key features that might otherwise have been stricken from Michael's original plans and vision, including the Daring Sea and the high-roller suites with their vistalike glass walls looking out into the waters beyond.

He was on the property, now free of the Maximus's rubble, twelve months later standing alongside Alexander, Naomi, and Las Vegas Mayor Oscar Goodman during the groundbreaking ceremony, when the first foundation forms were poured on a construction job that would continue nonstop for more than two years until the Seven Sins was completed.

"I'd like to congratulate a man of vision and determination," Mayor Goodman began into the microphone on the podium that had been erected. "Thanks to entrepreneurs like Michael Tiranno joining our community, the future of Las Vegas has never been more promising or brighter, in spite of the immense tragedy that occurred on this very site. This day heralds not only the beginning of a new casino but of a new era for the people of our great city, which has lost an iconic personality in Max Price, but gained one in Michael Tiranno."

As he listened to Goodman's words, Michael had the sense he, Alexander, Naomi, and all the others in attendance were actually attending a funeral, as concrete forever entombed the last remains of Max Price.

NINETY-THREE

PARIS, THE PRESENT

Alexander arrived at Michael's Plaza Athénée suite at 10:00 A.M., four hours after Raven Khan had left to return to Istanbul.

"Stolarchos," he greeted him, his voice flooded with relief. He'd taken the first flight available from Fontanarossa's Fillipo Eredia Airport into Rome, connecting with a direct flight into Paris's Orly Airport.

"Where's Naomi?" Michael asked.

"She insisted on staying behind. The scraps salvaged from the lawyer's briefcase yielded more than expected."

"Never mind that now. What have we learned about my old friend Amir Pharaon?"

"He's in Paris, continuing to avoid all our attempts to reach him."

"Then let's pay him a visit."

"You can come up now," Alexander said to Michael over his cell phone, thirty minutes after they reached Pharaon's penthouse apartment on Avenue Foche.

Michael had been sipping coffee at a sidewalk bistro within view of the building. Alexander buzzed him in and he rode the elevator to the penthouse through the garage to avoid being seen in the lobby, anxious over what exactly awaited him when the compartment doors opened again.

Alexander had made two stops on the way here, disappearing into innocuous-looking buildings to collect "materials" ordered from his underworld contacts in Paris. He emerged from the second with his entire demeanor changed, considerably more at ease now that he was armed. Still coiled and taut, but more like a snake than a band of steel.

Once on the building's top level, Michael proceeded to Pharaon's apartment at the end of the hall. Alexander opened the door before he could knock and led the way into the dining room, where Pharaon sat, shaking, at the head of a lavish mahogany table. As far as Michael could tell, the penthouse was otherwise deserted. But he caught a thin scent of blood in the air and remembered several dark smudges on the entry door and holes in the walls he had disregarded until now.

"Mr. Pharaon is ready for you, Stolarchos."

Cap tipped low over his forehead for disguise, Alexander flashed a fake badge identifying him as an inspector of the Police Judiciere to the concierge to gain entry to the building on Avenue Foche. They were barely inside when Alexander captured the man in a vicious chokehold. He was unconscious in seconds, then bound, gagged, and stuffed inside a closet less than a minute later.

Alexander took the elevator to the top floor, still not sure exactly what he'd encounter at Pharaon's penthouse. He emerged from the compartment to find a pair of burly guards posted before Pharaon's door and clipped his Police Judiciaire badge to his jacket, intending to give the men every opportunity to live.

"I need to see Monsieur Pharaon," he said in perfect French.

The two guards gazed at each other unsurely. They looked Arab, not altogether unusual in France, although neither seemed comfortable with the language.

"He is not available," one managed.

"Make him so or I will be forced to come back with a warrant. We have a few questions for him."

"What does this pertain to?" the other asked.

"That is between the police and Monsieur Pharaon."

The first man shrugged. "Wait here."

He had started to unlock the door, when Alexander caught a slight flicker of motion coming from the second man. His eyes recognized the glint of pistol steel emerging from beneath his jacket and lashed outward with his knife. He cut the man's throat before he could fully draw his gun and snapped the neck of the other man as he started to twist round from the door.

They'd left him no choice. So be it.

Alexander wheeled into the penthouse with a silenced Beretta in one hand and his knife still clasped in the other. Three other guards were clustered close together, easy to take with multiple shots. Alexander counted off nine bullets before swinging toward a fourth guard raising a cell phone to his ear. Two more shots downed this man, and Alexander used his twelfth and final bullet on a final gunman who spun out through a bedroom doorway. The man twisted at the last second, the bullet boring into his shoulder as he snapped his gun upward. In one single motion, Alexander hurled his knife forward, heard the distinctive hiss an instant before the blade tore through the man's throat, sticking in the wall behind him.

Leaving him standing there dead, Alexander moved to Amir Pharaon, who had crouched behind a couch for cover.

"Michael Tiranno would like to see you," Alexander told him calmly, not even breathing hard.

NINETY-FOUR

PARIS, THE PRESENT

"It's been a long time, Amir," Michael greeted him, taking the chair next to his old friend and mentor at the dining room table.

Pharaon's hands were trembling, his face pale with shock and fear, his eyes continuing to linger on Alexander.

"Don't worry, he won't kill you," Michael assured him. "Unless I tell him to."

Pharaon looked to be an altogether different man from the last time Michael had seen him, almost sickly thin with the bronze tone of better years spent in the sun only a memory. The declining spiral that had begun with Pharaon cutting off his son Samar had clearly continued unabated. Michael had heard he'd lost almost all of his fortune and been forced to sell off his grandest assets to even approximate his formerly lavish lifestyle and was being sued by many of the creditors he formerly entertained.

"Why did you do this, Michele? Why not just call me?"

"It's Michael now. And I tried, Amir, many times, to no avail, after others close to me had been murdered. I was worried. Imagine that."

"I did nothing against you, Michael!" Pharaon insisted. "I swear!"

"You don't want to make me mad today, trust me."

"I have thirty million in a Swiss account. It's yours. Just don't do this! Leave me alone!"

"Thirty million? Quite a sum for a man on the verge of bankruptcy just a few months ago." Michael slid his chair a bit closer. "What changed, Amir? Why did you sell me out?"

"I did not! I would not do that. It's not me!"

Michael shook his head. "Don't waste my time."

"I had no choice, Michael, you must believe that. If there's anything, and I mean *anything,* I can do to make amends, please, just tell me."

"How did you know so much about me, Amir?"

"I was always curious about you, suspicious even. How a young man like you could have been so connected and resourceful on his own. What that young man might have wanted from me. So after you rescued Samar, when we grew close . . ."

"Keep talking."

Pharaon suddenly seemed to choke on his words. "I hired private investigators to look into you. Discreet, of course, and highly professional. I had them follow you."

Michael just stared at him.

"That's how I learned about your connection to the Scagliones and the truth behind World Trade Agricola. All the details, everything. How you were orphaned. How your parents and sister were murdered. Even after we parted, I kept watch on you. Protectively, for your own good, I thought."

"And then you gave all this information to a journalist named Trumbull."

"I was forced."

"By *who*?"

"I . . . can't say."

"You'd better if you want to walk out of here alive."

Pharaon finally locked his gaze on Michael. "I had no choice!"

"If you had problems, you could have come to me."

"I could have come to Michele Nunziato, not Michael Tiranno. My pride never would've let me. Look at me, compared to the man you used to know."

"I never knew you."

"I even sold the *Atlantis* for a tenth of its value," Pharaon continued. "That's how desperate I was. Couldn't even afford the docking fees in Monte Carlo. Besides . . ."

"Besides what?"

Pharaon looked down, remaining silent.

Michael lurched forward and grabbed the arms of Pharaon's chair, twisting it around so they were face-to-face. "Listen to me, and listen to me carefully, Amir. People close to me, people who mattered in my life, are dead because you gave them up. Luciano Scaglione, Miranda Alvarez—do the names sound familiar from the private investigators you had following me? I want to know why. I want to know how you're connected to a group of assassins who call themselves Hashishin."

Pharaon's eyes bulged in fear. "I had no choice."

"You already said that."

"You don't understand."

"How much did you end up making for telling a prick reporter things about me nobody else knew?"

"I didn't believe the man at first, thought I was being set up. So I waited until the first half was deposited before I—"

Michael rose, looming over Pharaon. *"How much?"*

"One hundred million total. Fifty up front and fifty . . ." Pharaon's voice drifted off, the words trapped somewhere down his throat.

"After it's over," Michael completed for him. "After I'm dead and Vegas is gone."

"Yes! Yes!"

"Who paid you? What man?"

"I don't know! *I swear!*"

"You want to answer me or Alexander?"

"Listen to me, I'm begging you, Michael! The men he—Alexander—killed. They weren't my bodyguards, they were my captors. Placed here so I couldn't escape and get out of this mess."

"After taking your fee, why bother?"

"I was desperate. You don't know what it's like to lose *everything,* what it does to a man!"

Michael looked at Pharaon with revulsion. "You're not a man anymore."

"Michael—"

"What do you know about the Hashishin, the plot to destroy Vegas?"

"Nothing, and that's the truth."

"You're a whore, Amir."

"I'm at the mercy of the man who wants you and your world destroyed, the man who hired the Hashishin to destroy everything you ever loved and accomplished."

"Why didn't they just kill you once you'd done what they asked? Why leave you alive?"

"Because of their leader. He took the name of the group's founder, Hassan-i-Sabbah, but you and I both know him by another." Pharaon took a deep breath to steady himself. "Samar, Michael, my son."

NINETY-FIVE

Michael looked at Alexander, then at nothing at all.

Sam Pharaon, the friend he had made while in college purely to get close to his wealthy and powerful father. Sam Pharaon, the spoiled boy he had saved from both a drug overdose and the scandal that would have otherwise followed.

I should have let him die on the nightclub's bathroom floor. . . .

"I barely recognized him," Pharaon continued. "Every day, I have lunch at the Hotel Ritz in the restaurant called L'Espadon."

"You took me there once," Michael recalled. "It's on the veranda, frequented by rich Arabs like you are again, Amir, thanks to selling me out. They give you your private table back?"

"A figure dressed in robes and a kaffiyeh wearing very dark sunglasses approached while I was eating, accompanied by a trio of bodyguards. He sat down at the table without acknowledging me and took off his sunglasses. It took a few moments for me to realize it was Samar, he'd changed so drastically. A totally different man."

"What brought him back to you from his exile?"

Pharaon took a deep breath. "This man who paid for information about you also asked to be introduced to certain charities in the Arab world."

"Charities?"

"Financial fronts for terrorist groups. Said he was prepared to pay a billion dollars in cash for any one of them capable of burning Las Vegas to the ground."

"A group like the Hashishin."

"Samar told me he went to Afghanistan after I threw him out. That's where he realized his true destiny, he said. That's where he made himself into the living reincarnation of Hassan-i-Sabbah."

"And used his trust fund to rebuild the Hashishin."

"A pittance compared to the billion-dollar bounty on Las Vegas he came here to claim." Pharaon's eyes looked sad, empty. "That was months ago now, my last day of freedom. I've been held captive here by Samar's men ever since."

"Until Alexander intervened."

Pharaon nodded. "I'm a free man again, thanks to him."

"Not exactly. You're my bitch now and that means you answer my questions, starting with what happened to Samar?"

"He was wounded in Afghanistan, claimed a coma stripped him of a good part of his memory, including the drugs, the women, the embarrassment. He still remembered enough of his past to seek me out, though."

"What about me, Amir?"

"Your name was never mentioned. It was the money Samar, Hassan now, was after."

"Whose money?"

"I don't know, Michael, I swear I don't. All I have is a phone number I was able to trace to Macao."

Michael turned to Alexander. "Can you link an address to this phone number?"

"I can try."

Michael leaned closer to Pharaon. "How is Samar going to burn Las Vegas?"

"I don't know. I'd tell you if I did."

"Then we'll have to find this fucker together, won't we? You and I are going to Macao."

"Look at me, Michael," Pharaon continued, protesting. "What good can I possibly be to you?"

"You can get me through the door of the maniac behind all this."

"I don't even know this man!"

"But he knows you."

NINETY-SIX

Naomi Burns was waiting in the lobby when detectives began to arrive at the carabinieri post in Fontanarossa in the morning. Though she had already stated her business to the reception clerk, twenty minutes passed before another clerk ushered her to the desk of a plainclothes detective named Carlo Santapaola, who made no effort to hide his lack of interest in her presence.

"Naomi Burns, Inspector," she greeted him.

The detective took her extended hand, but didn't introduce himself. "So what can I do for you?" he asked.

He didn't offer her the chair before his desk, but Naomi sat down anyway. "Several weeks ago, a fellow attorney named Gianfranco Ferelli visited this post to inquire about a murder that occurred in 1975."

"The Nunziatos." The detective nodded. "Are you a reporter?"

"Not at all. You met Ferelli?"

"I heard about the reason for his visit. In spite of whatever you may have heard, Caltagirone is a peaceful village. That massacre has haunted this post and town for over thirty years now."

"Is that what you told Ferelli too?"

"If he had asked, one of us would have. But your fellow lawyer wasn't interested in the perpetrators of the Nunziato massacre, he was interested in the victims."

"Do you recall Ferelli's request for an exhumation?"

The detective pushed himself from his chair and moved to a filing cabinet. "He filed the request but never returned to fill it. Is that all?"

"No, I'd like to have the exhumation request filled now."

"Why? If you're not a reporter, why all this sudden interest?"

"I am an attorney and consigliere to a powerful man in America who has a personal interest in this story."

"Who is this mystery man?"

Naomi hesitated before responding, holding Santapaola's stare. "Attorney-client privilege."

"I'm afraid our meeting ends here, then."

Naomi didn't move. "Wouldn't you like to solve the case that has long haunted Caltagirone, Inspector?"

Santapaola's eyes widened slightly and stared at Naomi for a few seconds. "That's quite a suggestion."

"Would do wonders for your career, I'd imagine."

Santapaola studied her briefly, then yanked open a drawer and pulled a manila folder from inside it. "For what it's worth, Ferelli's exhumation request was never signed by a judge for lack of cause."

"Because he didn't know a police inspector driven and ambitious enough to help him."

Santapaola nodded and handed Naomi the document as he reached for his jacket. "If asked by my office, I imagine the judge will grant the request immediately."

Naomi looked at the form, focusing on the name of the corpse Santapaola was going to seek permission to exhume. She felt her heart skip a beat. The breath bottlenecked in her throat.

"Signora?"

The detective's voice sounded far away, heard only at the outskirts of her mind. The page before her held the answer to what Gianfranco Ferelli had uncovered, what he had tucked into his briefcase to share with Michael upon reaching Las Vegas.

"Signora Burns?"

Naomi rose awkwardly from her chair, the single sheet of the exhumation request floating to the floor.

"We need to get to the court, Inspector," she told Santapaola. "Now."

NINETY-SEVEN

Paris, the present

Before setting out for Macao, Michael placed a call to FBI agent Dell Slocumb's private line.

"Thought you might be dead, Tiranno. Where are you?"

"Doesn't matter. You need to move every resource you've got into Vegas," Michael told him. "The attack's coming tomorrow and it's real."

"This have anything to do with your bodyguards we found dead yesterday?"

"Yes, and it's just the beginning."

"And you know this because . . ."

"Sources."

"Same sources who told you to short stock in Price World Resorts? What's going on, Tiranno? Start answering my questions, or this is gonna be a real short phone call."

"FBI's got an 800 TIPS number now. You rather I just try that?"

"Nice timing, considering the city's filling up in anticipation of the big fight night at the Seven Sins Magnum Arena. Might be wise to call the whole thing off."

"When we met at the Riviera, you told me that would be pointless."

"That was before I knew somebody was planning to burn the city to the ground."

"City's already full, Agent Slocumb. Canceling the fight won't change that."

"I'll do my best, Tiranno. But when you get back to town, we'll need to talk."

"Whatever you say. Just get your people moving."

Michael hung up to find Alexander waiting patiently, slip of paper in hand.

"I've got the address in Macao." Alexander stopped short of handing it over to him. "But you should let me come with you."

"I need you in Vegas."

"You heard Slocumb: the FBI is taking the threat seriously."

"Not seriously enough. I want you there, Alexander. I'll be in touch from Macao."

Alexander knew there was no point in arguing. He recognized the look on Michael's face from times past when no amount of logic or argument could dissuade him from his chosen path. Michael's decision to pursue capture of a great white shark at all costs, for example, in spite of being rebuffed by scientists, fishermen, and investors alike. No matter what they did, no matter what they said, he refused to be denied. And, as always, it seemed, his stubborn, almost arrogant determination paid off.

NINETY-EIGHT

Pacific Ocean, 2007

Michael had insisted on the vast expense required to integrate the Daring Sea into the plans for the Seven Sins for the expressed purpose of having the first great white sharks ever in captivity. Toward that end, the environment had been designed by marine biologists not only to permit the survival of such creatures, but also to promote it and allow the sharks to thrive. The cost to manage all that was a staggering $450 million, amounting to 15 percent of the resort's total construction costs.

But catching the kind of sharks Michael's vision required proved to be as exorbitantly expensive as it was frustrating. His retaining a pair of commercial fishing vessels with the best equipment available resulted only in the sighting of three great whites, none over twelve feet. Michael, though, refused to be denied, earning the wrath and impatience of his investors and even Naomi Burns.

"This needs to end, Michael."

"Not until I get the perfect shark."

"It's been six months. We budgeted four million dollars and the cost is now over ten."

"What's your point?"

"I thought I just made it. It's bad enough we've built an ocean in the middle of the desert. Now we're building a zoo in addition to a casino, losing our asses while you're out playing Captain Nemo."

"Good idea."

"What?"

"A giant squid," Michael said sarcastically, referencing the Jules Verne classic novel he'd read as a young boy in Caltagirone. "Nobody's ever captured one of those either."

Michael hired a third vessel to patrol the waters of the Pacific off the coast of Southern California after sightings of a great white of mammoth proportions were confirmed there. Pictures taken by an amazed sailor showed a creature of thirty feet in length. Following the sighting of the shark, the coast guard was called in to patrol the coastline, and a long stretch of beaches were indefinitely closed down along the Southern California coast from Santa Barbara to San Diego.

A few days after the sighting, Michael received a call at 2:00 A.M. at Roma Vetus informing him that one of the fishing boats he had retained had a fix on the massive great white. He and Alexander sped off to McCarran, where a King Midas World corporate jet flew them into Santa Monica. They boarded an Air Royale helicopter, but with no way to land the chopper on any of the fishing boats, Michael had no choice but to drop onto the deck of the largest, tucking and rolling as Alexander instructed.

By that time all three of his vessels had converged on the area in an attempt to triangulate the territorial creature's position. Capturing it and transporting it alive to the Daring Sea would require both unprecedented strategy and equipment, including a giant wave pool capable of creating a current powerful enough for the shark to swim against. Several marine biologists were already part of the expedition, hired on retainer by King Midas World. The transportation of the creature from California would be handled via a C-130, already leased and on standby from the air force.

The shark started to feed at dawn behind Catalina Island, where a large colony of seals had settled. Hours later Michael caught his first glimpse of the magnificent monster rising out of the water to snatch a seal from its perch atop a rock formation. He watched the two smaller fishing boats converge from opposite angles and, along with Alexander and the other members of the crew, was shocked to see the shark turn and attack the nearest boat, hitting the vessel so hard it tore off a section of its stern. One of the sailors was knocked overboard and bitten in half, swallowed from the legs to the chest despite the efforts of the crew to pull him to safety.

Ultimately it fell to Michael's boat, the largest of the three, to wage the final battle, which lasted over six hours. Once, for reasons he didn't quite fathom himself, Michael was drawn to the gunwale, trying to help the crew as the battle raged. He slipped on the wet, muck-drenched deck and might have gone over into the monster's waiting jaws had Alexander not been there to grab hold of his arm and yank him back to safety. Minutes later, though, another sailor did not fare as well. He fell into the water trying to reel the shark in when it swung around the other side of the boat. While he screamed and waved desperately for help, the shark pounced and dragged him under.

The still-thrashing monster, exhausted from the struggle, was finally reeled in and hoisted by a custom-made winch into the tank Michael had commissioned and financed to ensure its survival during the trip by flatbed truck to the airstrip where the C-130 was waiting to fly the creature to Las Vegas. By the time a mild sedative was shot through the shark's steel-like skin, one fishing boat had almost sunk, another was disabled, and Michael's was a twisted mess from stem to stern, her crew equally battered by the battle that had won him his most prized possession.

Along with Alexander, he remained close to the tank for the entire trip.

"Assassino," Michael said at one point, Alexander turning to find him facing the tank. "I'm going to call him Assassino."

The deaths during the capture resulted in an investigation by the authorities that was opened and closed in a matter of days.

As a result, the publicity the man-eating shark garnered turned the Seven Sins into a must-see attraction on every visitor to Vegas's list. Hotel reservations soared overnight, the Daring Sea underwater suites booked one year in advance at a cost of $2,000 per night. Tickets for interior views of Red Water feeding time, meanwhile, sold out months ahead of time.

For his part, Michael's greatest concern was for the shark's well-being and survival. The Daring Sea marine facility had been constructed with the best advice in mind and finest technology money could buy. Since no one had ever cared for such a creature before, though, much about its eating and living habits had to be learned on the fly. Toward that end, for reasons even marine biologists could not fully explain, Assassino did not truly begin to thrive until another two far smaller great whites were added to the Daring Sea to complement the tigers, hammerheads, and bulls already present. It was as if this primordial monster needed to have its dominance exerted in order to live, and in that understanding Michael finally grasped the underlying meaning that defined his obsession.

He shared this realization only with Alexander, who embraced it in view of the legends Greek fishermen had long passed down about the bond between man and monster, believing that on some intrinsic level Assassino recognized, and even understood, Michael as well. Alexander became further convinced when his eyes met Assassino's one day while the shark was being vaccinated in the Intake Center, certain he caught a vague sense of recognition flash within them. The fact that this ran contrary to everything science said about a shark's lack of capacity for thought did nothing to dissuade him from the conviction that the mythical beast that defined the Seven Sins was to the sea what Michael Tiranno was to the land.

NINETY-NINE

PARIS, THE PRESENT

Michael and Amir Pharaon would be flying by private jet from Paris to Macao, accompanied by a pair of veterans of the French Foreign Legion that Alexander had retained in Paris, chosen for their allegiance to him.

"I checked out the address," Alexander reported. "It's a villa on Cologne Island."

King Midas World's planned expansion into Macao, a peninsula off mainland China located in the South China Sea sixty miles south of Hong Kong, had led to Michael making three trips there over the past twelve months. The province fascinated him for its contradictions and contrasts. Operating under the principle of "one country, two systems," Macao enjoyed autonomy from the Chinese government in all areas save for foreign matters and those dealing with defense. As such, it was able to maintain a robust economy based primarily on gambling, and maintained its own separate currency, customs territory, immigration controls, and police force.

First and foremost, though, the territory's identity was defined by gambling. By some estimates, Macao had already exceeded Vegas in terms of gambling revenues. And that was before the planned opening of the lavish Cotai Strip, modeled after Las Vegas Boulevard and to be occupied by several of the same megacasino resorts found there, including, eventually, the Seven Sins.

"I'll have a boat reserved to take you to Cologne Island," Alexander continued. "A rental car will be waiting at the marina there. As far as anyone knows, you're just another wealthy businessman looking to purchase a home." He hesitated. "I'd still rather be accompanying you myself."

"I already told you I need you in Vegas."

"We won't find the man behind this there, Stolarchos."

"No, I'm going to find him in Macao."

ONE HUNDRED

ISTANBUL, THE PRESENT

The phone inside Belas rang seconds after Raven Khan had closed the gallery's office door behind her. She answered it after the fourth ring, receiver held stiffly against her ear.

"You know what we want," a voice greeted in sharply accented English.

"Yes."

"If you want the old man back, you will bring the triggers to us. Specific instructions will be delivered to your gallery in twenty minutes. Deviate from them in the slightest and he dies. Do you understand?"

"I do."

Click.

The man didn't have to say she was being watched; it was obvious from the moment the phone rang to coincide with her entry. Raven moved back out into the gallery while awaiting the delivery. One way or another, she knew she would never be returning here again and studied her favorite pieces as if to bid them farewell. To anyone watching through Belas's windows overlooking Ortaköy Square, her motions were simply reflective and nostalgic, and it was almost impossible to see her lift a single object from the shelf and tuck it low, out of sight by her hip.

After her instructions were delivered in a thick envelope by private courier, Raven slid off toward the hidden door that led down into the secret basement room where the nuclear triggers were stored. She emerged from Belas three hours later carrying a padded, airtight case with the triggers safely inside. The case was of the diplomatic courier variety that would pass inspection at any airport security station, heavy and virtually impregnable. So long as it was accompanied by the proper paperwork, forged, of course, no airport security station worldwide would open it to inspect the contents.

Raven fully expected she'd be watched all the way to the airport; in fact, she hoped she would be, to offer assurance nothing was amiss.

And nothing would be, until she was in the same room as the leader of the Hashishin.

ONE HUNDRED ONE

MACAO, THE PRESENT

The private jet landed at Macao International Airport just before 9:00 A.M. local time. Michael's Cartier Tank Americaine watch told him it was 5:00 P.M. in Las Vegas, 5:00 P.M. *the day before,* actually, giving him the odd feeling he was traveling in time.

The two men assigned to him were a Frenchman named Pierre and a Greek named Stavros, and true to Alexander's word, they were clearly seasoned, battle-hardened men. For his part, Amir Pharaon took everything in impassively, a man resigned to the fate he had chosen for himself whether he lived or died today. He had uttered barely a word on the flight, no pleas for mercy to Michael or fond remembrances of their initial meetings. He was a different man now, while Michael clung to the same passions and values that had defined him for as long as his memory stretched. They were strangers now and no more.

A limousine took them from the airport to Kai Ho Port, located on Ilha de Coloane and the larger of Macao's two ports. Once there, Stavros and Pierre led Michael to the berth where the speedboat Alexander had arranged for them was moored. Pierre took the wheel and steered a straight course for the marina on Cologne Island.

For the first time since they had left Paris, Michael felt his insides knot up. Soon he would be face-to-face with whoever was behind the deaths of Luciano Scaglione, Miranda Alvarez, and Kenneth Cohan, the same man who had tried to destroy his casino along with his dreams.

Michael squeezed the medallion inside his shirt, as the speedboat flitted over the waves of the South China Sea, seeming to ride atop them.

ONE HUNDRED TWO

CALTAGIRONE, THE PRESENT

Naomi Burns stood alongside Inspector Carlo Santapaola of the carabinieri post at Fontanarossa, watching the workmen scoot around the piles of grave dirt they had made, as if afraid to touch them. They lowered themselves gingerly into the hole and skirted along the periphery toward the third coffin in the row, smaller since it was a child's.

Though there were three separate gravestones, the bodies of Michele Nunciato's parents and sister had been buried in a single grave. Naomi watched as the workmen lowered their hands beneath the child's coffin and hoisted it upward over the rim onto a flat patch of earth beyond. An old weathered forklift slid into position, the driver easing its tongs beneath the wood and then toting it over to a waiting carabinieri van where it was loaded into the rear. Then Santapaola accepted the fully executed document back from the groundskeeper and moved toward the van himself.

"Coming, signora?" he called to Naomi, who'd remained by the now open grave, lost in thought.

"Yes, Inspector," she said, falling into step behind Santapaola.

It would be several days, at least, before Naomi had the answers she was looking for, the answers the lawyer Gianfranco Ferelli had come to Caltagirone to find.

Answers that could change Michael Tiranno's life forever.

ONE HUNDRED THREE

"I need to blindfold you now," the Hashishin soldier told Raven Khan, once they were on board the helicopter.

"Try not to mess up my hair," Raven said, studying his flat, unwavering expression.

She had piloted her organization's own King Air 90 turbo propeller twin-engine plane into Khartoum to avoid additional scrutiny at commercial airport checkpoints, stopping to refuel in Cairo just past 2:00 A.M. Three of the same operatives who had been with her in the Black Sea accompanied her on the journey. Raven was under no illusions they'd be able to help her initially. If her plan succeeded, though, she would need their help getting out of the country, and the Kingair 90 was capable of landing on short, unpaved fields, another reason she had chosen it.

After clearing customs, Raven followed her instructions to proceed to the airport's private terminal, where her two Hashishin escorts stood in the shadow of the chopper shed, illuminated by the early morning sun. One offered to take her diplomatic case before she climbed on board but Raven refused, clutching the handle even tighter.

She maintained her hold throughout the entire flight, even when her blindfold was removed ninety minutes later upon landing in the ruins of an old fort constructed during the period of French colonialism in Western Africa. The Sudan was one of several countries France had laid claim to, thanks to forts like this that provided both bases and a resupply network for troops dating back as far as the seventeenth century.

The trip's flying time, along with the wooded brush and grasslands around the crumbling ruins of the fort, told Raven they had landed somewhere in the southern central area of the country, not far from the blood-soaked Darfur region. But the near total isolation of the fort made it a strange choice for the proposed exchange, especially since she saw no one else in evidence.

Raven's escorts guided her inside the fort's ruins toward a former cistern, down which a set of stairs had been erected. The stairs descended farther than she expected, ultimately ending at a steel door accessible via a keypad at eye level alongside it. One of her escorts entered the proper code and the door opened electronically, revealing a beautifully furnished foyer beyond.

Raven entered and heard the door click closed again behind her. Clearly, no expense had been spared in constructing and furnishing Hassan's headquarters in what had once been the storage chambers, catacombs, and escape tunnels of the old fort.

Her two escorts brought Raven to a majestic staircase that spiraled downward, where a man dressed in Muslim robes was waiting.

"I cannot bring you to the master until the contents of your case are inspected," he informed Raven in excellent English.

"Then we have a problem, because I have no intention of opening it until I am before him," she told him. The man looked as if he was ready to snatch the bag from her. "Go ahead," Raven continued. "But enter the wrong combination more than twice and the case will explode."

"Then perhaps we should just kill you and the old man now."

"In which case your master's chances of ever getting his hands on these nuclear triggers will die too."

The man seemed prepared for her response. "Very well," he said. "Come with me."

He led her down the narrow stairway to a smaller, second level and a set of ornate double doors. The man thrust open the doors and bid Raven to enter a beautifully appointed room furnished with priceless treasures of art that in normal times would have set her mind plotting. The dehumidified air was chilly, spilling in from vents located on the walls and ceiling. Raven could not even imagine what it had cost to build all this, much less while maintaining such meticulous attention to detail.

Her eyes continued to sweep the windowless room's confines,

locking finally on the sight of Adnan Talu seated in a chair, two black-robed guards with their faces concealed by veils and armed with submachine guns poised on either side of him. Raven felt a heaviness form in her stomach at the sight of his badly bruised face, one eye swollen shut. He wheezed with each breath, the wheezing growing more rapid at the sight of her. He mouthed her name. His lips trembled as he regarded her with dismay over the hopelessness of the situation in which they found themselves.

"At last," came a voice from the room's darkened rear corner, and Raven turned to see a figure striding toward her. "I am Hassan-i-Sabbah." The leader of the Hashishin had a fairly long beard untouched by gray and wore formal robes over his clearly thin frame. Hassan did not smile, remaining expressionless as his eyes fell on the diplomatic courier case that she was still holding. "So this is the pirate who stole the triggers I paid a hefty sum for," he greeted her in English, not smiling as he finally stopped a yard before her.

"Let the old man go and you can have them back."

"I'll have them back anyway."

"No, you won't."

He regarded Raven quizzically, surprised by her boldness. "You speak of him like he's your father."

"As close as I've got."

Hassan scowled. "I have no sympathy for fathers."

"You'd be wise to remember that I do." Raven lowered the case atop a map of Las Vegas spread across a glass table and looked back at Talu. "I'll unlock the case once you release him."

"You'll unlock the case or you'll watch him die."

"Am I to take you at your word?"

"I guarantee the old man's safe passage in return for the triggers. Not yours."

"Fair enough," Raven said, and entered the proper three numbers into the keypad.

Hassan stiffened as the courier case snapped open.

Raven started to open it.

"No!" Hassan ordered, storming toward her.

His guards eased forward, close enough to reach Raven before she could have managed any meaningful attack. Hassan's eyes were fixed on the now unlocked case, so resolute Raven felt certain he was going to open it there and then, until he took the case in his hands and just held it.

"No," he said, looking at her with a sly smile. "I don't think so."

Then he carried the case gingerly to Adnan Talu and laid it in his lap.

"I think I'll have the man you came here to save open it instead," Hassan continued.

Raven tensed visibly. Her eyes sought out Talu to warn him off, but he didn't meet them, as if resigned to his fate. She watched Talu flinch in fear as he started to raise the case's top, the wheezing sound coming rapidly and louder now.

Raven flinched. Talu closed his eyes, and in the next instant Leonardo da Vinci's ingenious spring trap, stolen from the Louvre in Paris, snapped forward on the coiled steel band that held the ancient arrow in place. It shot out in a blur, generating such force over an incredibly short distance that the arrow pierced Talu's breastbone and wedged in his chest. The force of the impact spilled his chair over backward and Raven rushed toward him, watching Hassan pluck the now open, blood-splattered case from his lap.

"I suppose neither of us is to be trusted," Hassan told her.

ONE HUNDRED FOUR

MACAO, THE PRESENT

Upon reaching the pier on Cologne Island, Stavros and Pierre escorted Michael off the speedboat and up the dock to the dark SUV that was waiting for them, complete with silenced Beretta pistols hidden beneath the driver's seat. Stavros and Pierre checked the weapons Alexander had arranged to be placed there, giving the haggard Amir Pharaon time to catch up.

Michael climbed into the backseat with him, his own nerves too frayed to do anything to calm Pharaon's. Here he was in a foreign city about to confront an enemy determined to annihilate him. He had long insulated himself from rash actions and unpredictable circumstances not his to manipulate. He thrived on thinking two moves beyond his opponents, beating them at their own game because he had learned to play it better than they. Today was the antithesis of all that. Today he was merely a piece on the chessboard instead of the player moving all such pieces into place. He wondered how it had come to this, where he had gone wrong, to create a vulnerability that had so exposed him.

Their SUV with Pierre driving wound crisply up the narrow roads that curved through the lush hillside, passing an array of secluded villas overlooking the sea that were hidden behind walls and blocked by the foliage. Unlike the rest of Macao, where real estate was the most rare of commodities, here on Cologne Island the richest of the rich claimed all the space they needed to live and breathe, no property smaller than two acres.

Pierre snailed the SUV to a halt just past the villa neighboring their destination, still a half mile down the road.

"You know the plan, Amir," Michael told Pharaon. "Time for you to take the wheel."

"What I did to you, Michael . . ."

"I don't want to hear it. Keep quiet."

"No, you need to understand how desperate I was. After all my success, to be on the verge of bankruptcy with creditors from all over the world knocking on my doors . . ."

"Sure, it was all about the money."

"You of all people should understand that."

"There's a difference between money and business, Amir, but I don't expect a man like you to understand that. You didn't just sell me out, you sold out yourself."

"I want to make it up to you, Michael."

"Then take the wheel and shut the fuck up."

ONE HUNDRED FIVE

Raven lunged toward Adnan Talu, dropping down to ease his head into her lap. The old man, frothy blood leaking from both sides of his mouth, looked up at her guiltily, seeming to sense what was behind her eyes.

Raven glanced up at Hassan-i-Sabbah's guards, then at Hassan himself as he lowered the diplomatic courier case gently to the glass table, resting it over the maps of Las Vegas strewn across the top.

"He's all yours," Hassan said to Raven, before easing his hands inside to peel back the protective padding and grasp one of the nuclear triggers she had stolen from him in the Black Sea. "Free to go. I am, after all, a man of my word."

Talu coughed more blood, whispered something. Raven stroked his face gently, trying to stop the bleeding by applying pressure to the wound. He started to whisper again and this time Raven lowered her ear to his mouth, straining to hear the words that emerged with the blood from his lips.

She went cold, her insides seizing up, not believing she could have heard Talu's words correctly. But she had; the look in his fading eyes confirmed it.

"No, Adnan, no . . . That can't be true. It can't be—"

She stopped when Talu's eyes locked open. She turned back to Hassan in time to see him removing one of the softball-sized triggers, his eyes mad and wide as he cradled it in both hands.

"Praise be to Allah," he said reverently, eyes locked on the trigger.

Counting the seconds since he had removed the first trigger from the case, Raven ducked low, pulling the body of the now dead Adnan Talu atop her. Any moment now the oily, viscous liquid she had poured into two dozen tiny holes drilled through each trigger's steel housing would ignite. The combination of glycerine and nitric acid, forming nitroglycerine, remained inert while the triggers were within the stable environment of the fortified diplomatic courier case. But the jolt caused by Hassan lifting the first trigger out of the bag activated the compound's exceptional volatility, soon to erupt in tandem with the trigger's already explosive contents.

She was looking right into his eyes when the nuclear trigger exploded, three pounds of steel turned instantly into a blizzard of deadly shrapnel and chemicals. The last thing Raven saw before she ducked all the way beneath Talu's corpse was Hassan's upper body seeming to disappear in a shower of red. She couldn't say for sure what exposure to polonium-210 and beryllium meant for her in the long term, leaving that consideration for another day if she managed to escape Hassan's fortress.

Raven heard the brief, awful, choking death screams of his guards before she peered back out to the sight of the pieces of the maps formerly atop the glass table fluttering to the floor.

One blood-drenched piece landed nearby, familiar words grabbing her attention, enough of the letters present to fill in the ones missing:

THE SEVEN SINS

Raven looked closer at the chunk of the map, realizing the final move in Hassan's deadly endgame to destroy Las Vegas. "Oh my God . . ."

ONE HUNDRED SIX

MACAO, THE PRESENT

A hundred feet from the gate, Pharaon pulled over to let Pierre and Stavros out. He let the SUV idle while the two men darted up the road, clinging to the brushy side to avoid cameras. Pierre and Stavros needed time to get the villa's gate open, eliminate any guards who were present, and then circle round the property to rendezvous with Pharaon and Michael in the front.

True to plan, the electronic gate had already swung inward when Pharaon snailed the SUV up to it. He drove on through after a quick glance toward Michael, following the steep private road that leveled out onto a circular driveway. Before them rose a modest white-stone villa that surprised Michael in its simplicity and lack of the kind of security he had expected.

Even though Pierre and Stavros were nowhere in sight, Michael gestured toward Pharaon to exit the SUV. They then walked together along the drive toward a set of immaculate steps leading to the mansion's entrance.

Pierre and Stavros appeared out of nowhere, pressed against the building in the last moments before they hurdled over the hand-molded steel rails and took posts on either side of the door, silenced pistols held in their hands. Michael remained at the foot of the stairs, while Pharaon mounted them and waited for Stavros's signal before ringing the buzzer set just beneath a gold-plated speaker.

A pause followed, then "Name" reverberated mechanically through the speaker.

"Amir," Pharaon stammered, "Amir Pharaon. It's an emergency. Please, open the door."

"Wait," the voice droned through the speaker.

Pharaon started to turn toward Michael, warned off by Pierre's ice-cold stare.

"Enter," the voice said, followed by the sound of the front door clicking open electronically.

Michael watched Pharaon lower his hand to the knob, as Pierre and Stavros prepared to spring, silenced pistols leveling out now. He saw Pharaon start to push the door inward and glimpsed a thin wire attached to the latch and doorjamb.

"No!" Michael screamed, already backpedaling.

The blast that followed rocketed him backward. Michael hit the soft ground and rolled to a stop, a hammerlike ringing in both ears, his mind numb. He saw he was splattered with blood, felt himself all over to make sure he hadn't been hit, and quickly realized the blood belonged to the men who had been just a few feet from him seconds before, nothing recognizable left of them now.

Amid the severed body parts and gore nearby, Michael saw one of the silenced pistols and crawled across the ground toward it. His hand closed on the blood-soaked handle just as a large figure burst through the smoke from the still-flaming carcass of the doorway.

The man swept his eyes about, inspecting the explosion's results. Michael lurched into a crouch, opening fire before the man was aware of his presence. He remembered Alexander's instructions to keep shooting until sure the target was down. He had no idea how many of his bullets actually struck the man, only that eventually he tumbled down the steps.

Michael's head continued to pound; he realized he hadn't heard the sound of his own gunshots going off through the ringing still claiming his ears. He tried to climb to his feet, stumbled, and sank back to his knees, the world swimming around him as time jumped from his control.

He closed his eyes, opened them when the ringing returned, louder. Michael realized he could hear again, although dimly, and that the ringing was his cell phone. It emerged from his pocket coated in blood from his hand.

"Hello, hello!"

"Michael!" he heard a voice call distantly.

"Hello!"

"Michael, can you hear me! It's Raven!"

"Who?"

"Raven Khan!"

"My ears . . . Talk louder, please. *Hello!*"

"I can't. Just listen to me. I know how they're going to do it. I know how they're going to burn Vegas to the ground. . . ."

ONE HUNDRED SEVEN

Las Vegas, the present

Alexander was walking amid the endless line of stalled cars along Las Vegas Boulevard when his phone rang. The traffic was evidence of the FBI's efforts to intensify security precautions throughout the city. All flights in and out of McCarran had been rerouted to avoid the immediate airspace, and the streets were closed to all trucks and vans. On his right, across the street, stood the Aladdin and the MGM Grand. On his left, beyond a construction fence, the multibillion-dollar Center City project rose as a naked steel monolith amid a never-ceasing cacophony of cranes and hydraulic air hammers.

He had returned to Vegas just before noon and spent all of the hours since crisscrossing the streets to answer a single question:

How is the Hashishin going to do it?

That answer began, and the clues lay, with what they had available to them. The Hashishin had already demonstrated possession and clear mastery of the kind of fertilizer bombs that had wreaked havoc at three, and nearly four casinos. But impact detonation was not an option here, given the much greater scope involved.

How would I burn the Strip?

Assume the words Pharaon had relayed had been literal and not figurative. Without an atomic device, much harder to obtain and render operational than most realized, what options did that leave?

Alexander had considered one after another, rejecting them all and always coming back to the materials he already knew the Hashishin had in their possession. He returned his attention to the skeletal steel behemoth of the Center City project just as a trio of Department of Public Works trucks were ushered onto the property to continue their inspection of the necessary sewer and storm drain relocation. Standard procedure in projects like this.

Something cold struck him, even as he was raising his cell phone to his ear, checking the caller ID on the way.

"Michael, are you all right?"

"It's the Daring Sea, Alexander!" Michael Tiranno blared loud enough to bubble Alexander's eyes. *The Daring Sea!*

ONE HUNDRED EIGHT

MACAO, THE PRESENT

Michael pocketed his phone and started toward the entrance to the villa. His ears continued to ring and he kept muttering to himself as if to retrain his hearing.

Halfway there, he stepped over Pierre's severed leg, stopping to pull a spare magazine from one of the side pockets of his bloodied cargo pants, where Alexander always stored his. He ejected the spent magazine from his pistol and snapped the fresh one into the slot, racking the slide to chamber a round. He climbed the steps gingerly, skirting the gore and debris en route to the charred doorway, which still had pools of stubborn flames flaring about it.

Michael entered the spacious foyer, glad to be free of the smell of blood and burned flesh. The villa was exquisitely furnished but felt somehow cold, as if the design had been lifted en masse from a decorating catalog with no thought given to originality. A winding stairway led to the second floor and Michael padded up it softly, aware he could hear his own footsteps now.

The pistol made him feel more secure than it should have. Another of Alexander's lessons: trust yourself, not the *pistola* that was merely an extension, not an independent force.

Almost to the top of the stairs, that thought made Michael

even more wary in the instant before a shape lunged at him
from behind the wall. Michael saw only a blur of white cloth-
ing and the telltale glint of light off steel. He had the presence
of mind to realize he could not get his pistol righted before the
steel found him, and he twisted aside, barely missing the razor-
sharp scalpel that would have otherwise sliced his throat.

Michael latched on to the wrist holding the blade, conscious
in that moment of a much larger man dressed as a nurse, close
enough for him to smell the odd mix of talcum powder and stale
sweat. The man tried to pull the scalpel back, giving Michael
the opportunity to hammer him in the face with the butt of the
pistol.

He felt the man's nose crush beneath the blow, heard him
grunt in pain. The man managed to tear his wrist free of
Michael's grasp, the next second unfolding in excruciatingly
slow motion.

First the glint of the blade coming at him again.

Then turning the pistol's barrel against the man's face and
firing.

And finally the thump of impact followed by the sight of a
face that had simply vanished into a mass of bone, blood, and
pulp from the nose up.

The man crumpled to the floor, his weight taking Michael
with him. Michael stumbled back to his feet and paused only
to steady his breathing before starting down the hall. He heard
a droning, melodic sound and steered toward it, reaching the
open door of what must have been the master bedroom.

Pistol raised before him, Michael entered a room steeped in
darkness. The windows overlooking the South China Sea beyond were blacked out or shuttered. The only light leaked down
from thin blue translucent strip bulbs recessed into the perime-
ter of the ceiling. The room smelled of alcohol, antiseptic, and
sweet air freshener that had failed to mask the other scents. The
beeping he had followed, along with a whirring sound, was all
that broke an impermeable silence; medical machines, Michael
thought, noticing the shape of what was clearly a hospital bed
against the far wall.

A shape stirred atop the bed; not stirred, so much as shifted, in the last moment before a soft light snapped on, illuminating a face Michael knew all too well.

"I can't fucking believe this," said Max Price between labored breaths.

ONE HUNDRED NINE

LAS VEGAS, THE PRESENT

"The Seven Sins is Ground Zero! It's the sewers, Alexander! They're going to blow up the sewers! . . ."

Alexander was charging down the sidewalk before Michael's warning was even complete, sprinting back toward the Seven Sins as dusk descended on the city.

While he ran, Alexander worked the details out in his mind of how the Hashishin must have done it. A few tanker trucks entering the storm drains at construction sites like that for Center City was all it would've taken. Trucks full of a combination of ammonium nitrate and diesel fuel to be sprayed throughout the sewer walls and ceiling beneath the Strip. With the storm drains bone dry, the exceptionally volatile aerosolized compound would cling to the walls as well as hang in the air, needing only a single triggering blast to be ignited. A liquid's explosive power was limited to its spread, a solid's to its size. But an aerosol suffered no such limitations. Once ignited, everything it had touched would catch, a shock wave spreading outward through the air in which it had collected. The result would be a series of massive blasts that would tear the integrity of Vegas's infrastructure away. The streets and roads would cave in, crumbling to the bedrock on which they had been laid and taking with them all the structures that rose above, their foundations compromised. The casinos would collapse to further fan the flames that engulfed them, creating an effect akin to that of a small nuclear explosion with the Seven Sins as Ground Zero.

Alexander continued his mad rush, shoving pedestrians aside and jumping atop cars slowed or stuck in the interminable traffic. He reached the main entrance to find the hotel teeming with celebrities and tourists alike. The three title fights to be broadcast all over the world from the Seven Sins Magnum Arena that were supposed to mark the unofficial reopening of Vegas instead were about to herald the city's ultimate destruction.

There was no sense calling FBI agent Dell Slocumb at this point, and nothing anyone else could do anyway, except for him.

Too late . . . No time . . .

The sun was gone, the evening clear, hot, and breezeless, which made for perfect conditions for the inferno to consume everything it touched. But Alexander knew he could stop all that if he could prevent the triggering blast he was certain would come at the Seven Sins during the live boxing broadcast. The explosives, likely in the form of several shape charges, he reasoned, must have already been laid in the Daring Sea, a cleanup or maintenance crew infiltrated by one or more of the Hashishin's men. And there was no way Alexander could find the explosive within such a massive underwater area in the mere minutes he had left. That meant his only chance lay in precluding the detonation itself.

Alexander's years in the French Foreign Legion had educated him on the terrorist mind-set. Not once could he recall a case where they relied on timer detonation. Blasts of their making were invariably of the suicide variety, detonated by those committed to martyring themselves, and this attack would be no different.

Alexander recalled Michael's description of the Hashishin assassin who had killed Vittorio and Francesco Scaglione in their Kabul hotel room. The *drakos* of lore from his childhood, the human monster he knew he'd been destined to face, had killed Michael's three bodyguards just two days ago outside Zefferino's. If luck was on his side, and he could only pray it was, the same man would still be in Las Vegas, charged with becoming a martyr by igniting the final deadly blast that would spread from the Daring Sea throughout the storm drains and sewers, eventually consuming Vegas in flames. In just a few minutes, Red Water, the sharks' feeding time, would begin in the hotel's retail area.

The perfect setting to hide in the open.

The perfect setting from which to trigger the blast.

ONE HUNDRED TEN

MACAO, THE PRESENT

In the eerie translucent light, Max Price didn't look real; nor would he have in any light.

Both his arms and legs were missing. Oxygen from a nearby tank was pumped into a clear plastic nose clip. Another device Michael knew was used only on terminal patients on life support pumped and whirred, pushing air into Max Price's lungs through a tube extending out his chest.

"Don't suppose that's your blood you got all over you," he continued, his words emerging between grunts and grimaces of pain. Price grabbed the breath he needed to continue. "What, you never seen a monster before?"

"Not since the last time we met," Michael said, advancing toward what was left of Max Price.

"Very funny, kiddo. I'd laugh if I still could. Problem is it hurts like hell, like everything else." His pale face twisted up in agony, taking on a milky complexion. "Ironic, ain't it? Me lying here right now 'cause I couldn't resist being the first guy to get fucked in the Maximus. So if it wasn't for Viagra, I'd've handed you your balls a long time ago." He turned his gaze briefly downward, the slight motion enough to draw a painful wince. "Lost those in the blast too, so I guess you can say I know what it's like to lose everything, just like you're about to."

"Guess you weren't expecting me."

"You're supposed to be dead already, you fucking pain in

the ass." Price continued speaking through his pained grimace. "Call it fate. Most important moment of your life and here you are spending it with me. Appropriate when you consider I'm only here 'cause of you. Works both ways, though, don't it? Ain't we a pair?" Price started to smile but the gesture quickly dissolved into a horrible cough that drew agonized gasps from him with each rasp. "What I did to you," he resumed finally, "that was business."

"So was my destroying the Maximus."

"See, you owe me your success, after all." Max Price's breathing became labored, wheezing between every word. "Didn't have the guts to do it yourself, though. Big, powerful man like you has to get others to do his dirty work for him."

"There's a first time for everything."

Price paused to catch his breath. "Come on, kiddo, you expect me to believe I was the first?"

"You're not dead. Yet."

"Lots of ways for a man to die. Like you today, for example, when you watch your fucking Vegas go up in flames."

Price shifted his head painfully against a control panel even with his left ear. Instantly a bank of television screens on the wall directly before him and behind Michael snapped to life.

"What, kiddo, you think you're the only one who likes to watch TV in his office?" he taunted, finding the strength and resolve to force the pain back behind gritted teeth. "Got live feeds from all the major news networks, local Vegas stations, even pay-per-view so you can watch your Seven Sins Magnum Arena blow up. Know what else? Vegas traffic cameras. That's their feeds on the top four screens. So I can watch the rest of the show live. Now we can watch together. Look, there's Mayor Goodman arriving at the Seven Sins. Wonder if he knows he's got a front-row seat for his city's destruction. Excuse my excitement. Don't get too much company these days. So, you make it to my funeral? Heard it was standing room only."

Michael took a few more steps closer to what was left of Max Price, the room's pungent antiseptic smell intensifying. "I made it to someone's funeral."

"Lemme tell you, setting that ruse up wasn't cheap either. Guess money really can buy anything." Price started to angle his gaze downward, but the pain was too great to manage the effort. "Except new limbs, of course. Force of the blast actually saved my life, you can believe that. Rocketed what was left of me into the air like a frigging astronaut. Landing in a fruit garden in a high-roller villa on the golf course saved my proverbial ass. Think about it. Here I am in the desert and a fruit garden saved my life. How's that for irony?"

"Nobody knew who you were."

"Nope, not at first. And by the time the folks at the hospital figured things out, the fix was in, if you know what I mean. Blowing up the Maximus might've won you Price World Resorts but I still had a couple billion in spare change, enough to finance my new dream. My only dream now. My life's shit otherwise, kiddo."

"Ruining me?"

"Hey, give me credit for patience. I wanted to wait until the dream was yours, till there was something for me to take away." Price heaved for breath painfully again. "Just like you waiting for the Maximus to open, the stock at ninety, before you destroyed it, you fucking little prick."

"You're wrong, Max."

"About you being a fucking little prick?"

"You can't kill my dream by blowing up a building or even a city. Because there are plenty of cities and plenty of places for me to build. You think I'm like you? Buying and selling, getting out only to get back in." Michael shook his head. "That's not me, not even close. I want to make a difference, not just money. I want to build on top of what I've already got instead of starting over a hundred times. You don't believe in what you do, Max, you never did. That's why you're lying there thinking you've beaten me when all you've done is beaten yourself. Again."

"Bullshit, kiddo. At heart, you're a two-bit hustler like all the rest of us. I was there, remember? Listening to your whole passionate spiel the first day we met. Was all I could do to keep from laughing. You thought you were playing me when I was playing you the whole time."

"That what you're doing now?"

"No. Now I'm gonna make this the worst day of your life."

"I watched my parents being shot, Max. I don't think you can top that."

"What a load of crap. I smell you, it's like my own armpits. I knew it the first time I saw you."

"Long time ago, Max. I've learned a lot since then."

"Yeah? Like what?"

"Goes back to my family's murder. I never thought I'd feel safe again. But I convinced myself I did once the Seven Sins was built. You want to talk about smells? Well, it smelled like home to me. Then you go after my hotel and my city, and all of a sudden, I don't feel safe anymore. But you know what? I never really did and I never will. I want it all, Max, not just the pieces other people don't."

"Who the fuck you think you are?" Max Price's eyes drifted back to the screens, unimpressed. "Pull up a chair, kiddo. Vegas's last show ever starts in about twenty minutes, round the same time the bell goes off on the first title bout at the Seven Sins."

Michael left his eyes on Price. "Guess you wanna make sure you get your money's worth from the Hashishin."

"I look worried to you?" Price challenged and then gasped as a fresh wave of pain coursed through him. He fought for air, looking as if he he'd forgotten how to breathe. His face turned crimson before slowly paling again. "I hated you and they hated Vegas," he continued, fighting the words out. "Match made in fucking heaven. Speaking of which, I got a plastic tube for a dick now. I wake up sometimes, I think it's still there and I reach down to scratch my balls, only there's nothing to reach with, so the itch doesn't go away. You get my meaning?"

"No."

Max Price's eyes darted back to his bank of television screens, then fixed again on Michael. "Vegas goes, my real itch is finally scratched. You may not be dead yet, but I will have killed you all the same. See, kiddo, I know what makes you tick. Know why? 'Cause I know what makes *me* tick. We're like brothers, and twenty minutes from now, we both might as well be dead."

"Along with tens of thousands of innocent people."

"Fuck 'em. I never gave a shit about those assholes other than to get their money. Here's the thing, kiddo: I *made* Las Vegas." Price fought off another cough. "If I can't have it, then nobody will, including a prick like you. *Especially* a prick like you." Price's words finally dissolved into a series of raspy, heaving coughs.

"I'm not the one who broke our deal," Michael said, after the spasm ceased.

"I been breaking deals since you were crapping your diapers," Price said hoarsely, his lips quivering now. "As I recall, you made seven mil on the deal, not exactly chump change. You leave me alone, maybe you got your own casino by now anyway and we're both winners. Now you're gonna lose it all, just like I did. And there's not gonna be anything left for anyone else to lay claim to. You can either watch the funeral on TV with me or walk out of here. Either way, our business is done."

Price's eyes moved from the screens to the pistol in Michael's hand.

"Unless you use that on me, which I don't think you've got the balls to do." Price refixed his milky, drug-laden gaze on the wall of television screens. "Hey, look, the preliminary bouts have started."

Michael continued to regard him as indifferently as he could, the hatred he felt for Max Price making it difficult to focus.

"What's the matter, can't do it?" Max taunted. "Yeah, that's what I figured. Some fucking tyrant. Know what you smelled like to me the first time we met? Diapers and baby powder. Just another punk with answers to all the wrong questions."

One of the televisions fizzled briefly and Michael swung back toward the bank of screens, his breath frozen in his throat.

"Showtime," Max Price said.

ONE HUNDRED ELEVEN

LAS VEGAS, THE PRESENT

The Seven Sins was as packed as Alexander had ever seen it, crowds still arriving for fight night at the Magnum Arena's grand opening. People made the best camouflage in which to hide, and he hoped the man he sought would be within view of the Daring Sea. More of the terrorist mind-set, explaining the progeny of the suicide bomber.

But the Seven Sins had a ready-made solution for the man in the form of Red Water, allowing him to hide amid others and witness the triggering of his blast at the same time. Knocking people from his path, Alexander charged wildly for the retail area, finding a jam-packed throng pressed up against the waist-high railings in anticipation of what was to come.

Not to disappoint them, Seven Sins personnel appeared wheeling buckets of bloody chum to attract the sharks and half a dozen sides of beef to feed them. The crowd began applauding madly as Alexander moved among it, searching for his *drakos* at or near the front, the best vantage point from which to witness his handiwork.

The next round of applause that greeted the massive Assassino's appearance betrayed his target's position, primarily because he was the one person *not* clapping. That and the fact he fit Michael's description of a human monster exactly, the monster Alexander knew he was fated to meet in battle since boyhood. And now that confrontation would take place with far more at stake than he could have ever possibly imagined.

His *drakos* stood thirty feet away across a section of the Daring Sea, towering over the rest of the crowd, which meant Alexander would have to circle all the way around in order to close in on him from the rear. Alexander crouched, pretending to tie a shoe as he freed his custom-made knife from the sheath strapped to his calf. He rose with his hand wrapped around the handle and the blade tucked under his sleeve.

His *drakos* hadn't moved an inch, staring down into the muck clinging to the surface of the water like everyone else. Alexander could see he was holding both hands low by his hips, one clearly grasping something.

The detonator!

Alexander would have to approach with extreme caution, then. No killing blow he struck, or bullet he fired, could totally preclude the simple jerk of a thumb needed to trigger the explosives set in the waters below. That meant every move had to be considered with the detonator in mind. Perhaps wrest it from the big man's grasp first—no easy task, considering his size and prowess, but the best choice.

Alexander slid back into the crowd and began to work his way around, keeping his target in sight the whole way. Finally he found himself at the rear of those squeezing expectantly forward, as Seven Sins handlers dropped the sides of beef into the water. He lost sight of his target in that moment, but quickly regained it and started to ease forward. Alexander regripped his knife so the blade was angled down and ready to use, slipping between the packed-together spectators adroitly without disturbing anyone—nothing that might draw attention to him now.

The next moment found him within killing range of the *drakos,* but his focus remained on the beefy hand closed around the detonator, thumb in the ready position. Wrench it away and he would buy himself the moments he needed to complete the kill.

Alexander shot his hand out in the same moment Assassino broke the water to clamp his jaws around one of the sides of beef, the crowd lurching backward en masse. Jostled, Alexander felt his timing thrown off just enough to strip the grace from his move. He managed to latch on to and pin the *drakos*'s thumb, but felt him twisting round before he could thrust his knife effectively forward.

His adversary deflected the strike and captured Alexander's arm under the elbow, jerking it upward to snap the bone. Alexander ducked inside the move enough to displace the pressure, but the big man still had leverage on his side and Alexander could not risk letting go of the hand grasping the

detonator. He could not beat the *drakos* on strength or savvy
alone, not if he wanted to save the Seven Sins and all of Las
Vegas. His only chance lay in the cold and now bloody waters
of the Daring Sea itself, where the big man's advantage would
be negated and the detonator possibly rendered useless.

Hesitating not at all, Alexander continued to force his weight
forward until the big man bent over the waist-high safety rail
and both of them tumbled into the Daring Sea.

Alexander landed atop the chunks of chum clinging to the surface, still engaged with the *drakos*. Above the crowd cheered,
believing they were witnessing part of the Red Water show.
The jolting impact had stripped the detonator from the big
man's grasp, and he flailed for it frantically amid the chum.

Alexander used that moment to lash out with his knife, quick
and sure. But the monster twisted inside the blow and snared the
detonator by its casing.

Alexander twisted the *drakos*'s hand and the detonator skittered away, slipping below the blood-laden water. He felt one
of the hammerhead sharks slice past him and caught sight of
the two smaller great whites fighting over another of the sides
of beef.

His opponent stretched a hand for the detonator again, then
pulled it back when one of the great whites slashed beneath
the surface, its jaws clamped around a hefty portion of the
beef side. Alexander seized the opportunity to latch on to his
adversary and drag him under, hoping to take advantage of
the fact that he was an excellent swimmer.

The *drakos* fought against him, the detonator fluttering
within both their grasps in perfect rhythm with their descent.
Alexander felt a grip like steel close on his wrist as a blade
similar to his own, though more curved, appeared in the giant's
other hand and slashed outward.

Alexander locked his grasp on the monster's wrist, resulting
in a strange pirouette with the two of them wheeling through
the water in search of some, *any* advantage. Alexander could
feel his lungs beginning to burn, his head filling with the pressure of the increasing depths.

Each man tried to use his feet, but it was Alexander who managed to plant both soles upon the *drakos*'s torso and push. His intention was to separate the man from his knife. But the man's grip on the hilt held firm and he actually managed to slash the blade outward, making a neat tear down the center of Alexander's palm. The big man then stretched a hand outward, paddling frantically for the detonator but failing to snare it in his grasp, as it continued to sink.

Alexander swam at him through the rising redness of his own blood spilling from the gash in his palm. The distance, he knew, was too great to do much damage, but cutting the right tendon would render the *drakos*'s hand—and thus the detonator—useless.

Alexander had just launched his strike when another of the whites came rushing at him. He lurched away at the last instant and slammed the side of the creature's head with a clenched fist, enough to send it temporarily on its way. Alexander rotated back around, expecting to fend off another shark, when he saw the big man finally catch hold of the detonator and reel it into his grasp. Their gazes locked, a mix of awe and fear filling the *drakos*'s as he struggled to move his thumb into position.

Alexander twisted round, coming face-to-face with Assassino himself bearing down, the creature's mouth still leaking bloody hunks of beef from his recent meal. He was swimming too fast for Alexander to do anything but look him in the eye and see the same flash of recognition he had sensed once before.

Assassino opened his massive jaws, coming straight for him.

Alexander readied his knife.

Assassino suddenly veered away, angling straight for the *drakos* instead. The big man tried to swim upward at the last moment, too late either to avoid the shark or press the button before Assassino's jaws clamped downward, slicing through the right side of his torso and swimming off with his body still thrashing about, spilling blood. The rest of the *drakos*'s torso and a single arm attached to the hand holding the detonator plunged into the cold, murky darkness below.

Assassino was gone again as quickly as he had come, and Alexander swam fast up through the blood-rich murky water, breaking the surface before a stunned and silent crowd.

ONE HUNDRED TWELVE

MACAO, THE PRESENT

Max Price kept checking the wall clock nervously, the first of the three title fights scheduled at the Seven Sins Magnum Arena now into its third round on the pay-per-view screen. On another, a local television station was interviewing Mayor Goodman in his front-row seat when Michael's cell phone rang.

"Go ahead, answer it," Price told him, his lips quivering from the pain now. "Tell whoever it is you're catching up with an old friend."

Michael listened to Alexander's voice on the other end, holding his gaze on Max Price.

"Your show's over, Max," he told him, gazing briefly at the television screens. Michael flipped the phone closed and stuck it back in his pocket. "The bomb in the Daring Sea's been diffused. An hour from now, the sewer systems are going to be flushed with water to dilute the explosives your goons planted there. Guess money really doesn't buy everything."

Price looked into Michael's eyes, came as close as he could to a shrug, which sent another bolt of agony through him. "Remember the first time we met, kiddo?" he asked through the haze of drugs and disappointment.

Michael recalled their lunch atop the Stratosphere and nodded.

"I was playing you even then. Bright-eyed kid all full of piss and vinegar—I'd been chewing through guys like you like the buffet at Sam's Casino. Okay, so Vegas doesn't burn, but know what? You're only part of the club because of me and the Maximus. I made you, kiddo, and deep down you know you owe everything you are, everything you built, to me. Fucking Tyrant," Price continued through the grimace stretched across his face. "You were nothing till you met me and you'll have to live with that forever."

Michael moved to the foot of Price's bed, pistol coming up in his hand. "You won't."

Price followed him, his glassy gaze hateful and dismissive. "You ain't got the balls and there's nobody here to do your dirty work for you."

"It won't work."

"Huh?"

"You don't really want to die, Max. You want me to spare your life and walk out of here, so you can come after me again."

"Got it all figured out, huh?"

"I always do."

"Just like you did when you sold me a bill of goods that first day over lunch. Thing is, you weren't selling, you were buying. You just didn't know it."

"I'm not buying now, Max."

"So it won't be me, kiddo," Price taunted, wheezing as the fear percolated in his eyes. "It'll be someone else down the road. You wanna know who your enemies are? Check the white pages."

Michael raised the pistol and aimed it straight for Max Price's head. "You fucked with the wrong guy . . . kiddo."

"See you in hell."

"Already been there," Michael said and fired.

EPILOGUE

THE MAN

"We need to talk," Naomi Burns said to Michael inside his glass office at the bottom of the Daring Sea ten days after he returned to Vegas from Macao, secure in the notion that no one would ever learn the true level of his involvement in saving the city.

"There's been something on your mind ever since you got back from Sicily."

"I didn't want to tell you and I'm still not sure I should."

"Tell me, Naomi."

She hesitated before resuming. "The body buried in your sister's grave, Michael. I had the remains exhumed and examined. The DNA didn't match hers, because the person buried in that grave wasn't Rosina; it was Daniela, the granddaughter of Attilio Cecchini."

Michael could only look at her, puzzled.

"According to the case file, the body of Cecchini's granddaughter Daniela was never found. No one paid any attention because the Sicilian authorities never knew she existed. But a young girl was brought to a house in Messina the day of the massacre, brought by a man who came back to get her just before the house was raided by the carabinieri." Naomi paused to hold Michael's stare. "Because all the toddlers inside had been stolen from their parents and sold on the black market. Sold by thieves, Michael. The man who brought the little girl there and then returned for her was their leader, a man who walked with a cane."

"What are you saying?"

"That Raven Khan, an orphan herself, hired the lawyer Ferelli to find out everything he could about you. But it looks like he ended finding out something about her too. I think he came to Vegas to ask for a sample of your DNA, Michael." Naomi hesitated again. "To prove Raven Khan was your sister, Rosina, and that she was the little girl Talu brought to Messina the day of the massacre."

Michael looked at Naomi for several moments before responding. "If she hadn't called me in Macao . . ."

Naomi shrugged. "There's been no sign of Raven Khan. We don't know if she's still alive."

"But there's no evidence she's dead, right?"

"No."

"And you can't be sure, not of any of this," Michael said, not sure what he was feeling. "Can you?"

Naomi remained silent.

SICILY, ONE WEEK LATER

A week later, Michael stood on the shore of Isola di Levanzo, in the Egadi chain, diagonally across the Mediterranean from the coastal town of Marsala. In the days following Naomi's revelation about Raven Khan, he had found himself distracted by memories he couldn't control and thoughts he should have been able to. Unable to focus on the business that so badly needed his undivided attention, he had come here to clear his mind and his own personal ledger, as Don Luciano might have put it.

. . . it doesn't offer immortality or even protection from harm's way, as much curse as blessing, perhaps even more *curse than blessing. . . .*

Everyone who had possessed the medallion prior to him had blazed their trails in blood and pain ultimately wrought back upon themselves. Even King Midas, the mythical figure based on the medallion's first-known owner, Mita, had been cursed by his ability to turn anything he touched into gold since it precluded contact with another human. That legend was an allegory to describe a man unable to trust another living soul due to his wealth and power, leaving him mired in loneliness. If Raven Khan was right, perhaps the same fate awaited Michael, in which case he, and the world, would be better off with the medallion returned to the same waters where his father had found it.

According to the tale so often told by his father, this was the very beach where Vito Nunziato had washed up with the medallion clutched in his hand. In the years since hearing that tale, Michael had learned that Caesar maintained several wine fields in Marsala and was reputed to have visited the area on several occasions. This sea had also been the site of numerous naval battles, including those waged by Caesar's nephew Octavian against pirates who called Sicily their home. Accordingly, these waters were laden with sunken ships, one of which had lost the medallion to the sea centuries before Michael's father had recovered it amid the wooden wreckage.

Hesitating no longer, Michael lifted the chain from his neck and clutched the medallion in his hand, wondering what his life might be like, how it might change, if he flung it into the sea here and now. He was tired of blood, tired of losing those he loved. But if Naomi Burns was right about Raven Khan, perhaps there was still someone to be gained instead. It made sense, explaining why Michael felt a strange sense of familiarity about her, as if they had known each other for a lifetime instead of the few fleeting moments when their fates had crossed.

His parents were gone. Miranda Alvarez, Luciano Scaglione, Amir Pharaon—all gone too. But Raven Khan was still out there, and if she was alive, Michael would find her. He owed her, and himself, that much. The mere thought gave him hope, made him see the world as both large and small at the same time.

Michael squeezed the medallion tighter, then took it by the chain in both hands . . .

His father would always end the story by making Michael promise that no matter what happened, once the medallion became his, he would never part with it until the day came to pass it on to his own son.

. . . and draped it over his neck, tucking the medallion into its accustomed spot beneath his shirt over his heart. Because it belonged to him, as it had to Mita, Caesar, and Charlemagne. It had been meant to be his, just as it had been meant to be theirs. They had conquered their empires, and now he would conquer his.

Michael's gaze drifted west out over the crystal waters enclosing Isola di Levanzo to the sun-lit horizon, promising a vast world that stretched beyond the boundaries of any map, there for the taking by someone with enough foresight to seize it. Las Vegas was out there too, beyond the scope of his eyes, but not his vision.

It was time to go home.

Turn the page for a preview of

✦

STRONG ENOUGH TO DIE

✦

J O N   L A N D

Available now from Forge Books

FORGE®

A FORGE HARDCOVER

ISBN-13: 978-0-7653-1258-7   ISBN-10: 0-7653-1258-1

"It's bad, Caitlin," Charlie Weeks said, head resting against
the boulder they'd taken cover behind. He squeezed a hand
against the spreading patch of red staining his khaki shirt,
looking shiny in the night. His other hand held fast to his SIG
P226R, standard-issue Texas Ranger pistol.

Caitlin Strong ejected the spent magazine from her Ruger
Mini-14 semiautomatic rifle and snapped a fresh one home.
"You die on me, Charlie, and I'll kill you myself, I swear," she
said, as a fresh barrage of gunfire chipped rock splinters out
of the boulder. Sharp flecks showered over them, feeling like
drizzle drops at the onset of a spring storm.

"This one's on me," Charlie said. "This ends bad, everyone
should know that."

"It ends when the last of those mules is down."

"Senior man," Charlie resumed, paying her no heed. "I
shoulda known better." Charlie ran his tongue over his parched
lips, his mouth crackling dryly. "Your dad be proud of you, your
granddad too, first woman Ranger and a damn fine one to boot.
I tell you that lately?"

"Can't hear it often enough."

Heat lightning lit up the sky, briefly illuminating the remaining gunmen firing from the other side of the arroyo. Then
the night went black again, the mules visible only from their
muzzle flashes taking brief bites out of the air in rhythm with
the staccato clacking of their assault rifles. The stiff breeze

carried the musky smell of chaparral and the sweet scent of mesquite, mixing uneasily with gun smoke.

"Shit, what a mess," Charlie Weeks said, trying to steady his SIG in a now trembling hand. His breaths were coming faster now and sounded soggy. At sixty, he was a dozen years younger to the day than Caitlin's father would've been if he were alive, the two of them having shared a birthday and much more.

Caitlin sighted on the muzzle flashes and fired off some rounds from the Ruger. Across the dry, water-carved gulley separating them from the drug mules, a yelp sounded, more animal than man. Even with two down now, that still left five more to contend with. Caitlin ran an ammo count in her head: fifteen shots left in her Ruger and eighteen, a magazine and a half, for her holstered SIG. Charlie's 12 gauge had all eight shells primed and ready, but he was down to the last bullets for his sidearm.

Caitlin tried to dab the sweat from her forehead with a shirtsleeve, but found it too soaked already. The blast-furnace heat of the day had given way to a windswept cool night that could do nothing to relieve the layers of perspiration gluing her shirt to her back and turning her jeans heavy with dampness.

The Texas Rangers had been called in after border patrolmen had unearthed a massive tunnel beneath the Chihuahuan Desert running back to the Mexican border, big enough to drive a vehicle through. The kind of energy and organization required for such an effort strongly suggested drug as opposed to people smuggling, later confirmed when Caitlin's own forensic check of the tunnel revealed clear traces of marijuana and a powder later identified as black tar heroin. The border patrol had discovered another three comparable tunnels along the Texas-Mexico border, and Rangers were dispatched to stake out each one.

Every night for the past eight, Charlie Weeks and Caitlin had parked their SUV behind the cover of a rock bed and hunkered low in the natural cover of the arroyo. They had positioned themselves a hundred feet across from each other in order to catch any emerging vehicle in their crossfire, if it came to that. As senior man, that had been Charlie's call, although the positioning left their rear flanks exposed, making them prime for an ambush. Not shy, Caitlin had pointed this out to Charlie, only to be rebuked.

She was eyeballing the culvert dug out of the desert floor from her position opposite Charlie's when chips of stone suddenly burst into the air around them. Caitlin recognized the gunfire an instant before there was a heavy *whump* followed by a sound like air being let out of a balloon, as Charlie Weeks hit the rock face hard and slumped, clutching his side.

Caitlin returned the fire blindly with her SIG, not on mark but enough to buy her the time she needed to reach Charlie and drag him back behind the trio of boulders beyond the arroyo. He collapsed just as they got there, Caitlin with gun in one hand and radio in the other.

"Officer down!" she told the nearest highway patrol dispatch, following with her call number and location. Except there wasn't a responding vehicle anywhere within hours of them, so unless the Rangers or highway patrol could get a chopper scrambled fast, she and Charlie Weeks would be fighting this battle alone.

The heat lightning and cool breeze meant storms would be dotting the air all the way across southwest Texas, playing hell with any chopper pilot crazy enough to fly into a gunfight to begin with. The gunfire from across the arroyo ratcheted up again, and Caitlin knew it was only a matter of time before the mules used their superior numbers of men and bullets to circle around to her exposed rear flank. That meant if she and Charlie were going to get the most out of their remaining ammo, it had to be now.

"Ready to get a move on, Charlie?" she asked the Texas Ranger who had fought battles like this a dozen times alongside her father.

"I think I just dreamed you saying that."

He took a deep breath that shook his chest when he let it back out. Caitlin propped him up higher against the boulder, the smell of his blood heavier now, its coating leaving a thick sheen across his midsection.

"We're gonna make a run for the vehicle, old man."

"Old man? Anyone calls me 'old man' better be able to take me in a bar fight and that includes you, Caitlin Strong."

"I'm buying soon as we get home."

Charlie Weeks gazed down past his waist. "I can't walk. My legs went dull a pint ago."

"I'll carry you."

"Good plan, if you had an extra pair of hands."

"I do," Caitlin told him.

"That's nuts."

"Alternative's worse."

"We use our ammo. Wait 'em out."

"They'll circle round and take us in a crossfire, soon as they realize we're down to our last shells. Better we take it to them, than wait for 'em to come."

"Who taught you that, your dad or your grandpa?"

"You, Charlie."

Charlie Weeks smiled through his own pain. "They ever tell you about the time we went after those moonshiners? Christ on a crutch, I don't think I was much older than you then, a damn rookie riding into trouble alongside two Ranger legends. Know what I remember thinking?"

"No."

"We was all wearing the same badge, theirs being a bit more scuffed and dulled than mine the only difference."

"Stop changing the subject, Charlie."

Caitlin took the 12 gauge in one hand, the Ruger in the other, testing their heft. Then she handed her SIG to Charlie Weeks.

"Ready, Ranger?"

"As I'll ever be," Charlie sighed, grimacing in pain as he pulled his knees into his chest.

Caitlin slid in against him so her shoulders were square with his chest. Charlie Weeks wrapped both his arms around her neck, a SIG clutched in either hand as Caitlin reached to take the 12 gauge in her left and Ruger in her right. Charlie's weight bent her spine inward when she tried to rise up. Their SUV was two hundred yards away, an interminable distance considering the pace at which it'd be covered.

Still, no choice.

Caitlin felt the warmth of Charlie's blood soaking through her damp shirt and hoisted the 12 gauge and Ruger into position.

"It's time, old man."

"I warned you not to call me that."

Caitlin visualized Charlie's smile dissolving into a pained grimace and lit out from behind the boulders. The drug mules' fire roared at them, answered immediately by the twin pistols in Charlie's grasp. The reports deafened Caitlin even before she started firing alternately with the 12 gauge and Ruger. The shotgun was semiauto with a cut-down barrel, but it was also little more than a gaudy noisemaker at this distance. Her shots from the Ruger stayed on line, though still serving more as distraction than anything else.

Bullets whizzed past her, the sensation curiously like mosquitoes buzzing near on a hot summer night. Caitlin felt something like a kick to her side just over her hip and knew she'd been hit, at least grazed, but kept going with the SUV just a hundred yards away now, fifty beyond the west bank of the arroyo.

One of Charlie Weeks's pistols clicked empty, the other on its last shells with the SUV still barely in sight and Caitlin's left leg beginning to stiffen.

"Put me down, for God's sake," he rasped at her.

"The hell you say," Caitlin shot back, still firing through the dark blanket of night.

A thin ribbon of moonlight opened up between the clouds, allowing her to spot the mules who'd emerged from their cover.

"Kill the fuckers!" one of them screamed in perfect English.

An American giving the orders to Mexican drug mules . . . What the hell was this?

Caitlin saw motion flash against the dark landscape, the mules opting for an all-out charge. She fired off rounds from the 12 gauge and Ruger to chase them back, slowing their attack. The same shaft of moonlight revealed the SUV to be closer than she thought. She was angling for it when something sharp bit into her back and sent the hard ground up to meet her.

BAHRAIN, 2008

The man stood before the plate-glass window in a place the signs, in both English and Arabic, called City Gardens. Squinting through the painful glare of light, he studied the reflection looking back at him, trying to place it. It had been so long since he'd seen a reflection of anything; the room he had known as home from the beginning of his memory had no windows or mirrors. There was a bowl of water to both wash and brush his teeth with twice a day. It would be there and then it would be gone, the man left trying to reconstruct the time in between.

He shuddered with fear, the sensation nearly paralyzing him even though he could not remember what it was that scared him. There had been another life before the new memories and the man wondered if it belonged to the face looking back at him in the window glass. Often the men who came to him in his room addressed him by name. But it wasn't his name. It may have been once, but it wasn't anymore.

He had no name. He told them that, but they never believed him.

The man noticed the reflection in the glass was shuddering too. He started to twist away, felt a bolt of searing pain rack his spine, and saw the reflection wince.

He started on again. His aching feet felt heavier, dragging across the road, the man too weak to lift them. His eyes hurt from the sunlight, telling him it was daytime. Night and day had ceased to have meaning long before, the distinctions between them as blurred as his very existence. More signs told him he was in a place called Bab Al Bahrain, surrounded by strangers in an outdoor market where handicrafts and brass coffeepots were on display amid elegantly woven carpets. Sharp-smelling spices roasted beneath the blazing sun.

His legs throbbed terribly, hot jabs rising through them

with each step. His arms hung limp by his side, the slightest movement causing his shoulder joints to feel disconnected from the muscles around them.

The man was aware of puzzled stares being cast upon him and swung round painfully, half expecting to find the reflection in the window glass staring back again. Words were being thrust his way in languages he did not understand until he passed under the shade of an overhang that turned the ache in his skin to a dull throb.

"Would you like some?"

The man turned to see a robe-clad merchant extending a glass that smelled like mint toward him.

"Yes," the man said, not recognizing his own voice. "Thank you."

He took the glass, sipped, and then drank the sweet brown tea. He could not remember drinking anything other than water, often tasting like soap or something worse.

The man handed his glass to the merchant who refilled it with a smile and handed it back.

"You have money?" the merchant asked him.

"Money?"

"Cash? Credit cards?"

The man touched his pockets, sank his hands in. "No."

The merchant winked, playing the game. "You like the tea?"

"Very much."

"You wish to see my wares. I have beautiful Bahrain pearls, wonderful pieces of jewelry for your woman. Is she with you?"

"Who?"

"Your woman."

"I don't have a woman."

"A man, boy perhaps?"

"No, no man. No boy."

"Just you then, eh?"

"Who?"

"You."

"No, not me. There is no me."

The glass felt suddenly too heavy to hold, so he returned it to the merchant with a trembling hand and moved on, aware that the hand ached badly now as well. He held it up to his face as if to look for the source of the pain, coming away only with the realization that the fingers looked gnarled and swollen.

He walked, as if trying to find a place where the pain would go away. If he closed his eyes and tried very hard to detach himself from his body, sometimes he could. But he couldn't close his eyes now, couldn't stop, spurred by the vague awareness of something out there worse than the pain that would catch up to him if he let it.

He approached the luscious smells of food roasting on spits and outdoor grates. The food sizzled and hissed amid the pungent scents of garlic and lemon. Merchants served heaping plates of it up to waiting customers who carried them away in search of a seat at the chairs and tables set in the shade of a crowded veranda.

The smells turned the man's shrunken stomach. He tried to remember eating, could not recall a single bite or swallow. He came to an empty spot at a table in the shade, abandoned with a half-full plate left behind. The man touched his hand to the thick sauce pooling on one side, swiped his tongue across his fingers.

Coughed, gagged, retched. Sank to his knees.

Soon he was surrounded by a circle of people looking down, seeming to see him. But that, of course, was impossible.

Because there was nothing to see. After all, he didn't exist.

WASHINGTON, D.C., 2008

Harmon Delladonne saw Clayton coming and snapped up from the bench overlooking the Mall. Delladonne's suit trousers flapped in the stiff breeze, and he ran his hands through his slicked-back dark hair before setting off down the street to let Clayton catch him in stride.

"Fifteen minutes late, Clayton," Delladonne greeted, feeling a slight drizzle dampening his shoulders. "Fifteen minutes."

"I came as soon as I could, sir."

"That's time I'll never get back, valuable time lost for good."

"We could have spoken by phone," Clayton suggested

weakly. Like Delladonne, he stood just over six feet, though much broader in the shoulders with narrow high-pitched cheekbones and a wide forehead that had an almost Neanderthal quality about it. "My line's secure."

"Never trust machines, Clayton," Delladonne told him. "Don't even use a cell phone. Too easy to track a man's movements with it. I know because my company does it. All the time. Anybody in the country. Anytime, anywhere. One of MacArthur-Rain's many government contracts."

Delladonne understood the technology he had helped create well enough to know how easy it was to become a victim of it. Even the outdoors weren't totally safe, not with surveillance cameras on every street corner and long-range listening devices that could hone in on a conversation from a quarter mile away. But stay on the move, keep your lips angled low when you speak, and you could feel relatively insulated. So whenever in Washington, Delladonne never took meetings in his satellite office, never took meetings at lunch, hardly ever took meetings at all. The one exception was the Senate hearing he had been called here to testify before, only to have an ally remove his name, temporarily anyway, from the witness list at the last moment. A good day indeed, until he heard about Bahrain.

"I assume you wanted to discuss another of those contracts with me," Clayton was saying.

"Your initial report about Bahrain has been confirmed. Now tell me how this happened."

Delladonne's route kept the Mall, Capitol Building and White House in view at all times. He liked it that way, liked the sense of ownership it implied, even if right now that ownership was going to hell. The day was gray and dismal with the promise of rain. Back in Houston it had been hot and sultry, the air holding signs of a blistering summer. But all that had been chased back by the dreariness of Washington, a city he had come to loath.

"Our Bahrain operatives panicked," Clayton reported. "Heard a U.S. government oversight inspection team was coming in."

"Government oversight," Delladonne repeated. "What a joke." But he didn't sound at all amused.

"The Bahrain facility wasn't supposed to be on the list released to the new administration. It was private, after all."

"They were all private, Clayton."

"But the CIA worked the site originally. Extra funds spent on soundproof padding the walls. You know the drill."

"MacArthur-Rain didn't retain your services to tell me what I already know."

Clayton remained silent, feeling Delladonne's stare boring into him. Clayton knew how to intimidate even those to whom he was subservient. But Delladonne was different. Delladonne might be thin enough to break over his knee but he was the first man, enemies and associates alike, who actually scared Clayton.

"May I speak plainly, sir?"

"Be careful, Clayton."

"My people in Bahrain went at this man for six months to get out what he was hiding in his head. They failed."

"You mean, you failed."

"Yes, sir."

"Then say it. Say you failed."

"I failed," Clayton conceded.

"Accepting responsibility—that's a good start. What comes next?"

"We find him."

Delladonne stopped and turned to face Clayton, his eyes like black daggers of ice. "What makes 9/11 such a great tragedy, Clayton? What's the first thing that comes to your mind?"

"This country attacked. All those deaths."

"This country being attacked, yes. But the real tragedy lay in not *enough* deaths."

Clayton just looked at him.

"We knew an attack was coming eventually," Delladonne continued. "We had the level of response the country would accept down to a cost-benefit analysis of the number of lives lost. The first reports putting the death toll over 20,000 would have been the best thing that ever happened to this country because people would've embraced everything MacArthur-Rain wanted to do overnight. But when it turned out to be barely 3,000 we had to scale back. The world did change that day, just not as much as it should have."

Clayton bristled. "I lost friends, sir, and, frankly, I don't understand what you're getting at."

"We all lost friends, and I'll tell you what I'm getting at. We're close to that point again. The gains we've made are incremental, but they're there. And what this man you lost has locked up in his brain can give us the power to accomplish everything we've always wanted. The key to securing the future, Clayton, and I am not exaggerating."

"If it's still in his brain, you mean, sir," Clayton cautioned.

"What I mean is that if we can't get it, you've got to make sure no one else does either."

HOUSTON, 2008

"Want a sandwich, Davis?"

His wife's voice drew him from his trance, and Davis S. Bonn looked up from his computer, flexing his fingers. His middle name was actually Lewis, but Bonn had adopted the *S* because it looked better on his byline. "Sure," he said, "I'd love one."

His wife Tayanna tried to see what he was writing but he shifted in his chair to block her view of the monitor. They had met a decade before while Davis Bonn had been researching a story about the Khmer Rouge's alleged intrusion into Thailand. The story had gone nowhere but Davis had fallen in love with his interpreter and managed to wrangle a visa for her to return with him to the States.

"Come on," she whined, "just a peek."

"Not until I'm finished. You know the rules."

"I just thought that this time . . ."

"This time especially," Davis told her, holding his ground.

Tayanna relented and started for the door, looking back at him before she closed it. "Just so long as you're sure about this."

"Why wouldn't I be?"

"Because these are dangerous people."

"All the more reason to bring them down."

"Always the crusader."

"Just a jounalist, Anna." Davis cracked a smile, as he always did when he called her that. "A journalist in search of a book deal."

"So long as you live to see it published."

"And the check cashed."

Tayanna smiled and, this time, closed the door behind her. She'd already mixed up the chicken salad and made sure the toast was just the way he liked it, the lettuce cut thin, before laying the sandwich on a plate surrounded by potato chips. Taking it in hand, she returned to Davis's office and entered without knocking.

"One sandwich made to—"

Tayanna stopped. The plate fell from her grasp and shattered on the floor, the twin halves of the sandwich leaping in opposite directions.

Davis Bonn lay slumped on the floor convulsing, bulging eyes fixed on the ceiling where a faint wisp of smoke had risen.

"Dtaay!" Tayanna screamed.

She rushed to her husband and dropped down, trying to still the spasmodic tremors in his arms and legs.

"Davis!" she screamed, noticing only then a thin trail of blood dribbling from his right ear. "Davis!"

His eyes failed to acknowledge her and then locked open altogether, his extremities settling stiffly. Tayanna bent over him and began administering CPR, continuing until exhaustion and hopelessness finally overcame her.

By the time she dialed 911, twenty minutes had slipped away into some mournful netherworld, and the stench of burnt wires she'd already forgotten was gone.